THE SIGNALMAN
& Other Ghost Stories

CHARLES DICKENS

THE SIGNALMAN
& Other Ghost Stories

SUTTON PUBLISHING

First published in this edition in 1990 by
Sutton Publishing Limited · Phoenix Mill
Thrupp · Stroud · Gloucestershire · GL5 2BU

Reprinted 1995, 1996

British Library Cataloguing in Publication Data

Dickens, Charles *1812–1870*
  The signalman and other ghost stories.
  1. Title
  823.8

ISBN 0 86299 858 1

Cover picture: Crown Copyright, National Railway Museum.

 ALAN SUTTON™ and SUTTON™ are the
trade marks of Sutton Publishing Limited

Typeset in 10/11 pt Bembo
Typesetting and origination by
Sutton Publishing Limited
Printed in Great Britain by
The Guernsey Press Company Limited,
Guernsey, Channel Islands.

CONTENTS

BIOGRAPHICAL NOTE

CHARLES DICKENS (1812–1870). A man of singular imagination, novelist, editor, journalist, theatrical producer, actor and a supporter of radical reform, Charles Dickens was one of the great Victorians. He was born in Portsmouth on 7 February 1812, the second child of John, a clerk in the Navy Pay Office, and Elizabeth, who were extroverts and continually living beyond their sufficient but modest means, apparently more interested in themselves than in their children. He spent a happy early childhood in Portsmouth, London and Chatham, entertained by the macabre stories of his nursemaid, and later by his own wide reading, and developing imagination. In 1822 John Dickens was reposted to London, and his financial situation, already perilous, quickly went from bad to worse. Charles was unable to attend school, and two years later was sent to work in a boot-blacking factory, where he met with some of the rougher elements of London life. Meanwhile his father was declared bankrupt, and escorted with his family to the Marshalsea, while Charles had lodgings near his work, and visited the prison frequently. Fortunately, this sad state of affairs lasted only a few months, and later in the year, at the age of twelve, Charles was sent back to school to complete his education. He left school at fifteen, and by the age of twenty-three had established himself as a journalist and man of the theatre.

Four years later he was a first ranking man of letters, a husband and a father. He had written the first of the *Sketches by Boz* in 1833, and, in 1836, *Pickwick* started to appear in serial form, to be followed by *Oliver Twist* (1838) and *Nicholas Nickleby* (1839). Dickens had become editor of *Bentley's Miscellany*, in which the first parts of *Mudfog* were published in 1837, and was receiving a steady income. He had married Catherine Hogarth in 1836, and had been devasted by the death, one year later, of Mary, his sister-in-law, whom he loved dearly. By 1839 he was able to move his impecunious parents to Devon, and buy a family house in London. His writings were based on his own experiences and concerns: childhood problems and poverty pervade *Oliver Twist*; ideas of education and the theatre appear in *Nicholas Nickleby*; while in *The Old Curiosity Shop* (1841), he invokes memories of the beloved Mary, and *Barnaby Rudge* (also 1841) reflects Dickens' visits to Newgate Prison, his intimate knowledge of the London underworld and his political sympathies.

Dickens' experiences were broadened in 1842, when he made a triumphant visit to America. Although he was warmly welcomed, he did not like America, and was profoundly affected by his encounters with slavery and a visit to a penal institute practising solitary confinement. His criticism of American society was lightly veiled in the ensuing *American Notes* (1842), and continued in *Martin Chuzzlewit* (1844), another study of a disturbed childhood, which included a journey to the States. Dickens' support for radical reformers in England developed with his reputation, and he was frequently a public speaker for charitable institutions. He was particularly concerned with the plight of children, and was inspired to write *Christmas Carol* (1843) by a visit to Miss Angela Burdett Coutts' Ragged School for deprived Cockney children, in order 'to present the poor in a favourable light to the rich.'

In 1844, after ten years of intensive work, Dickens took his family to Italy for a year's break. The family included five children and Georgina, Catherine's younger sister, who had lived with the family since 1842. Not unnaturally for a man of his temperament, Dickens missed London and his many friends, but was stimulated by an experiment in mesmerism with Madame de la Rue, an attractive English woman who suffered from hallucinations. This relationship and the foreign environment exacerbated problems in the relationship between Dickens and his wife, and marked the beginning of their final estrangement.

The next six years (1845–51) were busy ones. Besides spending nine months travelling and writing in Switzerland and Paris, Dickens was working as actor-manager of an amateur dramatic group, performing in London and touring the provinces. He was involved in an abortive attempt to establish a radical newspaper, but finally, in 1850, achieved his dream of producing his own journal, *Household Words*, which was an instant success, and employed many of Dickens' friends, his father and his father-in-law. Its purpose was to generate social awareness and press for social reform. Two years earlier Dickens had opened Urania Cottage, a home for reclaimed prostitutes, under the patronage of Angela Coutts, and he retained responsibility for it as an unpaid superintendent. During these years he worked on *Dombey and Son* (1848), a study in selfishness, and *David Copperfield* (1850), a semi-autobiographical novel, which explored once more Dickens' own unsatisfactory childhood. In 1851 a series of misfortunes afflicted the Dickens' household. After the birth of their ninth child, Catherine suffered a nervous breakdown and was taken to Malvern for treatment. While she was away, first Charles' father, and then this last child died. Restlessness and concern for Catherine's well-being induced Dickens to move the family to a new home in Tavistock Square, while ideas of a new book whirled through his mind.

Bleak House (1853), was completed when Dickens was forty-one, and the end of that year saw Dickens give the first of his famous public readings of his own work. But the years of frenzied activity had taken their toll, and during that same year Dickens had been forced to take holidays in Europe, to avoid a nervous breakdown. Although he escaped a breakdown, Dickens continued to be possessed by a restlessness and feverish energy which he never lost, in spite of taking regular working holidays in Folkestone and France. *Bleak House* is a vast rambling criticism of the British legal system, and, like it, his two subsequent novels were satirical comments on Victorian 'systems'. *Hard Times* (1854), comments on the effects of mechanization on society and education, while in *Little Dorrit* (1857), Dickens explored the way in which people are imprisoned in their social milieu. Little Dorrit herself was modelled on Georgina Hogarth, who had lived with the family for the last fourteen years, a companion to Catherine, nanny to the ten children and beloved 'sister' of Charles. In 1857 Dickens, still involved in theatricals, took a production of Wilkie Collins' melodrama *The Frozen Deep* to Manchester, and invited the actress Mrs Ternan and two of her daughters to take the female parts.

Ellen Ternan, the younger daughter, was an attractive eighteen-year-old. Dickens fell in love with her, and within the year, inspite of criticism from his friends, colleagues and readers had separated from Catherine, who moved out of Tavistock House. Since he now had three households to maintain, Tavistock House, Gad's Hill, which he had purchased as a country residence in 1857, and Mrs Dickens' new home in Gloucester Crescent, as well as the Ternans to support, Dickens needed to supplement his income, and this he did by making extensive tours to give public readings in England, Scotland and Ireland. At the same time, he continued his work as editor and journalist for *Household Words* until, through ill feeling, he changed publishers, and started producing a new journal called *All the Year Round*. The publication of the new magazine stimulated the writing of the next two serial novels: *A Tale of Two Cities* (1859), to establish a wide readership, and *Great Expectations* (1861) to maintain it. The first explored themes of death and resurrection against the violence of the French Revolution, while the second returned to thoughts of childhood and adolescent love in a plot involving mistaken identity. It also contained many shorter stories including 'The Signalman' (1866).

In 1860, Dickens sold Tavistock House, and the next few years were spent at Gad's Hill, or in London or Paris, giving regular readings and writing *Our Mutual Friend* (1865), a study of material greed and mistaken identity. He also paid regular visits to Ellen, who was now living in Slough. The years were beginning to tell, and although he was now a wealthy man, he continued to press himself beyond the limit. In 1865, he suffered the first of regular bouts of trouble with his feet, as well as being badly shaken in a rail accident. However, in 1867, at the age of fifty-five, he set out for a victorious five month reading tour of the States, returning to a hero's welcome. But his final tour of the English provinces was not completed because of ill health, and in January 1870, he gave his last readings in London. He died on 9 June 1870 of a cerebral haemorrhage, leaving his final novel, *Edwin Drood*, unfinished. He was buried in Poets' Corner, Westminster Abbey.

SHEILA MICHELL

INTRODUCTION

Dickens was a master of the ghost story, as this collection demonstrates. Even his mainstream work could frighten people – frequently ladies swooned during his public readings of the death of Nancy in *Oliver Twist* – but in these pieces he does more than shock: he chills.

Dickens liked to entertain his friends with readings of ghost stories at Christmas time in particular – as Jerome K. Jerome, in his collection of humorous ghost stories, observes, supernatural events always seem to happen on Christmas Eve, and Tennyson's 'Morte d'Arthur' is also set on that occasion, as one particularly suitable for story-telling.

The nearest one can come today to the atmosphere of one of these soirées is the performance of George Curry, a Dickens expert who, particularly when in costume, looks the image of the Great Man. His performance of 'The Signalman' has the audience completely under Dickens's spell, the hair on the back of their necks suitably raised, the denouement giving a palpable frisson of horror.

While 'The Signalman' is set in what was, for Dickens's contemporaries, a 'high-tech' environment (it first appeared at Christmas 1866), his other stories have more conventional, traditional settings, one of them being a graveyard. 'The Story of the Goblins Who Stole a Sexton' describes how on Christmas Eve Gabriel Grub, the misanthropic sexton and gravedigger, is transported to the underworld home of the goblins, where he is severely chastized for his miserable nature: 'he saw that men like himself, who snarled at the mirth and cheerfulness of others, were the foulest weeds on the fair surface of the earth . . .' The story has a clear moral, and after an initial atmosphere of menace ends on a happy note and an amusing use of puns in the final paragraph.

Punning was also the chief fame of Thomas Hood, the poet, until his last years, when he produced two great works of social protest, 'The Song of the Shirt' and 'The Bridge of Sighs'. These two works had an enormous impact on the Victorian public, and corresponded to the pressure for radical change and reform that Charles Dickens exerted through his novels.

Similarly, Hood wrote serious as well as humorous work, and two of his poems can be described as horror – 'The Dream of Eugene Arram' and 'The Haunted House'. 'The Dream of Eugene Arram' is not dissimilar to Dickens's 'A Madman's Manuscript' which is included in this volume, while it is interesting to compare Hood's poem, 'The Haunted House', with Dickens's story of the same name, which can also be read here.

Dickens's 'The Haunted House' formed part of the double Christmas number of his weekly magazine *All the Year Round* in 1859. He wrote the introduction 'The Mortals in the House', and 'The Ghost in Master B.'s Room', which are included here. Other chapters were contributed by different writers, among them George Augustus Sala, Wilkie Collins and Elizabeth Gaskell.

The story describes a haunted house that is shunned by the villagers. The narrator and his sister decide to fire the servants – who are nervous and unhappy – and arrange for a house-party of friends to come and stay for a few months in order to investigate the reputed hauntings. Dickens creates the sense of gloom and fear very effectively. The house does not look huge and menacing, but closed, decaying and obviously shunned. It is seen, not at night but in the morning, which makes it seem even more mysterious, as the deathly quiet of early morning can be more unnerving than the natural silence of midnight.

Hood, too, conveys an image of desolation, though his is more dramatic than Dickens's, as one would expect from a poem:

> Unhinged the iron gates half open hung,
> Jarr'd by the gusty gales of many winters,
> That from its crumbled pedestal had flung
> One marble globe in splinters . . .
>
> O'er all there hung a shadow and a fear;
> A sense of mystery the spirit daunted,
> And said, as plain as whisper in the ear,
> The place is Haunted!

The poem's narrator crosses the desolate courtyard and enters the house, climbing up the stairway towards the haunted room. As he makes his nervous way he is silently watched by the portraits of long-dead owners:

> On ev'ry lip a speechless horror dwelt;
> On ev'ry brow the burthen of affliction;
> The old Ancestral Spirits knew and felt
> The House's malediction.

Eventually the fatal bedchamber is reached, the evidence of murder staining the floor and casement:

> What human creature in the dead of night
> Had coursed like hunted hare that cruel distance?
> Had sought the door, the window, in his flight,
> Striving for dear existence?
>
> What shrieking Spirit in that bloody room
> Its mortal frame had violently quitted? –
> Across the sunbeam, with a sudden gloom,
> A ghostly shadow flitted.

The narrator of Dickens's 'Haunted House' stumbles across no such awful room, senses no apparition just out of sight, feels no such sense of barely restrained panic. The young people decide to confront whatever ghosts there may be in a rational manner, and the spirit that the narrator meets in Master B.'s bedroom (whose bell rings at odd hours to summon servants to an empty room) takes him on a very strange journey, but fails itself to terrify him.

In this respect the narrator resembles Dickens himself: though fascinated by supernatural phenomena he kept an open mind, writing to William Howitt in 1859 that:

> I have not yet met any Ghost Story that was proved to me, or that had not the noticeable peculiarity in it – that the alteration of some slight circumstance would bring it within the range of common natural probabilities. I have always had a strong interest in the subject, and never knowingly lose an opportunity of pursuing it.

He also never lost an opportunity of exorcizing his own ghost, for he was haunted and shamed by memories of that part of his childhood when he was forced, through his father's insolvency, to work in a blacking factory near the Strand. He drew on this experience in his novels, and comes back to it on many occasions, lightly disguising it in his fiction: in 'The Haunted House', for example, it is significant that the narrator's experience in Master B.'s bedroom brings him face to face with his own past. Wearing the transparent mask of the narrator, Dickens again alludes to his early life:

> I was taken home, and there was Debt at home as well as Death, and we had a sale there. My own little bed was so superciliously looked upon by a Power unknown to me, hazily called 'The Trade', that a brass coal-scuttle, a roasting-jack, and a birdcage, were obliged to be put into it to make a Lot of it, and then it went for a song. So I heard mentioned and I wondered what song, and thought what a dismal song it must have been to sing! . . .'
>
> Ah me, ah me! no other ghost has haunted the boy's room, my friends, since I have occupied it, than the ghost of my own childhood, the ghost of my own innocence, the ghost of my own airy belief. . . .

Other tales in this volume, for example 'To be Read at Dusk', in which a young bride is terrified by dreams of a sinister stranger who finally appears in the flesh, are more conventionally ghostly, while 'The Haunted House' remains the most interesting demonstration of Dickens's storytelling talent. As well as showing us the relish with which Victorians wrote and read ghost stories, the variety of stories in this collection gives us another glimpse into the mind of the greatest Victorian writer of them all.

PAUL WEBB

THE SIGNALMAN

'Halloa! Below there!'

When he heard a voice thus calling to him, he was standing at the door of his box, with a flag in his hand, furled round its short pole. One would have thought, considering the nature of the ground, that he could not have doubted from what quarter the voice came; but instead of looking up to where I stood on the top of the steep cutting nearly over his head, he turned about, and looked down the Line. There was something remarkable in his manner of doing so, though I could not have said for my life what. But I know it was remarkable enough to attract my notice, even though his figure was foreshortened and shadowed, down into the deep trench, and mine was high above him, so steeped in the glow of an angry sunset, that I had shaded my eyes with my hand before I saw him at all.

'Halloa! Below!'

From looking down the Line, he turned himself about again, and, raising his eyes, saw my figure high above him.

'Is there any path by which I can come down and speak to you?'

He looked up at me without replying, and I looked down at him without pressing him too soon with a repetition of my idle question. Just then there came a vague vibration in the earth and air, quickly changing into a violent pulsation, and an oncoming rush that caused me to start back, as though it had force to draw me down. When such vapour as rose to my height from this rapid train had passed me, and was skimming away over the landscape, I looked down again, and saw him refurling the flag he had shown while the train went by.

I repeated my inquiry. After a pause, during which he seemed to regard me with fixed attention, he motioned with his rolled-up flag towards a point on my level, some two or three hundred yards distant. I called down to him, 'All right!'

1

and made for that point. There, by dint of looking closely about me, I found a rough zigzag descending path notched out, which I followed.

The cutting was extremely deep, and unusually precipitate. It was made through a clammy stone, that became oozier and wetter as I went down. For these reasons, I found the way long enough to give me time to recall a singular aid of reluctance or compulsion with which he had pointed out the path.

When I came down low enough upon the zigzag descent to see him again, I saw that he was standing between the rails on the way by which the train had lately passed, in an attitude as if he were waiting for me to appear. He had his left hand at his chin, and that left elbow rested on his right hand, crossed over his breast. His attitude was one of such expectation and watchfulness that I stopped a moment, wondering at it.

I resumed my downward way, and stepping out upon the level of the railroad, and drawing nearer to him, saw that he was a dark sallow man, with a dark beard and rather heavy eyebrows. His post was in as solitary and dismal a place as ever I saw. On either side, a dripping-wet wall of jagged stone, excluding all view but a strip of sky; the perspective one way only a crooked prolongation of this great dungeon; the shorter perspective in the other direction termination in a gloomy red light, and the gloomier entrance to a black tunnel, in whose massive architecture there was a barbarous, depressing, and forbidding air. So little sunlight ever found its way to this spot, that it had an earthy, deadly smell; and so much cold wind rushed through it, that it struck chill to me, as if I had left the natural world.

Before he stirred, I was near enough to him to have touched him. Not even then removing his eyes from mine, he stepped back one step, and lifted his hand.

This was a lonesome post to occupy (I said), and it had riveted my attention when I looked down from up yonder. A visitor was a rarity, I should suppose; not an unwelcome rarity, I hoped? In me, he merely saw a man, who had been shut up within narrow limits all his life, and who being at last set free, had a newly-awakened interest in these great works. To such purpose I spoke to him; but I am far from sure of the terms I used; for, besides that I am not happy in opening any conversation, there was something in the man that daunted me.

He directed a most curious look towards the red light near the tunnel's mouth, and looked all about it, as if something were missing from it, and then looked at me.

That light was part of his charge? Was it not?

He answered in a low voice, – 'Don't you know it is?'

The monstrous thought came into my mind, as I perused the fixed eyes and the saturnine face, that this was a spirit, not a man. I have speculated since, whether there may have been infection in his mind.

In my turn, I stepped back. But in making the action, I detected in his eyes some latent fear of me. This put the monstrous thought into flight.

'You look at me,' I said, forcing a smile, 'as if you had a dread of me.'

'I was doubtful,' he returned, 'whether I had seen you before.'

'Where?'

He pointed to the red light he had looked at.

'There?' I said.

Intently watchful of me, he replied (but without sound), 'Yes.'

'My good fellow, what should I do there? However, be that as it may, I never was there, you may swear.'

'I think I may,' he rejoined. 'Yes; I am sure I may.'

His manner cleared, like my own. He replied to my remarks with readiness, and in well-chosen words. Had he much to do there? Yes; that was to say, he had enough responsibility to bear; but exactness and watchfulness were what was required of him, and of actual work – manual labour – he had next to none. To change that signal, to trim those lights, and to turn his iron handle now and then, was all he had to do under that head. Regarding those many long and lonely hours of which I seemed to make so much, he could only say that the routine of his life had shaped itself into that form, and he had grown used to it. He had taught himself a language down here, – if only to know it by sight, and to have formed his own crude ideas of its pronunciation, could be called learning it. He had also worked at fractions and decimals, and tried a little algebra; but he was, and had been as a boy, a poor hand at figures. Was it necessary for him when on duty always to remain in that channel of damp air, and could he never rise into the sunshine from between those high stone walls? Why, that depended upon times and circumstances. Under some conditions there would be less upon the Line than under others, and the same held good as to certain hours of the day and night. In bright weather, he did choose occasions for getting a little above these lower shadows; but, being at all times liable to be called by his electric bell, and at such times listening for it with redoubled anxiety, the relief was less than I would suppose.

He took me into his box, where there was a fire, a desk for an official book in which he had to make certain entries, a telegraphic instrument with its dial, face, and needles, and the little bell of which he had spoken. On my trusting that he would excuse the remark that he had been well educated, and (I hoped I might say without offence), perhaps educated above the station, he observed that instances of slight incongruity in such wise would rarely be found wanting among large bodies of men; that he had heard it was so in workhouses, in the police force, even in that last desperate resource, the army; and that he knew it was so, more or less, in any great railway staff. He had been, when young (if I could believe it, sitting in that hut, – he scarcely could), a student of natural philosophy, and had attended lectures; but he had run wild, misused his opportunities, gone down, and never risen again. He had no complaint to offer about that. He had made his bed, and he lay upon it. It was far too late to make another.

All that I have here condensed he said in a quiet manner, with his grave dark regards divided between me and the fire. He threw in a word, 'Sir,' from time to time, and especially when he referred to his youth – as though to request me to understand that he claimed to be nothing but what I found him. He was several times interrupted by the little bell, and had to read off messages, and send replies. Once he had to stand without the door, and display a flag as a trail passed, and make some verbal communication to the driver. In the discharge of his duties, I observed him to be remarkably exact and vigilant, breaking off his discourse at a syllable, and remaining silent until what he had to do was done.

In a word, I should have sent this man down as one of the safest men to be employed in that capacity, but for the circumstance that while he was speaking to me he twice broke off with a fallen colour, turned his face towards the little bell when it did NOT ring, opened the door of the hut (which was kept shut to exclude the unhealthy damp), and looked out towards the red light near the mouth of the tunnel. On both of those occasions, he came back to the fire with the inexplicable air upon him which I had remarked, without being able to define, when we were so far asunder.

Said I, when I rose to leave him, 'You almost make me think that I have met with a contented man.'

(I am afraid I must acknowledge that I said it to lead him on.)

'I believe I used to be so,' he rejoined, in the low voice in which he had first spoken; 'but I am troubled, Sir, I am troubled.'

He would have recalled the words if he could. He had said them, however, and I took them up quickly.

'With what? What is your trouble?'

'It is very difficult to impart, Sir. It is very, very difficult to speak of. If ever you make me another visit, I will try to tell you.'

'But I expressly intend to make you another visit. Say, when shall it be?'

'I go off early in the morning and I shall be on again at ten tomorrow night, Sir.'

'I will come at eleven.'

He thanked me, and went out at the door with me. 'I'll show my white light, Sir,' he said, in his peculiar low voice, "till you have found the way up. When you have found it, don't call out! And when you are at the top, don't call out!'

His manner seemed to make the place strike colder to me, but I said no more than, 'Very well.'

'And when you come down tomorrow night, don't call out! Let me ask you a parting question. What made you cry, "Halloa! Below there!" tonight?'

'Heavens knows,' said I. 'I cried something to that effect . . .'

'Not to that effect, Sir. Those were the very words. I know them well.'

'I admit those were the very words. I said them no doubt, because I saw you below.'

'For no other reason?'

'What other reason could I possibly have?'

'You had no feeling that they were conveyed to you in any supernatural way?'

'No.'

He wished me good night, and held up his light. I walked by the side of the down Line of rails (with a very disagreeable sensation of a train coming behind me) until I found the path. It was easier to mount than to descend, and I got back to my inn without any adventure.

Punctual to my appointment, I placed my foot on the first notch of the zigzag next night, as the distant clocks were striking eleven. He was waiting for me at the bottom, with his white light on. 'I have not called out,' I said, when we came close together; 'may I speak now?' 'By all means, Sir.' 'Good–night, then, and here's my hand.' 'Goodnight, Sir, and here's mine.' With that we walked side by side to his box, entered it, closed the door, and sat down by the fire.

'I have made up my mind, Sir,' he began, bending forward as soon as we were seated, and speaking in a tone but a little above a whisper, 'that you shall not have to ask me twice what troubles me. I took you for someone else yesterday evening. That troubles me.'

'That mistake?'

'No. That Some one else.'

'Who is it?'

'I don't know.'

'Like me?'

'I don't know. I never saw the face. The left arm is across the face and the right arm is waved – violently waved. This way.'

I followed his action with my eyes, and it was the action of an arm gesticulating with the utmost passion and vehemence, 'For God's sake, clear the way!'

'One moonlight night,' said the man, 'I was sitting here when I heard a voice cry, "Halloa! Below there!" I started up, looked from that door, and saw this Some one else standing by the red light near the tunnel, waving as I just now showed you. The voice seemed hoarse with shouting, and it cried, "Look out! Look out!" I caught up my lamp, turned it on red, and ran towards the figure calling, "What's wrong? What has happened? Where?" It stood just outside the blackness of the tunnel. I advanced so close upon it that I wondered at its keeping the sleeve across its eyes. I ran right up at it, and had my hand stretched out to pull the sleeve away, when it was gone.'

'Into the tunnel?' said I.

'No. I ran on into the tunnel, five hundred yards. I stopped, and held my lamp above my head, and saw the figures of the measured distance, and saw the wet stains stealing down the walls and trickling through the arch. I ran out again faster than I had run in (for I had a mortal abhorrence of the place upon me), and I looked all round the red light with my own red light, and I went up the iron ladder to the gallery atop of it, and I came down again, and ran back here. I telegraphed both ways. "An alarm has been given. Is anything wrong?" The answer came back, both ways, "All well."'

Resisting the slow touch of a frozen finger tracing out my spine, I showed him how that this figure must be a deception of his sense of sight; and how that figures, originating in disease of the delicate nerves that minister to the functions of the eye, were known to have often troubled patients, some of whom had become conscious of the nature of their affliction, and had even proved it by experiments upon themselves. 'As to an imaginary cry,' said I, 'do but listen for a moment to the wind in this unnatural valley while we speak so low, and to the wild harp it makes of the telegraph wires.'

That was all very well, he returned, after we had sat listening for a while, and he ought to know something of the wind and the wires, – he who so often passed long winter nights there, alone and watching. But he would beg to remark that he had not finished.

I asked his pardon, and he slowly added these words, touching my arm. –

'Within six hours after the Appearance, the memorable accident on this Line happened, and within ten hours the dead and wounded were brought along through the tunnel over the spot where the figure had stood.'

A disagreeable shudder crept over me, but I did my best against it. It was not to be denied, I rejoined, that this was a remarkable coincidence, calculated deeply to impress his mind. But it was unquestionable that remarkable coincidence did continually occur, and they must be taken into account in dealing with such a subject. Though to be sure I must admit, I added (for I thought I saw that he was going to bring the objection to bear upon me), men of common sense did not allow much for coincidences in making the ordinary calculations of life.

He again begged to remark that he had not finished.

I again begged his pardon for being betrayed into interruptions.

'This,' he said, again laying his hand upon my arm, and glancing over his shoulder with hollow eyes, 'was just a year ago. Six or seven months passed, and I had recovered from the surprise and shock, when one morning, as the day was breaking, I, standing at the door, looked towards the red light, and saw the spectre again.' He stopped, with a fixed look at me.

'Did it cry out?'

'No. It was silent.'

'Did it wave its arm?'

'No. It leaned against the shaft of light, with both hands before the face. Like this.'

Once more I followed his action with my eyes. It was an action of mourning. I have seen such an attitude in stone figures on tombs.

'Did you go up to it?'

'I came in and sat down, partly to collect my thoughts, partly because it had turned me faint. When I went to the door again, daylight was above me, and the ghost was gone.'

'But nothing followed? Nothing came of this?'

He touched me on the arm with his forefinger twice or thrice, giving a ghastly nod each time:-

'That very day, as a train came out of the tunnel, I noticed, at a carriage window on my side, what looked like a confusion of hands and heads, and something waved. I saw it just in time to signal the driver, Stop! He shut off, and put his brake on, but the train drifted past here a hundred and fifty yards or more. I ran after it, and, as I went along, heard terrible

screams and cries. A beautiful young lady had died instan-
taneously in one of the compartments, and was brought in
here, and laid down on this floor between us.'

Involuntarily I pushed my chair back, as I looked from the
boards at which he pointed to himself.

'True, Sir. True. Precisely as it happened, so I tell it you.'

I could think of nothing to say, to any purpose, and my
mouth was very dry. The wind and the wires took up the
story with a long lamenting wail.

He resumed. 'Now, Sir, mark this, and judge how my
mind is troubled. The spectre came back a week ago. Ever
since, it has been there, now and again, by fits and starts.'

'At the light?'

'At the Danger-light.'

'What does it seem to do?'

He repeated if possible with increased passion and vehemence, that former gesticulation of 'For God's sake, clear the
way!'

Then he went on. 'I have no peace or rest for it. It calls to
me, for many minutes together, in an agonised manner,
"Below there! Look out!" It stands waving to me. It rings my
little bell . . .'

I caught at that. 'Did it ring your bell yesterday evening
when I was here, and you went to the door?'

'Twice.'

'Why, see,' said I, 'how your imagination misleads you.
My eyes were on the bell, and my ears were open to the bell,
and if I am a living man, it did NOT ring at those times. No,
nor at any other time, except when it was rung in the natural
course of physical things by the station communicating with
you.'

He shook his head. 'I have never made a mistake as to that
yet, Sir. I have never confused the spectre's ring with the
man's. The ghost's ring is a strange vibration in the bell that it
derives from nothing else, and I have not asserted that the bell
stirs to the eye. I don't wonder that you failed to hear it. But I
heard it.'

'And did the spectre seem to be there, when you looked out?'

'It WAS there.'

'Both times?'

He repeated firmly: 'Both times.'

'Will you come to the door with me, and look for it now?'

He bit his under lip as though he were somewhat unwilling, but arose. I opened the door, and stood on the step, while he stood in the doorway. There was the Danger light. There was the dismal mouth of the tunnel. There were the high, wet stone walls of the cutting. There were the stars above them.

'Do you see it? I asked him, taking particular note of his face. His eyes were prominent and strained, but not very much more so, perhaps, than my own had been when I had directed them earnestly towards the same spot.

'No,' he answered. 'It's not there.'

'Agreed,' said I.

We went in again, shut the door, and resumed our seats. I was thinking how best to improve this advantage, if it might be called one, when he took up the conversation in such a matter-of-course way, so assuming that there could be no serious question of fact between us, that I felt myself placed in the weakest of positions.

'By this time you will fully understand, Sir,' he said, 'that what troubles me so dreadfully is the question, What does the spectre mean?'

I was not sure, I told him, that I did fully understand.

'What is its warning against?' he said, ruminating, with his eyes on the fire, and only by times turning them on me. 'What is the danger? Where is the danger? There is danger overhanging somewhere on the Line. Some dreadful calamity will happen. It is not to be doubted this third time, after what has gone before. But surely this a cruel haunting of *me*. What can *I* do?'

He pulled out his handkerchief, and wiped the drops from his heated forehead.

'If I telegraph Danger, on either side of me, or on both, I can give no reason for it,' he went on, wiping the palms of his hands. 'I should get into trouble, and do no good. They would think I was mad. This is the way it would work, – Message: "Danger! Take care!" Answer. "What Danger? Where?" Message: "Don't know. But for God's sake, take care!" They would displace me. What else could they do?'

His pain of mind was most pitiable to see. It was the mental torture of a conscientious man, oppressed beyond endurance by an unintelligible responsibility involving life.

'When it first stood under the Danger-light,' he went on, putting his dark hair back from his head, and drawing his hands outward and across his temples in an extremity of feverish distress, 'why not tell me where that accident was to happen, – if it might happen? Why not tell me how it could be averted, – if it could have been averted? When on its second coming it hid its face, why not tell me, instead, "She is going to die. Let them keep her at home"? If it came, on those two occasions, only to show me that its warnings were true, and so prepare me for the third, why not warn me plainly now? And I, Lord help me! A mere poor signalman on this solitary station! Why not go to somebody with credit to be believed and power to act?'

When I saw him in this state, I saw that for the poor man's sake, as well as for the public safety, what I had to do for the time was to compose his mind. Therefore, setting aside all question of reality or unreality between us, I represented to him that whoever thoroughly discharged his duty must do well, and that at least it was his comfort that he understood his duty, though he did not understand these confounding Appearances. In this effort I succeeded far better than in the attempt to reason him out of his conviction. He became calm; the occupations incidental to his post as the night advanced began to make larger demands on his attention: and I left him at two in the morning. I had offered to stay through the night, but he would not hear of it.

That I more than once looked back at the red light as I ascended the pathway, that I did not like the red light, and that I should have slept but poorly if my bed had been under it, I see no reason to conceal. Nor did I like the two sequences of the accident and the dead girl. I see no reason to conceal that either.

But what ran most in my thoughts was the consideration how ought I to act, having become the recipient of this disclosure? I had proved the man to be intelligent, vigilant, painstaking, and exact; but how long might he remain so, in his state of mind? Though in a subordinate position, still he held a most important trust, and would I (for instance) like to stake my own life on the chances of his continuing to execute it with precision?

Unable to overcome a feeling that there would be something treacherous in my communicating what he had told me to his superiors in the Company, without first being plain with himself and proposing a middle course to him, I ultimately resolved to offer to accompany him (otherwise keeping his secret for the present) to the wisest medical practitioner we could hear of in those parts, and to take his opinion. A change in his time of duty would come round next night, he had appraised me, and he would be off an hour or two after sunrise, and on again soon after sunset. I had appointed to return accordingly.

Next evening was a lovely evening, and I walked out early to enjoy it. The sun was not quite down when I traversed the field-path near the top of the deep cutting. I would extend my walk for an hour, I said to myself, half an hour on and half an hour back, and it would then be time to go to my signalman's box.

Before pursuing my stroll, I stepped to the brink, and mechanically looked down, from the point from which I had first seen him. I cannot describe the thrill that seized me, when, close at the mouth of the tunnel, I saw the appearance of a man, with his left sleeve across his eyes, passionately waving his right arm.

The nameless horror that oppressed me passed in a moment, for in a moment I saw this appearance of a man was a man indeed, and that there was a little group of other men, standing at a short distance, to whom he seemed to be rehearsing the gesture he made. The Danger-light was not yet lighted. Against its shaft, a little low hut, entirely new to me, had been made of some wooden supports and tarpaulin. It looked no bigger than a bed.

With an irresistible sense that something was wrong, – with a flashing self-reproachful fear that fatal mischief had come of my leaving the man there, and causing no one to be sent to overlook or correct what he did, – I descended the notched path with all the speed I could make.

'What is the matter?' I asked the men.

'Signalman killed this morning, Sir.'

'Not the man belonging to that box?'

'Yes, Sir.'

'Not the man I know?'

'You will recognise him, Sir, if you knew him,' said the man who spoke for the others, solemnly uncovering his own head, and raising an end of the tarpaulin, 'for his face is quite composed.'

'O, how did this happen, how did this happen?' I asked, turning from one to another as the hut closed in again.

'He was cut down by an engine, Sir. No man in England knew his work better. But somehow he was not clear of the outer rail. It was just at broad day. He had struck the light, and had the lamp in his hand. As the engine came out of the tunnel, his back was towards her, and she cut him down. That man drove her, and was showing how it happened. Show the gentleman, Tom.'

The man, who wore a rough dark dress, stepped back to his former place at the mouth of the tunnel.

'Coming round the curve in the tunnel, Sir,' he said, 'I saw him at the end, like as if I saw him down a perspective-glass. There was no time to check speed, and I knew him to be very careful. As he didn't seem to take heed of the whistle, I shut it off when we were running down upon him, and called to him as loud as I could call.'

'What did you say?'

'I said, "Below there! Look out! Look out! For God's sake, clear the way!"'

I started.

'Ah! it was a dreadful time, Sir. I never left off calling to him. I put this arm before my eyes not to see, and I waved this arm to the last; but it was no use.'

Without prolonging the narrative to dwell on any one of its curious circumstances more than on any other, I may, in closing it, point out the coincidence that the warning of the Engine-driver included, not only the words which the unfortunate Signalman had repeated to me as haunting him, but also the words which I myself – not he – had attached, and that only in my own mind, to the gesticulation he had imitated.

from *All the Year Round*

A MADMAN'S MANUSCRIPT

'Yes! – a madman's! How that word would have struck to my heart, many years ago! How it would have roused the terror that used to come upon me sometimes, sending the blood hissing and tingling through my veins, till the cold dew of fear stood in large drops upon my skin, and my knees knocked together with fright! I like it now though. It's a fine name. Show me the monarch whose angry frown was ever feared like the glare of a madman's eye – whose cord and axe were ever half so sure as a madman's gripe. Ho! ho! It's a grand thing to be mad! to be peeped at like a wild lion through the iron bars – to gnash one's teeth and howl, through the long still night, to the merry ring of a heavy chain – and to roll and twine among the straw, transported with such brave music. Hurrah for the madhouse! Oh, it's a rare place!

'I remember days when I was *afraid* of being mad; when I used to start from my sleep, and fall upon my knees, and pray to be spared from the curse of my race; when I rushed from the sight of merriment or happiness, to hide myself in some lonely place, and spend the weary hours in watching the progress of the fever that was to consume my brain. I knew that madness was mixed up with my very blood, and the marrow of my bones! that one generation had passed away without the pestilence appearing among them, and that I was the first in whom it would revive. I knew it *must* be so: that so it always had been, and so it ever would be: and when I cowered in some obscure corner of a crowded room, and saw men whisper, and point, and turn their eyes towards me, I knew they were telling each other of the doomed madman; and I slunk away again to mope in solitude.

'I did this for years; long, long years they were. The nights here are long sometimes – very long; but they are nothing to the restless nights, and dreadful dreams I had at that time. It makes me cold to remember them. Large dusky forms with

14

sly and jeering faces crouched in the corners of the room, and bent over my bed at night, tempting me to madness. They told me in low whispers, that the floor of the old house in which my father's father died was stained with his own blood, shed by his own hand in raging madness. I drove my fingers into my ears, but they screamed into my head till the room rang with it, that in one generation before him the madness slumbered, but that his grandfather had lived for years with his hands fettered to the ground, to prevent his tearing himself to pieces. I knew they told the truth – I knew it well. I had found it out years before, though they had tried to keep it from me. Ha! ha! I was too cunning for them, madman as they thought me.

'At last it came upon me, and I wondered how I could ever have feared it. I could go into the world now, and laugh and shout with the best among them. I knew I was mad, but they did not even suspect it. How I used to hug myself with delight, when I thought of the fine trick I was playing them after their old pointing and leering, when I was not mad, but only dreading that I might one day become so! And how I used to laugh for joy, when I was alone, and thought how well I kept my secret, and how quickly my kind friends would have fallen from me, if they had known the truth. I could have screamed with ecstasy when I dined alone with some fine roaring fellow, to think how pale he would have turned, and how fast he would have run, if he had known that the dear friend who sat close to him, sharpening a bright, glittering knife, was a madman with all the power, and half the will, to plunge it in his heart. Oh, it was a merry life!

'Riches became mine, wealth poured in upon me, and I rioted in pleasures enhanced a thousandfold to me by the consciousness of my well-kept secret. I inherited an estate. The law – the eagle-eyed law itself – had been deceived, and had handed over disputed thousands to a madman's hands. Where was the wit of the sharp-sighted men of sound mind? Where the dexterity of the lawyers, eager to discover a flaw? The madman's cunning had overreached them all.

'I had money. How I was courted! I spent it profusely. How I was praised! How those three proud, overbearing brothers humbled themselves before me! The old, white-headed father,

too – such deference – such respect – such devoted friendship –
he worshipped me! The old man had a daughter, and the
young men a sister; and all the five were poor. I was rich; and
when I married the girl, I saw a smile of triumph play upon
the faces of her needy relatives, as they thought of their well-
planned scheme, and their fine prize. It was for me to smile.
To smile! To laugh outright, and tear my hair, and roll upon
the ground with shrieks of merriment. They little thought
they had married her to a madman.

'Stay. If they had known it, would they have saved her? A
sister's happiness against her husband's gold. The lightest
feather I blow into the air, against the gay chain that orna-
ments my body!

'In one thing I was deceived with all my cunning. If I had
not been mad – for though we madmen are sharp-witted
enough, we get bewildered sometimes – I should have known
that the girl would rather have been placed, stiff and cold in a
dull leaden coffin, than borne an envied bride to my rich,
glittering house. I should have known that her heart was with
the dark-eyed boy whose name I once heard her breathe in her
troubled sleep; and that she had been sacrificed to me, to
relieve the poverty of the old, white-headed man and the
haughty brothers.

'I don't remember forms or faces now, but I know the girl
was beautiful. I *know* she was; for in the bright moonlight
nights, when I start up from my sleep, and all is quiet about
me, I see, standing still and motionless in one corner of this
cell, a slight and wasted figure with long black hair, which
streaming down her back, stirs with no earthly wind, and eyes
that fix their gaze on me, and never wink or close. Hush! the
blood chills at my heart as I write it down – that form is *hers;*
the face is very pale, and the eyes are glassy bright; but I know
them well. That figure never moves; it never frowns and
mouths as others do, that fill this place sometimes; but it is
much more dreadful to me, even than the spirits that tempted
me many years ago – it comes fresh from the grave; and is so
very death-like.

'For nearly a year I saw that face grow paler; for nearly a
year I saw the tears steal down the mournful cheeks, and never
knew the cause. I found it out at last though. They could not

keep it from me long. She had never liked me; I had never thought she did: she despised my wealth, and hated the splendour in which she lived; but I had not expected that. She loved another. This I had never thought of. Strange feelings came over me, and thought, forced upon me by some strange secret power, whirled round and round my brain. I did not hate her, though I hated the boy she still wept for. I pitied – yes, I pitied – the wretched life to which her cold and selfish relations had doomed her. I knew that she could not live long; but the thought that before her death she might give birth to some ill-fated being, destined to hand down madness to its offspring, determined me. I resolved to kill her.

'For many weeks I thought of poison, and then of drowning, and then of fire. A fine sight, the grand house in flames, and the madman's wife smouldering away to cinders. Think of the jest of a large reward, too, and of some sane man swinging in the wind for a deed he never did, and all through a madman's cunning! I thought often of this, but I gave it up at last. Oh! the pleasure of stropping the razor day after day, feeling the sharp edge, and thinking of the gash one stroke of its thin, bright edge would make!

'At last the old spirits who had been with me so often before whispered in my ear that the time was come, and thrust the open razor into my hand. I grasped it firmly, rose softly from the bed, and leaned over my sleeping wife. Her face was buried in her hands. I withdrew them softly, and they fell listlessly on her bosom. She had been weeping; for the traces of the tears were still wet upon her cheek. Her face was calm and placid; and even as I looked upon it, a tranquil smile lighted up her pale features. I laid my hand softly on her shoulder. She started – it was only a passing dream. I leaned forward again. She screamed, and woke.

'One motion of my hand, and she would never again have uttered cry or sound. But I was startled, and drew back. Her eyes were fixed on mine. I knew not how it was, but they cowed and frightened me; and I quailed beneath them. She rose from the bed, still gazing fixedly and steadily on me. I trembled; the razor was in my hand, but I could not move. She made towards the door. As she neared it, she turned, and withdrew her eyes from my face. The spell was broken. I bounded forward, and clutched her by the arm. Uttering shriek upon shriek, she sank upon the ground.

'Now I could have killed her without a struggle; but the house was alarmed. I heard the tread of footsteps on the stairs. I replaced the razor in its usual drawer, unfastened the door, and called loudly for assistance.

'They came, and raised her, and placed her on the bed. She lay bereft of animation for hours; and when life, look, and speech returned, her senses had deserted her, and she raved wildly and furiously.

'Doctors were called in – great men who rolled up to my door in easy carriages, with fine horses and gaudy servants. They were at her bedside for weeks. They had a great meeting, and consulted together in low and solemn voices in another room. One, the cleverest and most celebrated among them, took me aside, and bidding me prepare for the worst, told me – me, the madman! – that my wife was mad. He stood close beside me at an open window, his eyes looking in my face, and his hand laid upon my arm. With one effort, I could have hurled him into the street beneath. It would have been rare sport to have done it; but my secret was at stake, and I let him go. A few days after, they told me I must place her under some restraint: I must provide a keeper for her. *I!* I went into the open fields where none could hear me, and laughed till the air resounded with my shouts!

'She died next day. The white-haired old man followed her to the grave, and the proud brothers dropped a tear over the insensible corpse of her whose sufferings they had regarded in her lifetime with muscles of iron. All this was food for my secret mirth, and I laughed behind the white handkerchief which I held up to my face, as we rode home, till tears came into my eyes.

'But though I had carried out my object and killed her, I was restless and disturbed, and I felt that before long my secret must be known. I could not hide the wild mirth and joy which boiled within me, and made me when I was alone, at home, jump up and beat my hands together, and dance round and round, and roar aloud. When I went out, and saw the busy crowds hurrying about the streets; or the theatre, and heard the sound of music, and beheld the people dancing, I felt such glee, that I could have rushed among them, and torn them to pieces limb from limb, and howled in transport. But I ground my teeth, and struck my feet upon the floor, and drove my sharp nails into my hands. I kept it down; and no one knew I was a madman yet.

'I remember – though it's one of the last things I *can* remember: for now I mix up realities with my dreams, and having so much to do, and being always hurried here, have no time to separate the two, from some strange confusion in which they get involved – I remember how I let it out at last. Ha! ha! I think I see their frightened looks now, and feel the ease with which I flung them from me, and dashed my clenched fist into their white faces, and then flew like the wind, and left them screaming and shouting far behind. The strength of a giant comes upon me when I think of it. There – see how this iron bar bends beneath my furious wrench. I could snap it like a twig, only there are long galleries here with many doors – I don't think I could find my way along them; and even if I could, I know there are iron gates below which they keep locked and barred. They know what a clever madman I have been, and they are proud to have me here, to show.

'Let me see: yes, I had been found out. It was late at night when I reached home, and found the proudest of the three proud brothers waiting to see me – urgent business he said: I recollect it well. I hated that man with all a madman's hate. Many and many a time had my fingers longed to tear him. They told me he was there. I ran swiftly upstairs. He had a word to say to me. I dismissed the servants. It was late, and we were alone together – *for the first time*.

'I kept my eyes carefully from him at first, for I knew what he little thought – and I gloried in the knowledge – that the light of madness gleamed from them like fire. We sat in silence for a few minutes. He spoke at last. My recent dissipation, and strange remarks, made so soon after his sister's death, were an insult to her memory. Coupling together many circumstances which had at first escaped his observation, he thought I had not treated her well. He wished to know whether he was right in inferring that I meant to cast a reproach upon her memory, and a disrespect upon her family. It was due to the uniform he wore to demand this explanation.

'This man had a commission in the army – a commission, purchased with my money, and his sister's misery! This was the man who had been foremost in the plot to ensnare me, and grasp my wealth. This was the man who had been the main instrument in forcing his sister to wed me; well knowing that her heart was given to that puling boy. Due to *his* uniform! The livery of his degradation! I turned my eyes upon him – I could not help it – but I spoke not a word.

'I saw a sudden change that came upon him beneath my gaze. He was a bold man, but the colour faded from his face, and he drew back in his chair. I dragged mine nearer to him; and as I laughed – I was very merry then – I saw him shudder. I felt the madness rising within me. He was afraid of me.

'"You were very fond of your sister when she was alive," I said. – "Very."

'He looked uneasily round him, and I saw his hand grasp the back of his chair; but he said nothing.

'"You villain," said I, "I found you out; I discovered your hellish plots against me; I know her heart was fixed on some one else before you compelled her to marry me. I know it – I know it."

'He jumped suddenly from his chair, brandishing it aloft, and bid me stand back – for I took care to be getting closer to him all the time I spoke.

'I screamed rather than talked, for I felt tumultuous passions eddying through my veins, and the old spirits whispering and taunting me to tear his heart out.

'"Damn you," said I, starting up, and rushing upon him; "I killed her. I am a madman. Down with you. Blood, blood! I will have it!"

'I turned aside with one blow the chair he hurled at me in his terror, and closed with him; and with a heavy crash we rolled upon the floor together.

'It was a fine struggle that; for he was a tall, strong man, fighting for his life; and I, a powerful madman, thirsting to destroy him. I knew no strength could equal mine, and I was right. Right again, though a madman! His struggles grew fainter. I knelt upon his chest, and clasped his brawny throat firmly with both hands. His face grew purple; his eyes were starting from his head, and with protruded tongue, he seemed to mock me. I squeezed the tighter.

'The door was suddenly burst open with a loud noise and a crowd of people rushed forward, crying aloud to each other to secure the madman.

'My secret was out; and my only struggle now was for liberty and freedom. I gained my feet before a hand was on me, threw myself among my assailants, and cleared my way with my strong arm, as if I bore a hatchet in my hand, and hewed them down before me. I gained the door, dropped over the banisters, and in an instant was in the street.

'Straight and swift I ran, and no one dared to stop me, I heard the noise of feet behind, and redoubled my speed. It grew fainter and fainter in the distance, and at length died away altogether; but on I bounded, through marsh and rivulet, over fence and wall, with a wild shout which was taken up by strange beings that flocked around me on every side, and swelled the sound, till it pierced the air. I was borne upon the arms of demons who swept along upon the wind, and bore down bank and hedge before them, and spun me round and round with a rustle and a speed that made my head swim, until at last they threw me from them with a violent shock, and I fell heavily upon the earth. When I woke I found myself here – here in this grey cell, where the sunlight seldom comes, and the moon steals in, in rays which only serve to show the dark shadows about me, and that silent figure in its old corner. When I lie awake, I can sometimes hear strange shrieks and cries from distant parts of this large place. What they are, I know not; but they neither come from that pale form, nor does it regard them. For from the first shades of dusk till the earliest light of morning, it still stands motionless in the same place, listening to the music of my iron chain, and watching my gambols on my straw bed.'

from *The Pickwick Papers*

THE BAGMAN'S STORY

'One winter's evening, about five o'clock, just as it began to grow dusk, a man in a gig might have been seen urging his tired horse along the road which leads across Marlborough Downs, in the direction of Bristol. I say he might have been seen, and I have no doubt he would have been, if anybody but a blind man had happened to pass that way; but the weather was so bad, and the night so cold and wet, that nothing was out but the water, and so the traveller jogged along in the middle of the road, lonesome and dreary enough. If any bagman of that day could have caught sight of the little neck-or-nothing sort of gig, with clay-coloured body and red wheels, and the vixenish ill-tempered, fast-going bay mare, that looked like a cross between a butcher's horse and a two-penny post office pony, he would have known at once, that this traveller could have been no other than Tom Smart, of the great house of Bilson and Slum, Cateaton Street, City. However, as there was no bagman to look on, nobody knew anything at all about the matter; and so Tom Smart and his clay-coloured gig with the red wheels, and the vixenish mare with the fast pace, went on together, keeping the secret among them: and nobody was a bit the wiser.

'There are many pleasanter places even in this dreary world, than Marlborough Downs when it blows hard; and if you throw in beside, a gloomy winter's evening, a miry and sloppy road, and a pelting fall of heavy rain, and try the effect, by way of experiment, in your own proper person, you will experience the full force of this observation.

'The wind blew – not up the road or down it, though that's bad enough, but sheer across it, sending the rain slanting down like the lines they used to rule in the copy-books at school, to make the boys slope well. For a moment it would die away, and the traveller would begin to delude himself into the belief that, exhausted with its previous fury, it had quietly

22

lain itself down to rest, when, whoo! he would hear it growling and whistling in the distance, and on it would come rushing over the hilltops, and sweeping along the plain, gathering sound and strength as it drew nearer, until it dashed with a heavy gust against horse and man, driving the sharp rain into their ears, and its cold damp breath into their very bones; and past them it would scour, far, far away, with a stunning roar, as if in ridicule of their weakness, and triumphant in the consciousness of its own strength and power.

'The bay mare splashed away, through the mud and water, with drooping ears; now and then tossing her head as if to express her disgust at this very ungentlemanly behaviour of the elements, but keeping a good pace notwithstanding, until a gust of wind, more furious than any that had yet assailed them, caused her to stop suddenly and plant her four feet firmly against the ground, to prevent her being blown over. It's a special mercy that she did this for if she *had* been blown over, the vixenish mare was so light, and the gig was so light, and Tom Smart such a light weight into the bargain, that they must infallibly have all gone rolling over and over together, until they reached the confines of earth, or until the wind fell; and in either case the probability is, that neither the vixenish mare, nor the clay-coloured gig with the red wheels, nor Tom Smart, would ever have been fit for service again.

'"Well, damn my straps and whiskers," says Tom Smart, (Tom sometimes had an unpleasant knack of swearing), "Damn my straps and whiskers," says Tom, "if this ain't pleasant, blow me!"

'You'll very likely ask me why, as Tom Smart had been pretty well blown already, he expressed this wish to be submitted to the same process again. I can't say – all I know is, that Tom Smart said so – or at least he always told my uncle he said so, and it's just the same thing.

'"Blow me," says Tom Smart; and the mare neighed as if she were precisely of the same opinion.

'"Cheer up, old girl," said Tom, patting the bay on the neck with the end of his whip. "It won't do pushing on, such a night as this; the first house we come to we'll put up at, so the faster you go the sooner it's over. Soho, old girl – gently – gently."

'Whether the vixenish mare was sufficiently well acquainted with the tones of Tom's voice to comprehend his meaning, or whether she found it colder standing still than moving on, of course I can't say. But I can say that Tom had no sooner finished speaking, than she pricked up her ears, and started forward at a speed which made the clay-coloured gig rattle till you would have supposed every one of the red spokes were going to fly out on the turf of Marlborough Downs; and even Tom, whip as he was, couldn't stop or check her pace, until she drew up, of her own accord, before a roadside inn on the right-hand side of the way, about half a quarter of a mile from the end of the Downs.

'Tom cast a hasty glance at the upper part of the house as he threw the reins to the hostler, and stuck the whip in the box. It was a strange old place, built of a kind of shingle, inlaid, as it were, with cross-beams, with gabled-topped windows projecting completely over the pathway, and a low door with a dark porch, and a couple of steep steps leading down into the house, instead of the modern fashion of half a dozen ones leading up to it. It was a comfortable-looking place though, for there was a strong cheerful light in the bar-window, which shed a bright ray across the road, and even lighted up the hedges on the other side; and there was a red flickering light in the opposite window, one moment but faintly discernible, and the next gleaming strongly through the drawn curtains, which intimated that a rousing fire was blazing within. Marking these little evidences with the eye of an experienced traveller, Tom dismounted with as much agility as his half-frozen limbs would permit, and entered the house.

'In less than five minutes' time, Tom was ensconced in the room opposite the bar – the very room where he had imagined the fire blazing – before a substantial matter-of-fact roaring fire, composed of something short of a bushel of coals, and wood enough to make half a dozen decent gooseberry bushes, piled half way up the chimney, and roaring and crackling with a sound that of itself would have warmed the heart of any reasonable man. This was comfortable, but this was not all, for a smartly dressed girl, with a bright eye and a neat ankle, was laying a very clean white cloth on the table; and as Tom sat with his slippered feet on the fender, and his back to the open door, he saw a charming prospect of the bar reflected in the glass over the chimney-piece, with delightful rows of green bottles and gold labels, together with jars of pickles and preserves, and cheeses and boiled hams, and rounds of beef, arranged on shelves in the most tempting and delicious array. Well, this was comfortable too; but even this was not all – for in the bar, seated at tea at the nicest possible little table, drawn close up before the brightest possible little fire, was a buxom widow of some-where about eight and forty or thereabouts, with a face as comfortable as the bar, who was evidently the landlady of the house, and the supreme ruler over all these agreeable posses-sions. There was only one drawback to the beauty of the whole picture, and that was a tall man – a very tall man – in a brown coat and bright basket buttons, and black whiskers, and wavy black hair, who was seated at tea with the widow, and who it required no great penetration to discover was in a fair way of persuading her to be a widow no longer, but to confer upon him the privilege of sitting down in that bar, for and during the whole remainder of the term of his natural life.

'Tom Smart was by no means of an irritable or envious disposition, but somehow or other the tall man with the brown coat and the bright basket buttons did rouse what little gall he had in his composition, and did make him feel extremely indignant: the more especially as he could now and then observe, from his seat before the glass, certain little affectionate familiarities passing between the tall man and the widow, which sufficiently denoted that the tall man was as high in favour as he was in size. Tom was fond of hot punch – I may venture to say he was *very* fond of hot punch – and after he had seen the vixenish mare well fed and well littered down, and had eaten every bit of the nice little hot dinner which the widow tossed up for him with her own hands, he just ordered a tumbler of it, by way of experiment. Now, if there was one thing in the whole range of domestic art, which the widow could manufacture better than another, it was this identical article; and the first tumbler was adapted to Tom Smart's taste with such peculiar nicety, that he ordered a second with the least possible delay. Hot punch is a pleasant thing, gentlemen – an extremely pleasant thing under any circumstances – but in that snug old parlour, before the roaring fire, with the wind blowing outside till every timber in the old house creaked again, Tom Smart found it perfectly delightful. He ordered another tumbler, and then another – I am not quite certain whether he didn't order another after that – but the more he drank of the hot punch, the more he thought of the tall man.

'"Confound his impudence!" said Tom to himself, "what business has he in that snug bar? Such an ugly villain too!" said Tom. "If the widow had any taste, she might surely pick up some better fellow than that." Here Tom's eye wandered from the glass on the chimney-piece, to the glass on the table; and as he felt himself becoming gradually sentimental, he emptied the fourth tumbler of punch and ordered a fifth.

'Tom Smart, gentleman, had always been very much attached to the public line. It had long been his ambition to stand in a bar of his own, in a green coat, knee-cords, and tops. He had a great notion of taking the chair at convivial dinners, and he had often thought how well he could preside in a room of his own in the talking way, and what a capital example he could set to his customers in the drinking department. All these things passed rapidly through Tom's mind as he sat drinking the hot punch by the roaring fire, and he felt very justly and properly indignant that the tall man should be in a fair way of keeping such an excellent house, while he, Tom Smart, was as far off from it as ever. So, after deliberating over the two last tumblers, whether he hadn't a perfect right to pick a quarrel with the tall man for having contrived to get into the good graces of the buxom widow, Tom Smart at last arrived at the satisfactory conclusion that he was a very ill-used and persecuted individual, and had better go to bed.

'Up a wide and ancient staircase the smart girl preceded Tom, shading the chamber candle with her hand, to protect it from the currents of air which in such a rambling old place might have found plenty of room to disport themselves in, without blowing the candle out, but which did blow it out nevertheless; thus affording Tom's enemies an opportunity of asserting that it was he, and not the wind, who extinguished the candle, and that while he pretended to be blowing it alight again, he was in fact kissing the girl. Be this as it may, another light was obtained, and Tom was conducted through a maze of rooms, and a labyrinth of passages, to the apartment which had been prepared for his reception, where the girl bade him good night, and left him alone.

'It was a good large room with big closets, and a bed which might have served for a whole boarding-school, to say nothing of a couple of oaken presses that would have held the baggage of a small army; but what struck Tom's fancy most was a strange, grim-looking high-backed chair, carved in the most fantastic manner, with a flowered damask cushion, and the round knobs at the bottom of the legs carefully tied up in red cloth, as if it had got the gout in its toes. Of any other queer chair, Tom would only have thought it *was* a queer chair, and there would have been an end of the matter; but there was something about this particular chair, and yet he couldn't tell what it was, so odd and so unlike any other piece of furniture he had ever seen, that it seemed to fascinate him. He sat down before the fire, and stared at the old chair for half an hour; – Deuce take the chair, it was such a strange old thing, he couldn't take his eyes off it.

'"Well," said Tom, slowly undressing himself, and staring at the old chair all the while, which stood with a mysterious aspect by the bedside, "I never saw such a rum concern as that in my days. Very odd," said Tom, who had got rather sage with the hot punch, "Very odd." Tom shook his head with an air of profound wisdom, and looked at the chair again. He couldn't make anything of it though, so he got into bed, covered himself up warm, and fell asleep.

'In about half an hour, Tom woke up, with a start, from a confused dream of tall men and tumblers of punch: and the first object that presented itself to his waking imagination was the queer chair.

'"I won't look at it any more," said Tom to himself and he squeezed his eyelids together, and tried to persuade himself he was going to sleep again. No use; nothing but queer chairs danced before his eyes, kicking up their legs, jumping over each other's backs, and playing all kinds of antics.

'"I may as well see one real chair, as two or three complete sets of false ones," said Tom, bringing out his head from under the bed-clothes. There it was, plainly discernible by the light of the fire, looking as provoking as ever.

'Tom gazed at the chair; and, suddenly, as he looked at it, a most extraordinary change seemed to come over it. The carving of the back gradually assumed the lineaments and expression of an old shrivelled human face; the damask cushion became an antique, flapped waistcoat; the round knobs grew into a couple of feet, encased in red cloth slippers; and the old chair looked like a very ugly old man, of the previous century, with his arms a-kimbo. Tom sat up in bed, and rubbed his eyes to dispel the illusion. No. The chair was an ugly old gentleman; and what was more he was winking at Tom Smart.

'Tom was naturally a headlong, careless sort of dog, and he had had five tumblers of hot punch into the bargain; so, although he was a little startled at first, he began to grow rather indignant when he saw the old gentleman winking and leering at him with such an impudent air. At length he resolved that he wouldn't stand it; and as the old face kept winking away as fast as ever, Tom said, in a very angry tone:

'"What the devil are you winking at me for?"

'"Because I like it, Tom Smart," said the chair; or the old gentleman, whichever you like to call him. He stopped winking though, when Tom spoke, and began grinning like a superannuated monkey.

'"How do you know my name, old nut-cracker face!" inquired Tom Smart, rather staggered; – though he pretended to carry it off so well.

'"Come, come, Tom," said the old gentleman, "that's not the way to address solid Spanish Mahogany. Dam'me, you couldn't treat me with less respect if I was veneered." When the old gentleman said this, he looked so fierce that Tom began to grow frightened.

'"I didn't mean to treat you with any disrespect, sir," said Tom; in a much humbler tone than he had spoken in at first.

'"Well, well," said the old fellow, "perhaps not – perhaps not. Tom . . ."

'"Sir . . ."

'"I know everything about you, Tom; everything. You're very poor, Tom."

'"I certainly am," said Tom Smart. "But how came you to know that?"

"'Never mind that," said the old gentleman; "you're much too fond of punch, Tom."

'Tom Smart was just on the point of protesting that he hadn't tasted a drop since his last birthday, but when his eye encountered that of the old gentleman, he looked so knowing that Tom blushed, and was silent.

"'Tom," said the old gentleman, "the widow's a fine woman – remarkably fine woman – eh, Tom?" Here the old fellow screwed up his eyes, cocked up one of his wasted little legs, and looked altogether so unpleasantly amorous, that Tom was quite disgusted with the levity of his behaviour; – at his time of life, too!

"'I am her guardian, Tom," said the old gentleman.

"'Are you?" inquired Tom Smart.

"'I knew her mother, Tom," said the old fellow; "and her grandmother. She was very fond of me – made me this waistcoat, Tom."

"'Did she?" said Tom Smart.

"'And these shoes," said the old fellow, lifting up one of the red-cloth mufflers; "but don't mention it, Tom. I shouldn't like to have it known that she was so much attached to me. It might occasion some unpleasantness in the family." When the old rascal said this, he looked so extremely impertinent, that, as Tom Smart afterwards declared, he could have sat upon him without remorse.

"'I have been a great favourite among the women in my time, Tom," said the profligate old debauchee; "hundreds of fine women have sat in my lap for hours together. What do you think of that you dog, eh!" The old gentleman was proceeding to recount some other exploits of his youth, when he was seized with such a violent fit of creaking that he was unable to proceed.

"'Just served you right, old boy," thought Tom Smart; but he didn't say anything.

"'Ah!" said the old fellow, "I am a good deal troubled with this now. I am getting old Tom, and have lost nearly all my rails. I have had an operation performed, too – a small piece let into my back – and I found it a severe trial, Tom."

"'I dare say you did, sir," said Tom Smart.

"'However,' said the old gentleman, "that's not the point. Tom! I want you to marry the widow."

"'Me, sir!' said Tom.

"'You,' said the old gentleman.

"'Bless your reverend locks,' said Tom – (he had a few scattered horse-hairs left) – "bless your reverend locks, she wouldn't have me." And Tom sighed involuntarily, as he thought of the bar.

"'Wouldn't she?' said the old gentleman, firmly.

"'No, no,' said Tom; "there's somebody else in the wind. A tall man – a confoundedly tall man – with black whiskers."

"'Tom,' said the old gentleman, "she will never have him."

"'Won't she?' said Tom. "If you stood in the bar, old gentleman, you'd tell another story."

"'Pooh, pooh,' said the old gentleman. "I know all about that."

"'About what?' said Tom.

"'About kissing behind the door, and all that sort of thing, Tom,' said the old gentleman. And here he gave another impudent look, which made Tom very wroth, because as you all know, gentlemen, to hear an old fellow, who ought to know better, talking about these things, is very unpleasant – nothing more so.

"'I know all about that, Tom,' said the old gentleman. "I have seen it done very often in my time, Tom, between more people than I should like to mention to you; but it never came to anything after all."

"'You must have seen some queer things,' said Tom, with an inquisitive look.

"'You may say that, Tom,' replied the old fellow, with a very complicated wink. "I am the last of my family, Tom," said the old gentleman, with a melancholy sigh.

"'Was it a large one?' inquired Tom Smart.

"'There were twelve of us, Tom,' said the old gentleman; "fine straight-backed, handsome fellows as you'd wish to see. None of your modern abortions – all with arms, and with a degree of polish, though I say it that should not, which would have done your heart good to behold."

'"And what's become of the others, sir?" asked Tom Smart.

'The old gentleman applied his elbow to his eye as he replied, "Gone, Tom, gone. We had hard service, Tom, and they hadn't all my constitution. They got rheumatic about the legs and arms, and went into kitchens and hospitals; and one of 'em, with long service and hard usage, positively lost his senses: – he got so crazy that he was obliged to be burnt. Shocking thing that, Tom."

'"Dreadful!" said Tom Smart.

'The old fellow paused for a few minutes, apparently struggling with his feelings of emotion, and then said:

'"However, Tom, I am wandering from the point. This tall man, Tom, is a rascally adventurer. The moment he married the widow, he would sell off all the furniture, and run away. What would be the consequence? She would be deserted and reduced to ruin, and I should catch my death of cold in some broker's shop."

'"Yes, but . . ."

'"Don't interrupt me," said the old gentleman. "Of you, Tom, I entertain a very different opinion; for I well know that if you once settled yourself in a public house, you would never leave it, as long as there was anything to drink within its walls."

'"I am very much obliged to you for your good opinion, sir," said Tom Smart.

'"Therefore," resumed the old gentleman, in a dictatorial tone; "you shall have her, and he shall not."

'"What is to prevent it?" said Tom Smart, eagerly.

'"This disclosure," replied the old gentleman; "he is already married."

'"How can I prove it?" said Tom, starting half out of bed.

'The old gentleman untucked his arm from his side, and having pointed to one of the oaken presses, immediately replaced it in its old position.

'"He little thinks," said the old gentleman, "that in the right hand pocket of a pair of trousers in that press, he has left a letter, entreating him to return to his disconsolate wife, with six – mark me, Tom – six babes, and all of them small ones."

'As the old gentleman solemnly uttered these words, his features grew less and less distinct, and his figure more shadowy. A film came over Tom Smart's eyes. The old man

seemed gradually blending into the chair, the damask waistcoat to resolve into a cushion, the red slippers to shrink into
little red cloth bags. The light faded gently away, and Tom
Smart fell back on his pillow, and dropped asleep.

'Morning aroused Tom from the lethargic slumber, into
which he had fallen on the disappearance of the old man. He
sat up in bed, and for some minutes vainly endeavoured to
recall the events of the preceding night. Suddenly they rushed
upon him. He looked at the chair; it was a fantastic and grim-
looking piece of furniture, certainly, but it must have been a
remarkably ingenious and lively imagination that could have
discovered any resemblance between it and an old man.

'"How old are you, old boy?" said Tom. He was bolder in
the daylight – most men are.

'The chair remained motionless, and spoke not a word.

'"Miserable morning," said Tom. No. The chair would not
be drawn into conversation.

'"Which press did you point to? You can tell me that," said
Tom. Devil a word, gentlemen, the chair would say.

'"It's not much trouble to open it, any how," said Tom,
getting out of bed very deliberately. He walked up to one of
the presses. The key was in the lock; he turned it, and opened
the door. There *was* a pair of trousers there. He put his hand
into the pocket and drew forth the identical letter the old
gentleman had described!

'"Queer sort of thing, this," said Tom Smart; looking first
at the chair and then at the press, and then at the letter, and
then at the chair again. "Very queer," said Tom. But, as there
was nothing in either, to lessen the queerness, he thought he
might as well dress himself, and settle the tall man's business
at once – just to put him out of his misery.

'Tom surveyed the rooms he passed through, on his way
downstairs, with the scrutinising eye of a landlord; thinking it
not impossible, that before long, they and their contents
would be his property. The tall man was standing in the snug
little bar, with his hands behind him, quite at home. He
grinned vacantly at Tom. A casual observer might have
supposed he did it, only to show his white teeth; but Tom
Smart thought that a consciousness of triumph was passing
through the place where the tall man's mind would have been,

if he had had any. Tom laughed in his face; and summoned the landlady.

"'Good morning, ma'am" said Tom Smart, closing the door of the little parlour as the widow entered.

"'Good morning, sir," said the widow. "What will you take for breakfast, sir?"

'Tom was thinking how he should open the case, so he made no answer.

"'There's a very nice ham," said the widow, "and a beautiful cold larded fowl. Shall I send 'em in, sir?"

'These words roused Tom from his reflections. His admiration of the widow increased as she spoke. Thoughtful creature! Comfortable provider!

"'Who is that gentleman in the bar, ma'am?" inquired Tom.

"'His name is Jinkins, sir," said the widow, slightly blushing.

"'He's a tall man," said Tom.

"'He is a very fine man, sir," replied the widow, "and a very nice gentleman."

"'Ah!" said Tom.

"'Is there anything more you want, sir?" inquired the widow, rather puzzled by Tom's manner.

"'Why, yes," said Tom. "My dear ma'am, will you have the kindness to sit down for one moment?"

'The widow looked much amazed, but she sat down, and Tom sat down too, close beside her. I don't know how it happened, gentlemen, – indeed my uncle used to tell me that Tom Smart said *he* didn't know how it happened either – but somehow or other the palm of Tom's hand fell upon the back of the widow's hand, and remained there while he spoke.

"'My dear ma'am," said Tom Smart – he had always a great notion of committing the amiable – "My dear ma'am, you deserve a very excellent husband; – you do indeed."

"'Lor, sir!" said the widow – as well she might: Tom's mode of commencing the conversation being rather unusual, not to say startling: the fact of his never having set eyes upon her before the previous night, being taken into consideration. "Lor, sir!"

"'I scorn to flatter, my dear ma'am," said Tom Smart. "You deserve a very admirable husband, and whoever he is, he'll be a very lucky man." As Tom said this his eye involuntarily wandered from the widow's face, to the comforts around him.

'The widow looked more puzzled than ever, and made an effort to rise. Tom gently pressed her hand, as if to detain her, and she kept her seat. Widows, gentlemen, are not usually timorous, as my uncle used to say.

'"I am sure I am very much obliged to you, sir, for your good opinion," said the buxom landlady, half laughing; "and if I ever marry again . . ."

'"*If*," said Tom Smart, looking very shrewdly out of the right-hand corner of his left eye. "*If* . . .'

'"Well," said the widow, laughing outright this time. "*When* I do, I hope I shall have as good a husband as you describe."

'"Jinkins to wit," said Tom.

'"Lor, sir!" exclaimed the widow.

'"Oh, don't tell me," said Tom, "I know him."

'"I am sure nobody who knows him, knows anything bad of him," said the widow, bridling up at the mysterious air with which Tom had spoken.

'"Hem!" said Tom Smart.

'The widow began to think it was high time to cry, so she took out her handkerchief, and inquired whether Tom wished to insult her: whether he thought it like a gentleman to take away the character of another gentleman behind his back: why, if he had got anything to say, he didn't say it to the man, like a man, instead of terrifying a poor weak woman in that way; and so forth.

'"I'll say it to him fast enough," said Tom, "only I want you to hear it first."

'"What is it?" inquired the widow, looking intently in Tom's countenance.

'"I'll astonish you," said Tom, putting his hand in his pocket.

'"If it is, that he wants money," said the widow, "I know that already, and you needn't trouble yourself."

'"Pooh, nonsense, that's nothing," said Tom Smart, "*I* want money. 'Tan't that."

'"Oh, dear, what can it be?" exclaimed the poor widow.

'"Don't be frightened," said Tom Smart. He slowly drew forth the letter, and unfolded it. "You won't scream?" said Tom doubtfully.

'"No, no," replied the widow; "let me see it."

'"You won't go fainting away, or any of that nonsense?" said Tom.

'"No, no," returned the widow, hastily.

'"And don't run out, and blow him up," said Tom, "because I'll do all that for you; you had better not exert yourself."

'"Well, well," said the widow, "let me see it."

'"I will," replied Tom Smart; and, with these words, he placed the letter in the widow's hand.

'Gentlemen, I have heard my uncle say, that Tom Smart said, the widow's lamentations when she heard the disclosure would have pierced a heart of stone. Tom was certainly very tender-hearted, but they pierced his, to the very core. The widow rocked herself to and fro, and wrung her hands.

'"Oh, the deception and villainy of man!" said the widow.

'"Frightful, my dear ma'am; but compose yourself," said Tom Smart.

'"Oh, I can't compose myself," shrieked the widow. "I shall never find any one else I can love so much!"

'"Oh, yes you will, my dear soul," said Tom Smart, letting fall a shower of the largest sized tears, in pity for the widow's misfortunes. Tom Smart, in the energy of his compassion, had put his arm round the widow's waist; and the widow, in a passion of grief, had clasped Tom's hand. She looked up in Tom's face, and smiled through her tears. Tom looked down in her's, and smiled through his.

'I could never find out, gentlemen, whether Tom did or did not kiss the widow at that particular moment. He used to tell my uncle he didn't, but I have my doubts about it. Between ourselves, gentlemen, I rather think he did.

'At all events, Tom kicked the very tall man out at the front door half an hour after, and married the widow a month after. And he used to drive about the country, with the clay-coloured gig with red wheels, and the vixenish mare with the fast pace, till he gave up business many years afterwards, and went to France with his wife; and then the old house was pulled down.'

from *The Pickwick Papers*

THE STORY OF THE GOBLINS
WHO STOLE A SEXTON

'In an old abbey town, down in this part of the country, a long, long while ago – so long, that the story must be a true one, because our great grandfathers implicitly believed it – there officiated as sexton and grave-digger in the churchyard, one Gabriel Grub. It by no means follows that because a man is a sexton, and constantly surrounded by the emblems of mortality, therefore he should be a morose and melancholy man; your undertakers are the merriest fellows in the world; and I once had the honour of being on intimate terms with a mute, who in private life, and off duty, was as comical and jocose a little fellow as ever chirped out a devil-may-care song, without a hitch in his memory, or drained off the contents of a good stiff glass without stopping for breath. But, notwithstanding these precedents to the contrary, Gabriel Grub was an ill-conditioned, cross-grained, surly fellow – a morose and lonely man, who consorted with nobody but himself, and an old wicker bottle which fitted into his large waistcoat pocket – and who eyed each merry face, as it passed him by, with such a deep scowl of malice and ill-humour, as it was difficult to meet, without feeling something the worse for.

'A little before twilight, one Christmas Eve, Gabriel shouldered his spade, lighted his lantern, and betook himself towards the old churchyard; for he had got a grave to finish by next morning, and, feeling very low, he thought it might raise his spirits, perhaps, if he went on with his work at once. As he went his way, up the ancient street he saw the cheerful light of the blazing fires gleam through the old casements, and heard the loud laugh and the cheerful shouts of those who were assembled around them; he marked the bustling preparations for next day's cheer, and smelt the numerous savory odours consequent thereupon, as they steamed up from the kitchen

windows in clouds. All this was gall and wormwood to the
heart of Gabriel Grub; and when groups of children, bounded
out of the houses, tripped across the road, and were met,
before they could knock at the opposite door, by half a dozen
curly-headed little rascals who crowed round them as they
flocked upstairs to spend the evening in their Christmas
games, Gabriel smiled grimly, and clutched the handle of his
spade with a firmer grasp, as he thought of measles, scarlet
fever, thrush, whooping-cough, and a good many other
sources of consolation besides.

'In this happy frame of mind, Gabriel strode along:
returning a short, sullen growl to the good-humoured
greetings of such of his neighbours as now and then passed
him: until he turned into the dark lane which led to the
churchyard. Now, Gabriel had been looking forward to
reaching the dark lane, because it was, generally speaking, a
nice, gloomy, mournful place, into which the towns-people
did not much care to go, except in broad daylight, and
when the sun was shining; consequently, he was not a little
indignant to hear a young urchin roaring out some jolly
song about a merry Christmas, in this very sanctuary,
which had been called Coffin Lane ever since the days of
the old abbey, and the time of the shaven-headed monks.
As Gabriel walked on, and the voice grew nearer, he found
it proceeded from a small boy, who was hurrying alone, to
join one of the little parties in the old street, and who,
partly to keep himself company, and partly to prepare himself for the occasion, was shouting out the song at the
highest pitch of his lungs. So Gabriel waited until the boy
came up, and then dodged him into a corner, and rapped him
over the head with his lantern five or six times, to teach him to
modulate his voice. And as the boy hurried away with his
hand to his head, singing quite a different sort of tune, Gabriel
Grub chuckled very heartily to himself, and entered the
churchyard: locking the gate behind him.

'He took off his coat, put down his lantern, and getting into
the unfinished grave, worked at it for an hour or so, with
right good will. But the earth was hardened with the frost,
and it was no very easy matter to break it up, and shovel it
out; and although there was a moon, it was a very young one,

and shed little light upon the grave, which was in the shadow of the church. At any other time, these obstacles would have made Gabriel Grub very moody and miserable, but he was so well pleased with having stopped the small boy's singing, that he took little heed of the scanty progress he had made, and looked down into the grave, when he had finished work for the night, with grim satisfaction: murmuring as he gathered up his things:

> Brave lodgings for one, brave lodgings for one,
> A few feet of cold earth, when life is done;
> A stone at the head, a stone at the feet,
> A rich, juicy meal for the worms to eat;
> Rank grass over head, and damp clay around,
> Brave lodgings for one, these, in holy ground!

'"Ho! ho!" laughed Gabriel Grub, as he sat himself down on a flat tombstone which was a favourite resting-place of his; and drew forth his wicker bottle. "A coffin at Christmas! A Christmas Box. Ho! ho! ho!"

'"Ho! ho! ho!" repeated a voice which sounded close behind him.

'Gabriel paused, in some alarm, in the act of raising the wicker bottle to his lips: and looked round. The bottom of the oldest grave about him, was not more still and quiet, than the churchyard in the pale moonlight. The cold hoar-frost glistened on the tombstones, and sparkled like rows of gems, among the stone carvings of the old church. The snow lay hard and crisp upon the ground; and spread over the thickly-strewn mounds of earth, so white and smooth a cover, that it seemed as if corpses lay there, hidden only by the winding sheets. Not the faintest rustle broke the profound tranquillity of the solemn scene. Sound itself appeared to be frozen up, all was so cold and still.

'"It was the echoes," said Gabriel Grub, raising the bottle to his lips again.

'"It was *not*," said a deep voice.

'Gabriel started up, and stood rooted to the spot with astonishment and terror; for his eyes rested on a form that made his blood run cold.

'Seated on an upright tombstone, close to him, was a strange, unearthly figure, whom Gabriel felt at once, was no being of this world. His long fantastic legs which might have reached the ground, were cocked up, and crossed after a quaint, fantastic fashion; his sinewy arms were bare; and his hands rested on his knees. On his short round body, he wore a close covering, ornamented with small slashes; a short cloak dangled at his back; the collar was cut into curious peaks, which served the goblin in lieu of ruff or neckerchief; and his shoes curled up at his toes into long points. On his head, he wore a broad-brimmed sugar-loaf hat, garnished with a single feather. The hat was covered with the white frost; and the goblin looked as if he had sat on the same tombstone very comfortably, for two or three hundred years. He was sitting perfectly still; his tongue was put out, as if in derision; and he was grinning at Gabriel Grub with such a grin as only a goblin could call up.

'"It was *not* the echoes," said the goblin.

'Gabriel Grub was paralysed and could make no reply.

'"What do you do here on Christmas Eve?" said the goblin sternly.

'"I come to dig a grave, sir," stammered Gabriel Grub.

'"What man wanders among graves and churchyards on such a night as this?" cried the goblin.

'"Gabriel Grub! Gabriel Grub!" screamed a wild chorus of voices that seemed to fill the churchyard. Gabriel looked fearfully round – nothing was to be seen.

'"What have you got in that bottle?" said the goblin.

'"Hollands, sir," replied the sexton, trembling more than ever; for he had bought it of the smugglers, and he thought that perhaps his questioner might be in the excise department of the goblins.

'"Who drinks Hollands alone, and in a churchyard, on such a night as this?" said the goblin.

'"Gabriel Grub! Gabriel Grub!" exclaimed the wild voices again.

'The goblin leered maliciously at the terrified sexton, and then raising his voice, exclaimed:

'"And who, then, is our fair and lawful prize?"

'To this inquiry the invisible chorus replied, in a strain that sounded like the voices of many choristers singing to the mighty swell of the old church organ – a strain that seemed borne to the sexton's ears upon a wild wind, and to die away as it passed onward; but the burden of the reply was still the same, "Gabriel Grub! Gabriel Grub!"

'The goblin grinned a broader grin than before, as he said, "Well, Gabriel, what do you say to this?"

'The sexton gasped for breath.

'"What do you think of this, Gabriel?" said the goblin, kicking up his feet in the air on either side of the tombstone, and looking at the turned-up points with as much complacency as if he had been contemplating the most fashionable pair of Wellingtons in all Bond Street.

'"It's – it's – very curious, sir," replied the sexton, half dead with fright; "very curious, and very pretty, but I think I'll go back and finish my work, sir, if you please."

'"Work!" said the goblin, "what work?"

'"The grave, sir; making the grave," stammered the sexton.

'"Oh, the grave eh?" said the goblin; "who makes graves at a time when all other men are merry, and takes a pleasure in it?"

'Again the mysterious voices replied, "Gabriel Grub! Gabriel Grub!"

'"I'm afraid my friends want you, Gabriel," said the goblin, thrusting his tongue further into his cheek than ever – and a most astonishing tongue it was – "I'm afraid my friends want you, Gabriel," said the goblin.

'"Under favour, sir," replied the horror-stricken sexton, "I don't think they can, sir; they don't know me, sir; I don't think the gentlemen have ever seen me, sir."

'"Oh, yes they have," replied the goblin; "we know the man with the sulky face and grim scowl, that came down the street tonight, throwing his evil looks at the children, and grasping his burying spade the tighter. We know the man who struck the boy in the envious malice of his heart, because the boy could be merry, and he could not. We know him, we know him."

'Here, the goblin gave a loud shrill laugh, which the echoes returned twentyfold: and throwing his legs up in the air, stood on his head, or rather upon the very point of his sugar-loaf hat, on the narrow edge of the tombstone: whence he threw a somerset with extraordinary agility, right to the sexton's feet, at which he planted himself in the attitude in which tailors generally sit upon the shop-board.

"'I – I – am afraid I must leave you, sir," said the sexton, making an effort to move.

"'Leave us!" said the goblin, "Gabriel Grub going to leave us, Ho! ho! ho!"

'As the goblin laughed, the sexton observed, for one instant, a brilliant illumination within the windows of the church, as if the whole building were lighted up; it disappeared, the organ pealed forth a lively air, and whole troops of goblins, the very counterpart of the first one, poured into the churchyard, and began playing at leap-frog with the tombstones: never stopping for an instant to take breath, but "overing" the highest among them, one after the other, with the utmost marvellous dexterity. The first goblin was a most astonishing leaper, and none of the others could come near him; even in the extremity of his terror the sexton could not help observing, that while his friends were content to leap over the common-sized grave-stones, the first one took the family vaults, iron railings and all, with as much ease as if they had been so many street posts.

'At last the game reached to a most exciting pitch; the organ played quicker and quicker; and the goblins leaped faster and faster: coiling themselves up, rolling head over heels upon the ground, and bounding over the tombstones like footballs. The sexton's brain whirled round with the rapidity of the motion he beheld, and his legs reeled beneath him, as the spirits flew before his eyes: when the goblin king, suddenly darting towards him, laid his hand upon his collar, and sank with him through the earth.

'When Gabriel Grub had had time to fetch his breath, which the rapidity of his descent had for the moment taken away, he found himself in what appeared to be a large cavern, surrounded on all sides by crowds of goblins, ugly and grim; in the centre of the room, on an elevated seat, was stationed his friend of the churchyard; and close beside him stood Gabriel Grub himself, without power of motion.

"'Cold tonight," said the king of the goblins, "very cold. A glass of something warm, here!"

'At this command, half a dozen officious goblins, with a perpetual smile upon their faces, whom Gabriel Grub imagined to be courtiers, on that account, hastily disappeared, and presently returned with a goblet of liquid fire, which they presented to the king.

'"Ah!" cried the goblin, whose cheeks and throat were transparent, as he tossed down the flame, "This warms one, indeed! Bring a bumper of the same, for Mr. Grub."

'It was in vain for the unfortunate sexton to protest that he was not in the habit of taking anything warm at night; one of the goblins held him while another poured the blazing liquid down his throat; the whole assembly screeched with laughter as he coughed and choked, and wiped away the tears which gushed plentifully from his eyes, after swallowing the burning draught.

'"And now," said the king, fantastically poking the taper corner of his sugar-loaf hat into the sexton's eye, and thereby occasioning him the most exquisite pain: "And now, show the man of misery and gloom, a few of the pictures from our own great storehouse."

'As the goblin said this, a thick cloud which obscured the remoter end of the cavern, rolled gradually away, and disclosed, apparently at a great distance, a small and scantily furnished, but neat and clean apartment. A crowd of little children were gathered round a bright fire, clinging to their mother's gown, and gambolling around her chair. The mother occasionally rose, and drew aside the window-curtain, as if to look for some expected object; a frugal meal was ready spread upon the table; and an elbow chair was placed near the fire. A knock was heard at the door: the mother opened it, and the children crowded round her, and clapped their hands for joy, as their father entered. He was wet and weary, and shook the snow from his garments as the children crowded round him, and seizing his cloak, hat, stick, and gloves, with busy zeal, ran with them from the room. Then, as he sat down to his meal before the fire, the children climbed about his knee, and the mother sat by his side, and all seemed happiness and comfort.

'But a change came upon the view, almost imperceptibly. The scene was altered to a small bedroom, where the fairest and youngest child lay dying; the roses had fled from his cheek, and the light from his eye; and even as the sexton looked upon him with an interest he had never felt or known before, he died. His young brothers and sisters crowded round his little bed, and seized his tiny hand, so cold and heavy; but they shrunk back from its touch, and looked with awe on his infant face; for calm and tranquil as it was, and sleeping in rest and peace as the beautiful child seemed to be, they saw that he was dead, and they knew that he was an Angel looking down upon, and blessing them, from a bright and happy Heaven.

'Again the light cloud passed across the picture, and again the subject changed. The father and mother were old and helpless now, and the number of those about them was diminished more than half; but content and cheerfulness sat on every face, and beamed in every eye, as they crowded round the fireside, and told and listened to old stories of earlier and bygone days. Slowly and peacefully the father sank into the grave, and soon after, the sharer of all his cares and troubles followed him to a place of rest. The few, who yet survived them, knelt by their tomb, and watered the green turf which covered it, with their tears; then rose, and turned away: sadly and mournfully, but not with bitter cries, or despairing lamentations, for they knew that they should one day meet again; and once more they mixed with the busy world, and their content and cheerfulness were restored. The cloud settled upon the picture, and concealed it from the sexton's view.

'"What do you think of *that*?" said the goblin, turning his large face towards Gabriel Grub.

'Gabriel murmured out something about it being very pretty, and looked somewhat ashamed, as the goblin bent his fiery eyes upon him.

'"*You* a miserable man!" said the goblin, in a tone of excessive contempt. "You!" He appeared disposed to add more, but indignation choked his utterance, so he lifted up one of his very pliable legs, and flourishing it above his head a little, to insure his aim, administered a good sound kick to Gabriel Grub; immediately after which, all the goblins in waiting, crowded round the wretched sexton, and kicked him without mercy: according to the established and invariable

custom of courtiers upon earth, who kick whom royalty
kicks, and hug whom royalty hugs.

'"Show him some more!" said the king of the goblins.

'At these words, the cloud was dispelled, and a rich and
beautiful landscape was disclosed to view – there is just such
another, to this day, within half a mile of the old abbey town.
The sun shone from out the clear blue sky, the water sparkled
beneath his rays, and the trees looked greener, and the flowers
more gay, beneath his cheering influence. The water rippled
on, with a pleasant sound; the trees rustled in the light wind
that murmured among their leaves; the birds sang upon the
boughs; and the lark carolled on high, her welcome to the
morning. Yes, it was morning: the bright, balmy morning of
summer; the minutest leaf, the smallest blade of grass, was
instinct with life. The ant crept forth to her daily toil, the
butterfly fluttered and basked in the warm rays of the sun;
myriads of insects spread their transparent wings, and revelled
in their brief but happy existence. Man walked forth, elated
with the scene; and all was brightness and splendour.

'"*You* a miserable man!" said the king of the goblins in a
more contemptuous tone than before. And again the king of
the goblins gave his leg a flourish; again it descended on the
shoulders of the sexton; and again the attendant goblins
imitated the example of their chief.

'Many a time the cloud went and came, and many a lesson it
taught to Gabriel Grub, who, although his shoulders smarted
with pain from the frequent applications of the goblins' feet,
looked on with an interest that nothing could diminish. He
saw that men who worked hard, and earned their scanty bread
with lives of labour, were cheerful and happy; and that to the
most ignorant, the sweet face of nature was a never-failing
source of cheerfulness and joy. He saw those who had been
delicately nurtured, and tenderly brought up, cheerful under
privations, and superior to suffering, that would have crushed
many of a rougher grain, because they bore within their own
bosoms the materials of happiness, contentment, and peace.
He saw that women, the tenderest and most fragile of all
God's creatures, were the oftenest superior to sorrow, adversity, and distress; and he saw that it was because they bore, in
their own hearts, an inexhaustible well-spring of affection and

devotion. Above all, he saw that men like himself, who snarled at the mirth and cheerfulness of others, were the foulest weeds on the fair surface of the earth; and setting all the good of the world against the evil, he came to the conclusion that it was a very decent and respectable sort of world after all. No sooner had he formed it, than the cloud which closed over the last picture, seemed to settle on his senses, and lull him to repose. One by one, the goblins faded from his sight; and as the last one disappeared, he sunk to sleep.

'The day had broken when Gabriel Grub awoke, and found himself lying, at full length on the flat grave-stone in the churchyard, with the wicker bottle lying empty by his side, and his coat, spade, and lantern, all well whitened by the last night's frost, scattered on the ground. The stone on which he had first seen the goblin seated, stood bolt upright before him, and the grave at which he had worked, the night before, was not far off. At first, he began to doubt the reality of his adventures, but the acute pain in his shoulders when he attempted to rise, assured him that the kicking of the goblins was certainly not ideal. He was staggered again, by observing no traces of footsteps in the snow on which the goblins had played at leapfrog with the grave-stones, but he speedily accounted for this circumstance when he remembered that, being spirits, they would leave not visible impression behind them. So, Gabriel Grub got to his feet as well as he could, for the pain in his back; and brushing the frost off his coat, put it on, and turned his face towards the town.

'But he was an altered man, and he could not bear the thought of returning to a place where his repentance would be scoffed at, and his reformation disbelieved. He hesitated for a few moments; and then turned away to wander where he might, and seek his bread elsewhere.

'The lantern, the spade, and the wicker bottle, were found, that day, in the churchyard. There were a great many speculations about the sexton's fate, at first, but it was speedily determined that he had been carried away by the goblins; and there were not wanting some very credible witnesses who had distinctly seen him whisked through the air on the back of a chestnut horse blind in one eye, with the hind-quarters of a lion, and the tail of a bear. At length all this was devoutly believed; and the new sexton used to exhibit to the curious, for a trifling emolument, a good-sized piece of the church weathercock which had been accidently kicked off by the aforesaid horse in his aerial flight, and picked up by himself in the churchyard, a year or two afterwards.

'Unfortunately, these stories were somewhat disturbed by the unlooked-for reappearance of Gabriel Grub himself, some ten years afterwards, a ragged contented, rheumatic old man. He told his story to the clergyman, and also to the mayor; and in course of time it began to be received, as a matter of history, in which form it has continued down to this very day. The believers in the weathercock tale, having misplaced their confidence once, were not easily prevailed upon to part with it again, so they looked as wise as they could, shrugged their shoulders, touched their foreheads, and murmured something about Gabriel Grub having drunk all the Hollands, and then fallen asleep on the flat tombstone; and they affected to explain what he supposed he had witnessed in the goblins' cavern, by saying that he had seen the world, and grown wiser. But this opinion, which was by no means a popular one at any time, gradually died off; and be the matter how it may, as Gabriel Grub was afflicted with rheumatism to the end of his days, this story has at least one moral, if it teach no better one – and that is, that if a man turn sulky and drink by himself at Christmas time, he may make up his mind to be not a bit better for it: let the spirits be never so good, or let them be even as many degrees beyond proof, as those which Gabriel Grub saw in the goblin's cavern.'

from *The Pickwick Papers*

THE STORY OF THE BAGMAN'S UNCLE

'My uncle, gentlemen,' said the bagman, 'was one of the merriest, pleasantest, cleverest fellows that ever lived. I wish you had known him, gentlemen. On second thoughts, gentlemen, I *don't* wish you had known him, for if you had, you would have been all, by this time, in the ordinary course of nature, if not dead, at all events so near it, as to have taken to stopping at home and giving up company: which would have deprived me of the inestimable pleasure of addressing you at this moment. Gentlemen, I wish your fathers and mothers had known my uncle. They would have been amazingly fond of him, especially your respectable mothers; I know they would. If any two of his numerous virtues predominated over the many that adorned his character, I should say they were his mixed punch and his after-supper song. Excuse my dwelling on these melancholy recollections of departed worth; you won't see a man like my uncle every day in the week.

'I have always considered it a great point in my uncle's character, gentlemen, that he was the intimate friend and companion of Tom Smart, of the great house of Bilson and Slum, Cateaton Street, City. My uncle collected for Tiggin and Welps, but for a long time he went pretty near the same journey as Tom; and the very first night they met, my uncle took a fancy for Tom, and Tom took a fancy for my uncle. They made a bet of a new hat before they had known each other half an hour, who should brew the best quart of punch and drink it the quickest. My uncle was judged to have won the making, but Tom Smart beat him in the drinking by about half a salt-spoonful. They took another quart apiece to drink each other's health in, and were staunch friends ever afterwards. There's a destiny in these things, gentlemen; we can't help it.

'In personal appearance my uncle was a trifle shorter than the middle-size; he was a thought stouter too, than the

47

ordinary run of people, and perhaps his face might be a shade redder. He had the jolliest face you ever saw, gentlemen: something like Punch, with a handsomer nose and chin; his eyes were always twinkling and sparkling with good humour; and a smile – not one of your unmeaning wooden grins, but a real, merry, hearty, good-tempered smile – was perpetually on his countenance. He was pitched out of his gig once, and knocked, head first, against a mile-stone. There he lay, stunned, and so cut about the face with some gravel which had been heaped up alongside it, that, to use my uncle's own strong expression, if his mother could have revisited the earth, she wouldn't have known him. Indeed, when I come to think of the matter, gentlemen, I feel pretty sure she wouldn't, for she died when my uncle was two years and seven months old, and I think it's very likely that, even without the gravel, his top-boots would have puzzled the good lady not a little: to say nothing of his jolly red face. However, there he lay, and I have heard my uncle say, many a time, that the man said who picked him up that he was smiling as merrily as if he had tumbled out for a treat, and that after they had bled him, the first faint glimmerings of returning animation, were, his jumping up in bed, bursting out into a loud laugh, kissing the young woman who held the basin, and demanding a mutton chop and a pickled walnut. He was very fond of pickled walnuts, gentlemen. He said he always found that, taken without vinegar, they relished the beer.

'My uncle's great journey was in the fall of the leaf, at which time he collected debts, and took orders, in the north: going from London to Edinburgh, from Edinburgh to Glasgow, from Glasgow back to Edinburgh, and thence to London by the smack. You are to understand that his second visit to Edinburgh was for his own pleasure. He used to go back for a week, just to look up his old friends; and what with breakfasting with this one, lunching with that, dining with a third, and supping with another, a pretty tight week he used to make of it. I don't know whether any of you, gentlemen, ever partook of a real substantial hospitable Scotch breakfast, and then went out to a slight lunch of a bushel of oysters, a dozen or so of bottled ale, and a noggin or two of whiskey to close up with. If you ever did, you will agree with me that it requires a pretty strong head to go out to dinner and supper afterwards.

'But, bless your hearts and eyebrows, all this sort of thing was nothing to my uncle! He was so well seasoned, that it was mere child's play. I have heard him say that he could see the Dundee people out, any day, and walk home afterwards without staggering; and yet the Dundee people have as strong heads and as strong punch, gentlemen, as you are likely to meet with, between the poles. I have heard of a Glasgow man and a Dundee man drinking against each other for fifteen hours at a sitting. They were both suffocated, as nearly as could be ascertained, at the same moment, but with this trifling exception, gentlemen, they were not a bit the worse for it.

'One night, within four-and-twenty hours of the time when he had settled to take shipping for London, my uncle stopped at the house of a very old friend of his, a Baillie Mac something and four syllables after it, who lived in the old town of Edinburgh. There were the baillie's wife, and the baillie's three daughters, and the baillie's grown-up son, and three or four stout, bushy-eyebrowed, canny old Scotch fellows, that the baillie had got together to do honour to my uncle, and help to make merry. It was a glorious supper. There were kippered salmon, and Finnan haddocks, and a lamb's head, and a haggis – a celebrated Scotch dish, gentlemen, which my uncle used to say always looked to him, when it came to table, very much like a cupid's stomach – and a great many other things besides, that I forget the names of, but very good things notwithstanding. The lassies were pretty and agreeable; the baillie's wife was one of the best creatures that ever lived; and my uncle was in thoroughly good cue. The consequence of which was, that the young ladies tittered and giggled, and the old lady laughed out loud, and the baillie and the other fellows roared till they were red in the face, the whole mortal time. I don't quite recollect how many tumblers of whiskey toddy each man drank after supper; but this I know, that about one o'clock in the morning, the baillie's grown-up son became insensible while attempting the first verse of "Willie brewed a peck o'maut;" and he having been, for an hour before, the only other man visible above the mahogany, it occurred to my uncle that it was almost time to think about going, especially as drinking had set in at seven o'clock, in order that he might get home at a decent hour. But, thinking it might not be quite polite to go just then, my uncle voted himself into the chair, mixed another glass, rose to propose his own health, addressed himself in a neat and complimentary speech, and drank the toast with great enthusiasm. Still nobody woke; so my uncle took a little drop more – neat this time, to prevent the toddy from disagreeing with him – and, laying violent hands on his hat, sallied forth into the street.

'It was a wild gusty night when my uncle closed the baillie's door, and settling his hat firmly on his head, to prevent the wind from taking it, thrust his hands into his pockets, and looking upward, took a short survey of the state of the weather. The clouds were drifting over the moon at their giddiest speed: at one time wholly obscuring her: at another, suffering her to burst forth in full splendour and shed her light on all the objects around: anon, driving over her again, with increased velocity, and shrouding everything in darkness. "Really, this won't do," said my uncle, addressing himself to the weather, as if he felt himself personally offended. "This is not at all the kind of thing for my voyage. It will not do, at any price," said my uncle very impressively. Having repeated this, several times, he recovered his balance with some difficulty – for he was rather giddy with looking up into the sky so long – and walked merrily on.

'The baillie's house was in the Canongate, and my uncle was going to the other end of Leith Walk, rather better than a mile's journey. On either side of him, there shot up against the dark sky, tall gaunt straggling houses, with time-stained fronts, and windows that seemed to have shared the lot of eyes in mortals, and to have grown dim and sunken with age. Six, seven, eight storeys high, were the houses; storey piled above storey, as children build with cards – throwing their dark shadows over the roughly paved road, and making the dark night darker. A few oil lamps were scattered at long distances, but they only served to mark the dirty entrance to some narrow close, or to show where a common stair communicated, by steep and intricate windings, with the various flats above. Glancing at all these things with the air of a man who had seen them too often before, to think them worthy of much notice now, my uncle walked up the middle of the street, with a thumb in each waistcoat pocket, indulging from time to time in various snatches of song, chanted forth with such good will and spirit, that the quiet honest folk started from their first sleep and lay trembling in bed till the sound died away in the distance; when, satisfying themselves that it was only some drunken ne'er-do-well finding his way home, they covered themselves up warm and fell asleep again.

'I am particular in describing how my uncle walked up the middle of the street, with his thumbs in his waistcoat pockets, gentlemen, because, as he often used to say (and with great reason too) there is nothing at all extraordinary in this story, unless you distinctly understand at the beginning that he was not by any means of a marvellous or romantic turn.

'Gentlemen, my uncle walked on with his thumbs in his waistcoat pockets, taking the middle of the street to himself, and singing, now a verse of a love song, and then a verse of a drinking one, and when he was tired of both, whistling melodiously, until he reached the North Bridge, which, at this point, connects the old and new towns of Edinburgh. Here he stopped for a minute, to look at the strange irregular clusters of lights piled one above the other, and twinkling afar off so high, that they looked like stars, gleaming from the castle walls on the one side and the Calton Hill on the other, as if they illuminated veritable castles in the air; while the old picturesque town slept heavily on, in gloom and darkness below: its palace and chapel of Holyrood, guarded day and night, as a friend of my uncle's used to say, by old Arthur's Seat, towering surly and dark, like some gruff genius, over the ancient city he has watched so long. I say, gentlemen, my uncle stopped here, for a minute, to look about him; and then, paying a compliment to the weather which had a little cleared up, though the moon was sinking, walked on again, as royally as before; keeping the middle of the road with great dignity, and looking as if he would very much like to meet with somebody who would dispute possession of it with him. There was nobody at all disposed to contest the point, as it happened; and so, on he went, with his thumbs in his waistcoat pockets, like a lamb.

'When my uncle reached the end of Leith Walk, he had to cross a pretty large piece of waste ground which separated him from a short street which he had to turn down, to go direct to his lodging. Now, in this piece of waste ground, there was, at that time, an enclosure belonging to some wheelwright who contracted with the Post Office for the purchase of old worn-out mail coaches; and my uncle, being very fond of coaches, old, young, or middle-aged, all at once took it into his head to step out of his road for no other purpose than to peep between the palings at these mails – about a dozen of which, he remembered to have seen, crowded together in a very forlorn and dismantled state, inside. My uncle was a very enthusiastic, emphatic sort of person, gentlemen; so, finding that he could not obtain a good peep between the palings, he got over them, and sitting himself quietly down on an old axletree, began to contemplate the mail coaches with a deal of gravity.

'There might be a dozen of them, or there might be more – my uncle was never quite certain on this point, and being a man of very scrupulous veracity about numbers, didn't like to say – but there they stood, all huddled together in the most desolate condition imaginable. The doors had been torn from their hinges and removed: the linings had been stripped off: only a shred hanging here and there by a rusty nail; the lamps were gone, the poles had long since vanished, the ironwork was rusty, the paint was worn away; the wind whistled through the chinks in the bare woodwork; and the rain, which had collected on the roofs, fell, drop by drop, into the insides with a hollow and melancholy sound. They were the decaying skeletons of departed mails, and in that lonely place, at that time of night, they looked chill and dismal.

'My uncle rested his head upon his hands, and thought of the busy bustling people who had rattled about, years before, in the old coaches, and were now as silent and changed; he thought of the numbers of people whom one of those crazy mouldering vehicles had borne, night after night, for many years, and through all weathers, the anxiously expected intelligence, the eagerly looked-for remittance, the promised assurance of health and safety, the sudden announcement of sickness and death. The merchant, the lover, the wife, the widow, the mother, the schoolboy, the very child who tottered to the door at the postman's knock – how had they all looked forward to the arrival of the old coach. And where were they all now!

'Gentlemen, my uncle used to *say* that he thought all this at the time, but I rather suspect he learnt it out of some book afterwards, for he distinctly stated that he fell into a kind of doze, as he sat on the old axletree looking at the decayed mail coaches, and that he was suddenly awakened by some deep church-bell striking two. Now, my uncle was never a fast thinker, and if he had thought all these things, I am quite certain it would have taken him till full half-past two o'clock, at the very least. I am, therefore, decidedly of opinion, gentlemen, that my uncle fell into the kind of doze, without having thought about any thing at all.

'Be this as it may, a church bell struck two. My uncle woke, rubbed his eyes, and jumped up in astonishment.

'In one instant after the clock struck two, the whole of this deserted and quiet spot had become a scene of most extraordinary life and animation. The mail coach doors were on their hinges, the lining was replaced, the iron-work was as good as new, the paint was restored, the lamps were alight, cushions and great coats were on every coach box, porters were thrusting parcels into every boot, guards were stowing away letter-bags, hostlers were dashing pails of water against the renovated wheels; numbers of men were rushing about, fixing poles into every coach; passengers arrived, portmanteaus were handed up, horses were put to; in short, it was perfectly clear that every mail there, was to be off directly. Gentlemen, my uncle opened his eyes so wide at all this, that, to the very last moment of his life, he used to wonder how it fell out that he had ever been able to shut 'em again.

'"Now then!" said a voice, as my uncle felt a hand on his shoulder, "You're booked for one inside. You'd better get in."

'"*I* booked!" said my uncle, turning round.

'"Yes, certainly."

'My uncle, gentlemen, could say nothing; he was so very much astonished. The queerest thing of all, was, that although

there was such a crowd of persons, and although fresh faces
were pouring in, every moment, there was no telling where
they came from. They seemed to start up, in some strange
manner, from the ground, or the air, and disappear in the
same way. When a porter had put his luggage in the coach,
and received his fare, he turned round and was gone; and
before my uncle had well begun to wonder what had become
of him, half-a-dozen fresh ones started up, and staggered
along under the weight of parcels which seemed big enough
to crush them. The passengers were all dressed so oddly too!
Large, broad-skirted laced coats with great cuffs and no
collars; and wigs, gentlemen – great formal wigs with a tie
behind. My uncle could make nothing of it.

"'Now, *are* you going to get in?" said the person who had
addressed my uncle before. He was dressed as a mail guard,
with a wig on his head and most enormous cuffs to his coat,
and had a lantern in one hand, and a huge blunderbuss in the
other, which he was going to stow away in his little arm-
chest. "*Are* you going to get in, Jack Martin?" said the guard,
holding the lantern to my uncle's face.

"'Hallo!" said my uncle, falling back a step or two. "That's
familiar!"

"'It's so on the way-bill,"replied the guard.

"'Isn't there a Mister before it?" said my uncle. For he felt,
gentlemen, that for a guard he didn't know, to call him Jack
Martin, was a liberty which the Post Office wouldn't have
sanctioned if they had known it.

"'No, there is not," rejoined the guard coolly.

"'Is the fare paid?" enquired my uncle.

"'Of course it is," rejoined the guard.

"'It is, is it?" said my uncle. "Then here goes! Which
coach?"

"'This," said the guard, pointing to an old-fashioned Edinburgh and London Mail, which had the steps down, and the
door open. "Stop! Here are the other passengers. Let them get
in first."

'As the guard spoke, there all at once appeared, right in
front of my uncle, a young gentleman in a powdered wig, and
a sky-blue coat trimmed with silver, made very full and broad
in the skirts, which were lined with buckram. Tiggin and

Welps were in the printed calico and waistcoat piece line, gentlemen, so my uncle knew all the materials at once. He wore knee breeches, and a kind of leggings rolled up over his silk stockings, and shoes with buckles; he had ruffles at his wrists, a three-cornered hat on his head, and a long taper sword by his side. The flaps of his waistcoat came half way down his thighs, and the ends of his cravat reached to his waist. He stalked gravely to the coach-door, pulled off his hat, and held it above his head at arm's length: cocking his little finger in the air at the same time, as some affected people do, when they take a cup of tea. Then he drew his feet together, and made a low grave bow, and then put out his left hand. My uncle was just going to step forward, and shake it heartily, when he perceived that these attentions were directed, not towards him, but to a young lady who just then appeared at the foot of the steps, attired in an old-fashioned green velvet dress with a long waist and stomacher. She had no bonnet on her head, gentlemen, which was muffled in a black silk hood, but she looked round for an instant as she prepared to get into the coach, and such a beautiful face as she disclosed, my uncle had never seen – not even in a picture. She got into the coach, holding up her dress with one hand; and, as my uncle always said with a round oath, when he told the story, he wouldn't have believed it possible that legs and feet could have been brought to such a state of perfection unless he had seen them with his own eyes.

'But, in this one glimpse of the beautiful face, my uncle saw that the young lady cast an imploring look upon him, and that she appeared terrified and distressed. He noticed, too, that the young fellow in the powdered wig, notwithstanding his show of gallantry, which was all very fine and grand, clasped her tight by the wrist when she got in, and followed himself immediately afterwards. An uncommonly ill-looking fellow, in a close brown wig and a plum-coloured suit, wearing a very large sword, and boots up to his hips, belonged to the party; and when he sat himself down next to the young lady, who shrunk into a corner at his approach, my uncle was confirmed in his original impression that something dark and mysterious was going forward, or, as he always said to himself, that "there was a screw loose somewhere." It's quite surprising how quickly he made up his mind to help the lady at any peril, if she needed help.

"'Death and lightning!" exclaimed the young gentleman, laying his hand upon his sword as my uncle entered the coach.

"'Blood and thunder!' roared the other gentleman. With this, he whipped his sword out, and made a lunge at my uncle without further ceremony. My uncle had no weapon about him, but with great dexterity he snatched the ill-looking gentleman's three-cornered hat from his head, and, receiving the point of his sword right through the crown, squeezed the sides together, and held it tight.

"'Pink him behind!' cried the ill-looking gentleman to his companion, as he struggled to regain his sword.

"'He had better not,' cried my uncle, displaying the heel of one of his shoes, in a threatening manner. "I'll kick his brains out, if he has any, or fracture his skull if he hasn't." Exerting all his strength at this moment, my uncle wrenched the ill-looking man's sword from his grasp, and flung it clean out of the coach-window: upon which the younger gentleman vociferated "Death and lightning!" again, and laid his hand upon the hilt of his sword, in a very fierce manner, but didn't draw it. Perhaps, gentlemen, as my uncle used to say with a smile, perhaps he was afraid of alarming the lady.

"'Now, gentlemen,' said my uncle, taking his seat deliberately, "I don't want to have any death, with or without lightning, in a lady's presence, and we have had quite blood and thundering enough for one journey; so, if you please, we'll sit in our places like quiet insides. Here, guard, pick up that gentleman's carving-knife."

'As quickly as my uncle said the words, the guard appeared at the coach-window, with the gentleman's sword in his hand. He held up his lantern, and looked earnestly in my uncle's face, as he handed it in: when, by its light, my uncle saw, to his great surprise, that an immense crowd of mail-coach guards swarmed round the window, every one of whom had his eyes earnestly fixed upon him too. He had never seen such a sea of white faces, red bodies, and earnest eyes, in all his born days.

"'This is the strangest sort of thing I ever had anything to do with," thought my uncle; "allow me to return you your hat, sir."

'The ill-looking gentleman received his three-cornered hat in silence, looked at the hole in the middle with an inquiring air, and finally stuck it on the top of his wig with a solemnity the effect of which was a trifle impaired by his sneezing violently at the moment, and jerking it off again.

'"All right!" cried the guard with the lantern, mounting into his little seat behind. Away they went. My uncle peeped out of the coach-window as they emerged from the yard, and observed that the other mails, with coachmen, guards, horses, and passengers, complete, were driving round and round in circles, at a slow trot of about five miles an hour. My uncle burnt with indignation, gentlemen. As a commercial man, he felt that the mail bags were not to be trifled with, and he resolved to memorialise the Post Office on the subject, the very instant he reached London.

'At present, however, his thoughts were occupied with the young lady who sat in the farthest corner of the coach, with her face muffled closely in her hood; the gentleman with the sky-blue coat sitting opposite her; the other man in the plum-coloured suit, by her side; and both watching her intently. If she so much as rustled the folds of her hood, he could hear the ill-looking man clap his hand on his sword, and could tell by the other's breathing (it was so dark he couldn't see his face) that he was looking as big as if he were going to devour her at a mouthful. This roused my uncle more and more, and he resolved, come what might, to see the end of it. He had a great admiration for bright eyes, and sweet faces, and pretty legs and feet; in short, he was fond of the whole sex. It runs in our family, gentlemen – so am I.

'Many were the devices which my uncle practised, to attract the lady's attention, or at all events, to engage the mysterious gentlemen in conversation. They were all in vain; the gentlemen wouldn't talk, and the lady didn't dare. He thrust his head out of the coach-window at intervals, and bawled out to know why they didn't go faster? But he called till he was hoarse; nobody paid the least attention to him. He leant back in the coach, and thought of the beautiful face, and the feet and legs. This answered better; it wiled away the time, and kept him from wondering where he was going, and how it was that he found himself in such an odd situation. Not that this would have worried him much, any way – he was a mighty free and easy, roving, devil-may-care sort of person, was my uncle, gentlemen.

'All of a sudden the coach stopped. "Hallo!" said my uncle, "What's in the wind now?"

'"Alight here," said the guard, letting down the steps.

'"Here!" cried my uncle.

'"Here," rejoined the guard.

'"I'll do nothing of the sort," said my uncle.

'"Very well, then stop where you are," said the guard.

'"I will," said my uncle.

'"Do," said the guard.

'The other passengers had regarded this colloquy with great attention, and, finding that my uncle was determined not to alight, the younger man squeezed past him, to hand the lady out. At this moment, the ill-looking man was inspecting the hole in the crown of his three-cornered hat. As the young lady brushed past, she dropped one of her gloves into my uncle's hand, and softly whispered, with her lips, so close to his face that he felt her warm breath on his nose, the single word "Help!" Gentlemen, my uncle leaped out of the coach at once, with such violence that it rocked on the springs again.

'"Oh! You've thought better of it, have you?" said the guard when he saw my uncle standing on the ground.

'My uncle looked at the guard for a few seconds, in some doubt whether it wouldn't be better to wrench his blunder-buss from him, fire it in the face of the man with the big sword, knock the rest of the company over the head with the stock, snatch up the young lady, and go off in the smoke. On second thoughts, however, he abandoned this plan, as being a shade too melodramatic in the execution, and followed the two mysterious men, who, keeping the lady between them, were now entering an old house in front of which the coach had stopped. They turned into the passage, and my uncle followed.

'Of all the ruinous and desolate places my uncle had ever beheld, this was the most so. It looked as if it had once been a large house of entertainment; but the roof had fallen in, in many places, and the stairs were steep, rugged, and broken. There was a huge fireplace in the room into which they walked, and the chimney was blackened with smoke; but no warm blaze lighted it up now. The white feathery dust of burnt wood was still strewed over the hearth, but the stove was cold, and all was dark and gloomy.

'"Well," said my uncle, as he looked about him, "a mail travelling at the rate of six miles and a half an hour, and stopping for an indefinite time at such a hole as this, is rather an irregular sort of proceeding I fancy. This shall be made known. I'll write to the papers."

'My uncle said this in a pretty loud voice, and in an open unreserved sort of manner, with the view of engaging the two strangers in conversation if he could. But, neither of them took any more notice of him than whispering to each other, and scowling at him as they did so. The lady was at the farther end of the room, and once she ventured to wave her hand, as if beseeching my uncle's assistance.

'At length the two strangers advanced a little, and the conversation began in earnest.

'"You don't know this is a private room; I suppose, fellow?" said the gentleman in sky-blue.

'"No, I do not, fellow," rejoined my uncle. "Only if this is a private room specially ordered for the occasion, I should think the public room must be a *very* comfortable one;" with this my uncle took such an accurate measure of the gentleman, with his eyes, that Tiggin and Welps could have supplied him with printed calico for a suit, and not an inch too much or too little, from that estimate alone.

'"Quit this room," said both the men together, grasping their swords.

'"Eh?" said my uncle, not at all appearing to comprehend their meaning.

'"Quit the room, or you are a dead man," said the ill-looking fellow with the large sword, drawing it at the same time and flourishing it in the air.

'"Down with him!" cried the gentleman in sky-blue, drawing his sword also, and falling back two or three yards. "Down with him!" The lady gave a loud scream.

'Now, my uncle was always remarkable for great boldness, and a great presence of mind. All the time that he had appeared so indifferent to what was going on, he had been looking slyly about, for some missile or weapon of defence, and at the very instant when the swords were drawn, he espied, standing in the chimney corner, an old basket-hilted rapier in a rusty scabbard. At one bound, my uncle caught it in his hand, drew it, flourished it gallantly above his head, called aloud to the lady to keep out of the way, hurled the chair at the man in sky-blue, and the scabbard at the man in plum-colour, and taking advantage of the confusion, fell upon them both, pell-mell.

'Gentlemen, there is an old story – none the worse for being true – regarding a fine young Irish gentleman, who being asked if he could play the fiddle, replied he had no doubt he could, but he couldn't exactly say, for certain, because he had never tried. This is not inapplicable to my uncle and his fencing. He had never had a sword in his hand before, except once when he played Richard the Third at a private theatre: upon which occasion it was arranged with Richmond that he was to be run through, from behind, without showing fight at all. But here he was, cutting and slashing with two experienced swordsmen: thrusting and guarding and poking and slicing, and acquitting himself in the most manful and dexterous manner possible, although up to that time he had never been aware that he had the least notion of the science. It only shows how true the old saying is, that a man never knows what he can do, till he tries, gentlemen.

'The noise of the combat was terrific; each of the three combatants swearing like troopers, and their swords clashing with as much noise as if all the knives and steels in Newport market were rattling together, at the same time. When it was at its very height, the lady (to encourage my uncle most probably) withdrew her hood entirely from her face, and disclosed a countenance of such dazzling beauty, that he would have fought against fifty men, to win one smile from it, and die. He had done wonders before, but now he began to powder away like a raving mad giant.

'At this very moment, the gentleman in sky-blue turning round, and seeing the young lady with her face uncovered, vented an exclamation of rage and jealousy, and, turning his weapon against her beautiful bosom, pointed a thrust at her heart, which caused my uncle to utter a cry of apprehension that made the building ring. The lady stepped lightly aside, and snatching the young man's sword from his hand, before he had recovered his balance, drove him to the wall, and running it through him, and the panelling, up to the very hilt, pinned him there, hard and fast. It was a splendid example. My uncle, with a loud shout of triumph, and a strength that was irresistible, made his adversary retreat in the same direction, and plunging the old rapier into the very centre of a large red flower in the pattern of his waistcoat, nailed him beside his friend; there they both stood, gentlemen, jerking their arms and legs about, in agony, like the toy-shop figures that are moved by a piece of packthread. My uncle always said, afterwards, that this was one of the surest means he knew of, for disposing of an enemy; but it was liable to one objection on the ground of expense, inasmuch as it involved the loss of a sword for every man disabled.

"'The mail! the mail!' cried the lady, running up to my uncle and throwing her beautiful arms round his neck; "we may yet escape."

"'*May!*' cried my uncle; "why, my dear, there's nobody else to kill, is there?" My uncle was rather disappointed, gentlemen, for he thought a little quiet bit of love-making would be agreeable after the slaughtering, if it were only to change the subject.

"'We have not an instant to lose here," said the young lady. "He (pointing to the young gentleman in sky-blue) is the only son of the powerful Marquess of Filletoville."

"'Well, then, my dear, I'm afraid he'll never come to the title," said my uncle, looking coolly at the young gentleman as he stood fixed up against the wall, in the cockchafer fashion I have described. "You have cut off the entail, my love."

"'I have been torn from my home and friends by these villains," said the young lady, her features glowing with indignation. "That wretch would have married me by violence in another hour."

"'Confound his impudence!' said my uncle, bestowing a very contemptuous look on the dying heir of Filletoville.

"'As you may guess from what you have seen," said the young lady, "the party were prepared to murder me if I appealed to any one for assistance. If their accomplices find us here, we are lost. Two minutes hence may be too late! The mail!" With these words, overpowered by her feelings, and the exertion of sticking the young Marquess of Filletoville, she sunk into my uncle's arms. My uncle caught her up, and bore her to the house-door. There stood the mail, with four long-tailed, flowing-maned, black horses, ready harnessed; but no coachman, no guard, no hostler even, at the horses' heads.

'Gentlemen, I hope I do no injustice to my uncle's memory, when I express my opinion, that although he was a bachelor, he *had* held some ladies in his arms, before this time; I believe indeed, that he had rather a habit of kissing barmaids; and I know, that in one or two instances, he had been seen by credible witnesses, to hug a landlady in a very perceptible manner. I mention the circumstance, to show what a very uncommon sort of person this beautiful young lady must have been, to have affected my uncle in the way she did; he used to say, that as her long dark hair trailed over his arm, and her beautiful dark eyes fixed themselves upon his face when she recovered, he felt so strange and nervous that his legs trembled beneath him. But, who can look in a sweet soft pair of dark eyes, without feeling queer? *I* can't, gentlemen. I am afraid to look at some eyes I know, and that's the truth of it.

"'You will never leave me," murmured the young lady.

"'Never," said my uncle. And he meant it too.

"'My dear preserver!" exclaimed the young lady. "My dear, kind, brave preserver!"

"'Don't," said my uncle, interrupting her.

"'Why?" inquired the young lady.

"'Because your mouth looks so beautiful when you speak," rejoined my uncle, "that I'm afraid I shall be rude enough to kiss it."

'The young lady put up her hand as if to caution my uncle not to do so, and said – no, she didn't say anything – she smiled. When you are looking at a pair of the most delicious lips in the world, and see them gently break into a roguish smile – if you are very near them, and nobody else by – you cannot better testify your admiration of their beautiful form and colour than by kissing them at once. My uncle did so, and I honour him for it.

"'Hark!" cried the young lady, starting. "The noise of wheels and horses!"

'"So it is," said my uncle, listening. He had a good ear for wheels, and the trampling of hoofs; but there appeared to be so many horses and carriages rattling towards them, from a distance, that it was impossible to form a guess at their number. The sound was like that of fifty breaks, with six blood cattle in each.

'"We are pursued!" cried the young lady, clasping her hands. "We are pursued. I have no hope but in you!"

'There was such an expression of terror in her beautiful face, that my uncle made up his mind at once. He lifted her into the coach, told her not to be frightened, pressed his lips to hers once more, and then advising her to draw up the window to keep the cold air out, mounted to the box.

'"Stay, love," cried the young lady.

'"What's the matter?" said my uncle, from the coachbox.

'"I want to speak to you." said the young lady; "only a word. Only one word, dearest."

'"Must I get down?" inquired my uncle. The lady made no answer, but she smiled again. Such a smile, gentlemen! It beat the other one, all to nothing. My uncle descended from his perch in a twinkling.

'"What is it, my dear?" said my uncle, looking in at the coach window. The lady happened to bend forward at the same time, and my uncle thought she looked more beautiful than she had done yet. He was very close to her just then, gentlemen, so he really ought to know.

'"What is it, dear?" said my uncle.

'"Will you never love any one but me; never marry any one beside?" said the young lady.

'My uncle swore a great oath that he never would marry anybody else, and the young lady drew in her head, and pulled up the window. He jumped upon the box, squared his elbows, adjusted the ribands, seized the whip which lay on the roof, gave one flick to the off leader, and away went the four long-tailed, flowing-maned black horses, at fifteen good English miles an hour, with the old mail coach behind them. Whew! How they tore along!

'The noise behind grew louder. The faster the old mail went, the faster came the pursuers – men, horses, dogs, were leagued in the pursuit. The noise was frightful, but, above all, rose the voice of the young lady, urging my uncle on, and shrieking, "Faster! Faster!"

'They whirled past the dark trees, as feathers would be swept before a hurricane. Houses, gates, churches, haystacks, objects of every kind they shot by, with a velocity and noise like roaring waters suddenly let loose. Still the noise of pursuit grew louder, and still my uncle could hear the young lady wildly screaming, "Faster! Faster!"

'My uncle plied whip and rein, and the horses flew onward till they were white with foam; and yet the noise behind increased; and yet the young lady cried, "Faster! Faster!" My uncle gave a loud stamp on the boot in the energy of the moment, and – found that it was grey morning, and he was sitting in the wheelwright's yard, on the box of an old English mail, shivering with the cold and wet and stamping his feet to warm them! He got down, and looked eagerly inside for the beautiful young lady. Alas! There was neither door nor seat to the coach. It was a mere shell.

'Of course, my uncle knew very well that there was some mystery in the matter, and that everything had passed exactly as he used to relate it. He remained staunch to the great oath he had sworn to the beautiful young lady: refusing several eligible landladies on her account, and dying a bachelor at last. He always said, what a curious thing it was that he should have found out, by such a mere accident as his clambering over the palings, that the ghosts of mail-coaches and horses, guards, coachmen, and passengers, were in the habit of making journeys regularly every night. He used to add, that he believed he was the only living person who had ever been taken as a passenger on one of these excursions. And I think he was right, gentlemen – at least I never heard of any other.'

from *The Pickwick Papers*.

THE BARON OF GROGZWIG

'The Baron Von Koëldwethout, of Grogzwig in Germany, was as likely a young baron as you would wish to see. I needn't say that he lived in a castle, because that's of course; neither need I say that he lived in an old castle; for what German baron ever lived in a new one? There were many strange circumstances connected with this venerable building, among which, not the least startling and mysterious were, that when the wind blew, it rumbled in the chimneys, or even howled among the trees in the neighbouring forest; and that, when the moon shone, she found her way through certain small loopholes in the wall, and actually made some parts of the wide halls and galleries quite light, while she left others in gloomy shadow. I believe that one of the baron's ancestors, being short of money, had inserted a dagger in a gentleman who called one night to ask his way, and it *was* supposed that these miraculous occurrences took place in consequence. And yet I hardly know how that could have been, either, because the baron's ancestor, who was an amiable man, felt very sorry afterwards for having been so rash, and laying violent hands upon a quantity of stone and timber which belonged to a weaker baron, built a chapel as an apology, and so took a receipt from Heaven in full of all demands.

'Talking of the baron's ancestor puts me in mind of the baron's great claims to respect on the score of his pedigree. I am afraid to say, I am sure, how many ancestors the baron had; but I know that he had a great many more than any other man of his time; and I only wish that he had lived in these latter days, that he might have done more. It is a very hard thing upon the great men of past centuries, that they should have come into the world so soon, because a man who was born three or four hundred years ago cannot reasonably be expected to have had as many relations before him as a man who is born now. The last man, whoever he is – and he may

be a cobbler or some low vulgar dog for aught we know –
will have a longer pedigree than the greatest nobleman now
alive; and I contend that this is not fair.

'Well, but the Baron Von Koëldwethout of Grogzwig! He
was a fine swarthy fellow, with dark hair and large moustaches, who rode a-hunting in clothes of Lincoln green, with
russet boots on his feet, and a bugle slung over his shoulder
like the guard of a long stage. When he blew his bugle, four-
and-twenty other gentlemen of inferior rank, in Lincoln green
a little coarser, and russet boots with a little thicker soles,
turned out directly; and away galloped the whole train, with
spears in their hands like lacquered area railings, to hunt down
the boars, or perhaps encounter a bear: in which latter case the
baron killed him first, and greased his whiskers with him
afterwards.

'This was a merry life for the Baron of Grogzwig, and a
merrier still for the baron's retainers, who drank Rhine wine
every night till they fell under the table, and then had the
bottles on the floor, and called for pipes. Never were such
jolly, roystering, rollicking, merry-making blades as the
jovial crew of Grogzwig.

'But the pleasures of the table, or the pleasures of under the
table, require a little variety; especially when the same five-and-
twenty people sit daily down to the same board, to dicuss the
same subjects, and tell the same stories. The baron grew weary,
and wanted excitement. He took to quarrelling with his gentlemen, and tried kicking two or three of them every day after
dinner. This was a pleasant change at first; but it became
monotonous after a week or so, and the baron felt quite out of
sorts, and cast about, in despair, for some new amusement.

'One night, after a day's sport in which he had outdone
Nimrod or Gillingwater, and slaughtered "another fine bear,"
and brought him home in triumph, the Baron Von Koëldwethout. sat moodily at the head of his table, eyeing the
smoky roof of the hall with a discontented aspect. He
swallowed huge bumpers of wine, but, the more he swallowed, the more he frowned. The gentlemen who had been
honoured with the dangerous distinction of sitting on his right
and left, imitated him to a miracle in the drinking, and
frowned at each other.

'"I will!" cried the baron suddenly, smiting the table with his right hand, and twirling his moustache with his left. "Fill to the Lady of Grogzwig!"

'The four-and-twenty Lincoln greens turned pale, with the exception of the four-and-twenty noses, which were unchangeable.

'"I said to the Lady of Grogzwig," repeated the baron, looking round the board.

'"To the Lady of Grogzwig!" shouted the Lincoln greens; and down their four-and-twenty throats went four-and-twenty imperial pints of such rare old hock, that they smacked their eight-and-forty lips, and winked again.

'"The fair daughter of the Baron Von Swillenhausen," said Koëldwethout, condescending to explain. "We will demand her in marriage of her father ere the sun goes down tomorrow. If he refuses our suit, we will cut off his nose."

'A hoarse murmur arose from the company; every man touched, first the hilt of his sword, and then the tip of his nose, with appalling significance.

'What a pleasant thing filial piety is to contemplate! If the daughter of the Baron Von Swillenhausen had pleaded a preoccupied heart, or fallen at her father's feet and corned them in salt tears, or only fainted away, and complimented the old gentleman in frantic ejaculations, the odds are a hundred to one but Swillenhausen's Castle would have been turned out at window, or rather the baron turned out at window, and the castle demolished. The damsel held her peace, however, when an early messenger bore the request of Von Koëldwethout next morning, and modestly retired to her chamber, from the casement of which she watched the coming of the suitor and his retinue. She was no sooner assured that the horseman with the large moustaches was her proffered husband than she hastened to her father's presence, and expressed her readiness to sacrifice herself to secure his peace. The venerable baron caught his child to his arms, and shed a wink of joy.

'There was great feasting at the castle that day. The four-and-twenty Lincoln greens of Von Koëldwethout exchanged vows of eternal friendship with twelve Lincoln greens of Von Swillenhausen, and promised the old baron that they would drink his wine "Till all was blue" – meaning, probably, until their whole countenances had acquired the same tint as their noses. Everybody slapped everybody else's back when the time for parting came; and the Baron Von Koëldwethout and his followers rode gaily home.

'For six mortal weeks the bears and boars had a holiday. The house of Koëldwethout and Swillenhausen were united; the spears rusted; and the baron's bugle grew hoarse for lack of blowing.

'Those were great times for the four-and-twenty; but, alas! their high and palmy days had taken boots to themselves, and were already walking off.

'"My dear," said the baroness.

'"My love," said the baron.

'"Those coarse, noisy men . . ."

'"Which, ma'am?" said the baron, starting.

'The baroness pointed, from the window at which they stood, to the courtyard beneath, where the unconscious Lincoln greens were taking a copious stirrup-cup preparatory to issuing forth after a boar or two.

'"My hunting train, ma'am," said the baron.

'"Disband them, love," murmured the baroness.

'"Disband them!" cried the baron in amazement.

'"To please me, love," replied the baroness.

'"To please the devil, ma'am," answered the baron.

'Whereupon the baroness uttered a great cry, and swooned away at the baron's feet.

'What could the baron do? He called for the lady's maid, and roared for the doctor; and then, rushing into the yard, kicked the two Lincoln greens who were the most used to it, and cursing the others all round, bade them go . . . But never mind where. I don't know the German for it, or I would put it delicately that way.

'It is not for me to say by what means, or by what degrees, some wives manage to keep down some husbands as they do, although I may have my private opinion on the subject, and may think that no Member of Parliament ought to be married, inasmuch as three married members out of every four must vote according to their wive's consciences (if there be such things), and not according to their own. All I need say, just now, is, that the Baroness Von Koëldwethout somehow or other acquired great control over the Baron Von Koëldwethout, and that, little by little, and bit by bit, and day by day, and year by year, the baron got the worst of some disputed question, or was slyly unhorsed from some old hobby; and that, by the time he was a fat hearty fellow of forty-eight or thereabouts, he had no feasting, no revelry, no hunting train, and no hunting – nothing, in short, that he liked, or used to have; and that, although he was as fierce as a lion, and as bold as brass, he was decidedly snubbed and put down, by his own lady, in his own castle of Grogzwig.

'Nor was this the whole extent of the baron's misfortunes, About a year after his nuptials, there came into the world a lusty young baron, in whose honour a great many fireworks were let off, and a great many dozens of wine drunk; but next year there came a young baroness, and next year another young baron, and so on, every year, either a baron or baroness (and one year both together), until the baron found himself the father of a small family of twelve. Upon every one of these anniversaries the venerable Baroness Von Swillenhausen was nervously sensitive for the well-being of her child the Baroness Von Koëldwethout; and although it was not found that the good lady ever did anything material towards contributing to her child's recovery, still she made it a point of duty to be as nervous as possible at the castle of Grogzwig, and to divide her time between moral observations on the baron's housekeeping, and bewailing the hard lot of her unhappy daughter. And if the Baron of Grogzwig, a little hurt and irritated at this, took heart, and ventured to suggest that his wife was at least no worse off than the wives of other barons, the Baroness Von Swillenhausen begged all persons to take notice that nobody but she sympathised with her dear daughter's sufferings; upon which her relations and friends remarked that to be sure she did cry a great deal more than her son-in-law, and that, if there were a hard-hearted brute alive, it was the Baron of Grogzwig.

'The poor baron bore it all as long as he could, and, when he could bear it no longer, lost his appetite and his spirits, and sat himself gloomily and dejectedly down. But there were worse troubles yet in store for him, and, as they came on, his melancholy and sadness increased. Times changed. He got

into debt. The Grogzwig coffers ran low, though the Swillenhausen family had looked upon them as inexhaustible; and
just when the baroness was on the point of making a
thirteenth addition to the family pedigree, Von Koëldwethout
discovered that he had no means of replenishing them.

'"I don't see what is to be done," said the baron. "I think I'll
kill myself."

'This was a bright idea. The baron took an old hunting
knife from a cupboard hard by, and, having sharpened it on
his boot, made what boys call "an offer" at his throat.

'"Hem!" said the baron, stopping short. "Perhaps it's not
sharp enough."

'The baron sharpened it again, and made another offer,
when his hand was arrested by a loud screaming among the
young barons and baronesses, who had a nursery in an
upstairs tower, with irons bars outside the windows, to
prevent their tumbling out into the moat.

'"If I had been a bachelor," said the baron, sighing, "I might
have done it fifty times over without being interrupted. Hallo!
Put a flask of wine and the largest pipe in the little vaulted
room behind the hall."

'One of the domestics, in a very kind manner, executed the
baron's order in the course of half an hour or so, and Von
Koëldwethout, being appraised thereof, strode to the vaulted
room, the walls of which, being of dark shining wood,
gleamed in the light of the blazing logs which were piled upon
the hearth. The bottle and pipe were ready, and, upon the
whole, the place looked very comfortable.

'"Leave the lamp," said the baron.

'"Anything else, my lord?" inquired the domestic.

'"The room," replied the baron. The domestic obeyed, and
the baron locked the door.

'"I'll smoke a last pipe," said the baron, "and then I'll be
off." So putting the knife upon the table till he wanted it, and
tossing off a goodly measure of wine, the Lord of Grogzwig
threw himself back in his chair, stretched his legs out before
the fire, and puffed away.

'He thought about a great many things – about his present
troubles and past days of bachelorship, and about the Lincoln
greens, long since dispersed up and down the country, no one

knew whither; with the exception of two who had been
unfortunately beheaded, and four who had killed themselves
with drinking. His mind was running upon bears and boars,
when, in the process of draining his glass to the bottom, he
raised his eyes, and saw, for the first time and with
unbounded astonishment, that he was not alone.

'No, he was not; for, on the opposite side of the fire,
there sat with folded arms a wrinkled hideous figure, with
deeply-sunk and bloodshot eyes, and an immensely long
cadaverous face, shadowed by jagged and matted locks of
coarse black hair. He wore a kind of tunic of a dull bluish
colour, which, the baron observed, on regarding it attentively, was clasped or ornamented down the front with
coffin handles. His legs, too, were encased in coffin plates
as though in armour; and over his left shoulder he wore a
short dusky cloak, which seemed made of a remnant of
some pall. He took no notice of the baron, but was intently
eyeing the fire.

'"Halloa!" said the baron, stamping his foot to attract
attention.

'"Halloa!" replied the stranger, moving his eyes towards
the baron, but not his face or himself. "What now?"

'"What now!" replied the baron, nothing daunted by his
hollow voice and lustreless eyes. "*I* should ask that question. How did you get here?"

'"Through the door," replied the figure.

'"What are you?" says the baron.

'"A man," replied the figure.'

'"I don't believe it," says the baron.

'"Disbelieve it, then," says the figure.

'"I will," replied the baron.

'The figure looked at the bold Baron of Grogzwig for
some time, and then said familiarly,

'"There's no coming over you, I see. I am not a man!"

'"What are you, then?" asked the baron.

'"A genius," replied the figure.

'"You don't look much like one," returned the baron
scornfully.

'"I am the Genius of Despair and Suicide," said the apparition. "Now you know me."

'With these words the apparition turned towards the baron, as if composing himself for a talk – and what was very remarkable was, that he threw his cloak aside, and displaying a stake, which was run through the centre of his body, pulled it out with a jerk, and laid it on the table, as composedly as if it had been a walking stick.

'"Now," said the figure, glancing at the hunting knife, "are you ready for me?"

'"Not quite," rejoined the baron; "I must finish this pipe first."

'"Look sharp, then," said the figure.

'"You seem in a hurry," said the baron.

'"Why, yes, I am," answered the figure; "they're doing a pretty brisk business in my way over in England and France just now, and my time is a good deal taken up."

'"Do you drink?" said the baron, touching the bottle with the bowl of his pipe.

'"Nine times out of ten, and then very hard," rejoined the figure drily.

'"Never in moderation?"

'"Never," replied the figure with a shudder; "that breeds cheerfulness."

'The baron took another look at his new friend, whom he thought an uncommonly queer customer, and at length inquired whether he took any active part in such little proceedings as that which he had in contemplation.

'"No," replied the figure evasively; "but I am always present."

'"Just to see fair, I suppose?" said the baron.

'"Just that," replied the figure, playing with his stake, and examining the ferrule. "Be as quick as you can, will you? for there's a young gentleman who is afflicted with too much money and leisure wanting me now, I find."

'"Going to kill himself because he has too much money!" exclaimed the baron, quite tickled. "Ha! ha! that's a good one." (This was the first time the baron had laughed for many a long day.)

'"I say," expostulated the figure, looking very much scared; "don't do that again."

'"Why not?" demanded the baron.

'"Because it gives me pain all over," replied the figure. "Sigh as much as you please: that does me good."

'The baron sighed mechanically at the mention of the word; the figure, brightening up again, handed him the hunting knife with most winning politeness.

'"It's not a bad idea, though," said the baron, feeling the edge of the weapon; "a man killing himself because he has too much money."

'"Pooh!" said the apparition petulantly, "no better than a man's killing himself because he has none or little."

'Whether the genius unintentionally committed himself in saying this, or whether he thought the baron's mind was so thoroughly made up that it didn't matter what he said, I have no means of knowing. I only know that the baron stopped his hand all of a sudden, opened his eyes wide, and looked as if quite a new light had come upon him for the first time.

'"Why, certainly," said Von Koëldwethout, "nothing is too bad to be retrieved."

'"Except empty coffers," cried the genius.

'"Well; but they may be one day filled again," said the baron.

'"Scolding wives," snarled the genius.

'"Oh! They may be made quiet," said the baron.

'"Thirteen children," shouted the genius.

'"Can't all go wrong, surely," said the baron.

'The genius was evidently growing very savage with the baron for holding these opinions all at once; but he tried to laugh it off, and said if he would let him know when he had left off joking he should feel obliged to him.

'"But I am not joking; I was never farther from it," remonstrated the baron.

'"Well, I am glad to hear that," said the genius, looking very grim, "because a joke, without any figure of speech, *is* the death of me. Come! Quit this dreary world at once."

'"I don't know," said the baron, playing with the knife; "It's a dreary one certainly, but I don't think yours is much better, for you have not the appearance of being particularly comfortable. That puts me in mind – what security have I that I shall be any the better for going out of the world after all?" he cried, starting up; "I never thought of that."

'"Dispatch!" cried the figure, gnashing his teeth.

'"Keep off!" said the baron. "I'll brood over miseries no longer, but put a good face on the matter, and try the fresh air and the bears again; and, if that don't do, I'll talk to the baroness soundly, and cut the Von Swillenhausens dead." With this the baron fell into his chair, and laughed so loud and boisterously that the room rang with it.

'The figure fell back a pace or two, regarding the baron meanwhile with a look of intense terror, and, when he had ceased, caught up the stake, plunged it violently into his body, uttered a frightful howl, and disappeared.

'Von Koëldwethout never saw it again. Having once made up his mind to action, he soon brought the baroness and the Von Swillenhausens to reason, and died many years afterwards: not a rich man that I am aware of, but certainly a happy one: leaving behind him a numerous family, who had been carefully educated in bear and boar hunting under his own personal eye. And my advice to all men is, that if ever they become hipped and melancholy from similar causes (as very many men do), they look at both sides of the question, applying a magnifying glass to the best one; and if they still feel tempted to retire without leave, that they smoke a large pipe and drink a full bottle first, and profit by the laudable example of the Baron of Grogzwig.'

from *Nicholas Nickleby*

A CONFESSION FOUND IN A PRISON IN
THE TIME OF CHARLES THE SECOND

I held a lieutenant's commission in His Majesty's army, and served abroad in the campaigns of 1677 and 1678. The treaty of Nimegen being concluded, I returned home, and retiring from the service withdrew to a small estate lying a few miles east of London, which I had recently acquired in right of my wife.

This is the last night I have to live, and I will set down the naked truth without disguise. I was never a brave man, and had always been from my childhood of a secret, sullen, distrustful nature. I speak of myself as if I had passed from the world, for while I write this my grave is digging and my name is written in the black book of death.

Soon after my return to England, my only brother was seized with mortal illness. This circumstance gave me slight or no pain, for since we had been men we associated but very little together. He was open-hearted and generous, hand-somer than I, more accomplished, and generally beloved. Those who sought my acquaintance abroad or at home because they were friends of his, seldom attached themselves to me long, and would usually say in our first conversation that they were surprised to find two brothers so unlike in their manners and appearance. It was my habit to lead them on to this avowal, for I knew what comparisons they must draw between us, and having a rankling envy in my heart, I sought to justify it to myself.

We had married two sisters. This additional tie between us, as it may appear to some, only estranged us the more. His wife knew me well. I never struggled with any secret jealousy or gall when she was present but that woman knew it as well as I did. I never raised my eyes at such times but I found hers fixed upon me; I never bent them on the ground or looked another way, but I felt that she overlooked me always. It was

75

an inexpressible relief to me when we quarrelled, and a greater relief still when I heard abroad that she was dead. It seems to me now as if some strange and terrible foreshadowing of what has happened since, must have hung over us then. I was afriad of her, she haunted me; her fixed and steady look comes back upon me now like the memory of a dark dream and makes my blood run cold.

She died shortly after giving birth to a child – a boy. When my brother knew that all hope of his own recovery was past, he called my wife to his bed-side and confided this orphan, a child of four years old, to her protection. He bequeathed to him all the property he had, and willed that in case of the child's death, it should pass to my wife as the only acknow-ledgement he could make her for her care and love. He exchanged a few brotherly words with me, deploring our long separation, and being exhausted, fell into a slumber from which he never awoke.

We had no children; and as there had been a strong affection between the sisters, and my wife had almost supplied the place of a mother to this boy, she loved him as if he had been her own. The child was ardently attached to her; but he was his mother's image in face and spirit and always mistrusted me.

I can scarcely fix the date when the feeling first came upon me, but I soon began to be uneasy when this child was by. I never roused myself from some moody train of thought but I marked him looking at me: not with mere childish wonder, but with something of the purpose and meaning that I had so often noted in his mother. It was no effort of my fancy, founded on close resemblance of feature and expression. I never could look the boy down. He feared me, but seemed by some instinct to despise me while he did so; and even when he drew back beneath my gaze – as he would when we were alone, to get nearer to the door – he would keep his bright eyes upon me still.

Perhaps I hide the truth from myself, but I do not think that when this began, I meditated to do him any wrong. I may have thought how serviceable his inheritance would be to us, and may have wished him dead, but I believe I had no thought of compassing his death. Neither did the idea come upon me at once, but by slow degrees, presenting itself at first in dim shapes at a very great distance, as men may think of an earthquake or the last day – then drawing nearer and nearer and losing something of its horror and improbability – then coming to be part and parcel, nay nearly the whole sum and substance of my daily thoughts, and resolving itself into a question of means and safety; not of doing or abstaining from the deed.

While this was going on within me, I never could bear that the child should see me looking at him, and yet I was under a fascination which made it a kind of business with me to contemplate his slight and fragile figure and think how easily it might be done. Sometimes I would steal upstairs and watch him as he slept, but usually I hovered in the garden near the window of the room in which he learnt his little tasks, and there as he sat upon a low seat beside my wife, I would peer at him for hours together from behind a tree: starting like the guilty wretch I was at every rustling of a leaf, and still gliding back to look and start again.

Hard by our cottage, but quite out of sight, and (if there were any wind astir) of hearing too, was a deep sheet of water. I spent days in shaping with my pocket-knife a rough model of a boat, which I finished at last and dropped in the child's way. Then I withdrew to a secret place which he must pass if he stole away alone to swim this bauble, and lurked there for his coming. He came neither that day nor the next, though I waited from noon till nightfall. I was sure that I had him in my net for I had heard him prattling of the toy, and knew that in his infant pleasure he kept it by his side in bed, I felt no weariness or fatigue, but waited patiently, and on the third day he passed me, running joyously along, with his silken hair streaming in the wind and he singing – God have mercy upon me! – singing a merry ballad – who could hardly lisp the words.

I stole down after him, creeping under certain shrubs which grow in that place, and none but devils know with what terror I, a full-grown man, tracked the footsteps of that baby as he approached the water's brink. I was close upon him, had sunk upon my knee and raised my hand to thrust him in, when he saw my shadow in the stream and turned round.

His mother's ghost was looking from his eyes. The sun burst forth from behind a cloud: it shone in the bright sky, the glistening earth, the clear water, the sparkling drops of rain upon the leaves. There were eyes in everything. The whole great universe of light was there to see the murder done. I know not what he said; he came of bold and manly blood, and child as he was, he did not crouch or fawn upon me. I heard him cry that he would try to love me – not that he did – and then I saw him running back towards the house. The next I saw was my own sword naked in my hand and he lying at my feet stark dead – dabbled here and there with blood but otherwise no different from what I had seen him in his sleep – in the same attitude too, with his cheek resting upon his little hand.

I took him in my arms and laid him – very gently now that he was dead – in a thicket. My wife was from home that day and would not return until the next. Our bedroom window, the only sleeping room on that side of the house, was but a few feet from the ground, and I resolved to descend from it at night and bury him in the garden. I had no thought that I had failed in my design, no thought that the water would be dragged and nothing found, that the money must now lie waste since I must encourage the idea that the child was lost or stolen. All my thoughts were bound up and knotted together, in the one absorbing necessity of hiding what I had done.

How I felt when they came to tell me that the child was missing, when I ordered scouts in all directions, when I grasped and trembled at everyone's approach, no tongue can tell or mind of man conceive. I buried him that night. When I parted the boughs and looked into the dark thicket, there was a glow-worm shining like the visible spirit of God upon the murdered child. I glanced down into his grave when I had placed him there and still it gleamed upon his breast: an eye of fire looking up to Heaven in supplication to the stars that watched me at my work.

I had to meet my wife, and break the news, and give her hope that the child would soon be found. All this I did – with some appearance, I suppose, of being sincere, for I was the object of no suspicion. This done, I sat at the bedroom window all day long and watched the spot where the dreadful secret lay.

It was a piece of ground which had been dug up to be newly turfed, and which I had chosen on that account as the traces of my spade were less likely to attract attention. The men who laid

down the grass must have thought me mad. I called to them
continually to expedite their work, ran out and worked beside
them, trod down the turf with my feet, and hurried them with
frantic eagerness. They had finished their task before night,
and then I thought myself comparatively safe.

I slept – not as men do who wake refreshed and cheerful,
but I did sleep, passing from vague and shadowy dreams of
being hunted down, to visions of the plot of grass, through
which now a hand, and now a foot, and now the head itself
was starting out. At this point I always woke and stole to the
window to make sure that it was not really so. That done I
crept to bed again; and thus I spent the night in fits and starts,
getting up and lying down full twenty times, and dreaming
the same dream over and over again – which was far worse
than lying awake, for every dream had a whole night's
suffering of its own. Once I thought the child was alive and
that I had never tried to kill him. To wake from that dream
was the most dreadful agony of all.

The next day I sat at the window again, never once taking
my eyes from the place, which, although it was covered by
the grass, was as plain to me – its shape, its size, its depth, its
jagged sides, and all – as if it had been open to the light of day.
When a servant walked across it, I felt as if he must sink in;
when he had passed I looked to see that his feet had not worn
the edges. If a bird lighted there, I was in terror lest by some
tremendous interposition it should be instrumental in the
discovery; if a breath of air sighed across it, to me it whispered
murder. There was not a sight or sound – how ordinary mean
or unimportant soever – but was fraught with fear. And in this
state of ceaseless watching I spent three days.

On the fourth, there came to the gate one who had served
with me abroad, accompanied by a brother officer of his
whom I had never seen. I felt that I could not bear to be out of
sight of the place. It was a summer evening, and I bade my
people take a table and a flask of wine into the garden. Then I
sat down *with my chair upon the grave,* and being assured that
nobody could disturb it now, without my knowledge, tried
to drink and talk.

They hoped that my wife was well – that she was not
obliged to keep her chamber – that they had not frightened her

away. What could I do but tell them with a faltering tongue about the child? The officer whom I did not know was a down-looking man and kept his eyes upon the ground while I was speaking. Even that terrified me! I could not divest myself of the idea that he saw something there which caused him to suspect the truth. I asked him hurriedly if he supposed that – and stopped. 'That the child had been murdered?' said he, looking mildly at me. 'Oh no! what could a man gain by murdering a poor child?' *I* could have told him what a man gained by such a deed, no one better, but I held my peace and shivered with an ague.

Mistaking my emotion, they were endeavouring to cheer me with the hope that the boy would certainly be found – great cheer that was for me! – when we heard a low deep howl, and presently there sprung over the wall two great dogs, who, bounding into the garden, repeated the baying sound we had heard before.

'Blood-hounds!' cried my visitors.

What need to tell me that! I had never seen one of that kind in all my life, but I knew what they were and for what purpose they had come. I grasped the elbows of my chair, and neither spoke nor moved.

'They are of the genuine breed,' said the man whom I had known abroad, 'and being out of exercise have no doubt escaped from their keeper.'

Both he and his friend turned to look at the dogs, who with their noses to the ground moved restlessly about, running to and fro, and up and down, and across, and round in circles, careering about like wild things, and all this time taking no notice of us, but ever and again repeating the yell we had heard already, then dropping their noses to the ground again and tracking earnestly here and there. They now began to snuff the earth more eagerly than they had done yet, and although they were still very restless, no longer beat about in such wide circuits, but kept near to one spot, and constantly diminished the distance between themselves and me.

At last they came up close to the great chair on which I sat, and raising their frightful howl once more, tried to tear away the wooden rails that kept them from the ground beneath. I saw how I looked, in the faces of the two who were with me.

'They scent some prey,' said they, both together.

'They scent no prey!' cried I.

'In Heaven's name, move!' said the one I knew, very earnestly, 'or you will be torn to pieces.'

'Let them tear me limb from limb, I'll never leave this place!' cried I. 'Are dogs to hurry men to shameful deaths? Hew them down, cut them in pieces.'

'There is some foul mystery here!' said the officer whom I did not know, drawing his sword. 'In King Charles's name, assist me to secure this man.'

They both set upon me and forced me away, though I fought and bit and caught at them like a madman. After a struggle, they got me quietly between them, and then, my God! I saw the angry dogs tearing at the earth and throwing it up into the air like water.

What more have I to tell? That I fell upon my knees, and with chattering teeth confessed the truth, and prayed to be forgiven. That I have since denied, and now confess to it again. That I have been tried for the crime, found guilty, and sentenced. That I have not the courage to anticipate my doom, or to bear up manfully against it. That I have no compassion, no consolation, no hope, no friend. That my wife has happily lost for the time those faculties which would enable her to know my misery or hers. That I am alone in this stone dungeon with my evil spirit, and that I die tomorrow!

from *Master Humphrey's Clock*

TO BE READ AT DUSK

One, two, three, four, five. There were five of them.

Five couriers, sitting on a bench outside the convent on the summit of the Great St. Bernard in Switzerland, looking at the remote heights, stained by the setting sun, as if a mighty quantity of red wine had been broached upon the mountain top, and had not yet had time to sink into the snow.

This is not my simile. It was made for the occasion by the stoutest courier, who was a German. None of the others took any more notice of it than they took of me, sitting on another bench on the other side of the convent door, smoking my cigar, like them, and – also like them – looking at the reddened snow, and at the lonely shed hard by, where the bodies of belated travellers, dug out of it, slowly wither away, knowing no corruption in that cold region.

The wine upon the mountain top soaked in as we looked; the mountain became white; the sky, a very dark blue; the wind rose; and the air turned piercing cold. The five couriers buttoned their rough coats. There being no safer man to imitate in all such proceedings than a courier, I buttoned mine.

The mountain in the sunset had stopped the five couriers in a conversation. It is a sublime sight, likely to stop conversation. The mountain being now out of the sunset, they resumed. Not that I had heard any part of their previous discourse; for indeed, I had not then broken away from the American gentleman, in the travellers' parlour of the convent, who, sitting with his face to the fire, had undertaken to realise to me the whole progress of events which had led to the accumulation by the Honorable Ananias Dodger of one of the largest acquisitions of dollars ever made in one country.

'My God!' said the Swiss courier, speaking in French, which I do not hold (as some authors appear to do) to be such an all-sufficient excuse for a naughty word, that I have only to write it in that language to make it innocent; 'if you talk of ghosts . . .'

'But I *don't* talk of ghosts,' said the German.

'Of what then?' asked the Swiss.

'If I knew of what then,' said the German, 'I should probably know a great deal more.'

It was a good answer, I thought, and it made me curious. So I moved my position to that corner of my bench which was nearest to them, and leaning my back against the convent wall, heard perfectly, without appearing to attend.

'Thunder and lightning!' said the German, warming, 'when a certain man is coming to see you, unexpectedly; and, without his own knowledge, sends some invisible messenger, to put the idea of him into your head all day, what do you call that? When you walk along a crowded street – at Frankfurt, Milan, London, Paris – and think that a passing stranger is like your friend Heinrich, and then another passing stranger is like your friend Heinrich, and so begin to have a strange fore-knowledge that presently you'll meet your friend Heinrich – which you do, though you believed him at Trieste – what do you call *that*?"

'It's not uncommon, either,' murmured the Swiss and the other three.

'Uncommon!' said the German. 'It's as common as cherries in the Black Forest. It's as common as macaroni at Naples. And Naples reminds me! When the old Marchesa Senzanima shrieks at a card-party on the Chiaja – as I heard and saw her, for it happened in a Bavarian family of mine, and I was overlooking the service that evening – I say, when the old Marchesa starts up at the card-table, white through her rouge, and cries, "My sister in Spain is dead! I felt her cold touch on my back!" – and when that sister *is* dead at the moment – what do you call that?'

'Or when the blood of San Gennaro liquefies at the request of the clergy – as all the world knows that it does regularly once a year, in my native city,' said the Neopolitan courier after a pause, with a comical look, 'what do you call that?'

'*That!*' cried the German. 'Well, I think I know a name for that.'

'Miracle?' said the Neopolitan, with the same sly face.

The German merely smoked and laughed; and they all smoked and laughed.

'Bah!' said the German, presently. 'I speak of things that really do happen. When I want to see the conjurer, I pay to see a professional one, and have my money's worth. Very strange things do happen without ghosts. Ghosts! Giovanni Baptista, tell your story of the English bride. There's no ghost in that, but something full as strange. Will any man tell me what?'

As there was a silence among them, I glanced around. He whom I took to be Baptista was lighting a fresh cigar. He presently went on to speak. He was a Genoese, as I judged.

'The story of the English bride?' said he. 'Basta! One ought not to call so slight a thing a story. Well, it's all one. But it's true. Observe me well, gentlemen, it's true. That which glitters is not always gold: but what I am going to tell, is true.'

He repeated this more than once.

Ten years ago, I took my credentials to an English gentle-man at Long's Hotel, in Bond Street, London, who was about to travel – it might be for one year, it might be for two. He approved of them; likewise of me. He was pleased to make inquiry. The testimony that he received was favourable. He engaged me by the six months, and my entertainment was generous.

He was young, handsome, very happy. He was enamoured of a fair young English lady, with a sufficient fortune, and they were going to be married. It was the wedding-trip, in short, that we were going to take. For three months' rest in the hot weather (it was early summer then) he had hired an old place on the Riviera, at an easy distance from the city, Genoa, on the road to Nice. Did I know the place? Yes; I told him I knew it well. It was an old palace with great gardens. It was a little bare, and it was a little dark and gloomy, being close surrounded by trees; but it was spacious, ancient, grand, and on the sea-shore. He said it had been so described to him exactly, and he was well pleased that I knew it. For its being a little bare of furniture, all such places were. For its being a little gloomy, he had hired it principally for the gardens, and he and my mistress would pass the summer weather in their shade.

'So all goes well, Baptista?' said he.

'Indubitably, signore; very well.'

We had a travelling chariot for our journey, newly built for us, and in all respects complete. The marriage took place. They were happy. *I* was happy, seeing all was bright, being so well situated, going to my own city, teaching my language in the rumble to the maid, la bella Carolina, whose heart was gay with laughter; who was young and rosy.

The time flew. But I observed – listen to this, I pray! (and here the courier dropped his voice) – I observed my mistress sometimes brooding in a manner very strange; in a frightened manner; in an unhappy manner; with a cloudy, uncertain alarm upon her. I think that I began to notice this when I was walking up hills by the carriage side, and master had gone on in front. At any rate, I remember that it impressed itself upon my mind one evening in the South of France, when she called to me to call master back; and when he came back, and walked for a long way, talking encouragingly and affectionately to her, with his hand upon the open window, and hers in it. Now and then, he laughed in a merry way, as if he were bantering her out of something. By-and-by, she laughed, and then all went well again.

It was curious. I asked la bella Carolina, the pretty little one. Was mistress unwell? – No. – Out of spirits? – No. – Fearful of bad roads, or brigands? – No. And what made it more mysterious was, the pretty little one would not look at me in giving answer, but *would* look at the view.

But one day she told me the secret.

'If you must know,' said Carolina, 'I find, from what I have overheard, that mistress is haunted.'

'How haunted?'

'By a dream.'

'What dream?'

'By a dream of a face. For three nights before her marriage, she saw a face in a dream – always the same face, and only one.'

'A terrible face?'

'No. The face of a dark, remarkable-looking man, in black, with black hair and a grey moustache – a handsome man except for a reserved and secret air. Not a face she ever saw, or at all like a face she ever saw. Doing nothing in the dream but looking at her fixedly, out of darkness.'

'Does the dream come back?'

'Never. The recollection of it is all her trouble.'

'And why does it trouble her?'

Carolina shook her head.

'That's master's question,' said la bella. 'She don't know. She wonders why, herself. But I heard her tell him, only last night, that if she was to find a picture of that face in our Italian house (which she is afraid she will) she did not know how she could ever bear it.'

Upon my word, I was fearful after this (said the Genoese courier) of our coming to the old palazzo, lest some such ill-starred picture should happen to be there. I knew there were many there; and, as we got nearer and nearer to the place, I wished the whole gallery in the crater of Vesuvius. To mend the matter, it was a stormy dismal evening when we, at last, approached that part of the Riviera. It thundered; and the thunder of my city and its environs, rolling among the high hills, is very loud. The lizards ran in and out of the chinks in the broken stone wall of the garden, as if they were frightened; the frogs bubbled and croaked their loudest; the sea-wind moaned, and the wet trees dripped; and the lightning – body of San Lorenzo, how it lightened!

We all knew what an old palace in or near Genoa is – how time and the sea air have blotted it – how the drapery painted on the outer walls has peeled off in great flakes of plaster – how the lower windows are darkened with rusty bars of iron – how the courtyard is overgrown with grass – how the outer buildings are dilapidated – how the whole pile seems devoted to ruin. Our palazzo was one of the true kind. It had been shut up close for months. Months? – years! – it had an earthy smell, like a tomb. The scent of the orange trees on the broad back terrace, and of the lemons ripening on the wall, and of some shrubs that grew around a broken fountain, had got into the house somehow, and had never been able to get out again. There was, in every room, an aged smell, grown faint with confinement. It pined in all the cupboards and drawers. In the little rooms of communication between great rooms, it was stifling. If you turned a picture – to come back to the pictures – there it still was, clinging to the wall behind the frame, like a sort of bat.

The lattice-blinds were close shut, all over the house. There were two ugly grey old women in the house, to take care of it; one of them with a spindle, who stood winding and mumbling in the doorway, and who would as soon have let in the devil as the air. Master, mistress, la bella Carolina, and I, went all through the palazzo. I went first, though I have named myself last, opening the windows and the lattice-blinds, and shaking down on myself splashes of rain, and scraps of mortar, and now and then a dozing mosquito, or a monstrous, fat, blotchy, Genoese spider.

When I had let the evening light into a room, master, mistress, and la bella Carolina, entered. Then we looked round at all the pictures, and I went forward again into another room. Mistress secretly had a great fear of meeting with the likeness of that face – we all had; but there was no such thing. The Madonna and Bambino, San Francisco, San Sebastiano, Venus, Santa Caterina, Angels, Brigands, Friars, Temples at Sunset, Battles, White Horses, Forests, Apostles, Doges, all my old acquaintances many times repeated? – yes. Dark handsome man in black, reserved and secret, with black hair and grey moustache, looking fixedly at mistress out of darkness – no.

At last we got through all the rooms and all the pictures, and came out into the gardens. They were pretty well kept, being rented by a gardener, and were large and shady. In one place there was a rustic theatre, open to the sky; the stage a green slope; the coulisses, three entrances upon a side, sweet-smelling leafy screens. Mistress moved her bright eyes, even there, as if she looked to see the face come in upon the scene; but all was well.

'Now, Clara,' master said, in a low voice, 'you see that it is nothing? You are happy.'

Mistress was much encouraged. She soon accustomed herself to that grim palazzo, and would sing, and play the harp, and copy the old pictures, and stroll with master under the green trees and vines all day. She was beautiful. He was happy. He would laugh and say to me, mounting his horse for his morning ride before the heat:

'All goes well, Baptista!'

'Yes, signore, thank God, very well.'

We kept no company. I took la bella to the Duomo and Annunciata, to the Cafe, to the Opera, to the village Festa, to the Public Garden, to the Day Theatre, to the Marionetti. The pretty little one was charmed with all she saw. She learnt Italian – heavens! miraculously! Was mistress quite forgetful of that dream! I asked Carolina sometimes. Nearly, said la bella – almost. It was wearing out.

One day master received a letter, and called me.

'Baptista!'

'Signore!'

'A gentleman who is presented to me will dine here today. He is called the Signore Dellombra. Let me dine like a prince.'

It was an odd name. I did not know that name. But there had been many noblemen and gentlemen pursued by Austria on political suspicions, lately, and some names had changed. Perhaps this was one. Altro! Dellombra was as good a name to me as another.

When the Signor Dellombra came to dinner (said the Genoese courier in the low voice, into which he had subsided once before), I showed him into the reception-room, the great sala of the old palazzo. Master received him with cordiality and presented him to mistress. As she rose, her face changed, she gave a cry, and fell upon the marble floor.

Then I turned my head to the Signor Dellombra, and saw that he was dressed in black, and had a reserved and secret air, and was a dark remarkable-looking man, with black hair and a grey moustache.

Master raised mistress in his arms, and carried her to her own room, where I sent la bella Carolina straight. La bella told me afterwards that mistress was nearly terrified to death, and that she wandered in her mind about her dream, all night.

Master was vexed and anxious – almost angry, and yet full of solicitude. The Signore Dellombra was a courtly gentleman, and spoke with great respect and sympathy of mistress's being so ill. The African wind had been blowing for some days (they had told him at his hotel of the Maltese Cross), and he knew that it was often hurtful. He hoped the beautiful lady would recover soon. He begged permission to retire, and to renew his visit when he should have the happiness of hearing that she was better. Master would not allow of this, and they dined alone.

He withdrew early. Next day he called at the gate, on horseback, to inquire for mistress. He did so two or three times in that week.

What I observed myself, and what la bella Carolina told me, united to explain to me that master has now set his mind on curing mistress of her fanciful terror. He was all kindness, but he was sensible and firm. He reasoned with her, that to encourage such fancies was to invite melancholy, if not madness. That it rested with herself to be herself. That if she once resisted her strange weakness, so successfully as to receive Signor Dellombra as an English lady would receive any other guest, it was for ever conquered. To make an end, the signore came again, and mistress received him without marked distress (though with constraint and apprehension still), and the evening passed serenely. Master was so delighted with this change, and so anxious to confirm it, that the Signor Dellombra became a constant guest. He was accomplished in pictures, books, and music; and his society, in any grim palazzo, would have been welcome.

I used to notice, many times, that mistress was not quite recovered. She would cast down her eyes and droop her head, before Signore Dellombra, or would look at him with a terrified and fascinated glance, as if his presence had some evil influence or power upon her. Turning from her to him, I used to see him in the shaded gardens, or the large half-lighted sala, looking, as I might say, 'fixedly upon her out of darkness.' But, truly, I had not forgotten la bella Carolina's words describing the face in the dream.

After his second visit I heard master say:

'Now, see, my dear Clara, it's over! Dellombra has come and gone, and your apprehension is broken like glass.'

'Will he – will he ever come again?' asked mistress.

'Again? Why, surely, over and over again! Are you cold?' (she shivered).

'No, dear – but he terrifies me: are you sure that he need come again?'

'The surer for the question, Clara!' replied master, cheerfully.

But he was very hopeful of her complete recovery now, and

grew more and more so every day. She was beautiful. He was happy.

'All goes well, Baptista?' he would say to me again.

'Yes, signore, thank God; very well.'

We were all (said the Genoese courier, constraining himself to speak a little louder), we were all at Rome for the Carnival. I had been out, all day, with a Sicilian, a friend of mine, and a courier, who was there with an English family. As I returned at night to our hotel, I met the little Carolina, who never stirred from home alone, running distractedly along the Corso.

'Carolina! What's the matter?'

'O Baptista! O, for the Lord's sake! where is my mistress?'

'Mistress, Carolina?'

'Gone since morning – told me, when master went out on his day's journey, not to call her, for she was tired with not resting in the night (having been in pain), and would lie in bed until the evening; then get up refreshed. She is gone! – she is gone! Master has come back, broken down the door, and she is gone! My beautiful, my good, my innocent mistress!'

The pretty little one so cried, and raved, and tore herself that I could not have held her, but for her swooning on my arm as if she had been shot. Master came up – in manner, face, or voice, no more the master that I knew, than I was he. He took me (I laid the little one upon her bed in the hotel, and left her with the chamber-woman), in a carriage, furiously through the darkness, across the desolate Campagna. When it was day, and we stopped at a miserable post-house, all the horses had been hired twelve hours ago, and sent away in different directions. Mark me! by the Signor Dellombra, who had passed there in a carriage, with a frightened English lady crouching in one corner.

I never heard (said the Genoese courier, drawing a long breath) that she was ever traced beyond that spot. All I know is, that she vanished into infamous oblivion, with the dreaded face beside her that she had seen in her dream.

'What do you call *that*?' said the German courier, triumphantly. 'Ghosts! There are no ghosts *there*! What do you call

this, that I am going to tell you? Ghosts! There are no ghosts
here!'

I took an engagement once (pursued the German courier)
with an English gentleman, elderly and a bachelor, to travel
through my country, my Fatherland. He was a merchant who
traded with my country and knew the language, but who had
never been there since he was a boy – as I judge, some sixty
years before.

His name was James, and he had a twin-brother John, also a
bachelor. Between these brothers there was a great affection.
They were in business together, at Goodman's Fields, but
they did not live together. Mr James dwelt in Poland Street,
turning out of Oxford Street, London; Mr John resided by
Epping Forest.

Mr James and I were to start for Germany in about a week.
The exact day depended on business. Mr John came to Poland
Street (where I was staying in the house), to pass that week
with Mr James. But he said to his brother on the second day,
'I don't feel very well, James. There's not much the matter
with me; but I think I am a little gouty. I'll go home and put
myself under the care of my old housekeeper, who under-
stands my ways. If I get quite better, I'll come back and see
you before you go. If I don't feel well enough to resume my
visit where I leave it off, why *you* will come and see *me* before
you go.' Mr James, of course, said he would, and they shook
hands – both hands, as they always did – and Mr John ordered
out his old-fashioned chariot and rumbled home.

It was on the second night after that – that is to say, the
fourth in the week – when I was awoke out of my sound sleep
by Mr James coming into my bedroom in his flannel-gown,
with a lighted candle. He sat upon the side of my bed, and
looking at me, said:

'Wilhelm, I have reason to think I have got some strange
illness upon me.'

I then perceived that there was a very unusual expression in
his face.

'Wilhelm,' said he, 'I am not afraid or ashamed to tell you
what I might be afraid or ashamed to tell another man. You
come from a sensible country, where mysterious things are

inquired into and are not settled to have been weighed and
measured – or to have been unweighable and unmeasurable – or
in either case to have been completely disposed of, for all time –
ever so many years ago. I have just now seen the phantom of
my brother.'

I confess (said the German courier) that it gave me a little
tingling of the blood to hear it.

'I have just now seen,' Mr James repeated, looking full at me,
that I might see how collected he was, 'the phantom of my
brother John. I was sitting up in bed, unable to sleep, when it
came into my room, in a white dress, and regarding me
earnestly, passed to the end of the room, glanced at some
papers on my writing-desk, turned, and, still looking earnestly
at me as it passed the bed, went out at the door. Now, I am not
in the least mad, and am not in the least disposed to invest that
phantom with any external existence out of myself. I think it is
a warning to me that I am ill; and I think I had better be bled.'

I got out of bed directly (said the German courier) and began
to get on my clothes, begging him not to be alarmed, and
telling him that I would go myself to the doctor. I was just
ready, when we heard a loud knocking and ringing at the street
door. My room being an attic at the back, and Mr James's being
the second-floor room in the front, we went down to his room,
and put up the window, to see what was the matter.

'Is that Mr James?' said the man below, falling back to the
opposite side of the way to look up.

'It is,' said Mr James, 'and you are my brother's man,
Robert.'

'Yes, Sir. I am sorry to say, Sir, that Mr John is ill. He is very
bad, sir. It is even feared that he may be lying at the point of
death. He wants to see you, Sir. I have a chaise here. Pray come
to him. Pray lose no time.'

Mr James and I looked at one another. 'Wilhelm,' said he,
'this is strange. I wish you to come with me!' I helped him to
dress, partly there and partly in the chaise; and no grass grew
under the horses' iron shoes between Poland Street and the
Forest.

Now, mind! (said the German courier) I went with Mr James
into his brother's room, and I saw and heard myself what
follows.

His brother lay upon his bed, at the upper end of a long bed-chamber. His old housekeeper was there, and others were there: I think three others were there, if not four, and they had been with him since early in the afternoon. He was in white, like the figure – necessarily so, because he had his nightdress on. He looked like the figure – necessarily so, because he looked earnestly at his brother when he saw him come into the room.

But, when his brother reached the bed-side, he slowly raised himself in bed, and looking full upon him, said these words:

'*James, you have seen me before tonight – and you know it!*'
And so he died.

I waited, when the German courier ceased, to hear something said of this strange story. The silence was unbroken. I looked round, and the five couriers were gone: so noiselessly that the ghostly mountain might have absorbed them into its eternal snows. By this time, I was by no means in a mood to sit alone in that awful scene, with the chill air coming solemnly upon me – or, if I may tell the truth, to sit alone anywhere. So I went back into the convent-parlour, and finding the American gentleman still disposed to relate the biography of the Honourable Ananias Dodger, heard it all out.

from *The Keepsake*

THE TRIAL FOR MURDER

To be Taken with a Grain of Salt

I have always noticed a prevalent want of courage, even among persons of superior intelligence and culture, as to imparting their own psychological experiences when those have been of a strange sort. Almost all men are afraid that what they could relate in such wise would find no parallel or response in a listener's internal life, and might be suspected or laughed at. A truthful traveller, who should have seen some extraordinary creature in the likeness of a sea-serpent, would have no fear of mentioning it; but the same traveller, having had some singular presentiment, impulse, vagary of thought, vision (so called), dream, or other remarkable mental impression, would hesitate considerably before he would own to it. To this reticence I attribute much of the obscurity in which such subjects are involved. We do not habitually communicate our experiences of these subjective things as we do our experiences of objective creation. The consequence is that the general stock of experience in this regard appears exceptional, and really is so, in respect of being miserably imperfect.

In what I am going to relate, I have no intention of setting up, opposing, or supporting, any theory whatever. I know the history of the Bookseller of Berlin. I have studied the case of the wife of a late Astronomer Royal as related by Sir David Brewster, and I have followed the minutest details of a much more remarkable case of Spectral Illusion occurring within my private circle of friends. It may be necessary to state as to this last, that the sufferer (a lady) was in no degree, however distant, related to me. A mistaken assumption on that head might suggest an explanation of a part of my own case – but only a part – which would be wholly without foundation. It cannot be referred to my inheritance of any developed peculiarity, nor had I ever before any at all similar experience, nor have I ever had any at all similar experience since.

It does not signify how many years ago, or how few, a certain murder was committed in England, which attracted great attention. We hear more than enough of murderers as they rise in succession to their atrocious eminence, and I would bury the memory of this particular brute, if I could, as his body was buried, in Newgate Jail. I purposely abstain from giving any direct clue to the criminal's individuality.

When the murder was first discovered, no suspicion fell – or I ought rather to say, for I cannot be too precise in my facts, it was nowhere publicly hinted that any suspicion fell – on the man who was afterwards brought to trial. As no reference was at that time made to him in the newspapers, it is obviously impossible that any description of him can at that time have been given in the newpapers. It is essential that this fact be remembered.

Unfolding at breakfast my morning paper, containing the account of that first discovery, I found it to be deeply interesting, and I read it with close attention. I read it twice, if not three times. The discovery had been made in a bedroom, and, when I laid down the paper, I was aware of a flash – rush – flow – I do not know what to call it – no word I can find is satisfactorily descriptive – in which I seemed to see that bedroom passing through my room, like a picture impossibly painted on a running river. Though almost instantaneous in its passing, it was perfectly clear; so clear that I distinctly, and with a sense of relief, observed the absence of the dead body from the bed.

It was no romantic place that I had this curious sensation, but in chambers in Piccadilly, very near to the corner of St. James's Street. It was entirely new to me. I was in my easy-chair at the moment, and the sensation was accompanied with a peculiar shiver which started the chair from its position. (But it is to be noted that the chair ran easily on castors). I went to one of the windows (there are two in the room, and the room is on the second floor) to refresh my eyes with the moving objects down in Piccadilly. It was a bright autumn morning, and the street was sparkling and cheerful. The wind was high.

As I looked out, it brought down from the Park a quantity of fallen leaves, which a gust took, and whirled into a spiral pillar. As the pillar fell and the leaves dispersed, I saw two men on the opposite side of the way, going from West to East. They were one behind the other. The foremost man often looked back over his shoulder. The second man followed him, at a distance of some thirty paces, with his right hand menacingly raised. First, the singularity and steadiness of this threatening gesture in so public a thoroughfare attracted my attention; and next, the more remarkable circumstance that nobody heeded it. Both men threaded their way among the other passengers with a smoothness hardly consistent even with the action of walking on a pavement; and no single creature, that I could see, gave them place, touched them, or looked after them. In passing before my windows, they both stared up at me. I saw their two faces very distinctly, and I knew that I could recognise them anywhere. Not that I consciously noticed anything very remarkable in either face, except that the man who went first had an unusually lowering appearance, and that the face of the man who followed him was of the colour of impure wax.

I am a bachelor, and my valet and his wife constitute my whole establishment. My occupation is in a certain Branch Bank, and I wish that my duties as head of a Department were as light as they are popularly supposed to be. They kept me in town that autumn, when I stood in need of change. I was not ill, but I was not well. My reader is to make the most that can be reasonably made of my feeling jaded, having a depressing sense upon me of a monotonous life, and being "slightly dyspeptic." I am assured by my renowned doctor that my real state of health at that time justifies no stronger description, and I quote his own from his written answer to my request for it.

As the circumstances of the murder, gradually unravelling, took stronger and stronger possession of the public mind, I kept them away from mine by knowing as little about them as was possible in the midst of the universal excitement. But I knew that a verdict of Wilful Murder had been found against the suspected murderer, and that he had been committed to Newgate for trial. I also knew that his trial had been postponed over one Sessions of the Central Criminal Court, on the ground of general prejudice and want of time for the preparation of the defence. I may further have known, but I believe I did not, when, or about when, the Sessions to which his trial stood postponed would come on.

My sitting-room, bedroom, and dressing-room, are all on one floor. With the last there is no communication but through the bedroom. True, there is a door in it, once communicating with the staircase; but a part of the fitting of my bath has been – and had then been for some years – fixed across it. At the same period, and as a part of the same arrangement, the door had been nailed up and canvased over.

I was standing in my bedroom late one night, giving some directions to my servant before he went to bed. My face was towards the only available door of communication with the dressing-room, and it was closed. My servant's back was towards that door. While I was speaking to him I saw it open, and a man look in, who very earnestly and mysteriously beckoned to me. That man was the man who had gone second of the two along Piccadilly, and whose face was the colour of impure wax.

The figure, having beckoned, drew back, and closed the door. With no longer pause than was made by my crossing the bedroom, I opened the dressing-room door, and looked in. I had a lighted candle already in my hand. I felt no inward expectation of seeing the figure in the dressing-room, and I did not see it there.

Conscious that my servant stood amazed, I turned round to him, and said: 'Derrick, could you believe that in my cool senses I fancied I saw a . . .' As I there laid my hand upon his breast, with a sudden start he trembled violently, and said: 'O Lord, yes, Sir! A dead man beckoning!'

Now I do not believe that this John Derrick, my trusty and attached servant for more than twenty years, had any impression whatever of having seen any such figure, until I touched him. The change in him was so startling, when I touched him, that I fully believe he derived his impression in some occult manner from me at that instant.

I bade John Derrick bring some brandy, and I gave him a dram, and was glad to take one myself. Of what had preceded that night's phenomenon, I told him not a single word. Reflecting on it, I was absolutely certain that I had never seen that face before, except on the one occasion in Piccadilly. Comparing its expression when beckoning at the door with its expression when it had stared up at me as I stood at my window, I came to the conclusion that on the first occasion it had sought to fasten itself upon my memory, and that on the second it had made sure of being immediately remembered.

I was not very comfortable that night, though I felt a certainty, difficult to explain, that the figure would not return. At daylight I fell into a heavy sleep, from which I was awakened by John Derrick's coming to my bedside with a paper in his hand.

This paper, it appeared, had been the subject of an altercation at the door between its bearer and my servant. It was a summons to me to serve upon a Jury at the forthcoming Sessions of the Central Criminal Court at the Old Bailey. I had never before been summoned on such a Jury, as John Derrick well knew. He believed – I am not certain at this hour whether with reason or otherwise – that that class of Jurors were customarily chosen on a lower qualification than mine, and he had at first refused to accept the summons. The man who served it had taken the matter very coolly. He had said that my attendance or non-attendance was nothing to him; there the summons was; and I should deal with it at my own peril, and not at his.

For a day or two I was undecided whether to respond to this call, or take no notice of it. I was not conscious of the slightest mysterious bias, influence, or attraction, one way or other. Of that I am as strictly sure as of every other statement that I make here. Ultimately I decided, as a break in the monotony of my life, that I would go.

The appointed morning was a raw morning in the month of November. There was a dense brown fog in Piccadilly, and it became positively black and in the last degree oppressive East of Temple Bar. I found the passages and staircases of the Court-House flaringly lighted with gas, and the Court itself similarly illuminated. I *think* that, until I was conducted by officers into the Old Court and saw its crowded state, I did not know that the Murderer was to be tried that day. I *think*

that, until I was so helped into the Old Court with considerable difficulty, I did not know into which of the two
Courts sitting my summons would take me. But this must
not be received as a positive assertion, for I am not completely satisfied in my mind on either point.

I took my seat in the place appropriated to Jurors in
waiting, and I looked about the Court as well as I could
through the cloud of fog and breath that was heavy in it. I
noticed a black vapour hanging like a murky curtain outside
the great windows, and I noticed the stifled sound of wheels
on the straw or tan that was littered in the street; also, the
hum of the people gathered there, which a shrill whistle, or
a louder song or hail than the rest, occasionally pierced.
Soon afterwards the Judges, two in number, entered, and
took their seats. The buzz in the Court was awfully hushed.
The direction was given to put the Murderer to the bar. He
appeared there. And in that same instant I recognised in him
the first of the two men who had gone down Piccadilly.

If my name had been called then, I doubt if I could have
answered to it audibly. But it was called about sixth or
eight in the panel, and I was by that time able to say 'Here!'
Now, observe. As I stepped into the box, the prisoner,
who had been looking on attentively, but with no sign of
concern, became violently agitated, and beckoned to his
attorney. The prisoner's wish to challenge me was so manifest, that it occasioned a pause, during which the attorney,
with his hand upon the dock, whispered with his client, and
shook his head. I afterward had it from that gentleman, that
the prisoner's first affrighted words to him were: '*At all
hazards, challenge that man!*' But that, as he would give no
reason for it, and admitted that he had not ever known my
name until he heard it called and I appeared, it was not
done.

Both on the ground already explained, that I wish to
avoid reviving the unwholesome memory of that Murderer,
and also because a detailed account of his long trial is by no
means indispensable to my narrative, I shall confine myself
to such incidents in the ten days and nights during which
we, the Jury, were kept together, as directly bear on my
own curious personal experience. It is in that, and not in

the Murderer, that I seek to interest my reader. It is to that, and not to a page of the Newgate Calendar, that I beg attention.

I was chosen Foreman of the Jury. On the second morning of the trial, after evidence had been taken for two hours (I heard the church clocks strike), happening to cast my eyes over my brother jurymen, I found an inexplicable difficulty in counting them. I counted them several times, yet always with the same difficulty. In short, I made them one too many.

I touched the brother juryman whose place was next me, and I whispered to him: 'Oblige me by counting us.' He looked surprised by the request, but turned his head and counted. 'Why,' says he, suddenly, 'we are Thirt . . .; but not, it's not possible. No. We are twelve.'

According to my counting that day, we were always right in detail, but in the gross we were always one too many. There was no appearance – no figure – to account for it; but I had now an inward foreshadowing of the figure that was surely coming.

The Jury were housed at the London Tavern. We all slept in one large room on separate tables, and we were constantly in the charge and under the eye of the officer sworn to hold us in safe-keeping. I see no reason for suppressing the real name of that officer. He was intelligent, highly polite, and obliging, and (I was glad to hear) much respected in the City. He had an agreeable presence, good eyes, enviable black whiskers, and a fine sonorous voice. His name was Mr Harker.

When we turned into our twelve beds at night, Mr Harker's bed was drawn across the door. On the night of the second day, not being disposed to lie down, and seeing Mr Harker sitting on his bed, I went and sat beside him, and offered him a pinch of snuff. As Mr Harker's hand touched mine in taking it from my box, a peculiar shiver crossed him, and he said: 'Who is this?'

Following Mr Harker's eyes, and looking along the room, I saw again the figure I expected – the second of the two men who had gone down Piccadilly. I rose, and advanced a few steps; then stopped, and looked round at Mr Harker. He was quite unconcerned, laughed, and said in a pleasant way; 'I thought for a moment we had a thirteenth juryman, without a bed. But I see it is the moonlight.'

Making no revelation to Mr Harker, but inviting him to take a walk with me to the end of the room, I watched what the

figure did. It stood for a few moments by the bedside of each
of my eleven brother jurymen, close to the pillow. It always
went to the right-hand side of the bed, and always passed out
crossing the foot of the next bed. It seemed, from the action of
the head, merely to look down pensively at each recumbent
figure. It took no notice of me, or of my bed, which was the
nearest to Mr Harker's. It seemed to go out where the
moonlight came in, through a high window, as by an aerial
flight of stairs.

Next morning at breakfast, it appeared that everybody
present had dreamed of the murdered man last night, except
myself, and Mr Harker.

I now felt convinced that the second man who had gone
down Piccadilly was the murdered man (so to speak), as if it
had been borne into my comprehension by his immediate
testimony. But even this took place, and in a manner for
which I was not at all prepared.

On the fifth day of the trial, when the case for the
prosecution was drawing to a close, a miniature of the
murdered man, missing from his bedroom upon the discovery of the deed, and afterwards found in a hiding-place where
the Murderer had been seen digging, was put in evidence.
Having been identified by the witness under examination, it
was handed up to the Bench, and thence handed down to be
inspected by the Jury. As an officer in a black gown was
making his way with it across to me, the figure of the second
man who had gone down Piccadilly impetuously started from
the crowd, caught the miniature from the officer, and gave it
to me with his own hands, at the same time saying, in a low
and hollow tone – before I saw the miniature, which was in a
locket – *'I was younger then, and my face was not then drained of
blood.'* It also came between me and the brother juryman to
whom I would have given the miniature, and between him
and the brother juryman to whom he would have given it,
and so passed it on through the whole of our number, and
back into my possession. Not one of them, however, detected
this.

At table, and generally when we were shut up together in
Mr Harker's custody, we had from the first naturally discussed the day's proceedings a good deal. On that fifth day, the

case for the prosecution being closed, and we having that side of the question in a completed shape before us, our discussion was more animated and serious. Among our number was a vestry-man – the densest idiot I have ever seen at large – who met the plainest evidence with the most preposterous objections, and who was sided with by two flabby parochial parasites; all the three impanelled from a district so delivered over to Fever that they ought to have been upon their own trial for five hundred Murders. When these mischievous blockheads were at their loudest, which was towards midnight, while some of us were already pre-paring for bed, I again saw the murdered man. He stood grimly behind them, beckoning to me. On my going towards them, and striking into the conversation, he imme-diately retired. This was the beginning of a separate series of appearances, confined to that long room in which *we* were confined. Whenever a knot of my brother jurymen laid their heads together, I saw the head of the murdered man among them. Whenever their comparison of notes was going against him, he would solemnly and irresistably beckon to me.

It will be borne in mind that down to the production of the miniature, on the fifth day of the trial, I had never seen the Appearance in Court. Three changes occurred now that we entered on the case for the defence. Two of them I will mention together, first. The figure was now in Court conti-nually, and it never there addressed itself to me, but always to the person who was speaking at the time. For instance: the throat of the murdered man had been cut straight across. In the opening speech for the defence, it was sugges-ted that the deceased might have cut his own throat. At that very moment, the figure, with its throat in the dreadful condition referred to (this it had concealed before), stood at the speaker's elbow, motioning across and across its wind-pipe, now with the right hand, now with the left, vigor-ously suggesting to the speaker himself the impossibility of such a wound having been self-inflicted by either hand. For another instance: a witness to character, a woman, deposed to the prisoner's being the most amiable of mankind. The figure at that instant stood on the floor before her, looking

her full in the face, and pointing out the prisoner's evil
countenance with an extended arm and an outstretched finger.

   The third change now to be added impressed me strongly as
the most marked and striking of all. I do not theorise upon it; I
accurately state it, and there leave it. Although the Appearance
was not itself perceived by those whom it addressed, its
coming close to such persons was invariably attended by some
trepidation of disturbance on their part. It seemed to me as if it
were prevented, by laws to which I was not amenable, from
fully revealing itself to others, and yet as if it could visibly,
dumbly, and darkly overshadow their minds. When the
leading counsel for the defence suggested that hypothesis of
suicide, and the figure stood at the learned gentleman's elbow,
frightfully sawing at its severed throat, it is undeniable that the
counsel faltered in his speech, lost for a few seconds the thread
of his ingenious discourse, wiped his forehead with his
handkerchief, and turned extremely pale. When the witness to
character was confronted by the Appearance, her eyes most
certainly did follow the direction of its pointed finger, and rest
in great hesitation and trouble upon the prisoner's face. Two
additional illustrations will suffice. On the eighth day of the
trial, after a pause which was every day made early in the
afternoon for a few minutes' rest and refreshment, I came back
into court with the rest of the Jury some little time before the
return of the Judges. Standing up in the box and looking
about me, I thought the figure was not there, until, chancing
to raise my eyes to the gallery, I saw it bending forward, and
leaning over a very decent woman, as if to assure itself
whether the Judges had resumed their seats or not. Immediately afterwards that woman screamed, fainted, and was
carried out. So with the venerable, sagacious, and patient
Judge who conducted the trial. When the case was over, and
he settled himself and his papers to sum up, the murdered
man, entering the Judges' door, advanced to his Lordship's
desk, and looked eagerly over his shoulder at the pages of his
notes which he was turning. A change came over his Lordship's face; his hand stopped; the peculiar shiver, that I knew
so well, passed over him; he faltered: 'Excuse me, gentlemen,
for a few moments. I am somewhat oppressed by the vitiated
air,' and did not recover until he had drunk a glass of water.

Through all the monotony of six of those interminable ten days – the same Judges and others on the bench, the same Murderer in the dock, the same lawyers at the table, the same tones of question and answer rising to the roof of the Court, the same scratching of the Judge's pen, the same ushers going in and out, the same lights kindled at the same hour when there had been any natural light of day, the same foggy curtain outside the great windows when it was foggy, the same rain pattering and dripping when it was rainy, the same footmarks of turnkeys and prisoner day after day on the same sawdust, the same keys locking and unlocking the same heavy doors – through all the wearisome monotony which made me feel as if I had been Foreman of the Jury for a vast period of time, and Piccadilly had flourished coevally with Babylon, the murdered man never lost one trace of his distinctness in my eyes, nor was he at any moment less distinct than anybody else. I must not omit, as a matter of fact, that I never once saw the Appearance which I call by the name of the murdered man look at the Murderer. Again and again I wondered 'why does he not?' But he never did.

Nor did he look at me, after the production of the miniature, until the last closing minutes of the trial arrived. We retired to consider, at seven minutes before ten at night. The idiotic vestryman and his two parochial parasites gave us so much trouble that we twice returned into Court to beg to have certain extracts from the Judge's notes re-read. Nine of us had not the smallest doubt about these passages, neither, I believe, had any one in Court; the dunder-headed triumvirate, however, having no idea but obstruction, disputed them for that very reason. At length we prevailed, and finally the Jury returned into Court at ten minutes past twelve.

The murdered man at that time stood directly opposite the Jury box, on the other side of the Court. As I took my place, his eyes rested on me with great attention; he seemed satisfied, and slowly shook a great grey veil, which he carried on his arm for the first time, over his head and whole form. As I gave in our verdict, 'Guilty,' the veil collapsed, all was gone, and his place was empty.

The murderer, being asked by the Judge, according to usage, whether he had anything to say before sentence of

Death should be passed upon him, indistinctly muttered something which was described in the leading newspapers of the following day as 'a few rambling, incoherent, and half-audible words, in which he was understood to complain that he had not had a fair trial, because the Foreman of the Jury was prepossessed against him.' The remarkable declaration that he really made was this: '*My Lord, I knew I was a doomed man, when the Foreman of my Jury came into the box. My Lord, I knew he would never let me off, because, before I was taken, he somehow got to my bedside in the night, woke me, and put a rope round my neck.*'

from *All the Year Round*

A CHILD'S DREAM OF A STAR

There was once a child, and he strolled about a good deal, and thought of a number of things. He had a sister, who was a child too, and his constant companion. These two used to wonder all day long. They wondered at the beauty of the flowers; they wondered at the height and blueness of the sky; they wondered at the depth of the bright water; they wondered at the goodness and the power of God who made the lovely world.

They used to say to one another, sometimes, Supposing all the children upon earth were to die, would the flowers, and the water, and the sky, be sorry? They believed they would be sorry. For, said they, the buds are the children of the flowers, and the little playful streams that gambol down the hill-sides are the children of the water; and the smallest bright specks playing at hide-and-seek in the sky all night must surely be the children of the stars; and they would all be grieved to see their playmates, the children of men, no more.

There was one clear shining star that used to come out in the sky before the rest, near the church spire, above the graves. It was larger and more beautiful, they thought, than all the others, and every night they watched for it, standing hand in hand at a window. Whoever saw it first, cried out, 'I see the star!' And often they cried out both together, knowing so well when it would rise, and where. So they grew to be such friends with it, that, before lying down in their beds, they always looked out once again, to bid it good night; and when they were turning round to sleep, they used to say, 'God bless the star!'

But while she was still very young – oh, very, very young! – the sister drooped, and came to be so weak that she could no longer stand in the window at night; and then the child looked sadly out by himself, and when he saw the star, turned round and said to the patient pale face on the bed, 'I see the star!' and then a smile would come upon the face, and a little weak voice used to say, 'God bless my brother and the star!'

And so the time came all too soon when the child looked out alone, and when there was no face on the bed, and when there was a little grave among the graves, not there before; and when the star made long rays down towards him, as he saw it through his tears.

Now, these rays were so bright, and they seemed to make such a shining way from earth to Heaven, that when the child went to his solitary bed, he dreamed about the star; and dreamed that, lying where he was, he saw a train of people taken up that sparkling road by angels. And the star, opening, showed him a great world of light, where many more such angels waited to receive them.

All these angels, who were waiting, turned their beaming eyes upon the people who were carried up into the star; and some came out from the long rows in which they stood, and fell upon the people's necks, and kissed them tenderly, and went away with them down avenues of light, and were so happy in their company, that lying in his bed he wept for joy.

But, there were many angels who did not go with them, and among them one he knew. The patient face that once had lain upon the bed was glorified and radiant, but his heart found out his sister among all the host.

His sister's angel lingered near the entrance of the star, and said to the leader among those who had brought the people thither, 'Is my brother come?'

And he said, 'No.'

She was turning hopefully away, when the child stretched out his arms and cried, 'Oh, sister, I am here! Take me!' and then she turned her beaming eyes upon him, and it was night; and the star was shining into the room, making long rays down towards him as he saw it through his tears.

From that hour forth, the child looked out upon the star as on the home he was to go to, when his time should come; and he thought that he did not belong to the earth alone, but to the star too, because of his sister's angel gone before.

There was a baby born to be a brother to the child; and while he was so little that he never yet had spoken a word, he stretched his tiny form out on his bed, and died.

Again the child dreamed of the opened star, and of the company of angels, and the train of people, and the rows of angels with their beaming eyes all turned upon those people's faces.

Said his sister's angel to the leader, 'Is my brother come?'

And he said, 'Not that one, but another.'

As the child beheld his brother's angel in her arms, he cried, 'Oh, sister, I am here! Take me!' And she turned and smiled upon him, and the star was shining.

He grew to be a young man, and was busy at his books when an old servant came to him and said, 'Thy mother is no more. I bring her blessing on her darling son!'

Again at night he saw the star, and all that former company. Said his sister's angel to the leader, 'Is my brother come?'

And he said, 'Thy mother!'

A mighty cry of joy went forth through all the star, because the mother was reunited to her two children. And he stretched out his arms and cried, 'Oh, mother, sister, and brother, I am here! Take me!' And they answered him, 'Not yet,' and the star was shining.

He grew to be a man, whose hair was turning grey, and he was sitting in his chair by the fireside, heavy with grief, and with his face bedewed with tears, when the star opened once again.

Said his sister's angel to the leader, 'Is my brother come?'

And he said, 'Nay, but his maiden daughter.'

And the man who had been the child saw his daughter, newly lost to him, a celestial creature among those three, and he said, 'My daughter's head is on my sister's bosom, and her arm is round my mother's neck, and at her feet there is the baby of old time, and I can bear the parting from her, God be praised!'

And the star was shining.

Thus the child came to be an old man, and his once smooth face was wrinkled, and his steps were slow and feeble, and his back was bent. And one night as he lay upon his bed, his children standing round, he cried, as he had cried so long ago, 'I see the star!'

They whispered to one another, 'He is dying.'

And he said, 'I am. My age is falling from me like a garment, and I move towards the star as a child. And oh, my Father, now I thank thee that it has so often opened to receive those dear ones who await me!'

And the star was shining; and it shines upon his grave.

CHRISTMAS GHOSTS

I like to come home at Christmas. We all do, or we all *should*. We ought to come home for a holiday – the longer the better – from the great boarding school where we are for ever working at our arithmetical slates, to take and give a rest.

We travel home across a winter prospect; by low-lying mist grounds, through fens and fogs, up long hills, winding dark as caverns between thick plantations, almost shutting out the sparkling stars; so, out on broad heights, until we stop at last, with sudden silence, at an avenue. The gate bell has a deep, half-awful sound in the frosty air; the gate swings open on its hinges; and, as we drive up to a great house, the glancing lights grow larger in the windows, and the opposing rows of trees seem to fall solemnly back on either side, to give us place. At intervals, all day, a frightened hare has shot across this whitened turf; or the distant clatter of a herd of deer trampling the hard frost has, for the minute, crushed the silence too. Their watchful eyes beneath the fern may be shining now, if we could see them, like the icy dewdrops on the leaves; but they are still, and all is still. And so, the lights growing larger, and the trees falling back before us, and closing up again behind us, as if to forbid retreat, we come to the house.

There is probably a smell of roasted chestnuts and other good comfortable things all the time, for we are telling Winter Stories – Ghost Stories, or more shame for us – round the Christmas fire; and we have never stirred, except to draw a little nearer to it. But, no matter for that. We come to the house, and it is an old house, full of great chimneys where wood is burnt on ancient dogs upon the hearth, and grim portraits (some of them with grim legends, too) lower distrustfully from the oaken panels of the walls. We are a middle-aged nobleman, and we make a generous supper with our host and hostess and their guests – it being Christmas-

110

time, and the old house full of company – and then we go to
bed. Our room is a very old room. It is hung with tapestry.
We don't like the portrait of a cavalier in green, over the fire-
place. There are great black beams in the ceiling, and there is a
great black bedstead, supported at the foot by two great black
figures, who seem to have come off a couple of tombs in the
old baronial church in the park, for our particular accommodation. But, we are not a superstitious nobleman, and we
don't mind. Well! we dismiss our servant, lock the door, and
sit before the fire in our dressing-gown, musing about a great
many things. At length we go to bed. Well! we can't sleep. We
toss and tumble, and can't sleep. The embers on the hearth
burn fitfully, and make the room look ghostly. We can't help
peeping out, over the counterpane, at the two black figures
and the cavalier – that wicked-looking cavalier in green. In the
flickering light they seem to advance and retire: which,
though we are not by any means a superstitious nobleman, is
not agreeable. Well! we get nervous – more and more
nervous. We say, 'This is very foolish, but we can't stand this;
we'll pretend to be ill, and knock up somebody.' Well! we are
just going to do it, when the locked door opens, and there
comes in a young woman, deadly pale, and with long fair
hair, who glides to the fire, and sits down in the chair we have
left there, wringing her hands. Then, we notice that her
clothes are wet. Our tongue cleaves to the roof of our mouth,
and we can't speak; but, we observe her accurately. Her
clothes are wet; her long hair is dabbled with moist mud; she
is dressed in the fashion of two hundred years ago; and she has
at her girdle a bunch of rusty keys. Well! there she sits, and we
can't even faint, we are in such a state about it. Presently she
gets up, and tries all the locks in the room with the rusty keys,
which won't fit one of them; then, she fixes her eyes on the
portrait of the cavalier in green, and says, in a low, terrible
voice, 'The stags know it!' After that, she wrings her hands
again, passes the bedside, and goes out at the door. We hurry
on our dressing-gown, seize our pistols (we always travel
with pistols), and are following, when we find the door
locked. We turn the key, look out into the dark gallery; no
one there. We wander away, and try to find our servant. Can't
be done. We pace the gallery till daybreak; then return to our

deserted room, fall asleep, and are awakened by our servant (nothing ever haunts *him*) and the shining sun. Well! we make a wretched breakfast, and all the company say we look queer. After breakfast, we go over the house with our host, and then we take him to the portrait of the cavalier in green, and then it all comes out. He was false to a young housekeeper once attached to that family, and famous for her beauty, who drowned herself in a pond, and whose body was discovered, after a long time, because the stags refused to drink the water. Since which it has been whispered that she traverses the house at midnight (but goes especially to that room, where the cavalier in green was wont to sleep), trying the old locks with the rusty keys. Well! we tell our host of what we have seen, and a shade comes over his features, and he begs it may be hushed up; and so it is. But, it's all true; and we said so, before we died (we are dead now), to many responsible people.

There is no end to the old houses, with resounding galleries, and dismal state bedchambers, and haunted wings shut up for many years, through which we may ramble, with an agreeable creeping up our back, and encounter any number of ghosts, but (it is worthy of remark perhaps) reducible to a very few general types and classes; for, ghosts have little originality, and 'walk' in a beaten track. Thus, it comes to pass that a certain room in a certain old hall, where a certain bad lord, baronet, knight, or gentleman shot himself, has certain planks in the floor from which the blood *will not* be taken out. You may scrape and scrape, as the present owner has done, or plane and plane, as his father did, or scrub and scrub, as his grandfather did, or burn and burn with strong acids, as his great-grandfather did, but there the blood will still be – no redder and no paler – no more and no less – always just the same. Thus, in such another house there is a haunted door that never will keep open; or another door that never will keep shut; or a haunted sound of a spinning-wheel, or a hammer, or a footstep, or a cry, or a sigh, or a horse's tramp, or the rattling of a chain. Or else there is a turret clock, which, at the midnight hour, strikes thirteen when the head of the family is going to die; or a shadowy, immovable black carriage which at such a time is always seen by somebody, waiting near the great gates in the stable-yard. Or thus, it came to pass how

Lady Mary went to pay a visit at a large wild house in the Scottish Highlands, and, being fatigued with her long journey, retired to bed early, and innocently said, next morning, at the breakfast-table, 'How odd to have so late a party last night in this remote place, and not to tell me of it before I went to bed!' Then, every one asked Lady Mary what she meant. Then, Lady Mary replied, 'Why, all night long, the carriages, were driving round and round the terrace, underneath my window!' Then, the owner of the house turned pale, and so did his Lady, and Charles Macdoodle of Macdoodle signed to Lady Mary to say no more, and everyone was silent. After breakfast, Charles Macdoodle told Lady Mary that it was a tradition in the family that those rumbling carriages on the terrace betokened death. And so it proved, for, two months afterwards, the Lady of the mansion died. And Lady Mary, who was a Maid of Honour at Court, often told this story to the old Queen Charlotte; by this token, that the old King always said, 'Eh, eh? What, what? Ghosts, ghosts? No such thing, no such thing!' And never left off saying so until he went to bed.

Or, a friend of somebody's whom most of us know, when he was a young man at college, had a particular friend, with whom he made the compact that, if it were possible for the Spirit to return to this earth after its separation from the body, he of the twain who first died should reappear to the other. In course of time this compact was forgotten by our friend; the two young men having progressed in life, and taken diverging paths and were wide asunder. But one night, many years afterwards, our friend being in the North of England, and staying for the night in an inn on the Yorkshire Moors, happened to look out of bed; and there, in the moonlight, leaning on a bureau near the window, steadfastly regarding him, saw his old college friend! The appearance being solemnly addressed, replied, in a kind of whisper, but very audibly, 'Do not come near me. I am dead. I am here to redeem my promise. I come from another world, but may not disclose its secrets!' Then, the whole form becoming paler, melted, as it were, into the moonlight, and faded away.

Or, there was the daughter of the first occupier of the picturesque Elizabethan house, so famous in our neighbourhood. You have heard about her? No! Why, *she* went out one summer evening at twilight, when she was a beautiful girl, just seventeen years of age, to gather flowers in the garden; and presently came running, terrified, into the hall to her father, saying, 'Oh, dear father, I have met myself!' He took her in his arms, and told her it was fancy, but she said, 'Oh no! I met myself in the broad walk, and I was pale and gathering withered flowers, and I turned my head and held them up!' And, that night, she died; and a picture of her story was begun, though never finished, and they say it is somewhere in the house to this day, with its face to the wall.

Or, the uncle of my brother's wife was riding home on horseback, one mellow evening at sunset, when, in a green lane close to his own house, he saw a man standing before him, in the very centre of the narrow way. 'Why does that man in the cloak stand there?' he thought. 'Does he want me to ride over him?' But the figure never moved. He felt a strange sensation at seeing it so still, but slackened his trot and rode forward. When he was so close to it as almost to touch it with his stirrup, his horse shied, and the figure glided up the bank in a curious, unearthly manner – backward, and without seeming to use its feet – and was gone. The uncle of my brother's wife exclaiming, 'Good Heaven! It's my cousin Harry, from Bombay!' put spurs to his horse, which was suddenly in a profuse sweat, and, wondering at such strange behaviour, dashed round to the front of his house. There, he saw the same figure, just passing in at the long French window of the drawing-room opening on the ground. He threw his bridle to a servant, and hastened in after it. His sister was sitting there alone.

'Alice, where's my cousin Harry?'

'Your cousin Harry, John?'

'Yes. From Bombay. I met him in the lane just now, and saw him enter here this instant.'

Not a creature had been seen by any one; and in that hour and minute, as it afterwards appeared, this cousin died in India.

Or, it was a certain sensible old maiden lady, who died at ninety-nine, and retained her faculties to the last, who really did see the Orphan Boy; a story which has often been

incorrectly told, but of which the real truth is this – because it
is, in fact, a story belonging to our family – and she was a
connection of our family. When she was about forty years of
age, and still an uncommonly fine woman (her lover died
young, which was the reason why she never married, though
she had many offers), she went to stay at a place in Kent,
which her brother, an Indian merchant, had newly bought.

There was a story that this place had once been held in trust
by the guardian of a young boy; who was himself the next
heir, and who killed the young boy by harsh and cruel
treatment. She knew nothing of that. It has been said that
there was a cage in her bedroom, in which the guardian used
to put the boy. There was no such thing. There was only a
closet. She went to bed, made no alarm whatever in the night,
and in the morning said composedly to her maid, when she
came in, 'Who is the pretty forlorn-looking child who has
been peeping out of that closet all night?' The maid replied by
giving a loud scream, and instantly decamping. She was
surprised; but, she was a woman of remarkable strength of
mind, and she dressed herself and went downstairs, and
closeted herself with her brother. 'Now, Walter,' she said, 'I
have been disturbed all night by a pretty, forlorn-looking
boy, who has been constantly peeping out of that closet in my
room, which I can't open. This is some trick.'

'I am afraid not, Charlotte,' said he, 'for it is the legend of
the house. It is the Orphan Boy. What did he do?'

'He opened the door softly,' said she, 'and peeped out.
Sometimes, he came a step or two into the room. Then, I
called to him, to encourage him, and he shrunk, and shuddered, and crept in again, and shut the door.

'The closet has no communication, Charlotte,' said her
brother, 'with any other part of the house, and it's nailed up.'

This was undeniably true, and it took two carpenters a
whole forenoon to get it open for examination. Then, she was
satisfied that she had seen the Orphan Boy. But the wild and
terrible part of the story is, that he was also seen by three of
her brother's sons in succession, who all died young. On the
occasion of each child being taken ill, he came home in a heat,
twelve hours before, and said, Oh, Mamma, he had been
playing under a particular oak-tree, in a certain meadow, with

a strange boy – a pretty, forlorn-looking boy, who was very timid, and made signs! From fatal experience, the parents came to know that this was the Orphan Boy, and that the course of that child whom he chose for his little playmate was surely run.

THE HANGED MAN'S BRIDE

The house was a genuine old house of a very quaint description, teeming with old carving, and beams, and panels, and having an excellent old staircase, with a gallery or upper staircase, cut off from it by a curious fence-work of old oak, or of the old Honduras Mahogany wood. It was, and is, and will be, for many a long year to come, a remarkably picturesque house; and a certain grave mystery lurking in the depth of the old mahogany panels, as if they were so many deep pools of dark water – such, indeed, as they had been much among when they were trees – gave it a very mysterious character after nightfall.

When Mr. Goodchild and Mr. Idle had first alighted at the door, and stepped into the sombre handsome old hall, they had been received by half-a-dozen noiseless old men in black, all dressed exactly alike, who glided up the stairs with the obliging landlord and waiter – but without appearing to get into their way, or to mind whether they did or no – and who had filed off to the right and left on the old staircase, as the guests entered their sitting-room. It was then broad, bright day. But, Mr. Goodchild had said, when their door was shut, 'Who on earth are those old men?' And afterwards, both on going out and coming in, he had noticed that there were no old men to be seen.

Neither, had the old men, or any one of the old men, reappeared since. The two friends had passed a night in the house, but had seen nothing more of the old men. Mr. Goodchild, in rambling about it, had looked along passages, and glanced in at doorways, but had encountered no old men; neither did it appear that any old men were, by any member of the establishment, missed or expected.

Another odd circumstance impressed itself on their attention. It was, that the door of their sitting-room was never left untouched for a quarter of an hour. It was opened with hesitation, opened with confidence, opened a little way, opened a good way, always clapped-to again without a word of explanation. They were reading, they were writing, they were eating, they were drinking, they were talking, they were dozing; the door was always opened at an unexpected moment, and they looked towards it, and it was clapped-to again, and nobody was to be seen. When this had happened fifty times or so, Mr. Goodchild had said to his companion, jestingly: 'I begin to think, Tom, there was something wrong with those six old men.'

Night had come again, and they had been writing for two or three hours: writing, in short, a portion of the lazy notes from which these lazy sheets are taken. They had left off writing, and glasses were on the table between them. The house was closed and quiet. Around the head of Thomas Idle, as he lay upon his sofa, hovered light wreaths of fragrant smoke. The temples of Francis Goodchild, as he leaned back in his chair, with his two hands clasped behind his head, and his legs crossed, were similarly decorated.

They had been discussing several idle subjects of specula-tion, not omitting the strange old men, and were still so occupied, when Mr. Goodchild abruptly changed his attitude to wind up his watch. They were just becoming drowsy enough to be stopped in their talk by any such slight check. Thomas Idle, who was speaking at the moment, paused and said, 'How goes it?'

'One,' said Goodchild.

As if he had ordered one old man, and the order were promptly executed (truly, all orders were so, in that excellent hotel), the door opened, and one old man stood there.

He did not come in, but stood with the door in his hand.

'One of the six, Tom, at last!' said Mr. Goodchild, in a surprised whisper. 'Sir, your pleasure?'

'Sir, *your* pleasure?' said the one old man.

'I didn't ring.'

'The bell did,' said the one old man.

He said *bell*, in a deep strong way, that would have expressed the church bell.

'I had the pleasure, I believe, of seeing you, yesterday?' said Goodchild.

'I cannot undertake to say for certain,' was the grim reply of the one old man.

'I think you saw me. Did you not?'

'Saw *you*?' said the old man. 'O yes, I saw *you*. But, I see many who never see me.'

A chilled, slow, earthy, fixed old man. A cadaverous old man of measured speech. An old man who seemed as unable to wink, as if his eyelids had been nailed to his forehead. An old man whose eyes – two spots of fire – had no more motion than if they had been connected with the back of his skull by screws driven through it, and riveted and bolted outside, among his grey hair.

The night had turned so cold, to Mr. Goodchild's sensations, that he shivered. He remarked lightly, and half apologetically, 'I think somebody is walking over my grave.'

'No,' said the weird old man, 'there is no one there.'

Mr. Goodchild looked at Idle, but Idle lay with his head enwreathed in smoke.

'No one there?' said Goodchild.

'There is no one at your grave, I assure you,' said the old man.

He had come in and shut the door, and he now sat down. He did not bend himself to sit as other people do, but seemed to sink bolt upright, as if in water, until the chair stopped him.

'My friend, Mr. Idle,' said Goodchild, extremely anxious to introduce a third person into the conversation.

'I am,' said the old man, without looking at him, 'at Mr. Idle's service.'

'If you are an old inhabitant of this place,' Francis Goodchild resumed:

'Yes.'

'Perhaps you can decide a point my friend and I were in doubt upon this morning. They hang condemned criminals at the castle, I believe?'

'*I* believe so,' said the old man.

'Are their faces turned towards that noble prospect?'

'Your face is turned,' replied the man, 'to the castle wall. When you are tied up, you see its stones expanding and contracting violently, and a similar expansion and contraction seems to take place in your own head and breast. Then, there is a rush of fire and an earthquake, and the castle springs into the air, and you tumble down a precipice.'

His cravat appeared to trouble him. He put his hand to his throat, and moved his neck from side to side. He was an old man of a swollen character of face, and his nose was immovably hitched up on one side, as if by a little hook inserted in that nostril. Mr. Goodchild felt exceedingly uncomfortable, and began to think the night was hot, and not cold.

'A strong description, sir,' he observed.

'A strong sensation,' the old man rejoined.

Again, Mr. Goodchild looked to Mr. Thomas Idle; but Thomas lay on his back with his face attentively turned towards the one old man, and made no sign. At this time Mr. Goodchild believed that he saw threads of fire stretch from the old man's eyes to his own, and there attach themselves. (Mr. Goodchild writes the present account of his experience, and, with the utmost solemnity, protests that he had the strongest sensation upon him of being forced to look at the old man along those two fiery films, from that moment.)

'I must tell it to you,' said the old man, with a ghastly and a stony stare.

'What?' asked Francis Goodchild.

'You know where it took place. Yonder!'

Whether he pointed to the room above, or to the room below, or to any room in that old house, or to a room in some other old house in that old town, Mr. Goodchild was not, nor is, nor ever can be, sure. He was confused by the circumstance that the right forefinger of the one old man seemed to dip itself in one of the threads of fire, light itself, and make a fiery start in the air, as it pointed somewhere. Having pointed somewhere, it went out.

'You know she was a bride,' said the old man.

'I know they still send up bride-cake,' Mr. Goodchild faltered. 'This is a very oppressive air.'

She was a bride, said the old man. She was a fair, flaxen-haired, large-eyed girl, who had no character, no purpose. A weak, credulous, incapable, helpless nothing. Not like her mother. No, no. It was her father whose character she reflected.

Her mother had taken care to secure everything to herself, for her own life, when the father of this girl (a child at that time) died – of sheer helplessness; no other disorder – and then he renewed the acquaintance that had once subsisted between the mother and him. He had been put aside for the flaxen-haired, large-eyed man (or nonentity) with money. He could overlook that for money. He wanted compensation in money.

So, he returned to the side of that woman the mother, made love to her again, danced attendance on her, and submitted himself to her whims. She wreaked upon him every whim she had, or could invent. He bore it. And the more he bore, the more he wanted compensation in money, and the more he was resolved to have it.

But, lo! Before he got it, she cheated him. In one of her imperious states, she froze, and never thawed again. She put her hands to her head one night, uttered a cry, stiffened, lay in that attitude certain hours, and died. And he had got no compensation from her in money, yet. Blight and Murrain on her! Not a penny.

He had hated her throughout that second pursuit, and had longed for retaliation on her. He now counterfeited her signature to an instrument, leaving all she had to leave, to her daughter – ten years old then – to whom the property passed absolutely, and appointing himself the daughter's Guardian. When he slid it under the pillow of the bed on which she lay, he bent down in the deaf ear of Death, and whispered: 'Mistress Pride, I have determined a long time that, dead or alive, you must make me compensation in money.'

So, now there were only two left. Which two were, he, and the fair flaxen-haired, large-eyed foolish daughter, who afterwards became the bride.

He put her to school. In a secret, dark, oppressive, ancient house, he put her to school with a watchful and unscrupulous woman. 'My worthy lady,' he said, 'here is a mind to be formed; will you help me to form it?' She accepted the trust. For which she, too, wanted compensation in money, and had it.

The girl was formed in the fear of him, and in the conviction, that there was no escape from him. She was taught, from the first, to regard him as her future husband – the man who must marry her – the destiny that overshadowed her – the appointed certainty that could never be evaded. The poor fool was soft white wax in their hands, and took the impression that they put upon her. It hardened with time. It became a part of herself. Inseparable from herself, and only to be torn away from her, by tearing life away from her.

Eleven years she had lived in the dark house and its gloomy garden. He was jealous of the very light and air getting to her, and they kept her close. He stopped the wide chimneys, shaded the little windows, left the strong-stemmed ivy to wander where it would over the house-front, the moss to accumulate on the untrimmed fruit-trees in the red-walled garden, the weeds to over-run its green and yellow walks. He surrounded her with images of sorrow and desolation. He caused her to be filled with fears of the place and of the stories that were told of it, and then on pretext of correcting them, to be left in it in solitude, or made to shrink about it in the dark. When her mind was most depressed and fullest of terrors, then, he would come out of one of the hiding-places from which he overlooked her, and present himself as her sole resource.

Thus, by being from her childhood the one embodiment her life presented to her of power to coerce and power to relieve, power to bind and power to loose, the ascendancy over her weakness was secured. She was twenty-one years and twenty-one days old, when he brought her home to the gloomy house, his half-witted, frightened, and submissive bride of three weeks.

He had dismissed the governess by that time – what he had left to do, he could best do alone – and they came back, upon a rainy night, to the scene of her long preparation. She turned to him upon the threshold, as the rain was dripping from the porch, and said, 'Oh sir, it is the Death-watch ticking for me!'

'Well!' he answered. 'And if it were?'

'O sir!' she returned to him, 'look kindly on me, and be merciful to me! I beg your pardon. I will do anything you wish, if you will only forgive me!'

That had become the poor fool's constant song: 'I beg your pardon,' and 'Forgive me!'

She was not worth hating; he felt nothing but contempt for her. But she had long been in the way, and he had long been weary, and the work was near its end, and had to be worked out.

'You fool,' he said. 'Go up the stairs!'

She obeyed very quickly, murmuring, 'I will do anything you wish!' When he came into the bride's chamber, having been a little retarded by the heavy fastenings of the great door (for they were alone in the house, and he had arranged that the people who attended on them should come and go in the day), he found her withdrawn to the furthest corner, and there standing pressed against the panelling as if she would have shrunk through it: her flaxen hair all wild about her face, and her large eyes staring at him in vague terror.

'What are you afraid of? Come and sit down by me.'

'I will do anything you wish. I beg your pardon, sir. Forgive me!' Her monotonous tune as usual.

'Ellen, here is a writing that you must write out tomorrow, in your own hand. You may as well be seen by others, busily engaged upon it. When you have written it all fairly, and corrected all mistakes, call in any two people there may be about the house, and sign your name to it before them. Then, put it in your bosom to keep it safe, and when I sit here again tomorrow night, give it to me.'

'I will do it all, with the greatest care. I will do anything you wish.'

'Don't shake and tremble, then.'

'I will try my utmost not to do it – if you will only forgive me!'

Next day, she sat down at her desk, and did as she had been told. He often passed in and out of the room, to observe her, and always saw her slowly and laboriously writing: repeating to herself the words she copied, in appearance quite mechanically, and without caring or endeavouring to comprehend them, so that she did her task. He saw her follow the direction she had received, in all particulars; and at night, when they were alone again in the same bride's chamber, and he drew his chair to the hearth, she timidly approached him from her distant seat, took the paper from her bosom, and gave it into his hand.

It secured all her possessions to him, in the event of her death. He put her before him, face to face, that he might look at her steadily; and he asked her, in so many plain words, neither fewer nor more, did she know that?

There were spots of ink upon the bosom of her white dress, and they made her face look whiter and her eyes look larger as she nodded her head. There were spots of ink upon the hand with which she stood before him, nervously plaiting and folding her white skirts.

He took her by the arm, and looked her, yet more closely and steadily, in the face. 'Now, die! I have done with you.'

She shrunk, and uttered a low, suppressed cry.

'I am not going to kill you. I will not endanger my life for yours. Die!'

He sat before her in the gloomy bride's chamber, day after day, night after night, looking the word at her when he did not utter it. As often as her large unmeaning eyes were raised from the hands in which she rocked her head, to the stern figure, sitting with crossed arms and knitted forehead, in the chair, they read in it, 'Die!' When she dropped asleep in exhaustion, she was called back to shuddering consciousness, by the whisper, 'Die!' When she fell upon her old entreaty to be pardoned, she was answered, 'Die!' When she had out-watched and out-suffered the long night, and the rising sun flamed into the sombre room, she heard it hailed with, 'Another day and not dead? Die!'

Shut up in the deserted mansion, aloof from all mankind, and engaged alone in such a struggle without any respite, it came to this – that either he must die, or she. He knew it very well, and concentrated his strength against her feebleness. Hours upon hours he held her by the arm when her arm was black where he held it, and bade her Die!

It was done, upon a windy morning, before sunrise. He computed the time to be half-past four; but, his forgotten watch had run down, and he could not be sure. She had broken away from him in the night, with loud and sudden cries – the first of that kind to which she had given vent – and he had had to put his hands over her mouth. Since then, she had been quiet in the corner of the panelling

where she had sunk down; and he had left her, and had gone
back with his folded arms and his knitted forehead to his chair.

Paler in the pale light, more colourless than ever in the
leaden dawn, he saw her coming, trailing herself along the
floor towards him – a white wreck of hair, and dress, and wild
eyes, pushing itself on by an irresolute and bending hand.

'O, forgive me! I will do anything. O, sir, pray tell me I
may live!'

'Die!'

'Are you so resolved? Is there no hope for me?'

'Die!'

Her large eyes strained themselves with wonder and fear;
wonder and fear changed to reproach; reproach to blank
nothing. It was done. He was not at first so sure it was done,
but that the morning sun was hanging jewels in her hair – he
saw the diamond, emerald, and ruby, glittering among it in
little points, as he stood looking down at her – when he lifted
her and laid her on her bed.

She was soon laid in the ground. And now they were all
gone, and he had compensated himself well.

He had a mind to travel. Not that he meant to waste his
money, for he was a pinching man and liked his money dearly
(like nothing else, indeed), but, that he had grown tired of the
desolate house and wished to turn his back upon it and have
done with it. But, the house was worth money, and money
must not be thrown away. He determined to sell it before he
went. That it might look the less wretched and bring a better
price, he hired some labourers to work in the overgrown
garden; to cut out the dead wood, trim the ivy that drooped in
heavy masses over the windows and gables, and clear the
walks in which the weeds were growing mid-leg high.

He worked, himself, along with them. He worked later
than they did, and, one evening at dusk, was left working
alone, with his bill-hook in his hand. One autumn evening,
when the bride was five weeks dead.

'It grows too dark to work longer,' he said to himself, 'I
must give over for the night.'

He detested the house, and was loath to enter it. He looked
at the dark porch waiting for him like a tomb, and felt that it
was an accursed house. Near to the porch, and near to where

he stood, was a tree whose branches waved before the old bay-window of the bride's chamber, where it had been done. The tree swung suddenly, and made him start. It swung again, although the night was still. Looking up into it, he saw a figure among the branches.

It was the figure of a young man. The face looked down, as his looked up; the branches cracked and swayed; the figure rapidly descended, and slid upon its feet before him. A slender youth of about her age, with long light brown hair.

'What thief are you?' he said, seizing the youth by the collar.

The young man, in shaking himself free, swung him a blow with his arm across the face and throat. They closed, but the young man got from him and stepped back, crying, with great eagerness and horror, 'Don't touch me! I would as lieve be touched by the Devil!'

He stood still, with his bill-hook in his hand, looking at the young man. For, the young man's look was the counterpart of her last look, and he had not expected ever to see that again.

'I am not a thief. Even if I were, I would not have a coin of your wealth, if it would buy me the Indies. You murderer!'

'What!'

'I climbed it,' said the young man, pointing up into the tree, 'for the first time, nigh four years ago. I climbed it, to look at her. I saw her. I spoke to her. I have climbed it, many a time, to watch and listen for her. I was a boy, hidden among its leaves, when from that bay-window she gave me this!'

He showed a tress of flaxen hair, tied with a mourning ribbon.

'Her life,' said the young man, 'was a life of mourning. She gave me this, as a token of it, and a sign that she was dead to every one but you. If I had been older, if I had seen her sooner, I might have saved her from you. But, she was fast in the web when I first climbed the tree, and what could I do then to break it!'

In saying these words, he burst into a fit of sobbing and crying: weakly at first, then passionately, 'Murderer! I climbed the tree on the night when you brought her back. I heard her, from the tree, speak of the Death-watch at the door. I was three times in the tree while you were shut up with her, slowly killing her. I saw her, from the tree, lie dead upon her bed. I have watched you, from the tree, for proofs and traces of your guilt. The manner of it, is a mystery to me yet, but I will pursue you until you have rendered up your life to the hangman. You shall never, until then, be rid of me. I loved her! I can know no relenting towards you. Murderer, I loved her!'

The youth was bare-headed, his hat having fluttered away in his descent from the tree. He moved towards the gate. He had to pass – him – to get to it. There was breadth for two old-fashioned carriages abreast; and the youth's abhorrence, openly expressed in every feature of his face and limb of his body, and very hard to bear, had verge enough to keep itself at a distance in. He (by which I mean the other) had not stirrèd hand or foot, since he had stood still to look at the boy. He faced round, now, to follow him with his eyes. As the back of the bare light brown head was turned to him, he saw a red curve stretch from his hand to it. He knew, before he threw the bill-hook, where it had alighted – I say, had alighted, and not would alight; for, to his clear perception the thing was done before he did it. It cleft the head, and it remained there, and the boy lay on his face.

He buried the body in the night, at the foot of the tree. As soon as it was light in the morning, he worked at turning up all the ground near the tree, and hacking and hewing at the neighbouring bushes and undergrowth. When the labourers came, there was nothing suspicious, and nothing suspected.

But, he had, in a moment, defeated all his precautions, and destroyed the triumph of the scheme he had so long concerted, and so successfully worked out. He had got rid of the bride, and had acquired her fortune without endangering his life; but now, for a death by which he had gained nothing, he had evermore to live with a rope around his neck.

Beyond this, he was chained to the house of gloom and horror, which he could not endure. Being afraid to sell it or to quit it, lest discovery should be made, he was forced to live in it. He hired two old people, man and wife, for his servants; and dwelt in it, and dreaded it. His great difficulty, for a long time, was the garden. Whether he should keep it trim, whether he should suffer it to fall into its former state of neglect, what would be the least likely way of attracting attention to it?

He took the middle course of gardening himself, in his evening leisure, and of then calling the old serving-man to help him; but, of never letting him work there alone. And he made himself an arbour over against the tree, where he could sit and see that it was safe.

As the seasons changed, and the tree changed, his mind perceived dangers that were always changing. In the leafy time, he perceived that the upper boughs were growing into the form of the young man – that they made the shape of him exactly, sitting in a forked branch swinging in the wind. In the time of the falling leaves, he perceived that they came down from the tree, forming tell-tale letters on the path, or that they had a tendency to heap themselves into a churchyard-mound above the grave. In the winter, when the trees were bare, he perceived that the boughs swung at him the ghost of the blow the young man had given, and that they threatened him openly. In the spring, when the sap was mounting in the trunk, he asked himself, were the dried-up particles of blood mounting with it: to make out more obviously this year than last, the leaf-screened figure of the young man, swinging in the wind?

However, he turned his money over and over, and still over. He was in the dark trade, and gold-dust trade, and most secret trades that yielded great returns. In ten years, he had turned his money over, so many times, that the traders and shippers who had dealings with him, absolutely did not lie – for once – when they declared that he had increased his fortune, twelve hundred per cent.

He possessed his riches one hundred years ago, when people could be lost easily. He had heard who the youth was, from hearing of the search that was made after him; but, it died away, and the youth was forgotten.

The annual round of changes in the tree had been repeated ten times since the night of the burial at its foot, when there was a great thunder-storm over this place. It broke at midnight, and raged until morning. The first intelligence he heard from his old serving-man that morning, was, that the tree had been struck by lightning.

It had been driven down the stem, in a very surprising manner, and the stem lay in two blighted shafts: one resting against the house, and one against a portion of the old red garden-wall in which its fall had made a gap. The fissure went down the tree to a little above the earth, and there stopped. There was great curiosity to see the tree, and, with most of his former fears revived, he sat in his arbour – grown quite an old man – watching the people who came to see it.

They quickly began to come, in such dangerous numbers, that he closed his garden-gate and refused to admit any more. But, there were certain men of science who travelled from a distance to examine the tree, and, in an evil hour, he let them in – Blight and Murrain on them, let them in!

They wanted to dig up the ruin by the roots, and closely examine it, and the earth about it. Never, while he lived! They offered money for it. They! Men of science, whom he could have bought by the gross, with a scratch of his pen! He showed them the garden-gate again, and locked and barred it.

But they were bent on doing what they wanted to do, and they bribed the old serving-man – a thankless wretch who regularly complained when he received his wages, of being underpaid – and they stole into the garden by night with their lanterns, picks, and shovels, and fell to at the tree. He was lying in a turret-room on the other side of the house (the bride's chamber had been unoccupied ever since), but he soon dreamed of picks and shovels, and got up.

He came to an upper window on that side, whence he could see their lanterns, and them, and the loose earth in a heap which he had himself disturbed and put back, when it was last turned to the air. It was found! They had that minute lighted on it. They were all bending over it. One of them said, 'The skull is fractured;' and another, 'See here the bones;' and another, 'See here the clothes;' and then the first struck in again, and said, 'A rusty bill-hook!'

He became sensible, next day, that he was already put under a strict watch, and that he could go nowhere without being followed. Before a week was out, he was taken and laid in hold. The circumstances were gradually pieced together against him, and with a desperate malignity, and an appalling ingenuity. But, see the justice of men, and how it was extended to him! He was further accused of having poisoned that girl in the bride's chamber. He, who had carefully and expressly avoided imperilling a hair of his head for her, and who had seen her die of her own incapacity!

There was doubt for which of the two murders he should be first tried; but, the real one was chosen, and he was found guilty, and cast for death. Bloodthirsty wretches! They would have made him guilty of anything, so set they were upon having his life.

His money could do nothing to save him, and he was hanged. *I* am he, and I was hanged at Lancaster Castle with my face to the wall, a hundred years ago!

At this terrific announcement, Mr. Goodchild tried to rise and cry out. But, the two fiery lines extending from the old man's eyes to his own, kept him down, and he could not utter a sound. His sense of hearing, however, was acute, and he could hear the clock strike two. No sooner had he heard the clock strike Two, than he saw before him two old men!

Two.

The eyes of each, connected with his eyes by two films of fire: each, exactly like the other: each, addressing him at precisely one and the same instant: each, gnashing the same teeth in the same head, with the same twitched nostril above them, and the same suffused expression around it. Two old men. Differing in nothing, equally distinct to the sight, the copy no fainter than the original, the second as real as the first.

'At what time,' said the two old men, 'did you arrive at the door below?'

'At six.'

'And there were six old men upon the stairs!'

Mr. Goodchild having wiped the perspiration from his brow, or tried to do it, the two old men proceeded in one voice, and in the singular number:

I had been anatomised, but had not yet had my skeleton put together and rehung on an iron hook, when it began to be whispered that the bride's chamber was haunted. It *was* haunted, and I was there.

We were there. She and I were there. I, in the chair upon the hearth; she, a white wreck again, trailing itself towards me on the floor. But, I was the speaker no more, and the one word that she said to me from midnight until dawn was, 'Live!'

The youth was there, likewise. In the tree outside the window. Coming and going in the moonlight, as the tree bent and gave. He has, ever since, been there, peeping in at me in my torment; revealing to me by snatches, in the pale lights and slaty shadows where he comes and goes, bare-headed – a bill-hook, standing edgewise in his hair.

In the bride's chamber, every night from midnight until dawn – one month in the year excepted, as I am going to tell you – he hides in the tree, and she comes towards me on the floor; always approaching; never coming nearer; always visible as if by moonlight, whether the moon shines or no; always saying, from midnight until dawn, her one word, 'Live!'

But, in the month wherein I was forced out of this life – this present month of thirty days – the bride's chamber is empty and quiet. Not so my old dungeon. Not so the rooms where I was restless and afraid, ten years. Both are fitfully haunted then. At one in the morning, I am what you saw me when the clock struck that hour – one old man. At two in the morning, I am two old men. At three, I am three. By twelve at noon, I am twelve old men, one for every hundred per cent of old gain. Every one of the twelve, with twelve times my old power of suffering and agony. From that hour until twelve at night, I, twelve old men in anguish and fearful foreboding, wait for the coming of the executioner. At twelve at night, I, twelve old men turned off, swing invisible outside Lancaster Castle, with twelve faces to the wall!

When the bride's chamber was first haunted, it was known to me that this punishment would never cease, until I could make its nature, and my story, known to two living men together. I waited for the coming of two living men together into the bride's chamber, years upon years. It was infused into my knowledge (of the means I am ignorant) that if two living men, with their eyes open, could be in the bride's chamber at one in the morning, they would see me sitting in my chair.

At length, the whispers that the room was spiritually troubled, brought two men to try the adventure. I was scarcely struck upon the hearth at midnight (I came there as if the lightning blasted me into being), when I heard them ascending the stairs. Next, I saw them enter. One of them was a bold, gay, active man, in the prime of life, some five and forty years of age; the other, a dozen years younger. They brought provisions with them in a basket, and bottles. A young woman accompanied them, with wood and coals for the lighting of the fire. When she had lighted it, the bold, gay, active man accompanied her along the gallery outside the room, to see her safely down the staircase, and came back laughing.

He locked the door, examined the chamber, put out the contents of the basket on the table before the fire – and filled the glasses, and ate and drank. His companion did the same, and was as cheerful and confident as he: though he was the leader. When they had supped, they laid pistols on the table, turned to the fire, and began to smoke their pipes of foreign make.

They had travelled together, and had been much together, and had an abundance of subjects in common. In the midst of their talking and laughing, the younger man made a reference to the leader's being always ready for any adventure; that one, or any other. He replied in these words: 'Not quite so, Dick; if I am afraid of nothing else, I am afraid of myself.'

His companion seeming to grow a little dull, asked him, in what sense? How?

'Why, thus,' he returned. 'Here is a Ghost to be disproved. Well! I cannot answer for what my fancy might do if I were alone here, or what tricks my senses might play with me if they had me to themselves. But, in company with another man, and especially with you, Dick, I would consent to outface all the ghosts that were ever told of in the universe.'

'I had not the vanity to suppose that I was of so much importance tonight,' said the other.

'Of so much,' rejoined the leader, more seriously than he had spoken yet, 'that I would, for the reason I have given, on no account have undertaken to pass the night here alone.'

It was within a few minutes of one. The head of the younger man had drooped when he made his last remark, and it drooped lower now.

'Keep awake, Dick!' said the leader, gaily. 'The small hours are the worst.'

He tried, but his head drooped again.

'Dick!' urged the leader. 'Keep awake!'

'I can't,' he indistinctly muttered. 'I don't know what strange influence is stealing over me. I can't.'

His companion looked at him with a sudden horror, and I, in my different way, felt a new horror also; for, it was on the stroke of one, and I felt that the second watcher was yielding to me, and that the curse was upon me that I must send him to sleep.

'Get up and walk, Dick,' cried the leader. 'Try!'

It was in vain to go behind the slumberer's chair and shake him. One o'clock sounded, and I was present to the elder man, and he stood transfixed before me.

To him alone, I was obliged to relate my story, without hope of benefit. To him alone, I was an awful phantom making a quite useless confession. I foresee it will ever be the same. The two living men together will never come to release me. When I appear, the sense of one of the two will be locked in sleep; he will neither see nor hear me; my communication will ever be made to a solitary listener, and will ever be unserviceable. Woe! Woe! Woe!

As the two old men, with these words, wrung their hands, it shot into Mr. Goodchild's mind that he was in the terrible situation of being virtually alone with the spectre, and that Mr. Idle's immovability was explained by his having been charmed asleep at one o'clock. In the terror of this sudden discovery which produced an indescribable dread, he struggled so hard to get free from the four fiery threads, that he snapped them, after he had pulled them out to a great width. Being then out of bonds, he caught up Mr. Idle from the sofa, and rushed downstairs with him.

'What are you about, Francis?' demanded Mr. Idle. 'My bedroom is not down here. What the deuce are you carrying me at all for? I can walk with a stick now. I don't want to be carried. Put me down.'

Mr. Goodchild put him down in the old hall, and looked about him wildly.

'What are you doing? Idiotically plunging at your own sex, and rescuing them or perishing in the attempt?' asked Mr. Idle, in a highly petulant state.

'The one old man!' cried Mr. Goodchild, distractedly, 'and the two old men!'

Mr. Idle deigned no other reply than, 'The one old woman, I think you mean,' as he began hobbling his way back up the staircase, with the assistance of its broad balustrade.

'I assure you, Tom,' began Mr. Goodchild, attending at his side, 'that since you fell asleep —'

'Come, I like that!' said Thomas Idle, 'I haven't closed an eye!'

With the peculiar sensitiveness on the subject of the disgraceful action of going to sleep out of bed, which is the lot of all mankind, Mr. Idle persisted in this declaration. The same peculiar sensitiveness impelled Mr. Goodchild, on being taxed with the same crime, to repudiate it with honourable resentment. The settlement of the question of the one old man and the two old men was thus presently complicated, and soon made quite impracticable. Mr. Idle said it was all bride-cake, and fragments, newly arranged, of things seen and thought about in the day. Mr. Goodchild said how could that be, when he hadn't been asleep? Mr. Idle said he had never been asleep, and never did go to sleep, and that Mr. Goodchild, as a general rule, was always asleep. They consequently parted for the rest of the night, at their bedroom doors, a little ruffled. Mr. Goodchild's last words were, that he had had, in that real and tangible old sitting-room of that real and tangible old Inn (he supposed Mr. Idle denied its existence?), every sensation and experience, the present record of which is now within a line or two of completion; and that he would write it out and print it every word. Mr. Idle returned that he might if he liked — and he did like, and has now done it.

from *The Lazy Tour of Two Idle Apprentices*

MR TESTATOR'S VISITATION

Mr. Testator took a set of chambers in Lyons Inn when he had but very scanty furniture for his bedroom, and none for his sitting-room. He had lived some wintry months in this condition, and had found it very bare and cold. One night, past midnight, when he sat writing, and still had writing to do that must be done before he went to bed, he found himself out of coals. He had coals downstairs, but had never been to his cellar; however, the cellar key was on his mantel-shelf, and, if he went down and opened the cellar it fitted, he might fairly assume the coals in that cellar to be his. As to his laundress, she lived among the coal-waggons and Thames watermen – for there were Thames watermen at that time – in some unknown rat-hole by the river, down lanes and alleys on the other side of the Strand. As to any other person to meet him or obstruct him, Lyons Inn was dreaming, drunk, maudlin, moody, betting, brooding over bill discounting or renewing – asleep or awake, minding its own affairs. Mr. Testator took his coal-scuttle in one hand, his candle and key in the other, and descended to the dismallest underground dens of Lyons Inn, where the late vehicles in the streets became thunderous, and all the water-pipes in the neighbourhood seemed to have Macbeth's Amen sticking in their throats, and to be trying to get it out. After groping here and there among low doors to no purpose, Mr. Testator at length came to a door with a rusty padlock which his key fitted. Getting the door open with much trouble, and looking in, he found, no coals, but a confused pile of furniture. Alarmed by this intrusion on another man's property, he locked the door again, found his own cellar, filled his scuttle, and returned upstairs.

But the furniture he had seen ran on casters across and across Mr. Testator's mind incessantly, when, in the chill hour of five in the morning, he got to bed. He particularly wanted a table to write at, and a table expressly made to be

written at had been the piece of furniture in the foreground of
the heap. When his laundress emerged from her burrow in the
morning to make his kettle boil he artfully led up to the subject
of the cellars and furniture; but the two ideas had evidently no
connection in her mind. When she left him, and he sat at his
breakfast, thinking about the furniture, he recalled the rusty
state of the padlock, and inferred that the furniture must have
been stored in the cellars for a long time – was perhaps
forgotten – owner dead, perhaps? After thinking it over a few
days, in the course of which he could pump nothing out of
Lyons Inn about the furniture, he became desperate, and
resolved to borrow the table. He did so that night. He had not
had the table long, when he made up his mind to borrow an
easy-chair; he had not had that long, when he made up his mind
to borrow a book-case; then, a couch; then, a carpet and rug.
By that time, he felt he was 'in furniture stepped in so far,' as
that it could be no worse to borrow it all. Consequently, he
borrowed it all, and locked up the cellar for good. He had
always locked it after every visit. He had carried up every
separate article in the dead of night, and, at the best, had felt as
wicked as a resurrection man. Every article was blue and furry
when brought into his rooms, and he had had, in a murderous
and guilty sort of way, to polish it up while London slept.

Mr. Testator lived in his furnished chambers two or three
years, or more, and gradually lulled himself into the opinion
that the furniture was his own. This was his convenient state of
mind when, late one night, a step came up the stairs, and a hand
passed over his door, feeling for his knocker, and then one deep
and solemn rap was rapped, that might have been a spring in
Mr. Testator's easy-chair to shoot him out of it; so promptly
was it attended with that effect.

With a candle in his hand, Mr. Testator went to the door, and
found there a very pale and very tall man; a man who stooped; a
man with very high shoulders, a very narrow chest, and a very
red nose; a shabby-genteel man. He was wrapped in a long
threadbare black coat, fastened up the front with more pins
than buttons, and under his arm he squeezed an umbrella
without a handle, as if he were playing bagpipes. He said, 'I ask
your pardon, but can you tell me —' and stopped; his eyes
resting on some object within the chambers.

'Can I tell you what?' asked Mr. Testator, noting his stoppage with quick alarm.

'I ask your pardon,' said the stranger, 'but – this is not the inquiry I was going to make – *do* I see in there any small article of property belonging to *me*?'

Mr. Testator was beginning to stammer that he was not aware – when the visitor slipped past him into the chambers. There, in a goblin way which froze Mr. Testator to the marrow, he examined, first, the writing-table, and said, 'Mine', then, the easy-chair, and said 'Mine', then, the book-case, and said, 'Mine'; then, turned up a corner of the carpet, and said, 'Mine!' In a word, inspected every item of furniture from the cellar in succession, and said, 'Mine!' Towards the end of this investigation, Mr. Testator perceived that he was sodden with liquor, and that the liquor was gin. He was not unsteady with the gin, either in his speech or carriage; but he was stiff with gin in both particulars.

Mr. Testator was in a dreadful state, for (according to his making out of the story) the possible consequences of what he had done in recklessness and hardihood flashed upon him in their fulness for the first time. When they had stood gazing at one another for a little while, he tremulously began, 'Sir, I am conscious that the fullest explanation, compensation, and restitution are your due. They shall be yours. Allow me to entreat that, without temper, without even natural irritation on your part, we may have a little —'

'Drop of something to drink,' interposed the stranger. 'I am agreeable.'

Mr. Testator had intended to say, 'a little quiet conversation,' but with great relief of mind adopted the amendment. He produced a decanter of gin, and was bustling about for hot water and sugar, when he found that his visitor had already drunk half the decanter's contents. With hot water and sugar the visitor drank the remainder before he had been an hour in the chambers by the chimes of the church of St Mary in the Strand; and during the process he frequently whispered to himself, 'Mine!'

The gin gone, and Mr. Testator wondering what was to follow it, the visitor rose and said, with increased stiffness, 'At what hour of the morning, sir, will it be convenient?'

Mr. Testator hazarded, 'At ten?'

'Sir,' said the visitor, 'at ten, to the moment, I shall be here.' He then contemplated Mr. Testator somewhat at leisure, and said, 'God bless you! How is your wife?'

Mr. Testator (who never had a wife) replied, with much feeling, 'Deeply anxious, poor soul, but otherwise well.'

The visitor thereupon turned and went away, and fell twice in going downstairs. From that hour he was never heard of. Whether he was a ghost, or a spectral illusion of conscience, or a drunken man who had no business there, or the drunken rightful owner of the furniture, with a transitory gleam of memory; whether he got safe home, or had no home to get to; whether he died of liquor on the way, or lived in liquor ever afterwards; he never was heard of more. This was the story, received with the furniture, and held to be as substantial, by its second possessor in an upper set of chambers in grim Lyons Inn.

from *The Uncommercial Traveller*

THE HAUNTED MAN

THE GIFT BESTOWED

Everybody said so.

Far be it from me to assert that what everybody says must be true. Everybody is, often, as likely to be wrong as right. In the general experience, everybody has been wrong so often, and it has taken, in most instances, such a weary while to find out how wrong, that authority is proved to be fallible. Everybody may sometimes be right; 'but *that's* no rule,' as the ghost of Giles Scroggins says in the ballad.

The dread word, GHOST, recalls me.

Everybody said he looked like a haunted man. The extent of my present claim for everybody is, that they were so far right. He did.

Who could have seen his hollow cheeks; his sunken, brilliant eye; his black-attired figure, indefinably grim, although well knit and well proportioned; his grizzled hair hanging, like tangled seaweed, about his face – as if he had been, through his whole life, a lonely mark for the chafing and beating of the great deep of humanity – but might have said he looked like a haunted man?

Who could have observed his manner, taciturn, thoughtful, gloomy, shadowed by habitual reserve, retiring always, and jocund never, with a distraught air of reverting to a bygone place and time, or of listening to some old echoes in his mind, but might have said it was the manner of a haunted man?

Who could have heard his voice, slow-speaking, deep, and grave, with a natural fulness and melody in it which he seemed to set himself against and stop, but might have said it was the voice of a haunted man?

Who that had seen him in his inner chamber, part library and part laboratory – for he was, as the world knew, far and wide, a learned man in chemistry, and a teacher on whose lips and hands a crowd of aspiring ears and eyes hung daily – who that had seen him there, upon a winter night, alone, sur-

rounded by his drugs and instruments and books; the shadow
of his shaded lamp a monstrous beetle on the wall, motionless
among a crowd of spectral shapes raised there by the flickering
of the fire upon the quaint objects around him; some of these
phantoms (the reflection of glass vessels that held liquids)
trembling at heart like things that knew his power to uncom-
bine them, and to give back their component parts to fire and
vapour; – who that had seen him then, his work done, and he
pondering in his chair before the rusted grate and red flame,
moving his thin mouth as if in speech, but silent as the dead,
would not have said that the man seemed haunted, and the
chamber too?

Who might not, by a very easy flight of fancy, have believed
that everything about him took this haunted tone, and that he
lived on haunted ground?

His dwelling was so solitary and vault-like – an old, retired
part of an ancient endowment for students, once a brave
edifice planted in an open place, but now the obsolete whim of
forgotten architects; smoke-age-and-weather darkened,
squeezed on every side by the overgrowing of the great city,
and choked, like an old well, with stones and bricks; its small
quadrangles, lying down in very pits formed by the streets and
buildings, which, in course of time, had been constructed
above its heavy chimney-stacks; its old trees, insulted by the
neighbouring smoke, which deigned to droop so low when it
was very feeble, and the weather very moody; its grass-plots,
struggling with the mildewed earth to be grass, or to win any
show of compromise; its silent pavement, unaccustomed to
the tread of feet, and even to the observation of eyes, except
when a stray face looked down from the upper world,
wondering what nook it was; its sun-dial in a little bricked-up
corner, where no sun had straggled for a hundred years, but
where, in compensation for the sun's neglect, the snow would
lie for weeks when it lay nowhere else, and the black east wind
would spin like a huge humming-top, when in all other places
it was silent and still.

His dwelling, at its heart and core – within doors – at his
fireside – was so lowering and old, so crazy, yet so strong,
with its worm-eaten beams of wood in the ceiling, and its
sturdy floor shelving downward to the great oak chimney-

piece; so environed and hemmed in by the pressure of the town, yet so remote in fashion, age, and custom; so quiet, yet so thundering with echoes when a distant voice was raised, or a door was shut – echoes not confined to the many low passages and empty rooms, but rumbling and grumbling till they were stifled in the heavy air of the forgotten crypt where the Norman arches were half buried in the earth.

You should have seen him in his dwelling about twilight, in the dead winter-time.

When the wind was blowing shrill and shrewd, with the going down of the blurred sun. When it was just so dark as that the forms of things were indistinct and big – but not wholly lost. When sitters by the fire began to see wild faces and figures, mountains and abysses, ambuscades and armies, in the coals. When people in the streets bent down their heads, and ran before the weather. When those who were obliged to meet it were stopped at angry corners, stung by wandering snow-flakes alighting on the lashes of their eyes – which fell too sparingly, and were blown away too quickly, to leave a trace upon the frozen ground. When windows of private houses closed up tight and warm. When lighted gas began to burst forth in the busy and the quiet streets, fast blackening otherwise. When stray pedestrians, shivering along the latter, looked down at the glowing fires in the kitchens, and sharpened their sharp appetites by sniffing up the fragrance of whole miles of dinners.

When travellers by land were bitter cold, and looked wearily on gloomy landscapes, rustling and shuddering in the blast. When mariners at sea, outlying upon icy yards, were tossed and swung above the howling ocean dreadfully. When lighthouses, on rocks and headlands, showed solitary and watchful; and benighted sea birds breasted on against their ponderous lanterns; and fell dead. When little readers of story books, by the firelight, trembled to think of Cassim Baba cut into quarters, hanging in the Robbers' Cave, or had some small misgivings that the fierce old woman, with the crutch, who used to start out of the box in the merchant Abudah's bedroom, might, one of these nights, be found upon the stairs, in the long, cold, dusky journey up to bed.

When, in rustic places, the last glimmering of daylight died away from the ends of avenues; and the trees, arching overhead, were sullen and black. When, in parks and woods, the high wet fern and sodden moss and beds of fallen leaves, and trunks of trees, were lost to view, in masses of impenetrable shade. When mists arose from dyke, and fen, and river. When lights in old halls and in cottage windows were a cheerful sight. When the mill stopped, the wheelwright and the blacksmith shut their workshops, the turnpike-gate closed, the plough and harrow were left lonely in the fields, the labourer and team went home, and the striking of the church clock had a deeper sound than at noon, and the churchyard wicket would be swung no more that night.

When twilight everywhere released the shadows, prisoned up all day, that now closed in and gathered like mustering swarms of ghosts. When they stood lowering in corners of rooms, and frowned out from behind half-opened doors. When they had full possession of unoccupied apartments. When they danced upon the floors, and walls, and ceilings of inhabited chambers while the fire was low, and withdrew like ebbing waters when it sprung into a blaze. When they fantastically mocked the shapes of household objects, making the nurse an ogress, the rocking-horse a monster, the wondering child, half scared and half amused, a stranger to itself – the very tongs upon the hearth a straddling giant with his arms a-kimbo, evidently smelling the blood of Englishmen, and wanting to grind people's bones to make his bread.

When these shadows brought into the minds of older people other thoughts, and showed them different images. When they stole from their retreats, in the likenesses of forms and faces from the past, from the grave, from the deep, deep gulf, where the things that might have been, and never were, are always wandering.

When he sat, as already mentioned, gazing at the fire. When, as it rose and fell, the shadows went and came. When he took no heed of them with his bodily eyes; but, let them come or let them go, looked fixedly at the fire. You should have seen him then.

When the sounds that had arisen with the shadows, and come out of their lurking-places at the twilight summons, seemed to make a deeper stillness all about him. When the wind was rumbling in the chimney, and sometimes crooning, sometimes howling, in the house. When the old trees outward were so shaken and beaten, that one querulous old rook, unable to sleep, protested now and then in a feeble, dozy, high-up 'Caw!' When, at intervals, the window trembled, the rusty vane upon the turret-top complained, the clock beneath it recorded that another quarter of an hour was gone, or the fire collapsed and fell in with a rattle.

— When a knock came at his door, in short, as he was sitting so, and roused him.

'Who's that?' said he. 'Come in!'

Surely there had been no figure leaning on the back of his chair; no face looking over it. It is certain that no gliding footstep touched the floor as he lifted up his head with a start, and spoke. And yet there was no mirror in the room on whose surface his own form could have cast its shadow for a moment: and Something had passed darkly and gone!

'I'm humbly fearful, sir,' said a fresh-coloured busy man, holding the door open with his foot for the admission of himself and a wooden tray he carried, and letting it go again by very gentle and careful degrees, when he and the tray had got in, lest it should close noisily, 'that it's a good bit past the time tonight. But Mrs. William had been taken off her legs so often —'

'By the wind? Ay! I have heard it rising.'

'— By the wind, sir – that it's a mercy she got home at all. Oh dear, yes! Yes. It was by the wind, Mr. Redlaw. By the wind.'

He had, by this time, put down the tray for dinner, and was employed in lighting the lamp, and spreading a cloth on the table. From this employment he desisted in a hurry, to stir and feed the fire, and then resumed it; the lamp he had lighted, and the blaze that rose under his hand, so quickly changing the appearance of the room, that it seemed as if the mere coming in of his fresh red face and active manner had made the pleasant alteration.

'Mrs. William is of course subject at any time, sir, to be taken off her balance by the elements. She is not formed superior to *that*.'

'No,' returned Mr. Redlaw good-naturedly, though abruptly.

'No, sir. Mrs. William may be taken off her balance by Earth; as, for example, last Sunday week, when sloppy and greasy, and she going out to tea with her newest sister-in-law, and having a pride in herself, and wishing to appear perfectly spotless, though pedestrian. Mrs. William may be taken off her balance by Air; as being once over-persuaded by a friend to try a swing at Peckham Fair, which acted on her constitution instantly like a steamboat. Mrs. William may be taken off her balance by Fire; as on a false alarm of engines at her mother's when she went two miles in her nightcap. Mrs. William may be taken off her balance by Water; as at Battersea, when rowed into the piers by her young nephew, Charley Swidger, junior, aged twelve, which had no idea of boats whatever. But these are elements. Mrs. William must be taken out of elements for the strength of *her* character to come into play.'

As he stopped for a reply, the reply was 'Yes,' in the same tone as before.

'Yes, sir. Oh dear, yes!' said Mr. Swidger, still proceeding with his preparations, and checking them off as he made them. 'That's where it is, sir. That's what I always say myself, sir. Such a many of us Swidgers! Pepper. Why, there's my father, sir, superannuated keeper and custodian of this Institution, eighty-seven years old. He's a Swidger! Spoon.'

'True, William,' was the patient and abstracted answer when he stopped again.

'Yes, sir,' said Mr. Swidger. 'That's what I always say, sir. You may call him the trunk of the tree! Bread. Then you come to his successor, my unworthy self – salt – and Mrs. William, Swidgers both. Knife and fork. Then you come to all my brothers and their families, Swidgers, man and woman, boy and girl. Why, what with cousins, uncles, aunts, and relationships of this, that, and t'other degree, and what-not degree, and marriages, and lyings-in, the Swidgers – tumbler – might take hold of hands, and make a ring round England!'

Receiving no reply at all here from the thoughtful man whom he addressed, Mr. William approached him nearer, and made a feint of accidentally knocking the table with a decanter to rouse him. The moment he succeeded, he went on, as if in great alacrity of aquiescence.

'Yes, sir! That's just what I say myself, sir. Mrs. William and me have often said so. "There's Swidgers enough," we say, "without *our* voluntary contributions." Butter. In fact, sir, my father is a family in himself – casters – to take care of; and it happens all for the best that we have no child of our own, though it's made Mrs. William rather quiet-like, too. Quite ready for the fowl and mashed potatoes, sir? Mrs. William said she'd dish in ten minutes when I left the Lodge.'

'I am quite ready,' said the other, waking as from a dream, and walking slowly to and fro.

'Mrs. William has been at it again, sir!' said the keeper, as he stood warming a plate at the fire, and pleasantly shading his face with it. Mr. Redlaw stopped in his walking, and an expression of intent appeared in him.

'What I always say myself, sir. She *will* do it! There's a motherly feeling in Mrs. William's breast that must and will have went.'

'What has she done?'

'Why, sir, not satisfied with being a sort of mother to all the young gentlemen that come up from a variety of parts, to attend your courses of lectures at this ancient foundation – It's surprising how stone-chaney catches the heat, this frosty weather, to be sure!' Here he turned the plates, and cooled his fingers.

'Well?' said Mr. Redlaw.

'That's just what I say myself, sir,' returned Mr. William, speaking over his shoulder, as if in ready and delighted assent. 'That's exactly where it is, sir! There ain't one of our students but appears to regard Mrs. William in that light. Every day, right through the course, they put their heads into the Lodge, one after another, and have all got something to tell her, or something to ask her. "Swidge" is the appellation by which they speak of Mrs. William in general, among themselves, I'm told; but that's what I say, sir. Better be called ever so far out of your name, if it's done in real liking, than have it made ever so much of, and not cared about! What's a name for? To know a person by. If Mrs. William is known by something better than her name – I allude to Mrs. William's qualities and disposition – never mind her name, though it *is* Swidger, by rights. Let 'em call her Swidge, Widge, Bridge – Lord!

London Bridge, Blackfriars, Chelsea, Putney, Waterloo, or
Hammersmith Suspension – if they like!'

The close of this triumphant oration brought him and the
plate to the table, upon which he half laid and half dropped it,
with a lively sense of its being thoroughly heated, just as the
subject of his praises entered the room, bearing another tray
and a lantern, followed by a venerable old man with long grey
hair.

Mrs. William, like Mr. William, was a simple innocent-
looking person, in whose smooth cheeks the cheerful red of
her husband's official waistcoat was very pleasantly repeated.
But whereas Mr. William's light hair stood on end all over his
head, and seemed to draw his eyes up with it in an excess of
bustling readiness for anything, the dark brown hair of Mrs.
William was carefully smoothed down, and waved away
under a trim, tidy cap, in the most exact and quiet manner
imaginable. Whereas Mr. William's very trousers hitched
themselves up at the ankles, as if it were not in their iron-grey
nature to rest without looking about them, Mrs. William's
neatly-flowered skirts – red and white, like her own pretty
face – were as composed and orderly as if the very wind that
blew so hard out of doors could not disturb one of their folds.
Whereas his coat had something of a fly-away and half-off
appearance about the collar and breast, her little bodice was so
placid and neat, that there should have been protection for her
in it, had she needed any, with the roughest people. Who
could have had the heart to make so calm a bosom swell with
grief, or throb with fear, or flutter with a thought of shame?
To whom would its repose and peace have not appealed
against disturbance, like the innocent slumber of a child?

'Punctual, of course, Milly,' said her husband, relieving her
of the tray, 'or it wouldn't be you. Here's Mrs. William, sir!
He looks lonelier than ever tonight,' whispering to his wife as
he was taking the tray, 'and ghostlier altogether.'

Without any show of hurry or noise, or any show of herself
even, she was so calm and quiet, Milly set the dishes she had
brought upon the table, Mr. William, after much clattering
and running about, having only gained possession of a
butter-boat of gravy, which he stood ready to serve.

'What is that the old man has in his arms?' asked Mr.

Redlaw as he sat down to his solitary meal.

'Holly, sir,' replied the quiet voice of Milly.

'That's what I say myself, sir,' interposed Mr. William, striking in with the butter-boat. 'Berries is so seasonable to the time of year! Brown gravy!'

'Another Christmas come, another year gone!' murmured the Chemist with a gloomy sigh. 'More figures in the lengthening sum of recollection that we work and work at to our torment, till Death idly jumbles all together, and rubs all out. So, Philip!' breaking off, and raising his voice as he addressed the old man standing apart, with his glistening burden in his arms, from which the quiet Mrs. William took small branches, which she noiselessly trimmed with his scissors, and decorated the room with, while her aged father-in-law looked on, much interested in the ceremony.

'My duty to you, sir,' returned the old man. 'Should have spoke before, sir, but know your ways, Mr. Redlaw – proud to say – and wait till spoke to! Merry Christmas, sir, and happy New Year, and many of 'em. Have had a pretty many of 'em myself – ha, ha! – and may take the liberty of wishing 'em. I'm eighty-seven!'

'Haven't you had so many that were merry and happy?' asked the other.

'Ay, sir, ever so many,' returned the old man.

'Is his memory impaired with age? It is to be expected now,' said Mr. Redlaw, turning to the son, and speaking lower.

'Not a morsel of it, sir,' replied Mr. William. 'That's exactly what I say myself, sir. There never was such a memory as my father's. He's the most wonderful man in the world. He don't know what forgetting means. It's the very observation I'm always making to Mrs. William, sir, if you'll believe me!'

Mr Swidger, in his polite desire to seem to acquiesce at all events, delivered this as if there were no iota of contradiction in it, and it were all said in unbounded and unqualified assent.

The Chemist pushed his plate away, and, rising from the table, walked across the room to where the old man stood looking at a little sprig of holly in his hand.

'It recalls the time when many of those years were old and new, then?' he said, observing him attentively, and touching him on the shoulder. 'Does it?'

'Oh, many, many!' said Philip, half awaking from his reverie. 'I'm eighty-seven!'

'Merry and happy, was it?' asked the Chemist in a low voice. 'Merry and happy, old man?'

'Maybe as high as that, no higher,' said the old man, holding out his hand a little way above the level of his knee, and looking retrospectively at his questioner, 'when I first remember 'em! Cold, sunshiny day it was, out a walking, when someone – it was my mother as sure as you stand there, though I don't know what her blessed face was like, for she took ill and died that Christmas-time – told me they were food for birds. The pretty little fellow thought – that's me, you understand – that birds' eyes were so bright, perhaps, because the berries that they lived on in the winter were so bright. I recollect that. And I'm eighty-seven!'

'Merry and happy!' mused the other, bending his dark eyes upon the stooping figure, with a smile of compassion. 'Merry and happy – and remember well?'

'Ay, ay, ay!' resumed the old man, catching the last words. 'I remember 'em well in my school-time, year after year, and all the merry-making that used to come along with them. I was a strong chap then, Mr. Redlaw; and, if you'll believe me, hadn't my match at football within ten mile. Where's my son William? Hadn't my match at football, William, within ten mile!'

'That's what I always say, father!' returned the son promptly, and with great respect. 'You *are* a Swidger, if ever there was one of the family!'

'Dear!' said the old man, shaking his head as he again looked at the holly. 'His mother – my son William's my youngest son – and I, have sat among 'em all, boys and girls, little children and babies, many a year, when the berries like these were not shining half so bright all round us, as their bright faces. Many of 'em are gone; she's gone; and my son George (our eldest, who was her pride more than all the rest) is fallen very low: but I can see them, when I look here, alive and healthy, as they used to be in those days; and I can see him, thank God, in his innocence. It's a blessed thing to me, at eighty-seven.'

The keen look that had been fixed upon him with so much earnestness had gradually sought the ground.

'When my circumstances got to be not so good as formerly, through not being honestly dealt by, and I first come here to be custodian,' said the old man, '– which was upwards of fifty years ago – where's my son William? More than half a century ago, William!'

'That's what I say, father,' replied the son as promptly and dutifully as before, 'that's exactly where it is. Two times ought's an ought, and twice five ten, and there's a hundred of 'em.'

'It was quite a pleasure to know that one of our founders – or, more correctly speaking,' said the old man, with a great glory in his subject and his knowledge of it, 'one of the learned gentlemen that helped endow us in Queen Elizabeth's time, for we were founded afore her day – left in his will, among the other bequests he made us, so much to buy holly, for garnishing the walls and windows come Christmas. There was something homely and friendly in it. Being but strange here then, and coming at Christmas-time, we took a liking for his very picter that hangs in what used to be, anciently, afore our ten poor gentlemen commuted for an annual stipend in money, our great Dinner Hall. A sedate gentleman in a peaked beard, with a ruff round his neck, and a scroll below him, in old English letters, "Lord, keep my memory green!" You know all about him, Mr. Redlaw?'

'I know the portrait hangs there, Philip.'

'Yes, sure, it's the second on the right, above the panelling. I was going to say – he has helped to keep *my* memory green, I thank him; for going round the building every year, as I'm a doing now, and freshening up the bare rooms with these branches and berries, freshens up my bare old brain. One year brings back another, and that year another, and those others numbers! At last, it seems to me as if the birth-time of our Lord was the birth-time of all I have ever had affection for, or mourned for, or delighted-in, and they're a pretty many, for I'm eighty-seven!'

'Merry and happy,' murmured Redlaw to himself.

The room began to darken strangely.

'So you see, sir,' pursued old Philip, whose hale, wintry cheek had warmed into a ruddier glow and whose blue eyes had brightened while he spoke, 'I have plenty to keep, when I keep this present season. Now, where's my quiet Mouse? Chattering's the sin of my time of life, and there's half the building to do yet, if the cold don't freeze us first, or the wind don't blow us away, or the darkness don't swallow us up.'

The quiet Mouse had brought her calm face to his side, and silently taken his arm, before he finished speaking.

'Come away, my dear,' said the old man. 'Mr. Redlaw won't settle to his dinner, otherwise, till it's cold as the winter. I hope you'll excuse me rambling on sir, and I wish you good night, and, once again, a merry —'

'Stay!' said Mr. Redlaw, resuming his place at the table, more, it would have seemed from his manner, to reassure the old keeper, than in any remembrance of his own appetite. 'Spare me another moment Philip. William, you were going to tell me something to your excellent wife's honour. It will not be disagreeable to her to hear you praise her. What was it?'

'Why, that's where it is, you see, sir,' returned Mr. William Swidger, looking towards his wife in considerable embarrassment. 'Mrs. William's got her eye upon me.'

'But you're not afraid of Mrs. William's eye?'

'Why, no, sir,' returned Mr. Swidger, 'that's what I say myself. It wasn't made to be afraid of. It wouldn't have been made so mild, if that was the intention. But I wouldn't like to – Milly! – him, you know. Down in the Buildings.'

Mr. William, standing behind the table, and rummaging disconcertedly among the objects upon it, directed persuasive glances at Mrs. William, and secret jerks of his head and thumb at Mr. Redlaw, as alluring her towards him.

'Him, you know, my love,' said Mr. William. 'Down in the Buildings. Tell, my dear! You're the works of Shakespeare in comparison with myself. Down in the Buildings, you know, my love. Student.'

'Student!' repeated Mr. Redlaw, raising his head.

'That's what I say, sir!' cried Mr. William in the utmost animation of assent. 'If it wasn't the poor student down in the Buildings, why should you wish to hear it from Mrs. William's lips? Mrs. William, my dear – Buildings.'

'I didn't know,' said Milly with a quiet frankness, free from any haste or confusion, 'that William had said anything about it, or I wouldn't have come. I asked him not to. It's a sick

young gentleman, sir – and very poor, I am afraid – who is too
ill to go home this holiday-time, and lives, unknown to any
one, in but a common kind of lodging for a gentleman, down
in Jerusalem Buildings. That's all, sir.'

'Why have I never heard of him?' said the Chemist, rising
hurriedly. 'Why has he not made his situation known to me?
Sick! Give me my hat and cloak. Poor! What house? – what
number?'

'Oh, you mustn't go there, sir!' said Milly, leaving her
father-in-law, and calmly confronting him with her collected
little face and folded hands.

'Not go there?'

'Oh dear, no!' said Milly, shaking her head as at a most
manifest and self-evident impossibility. 'It couldn't be thought
of!'

'What do you mean? Why not?'

'Why, you see, sir,' said Mr. William Swidger persuasively
and confidentially, 'that's what I say. Depend upon it, the
young gentleman would never have made his situation known
to one of his own sex. Mrs. William has got into his
confidence, but that's quite different. They all confide in Mrs.
William; they all trust *her*. A man, sir, couldn't have got a
whisper out of him; but woman, sir, and Mrs. William
combined —!'

'There is good sense and delicacy in what you say, William,'
returned Mr. Redlaw, observant of the gentle and composed
face at his shoulder. And laying his finger on his lip, he
secretly put his purse into her hand.

'Oh dear, no, sir!' cried Milly, giving it back again. 'Worse
and worse! Couldn't be dreamed of!'

Such a staid, matter-of-fact housewife she was, and so
unruffled by the momentary haste of this rejection, that, an
instant afterwards, she was tidily picking up a few leaves
which had strayed from between her scissors and her apron
when she had arranged the holly.

Finding, when she rose from her stooping posture, that Mr.
Redlaw was still regarding her with doubt and astonishment,
she quietly repeated – looking about, the while, for any other
fragments that might have escaped her observation:

'Oh dear, no, sir! He said that of all the world he would not be known to you, or receive help from you – though he is a student in your class. I have made no terms of secrecy with you, but I trust to your honour completely.'

'Why did he say so?'

'Indeed I can't tell, sir,' said Milly, after thinking a little, 'because I am not at all clever, you know; and I wanted to be useful to him in making things neat and comfortable about him, and employed myself that way. But I know he is poor and lonely, and I think he is somehow neglected too. How dark it is!'

The room had darkened more and more. There was a very heavy gloom and shadow gathering behind the Chemist's chair.

'What more about him?' he asked.

'He is engaged to be married when he can afford it,' said Milly, 'and is studying, I think, to qualify himself to earn a living. I have seen, a long time, that he has studied hard, and denied himself much. How very dark it is!'

'It's turned colder, too,' said the old man, rubbing his hands. 'There's a chill and dismal feeling in the room. Where's my son William? William, my boy, turn the lamp, and rouse the fire!'

Milly's voice resumed, like quiet music very softly played: 'He muttered in his broken sleep yesterday afternoon, after talking to me' (this as to herself), 'about someone dead, and some great wrong done that could never be forgotten; but whether to him or to another person, I don't know. Not *by* him, I am sure.'

'And, in short, Mrs. William, you see – which she wouldn't say herself, Mr. Redlaw, if she was to stop here till the new year after this next one,' said Mr. William, coming up to him to speak in his ear – 'has done him worlds of good! Bless you, worlds of good! All at home just the same as ever – my father made as snug and comfortable – not a crumb of litter to be found in the house, if you were to offer fifty pound ready money for it – Mrs. William apparently never out of the way – yet Mrs. William backwards and forwards, backwards and forwards, up and down, up and down, a mother to him!'

The room turned darker and colder, and the gloom and shadow gathering behind the chair was heavier.

'Not content with this, sir, Mrs. William goes and finds,
this very night, when she was coming home (why, it's not
above a couple of hours ago), a creature more like a young
wild beast than a young child, shivering upon a doorstep.
What does Mrs. William do, but brings it home to dry it, and
feed it, and keep it till our old Bounty of food and flannel is
given away on Christmas morning! If it ever felt a fire before,
it's as much as it ever did; for it's sitting in the old Lodge
chimney, staring at ours as if its ravenous eyes would never
shut again. It's sitting there, at least,' said Mr. William,
correcting himself, on reflection, 'unless it's bolted!'

'Heaven keep her happy!' said the Chemist aloud, 'and you
too, Philip! and you, William! I must consider what to do in
this. I may desire to see this student. I'll not detain you longer
now. Good night!'

'I thankee, sir, I thankee!' said the old man, 'for Mouse, and
for my son William, and for myself. Where's my son William?
William, you take the lantern, and go on first, through them
long dark passages, as you did last year and the year afore. Ha,
ha! I remember – though I'm eighty-seven! "Lord, keep my
memory green!" It's a very good prayer, Mr. Redlaw, that of
the learned gentlemen in the peaked beard, with a ruff round
his neck – hangs up, second on the right above the panelling,
in what used to be, afore our ten poor gentleman commuted,
our great Dinner Hall. "Lord, keep my memory green!" It's
very good and pious, sir. Amen! Amen!'

As they passed out and shut the heavy door, which,
however carefully withheld, fired a long train of thundering
reverberations when it shut at last, the room turned darker.

As he fell a musing in his chair alone, the healthy holly
withered on the wall, and dropped – dead branches.

As the gloom and shadow thickened behind him, in that
place where it had been gathering so darkly, it took, by slow
degrees, or out of it there came, by some unreal, unsubstantial
process, not to be traced by any human sense, an awful
likeness of himself.

Ghastly and cold, colourless in its leaden face and hands, but
with his features, and his bright eyes, and his grizzled hair, and
dressed in the gloomy shadow of his dress, it came into its
terrible appearance of existence, motionless, without a sound.

As *he* leaned his arm upon the elbow of his chair, ruminating before the fire, *it* leaned upon the chair-back, close above him, with its appalling copy of his face looking where his face looked, and bearing the expression his face bore.

This, then, was the Something that had passed and gone already. This was the dead companion of the haunted man!

It took, for some moments, no more apparent heed of him than he of it. The Christmas Waits were playing somewhere in the distance, and, through his thoughtfulness, he seemed to listen to the music. It seemed to listen too.

At length he spoke; without moving or lifting up his face.

'Here again!' he said.

'Here again!' replied the Phantom.

'I see you in the fire,' said the haunted man. 'I hear you in music, in the wind, in the dead stillness of the night.'

The Phantom moved his head, assenting.

'Why do you come to haunt me thus?'

'I come as I am called,' replied the Ghost.

'No. Unbidden!' exclaimed the Chemist.

'Unbidden be it,' said the Spectre. 'It is enough. I am here.'

Hitherto the light of the fire had shone on the two faces – if the dread lineaments behind the chair might be called a face – both addressed towards it, as at first, and neither looking at the other. But, now, the haunted man turned suddenly, and stared upon the Ghost. The Ghost, as sudden in its motion, passed to before the chair, and stared on him.

The living man, and the animated image of himself dead, might so have looked, the one upon the other. An awful survey, in a lonely and remote part of an empty old pile of building, on a winter night, with the loud wind going by upon its journey of mystery – whence, or whither, no man knowing since the world began – and the stars, in unimaginable millions, glittering through it, from eternal space, where the world's bulk is as a grain, and its hoary age is infancy.

'Look upon me!' said the Spectre. 'I am he, neglected in my youth, and miserably poor, who strove and suffered, and still strove and suffered, until I hewed out knowledge from the mine where it was buried, and made rugged steps thereof, for my worn feet to rest and rest on.'

'I *am* that man,' returned the Chemist.

'No mother's self-denying love,' pursued the Phantom, 'no father's counsel, aided *me*. A stranger came into my father's place when I was but a child, and I was easily an alien from my mother's heart. My parents, at the best, were of that sort whose care soon ends, and whose duty is soon done; who cast their offspring loose early, as birds do theirs; and, if they do well, claim the merit; if ill, the pity.'

It paused, and seemed to tempt and goad him with its look, and with the manner of its speech, and with its smile.

'I am he,' pursued the Phantom, 'who, in this struggle upward, found a friend. I made him – won him – bound him to me! We worked together, side by side. All the love and confidence that in my ealier youth had had no outlet, and found no expression, I bestowed on him.'

'Not all,' said Redlaw hoarsely.

'No, not all,' returned the Phantom. 'I had a sister.'

The haunted man, with his head resting on his hands, replied, 'I had!' The Phantom, with an evil smile, drew closer to the chair, and resting its chin upon its folded hands, its folded hands upon the back, and looking down into his face with searching eyes, that seemed instinct with fire, went on:

'Such glimpses of the light of home as I had ever known, had streamed from her. How young she was, how fair, how loving! I took her to the first poor roof that I was master of, and made it rich. She came into the darkness of my life, and made it bright. She is before me!'

'I saw her, in the fire, but now. I hear her in music, in the wind, in the dead stillness of the night,' returned the haunted man.

'*Did* he love her?' said the Phantom, echoing his contemplative tone. 'I think he did once. I am sure he did. Better had she loved him less – less secretly, less dearly, from the shallower depths of a more divided hearth!'

'Let me forget it,' said the Chemist with an angry motion of his hand. 'Let me blot it from my memory!'

The Spectre, without stirring, and with its unwinking, cruel eyes still fixed upon his face, went on: 'A dream, like hers, stole upon my own life.'

'It did,' said Redlaw.

'A love, as like hers,' pursued the Phantom, 'as my inferior nature might cherish, arose in my own heart. I was too poor to bind its object to my fortune, then, by any thread of promise or entreaty. I loved her far too well to seek to do it. But, more than ever I had striven in my life, I strove to climb! Only an inch gained, brought me something nearer to the height. I toiled up! In the late pauses of my labour at that time – my sister (sweet companion!) still sharing with me the expiring embers and the cooling hearth – when day was breaking, what pictures of the future did I see!'

'I saw them in the fire but now,' he murmured. 'They come back to me in music, in the wind, in the dead stillness of the night, in the revolving years.'

'— Pictures of my own domestic life, in after-time, with her who was the inspiration of my toil. Pictures of my sister, made the wife of my dear friend, on equal terms – for he had some inheritance, we none – pictures of our sobered age and mellowed happiness, and of the golden links, extending back so far, that should bind us, and our children, in a radiant garland,' said the Phantom.

'Pictures,' said the haunted man, 'that were delusions. Why is it my doom to remember them too well?'

'Delusions,' echoed the Phantom in its changeless voice, and glaring on him with its changeless eyes. 'For my friend (in whose breast my confidence was locked as in my own), passing between me and the centre of the system of my hopes and struggles, won her to himself, and shattered my frail universe. My sister, doubly dear, doubly devoted, doubly cheerful in my home, lived on to see me famous, and my old ambition so rewarded when its spring was broken, and then —'

'Then died,' he interposed. 'Died, gentle as ever, happy, and with no concern but for her brother. Peace!'

The Phantom watched him silently.

'Remembered!' said the haunted man after a pause. 'Yes. So well remembered, that even now, when years have passed, and nothing is more idle or more visionary to me than the boyish love so long outlived, I think of it with sympathy, as if it were a younger brother's or a son's. Sometimes I even wonder when her heart first inclined to him, and how it had been affected towards me. Not lightly, once, I think. — But that is nothing. Early unhappiness, a wound from a hand I loved and trusted, and a loss that nothing can replace, outlive such fancies.'

'Thus,' said the Phantom, 'I bear within me a Sorrow and a Wrong. Thus I prey upon myself. Thus, memory is my curse; and, if I could forget my sorrow and my wrong, I would!'

'Mocker!' said the Chemist, leaping up, and making, with a wrathful hand, at the throat of his other self. 'Why have I always that taunt in my ears?'

'Forbear!' exclaimed the Spectre in an awful voice. 'Lay a hand on me, and die!'

He stopped midway, as if its words had paralysed him, and stood looking on it. It had glided from him; it had its arm raised high in warning; and a smile passed over its unearthly features as it reared its dark figure in triumph.

'If I could forget my sorrow and wrong, I would,' the Ghost repeated. 'If I could forget my sorrow and wrong, I would!'

'Evil spirit of myself,' returned the haunted man in a low, trembling tone, 'my life is darkened by that incessant whisper.'

'It is an echo,' said the Phantom.

'If it be an echo of my thoughts – as now, indeed, I know it is,' rejoined the haunted man, 'why should I, therefore, be tormented? It is not a selfish thought. I suffer it to range beyond myself. All men and women have their sorrows; most of them their wrongs; ingratitude, and sordid jealousy, and interest besetting all degrees of life. Who would not forget their sorrows and their wrongs?'

'Who would not, truly, and be the happier and better for it? said the Phantom.

'These revolutions of years, which we commemorate,' proceeded Redlaw, 'what do *they* recall? Are there any minds in which they do not re-awaken some sorrow, or some trouble? What is the remembrance of the old man who was here tonight? A tissue of sorrow and trouble.'

'But common natures,' said the Phantom, with its evil smile upon its glassy face, 'unenlightened minds and ordinary spirits, do not feel or reason on these things like men of higher cultivation and profounder thought.'

'Tempter,' answered Redlaw, 'whose hollow look and voice I dread more than words can express, and from whom some dim foreshadowing of greater fear is stealing over me while I speak, I hear again an echo of my own mind.'

'Receive it as a proof that I am powerful,' returned the Ghost. 'Hear what I offer! Forget the sorrow, wrong, and trouble you have known!'

'Forget them!' he repeated.

'I have the power to cancel their remembrance – to leave but very faint, confused traces of them, that will die out soon,' returned the Spectre. 'Say! Is it done?'

'Stay!' cried the haunted man, arresting by a terrified gesture the uplifted hand. 'I tremble with distrust and doubt of you; and the dim fear you cast upon me deepens into a nameless horror I can hardly bear. I would not deprive myself of any kindly recollection, or any sympathy that is good for me, or others. What shall I lose if I assent to this? What else will pass from my remembrance?'

'No knowledge; no result of study; nothing but the inter-twisted chain of feelings and associations; each in its turn dependent on, and nourished by, the banished recollections. Those will go.'

'Are they so many?' said the haunted man, reflecting in alarm.

'They have been wont to show themselves in the fire, in music, in the wind, in the dead stillness of the night, in the revolving years,' returned the Phantom scornfully.

'In nothing else?'

The Phantom held its peace.

But, having stood before him, silent, for a little while, it moved towards the fire; then stopped.

'Decide!' it said, 'before the opportunity is lost!'

'A moment! I call Heaven to witness,' said the agitated man, 'that I have never been a hater of my kind – never morose, indifferent, or hard to anything around me. If, living here alone, I have made too much of all that was and might have been, and too little of what is, the evil, I believe, has fallen on me, and not on others. But, if there were poison in my body, should I not, possessed of antidotes and knowledge how to use them, use them? If there be poison in my mind, and through this fearful shadow I can cast it out, shall I not cast it out?'

'Say,' said the Spectre, 'is it done?'

'A moment longer!' he answered hurriedly. '*I would forget it if I could*! Have *I* thought that alone, or has it been the thought of thousands upon thousands, generation after generation? All human memory is fraught with sorrow and trouble. My memory is as the memory of other men, but other men have not this choice. Yes, I close the bargain. Yes! I *will* forget my sorrow, wrong and trouble!'

'Say,' said the Spectre, 'is it done?'

'It is!'

'*It is*. And take this with you, man whom I here renounce! The gift that I have given, you shall give again, go where you will. Without recovering yourself the power that you have yielded up, you shall henceforth destroy its like in all whom you approach. Your wisdom has discovered that the memory of sorrow, wrong, and trouble is the lot of all mankind, and that mankind would be the happier, in its other memories, without it. Go! Be its benefactor! Freed from such remembrance, from this hour, carry involuntarily the blessing of such freedom with you. Its diffusion is inseparable and inalienable from you. Go! Be happy in the good you have won, and in the good you do!'

The Phantom, which had held its bloodless hand above him while it spoke, as if in some unholy invocation, or some ban; and which had gradually advanced its eyes so close to his, that he could see how they did not participate in the terrible smile upon its face, but were a fixed, unalterable, steady horror; melted from before him, and was gone.

As he stood rooted to the spot, possessed by fear and wonder, and imagining he heard repeated in melancholy echoes dying away fainter and fainter, the words, 'Destroy its like in all whom you approach!' a shrill cry reached his ears. It came, not from the passages beyond the door, but from another part of the old building, and sounded like the cry of someone in the dark who had lost the way.

He looked confusedly upon his hands and limbs, as if to be assured of his identity, and then shouted in reply, loudly and wildly; for there was a strangeness and terror upon him, as if he, too, were lost.

The cry responding, and being nearer, he caught up the lamp, and raised a heavy curtain in the wall, by which he was accustomed to pass into and out of the theatre where he lectured, which adjoined his room. Associated with youth and animation, and a high amphitheatre of faces which his entrance charmed to interest in a moment, it was a ghostly place when all this life was faded out of it, and stared upon him like an emblem of Death.

'Holloa!' he cried. 'Holloa! This way! Come to the light!' When, as he held the curtain with one hand, and with the other raised the lamp and tried to pierce the gloom that filled the place, something rushed past him into the room like a wild cat, and crouched down in a corner.

'What is it?' he said hastily.

He might have asked, 'What is it?' even had he seen it well, as presently he did when he stood looking at it gathered up in its corner.

A bundle of tatters, held together by a hand, in size and form almost an infant's, but in its greedy, desperate little clutch, a bad old man's. A face round and smoothed by some half-dozen years, but pinched and twisted by the experiences of a life. Bright eyes, but not youthful. Naked feet, beautiful in their childish delicacy, ugly in the blood and dirt that cracked upon them. A baby savage, a young monster, a child who had never been a child, a creature who might live to take the outward form of man, but who, within, would live and perish a mere beast.

Used, already, to be worried and hunted like a beast, the boy crouched down as he was looked at, and looked back again, and interposed his arm to ward off the expected blow.

'I'll bite,' he said, 'if you hit me!'

The time had been, and not many minutes since, when such a sight as this would have wrung the Chemist's heart. He looked upon it now coldly, but with a heavy effort to remember something – he did not know what – he asked the boy what he did there, and whence he came.

'Where's the woman?' he replied. 'I want to find the woman.'

'Who?'

'The woman. Her that brought me here, and set me by the

large fire. She was so long gone, that I went to look for her, and lost myself. I don't want you. I want the woman.'

He made a spring, so suddenly, to get away, that the dull sound of his naked feet upon the floor was near the curtain, when Redlaw caught him by his rags.

'Come! you let me go!' muttered the boy, struggling, and clenching his teeth. 'I've done nothing to you. Let me go, will you, to the woman?'

'That is not the way. There is a nearer one,' said Redlaw, detaining him, in the same blank effort to remember some association that ought of right to bear upon this monstrous object. 'What is your name?'

'Got none.'

'Where do you live?'

'Live! What's that?'

The boy shook his hair from his eyes to look at him for a moment, and then, twisting round his legs and wrestling with him, broke again into his repetition of, 'You let me go, will you? I want to find the woman.'

The Chemist led him to the door. 'This way,' he said, looking at him still confusedly, but with repugnance and avoidance, growing out of his coldness. 'I'll take you to her.'

The sharp eyes in the child's head, wandering round the room, lighted on the table where the remnants of the dinner were.

'Give me some of that!' he said covetously.

'Has she not fed you?'

'I shall be hungry again tomorrow, shan't I? Ain't I hungry every day?'

Finding himself released, he bounded at the table like some small animal of prey, and hugging to his breast bread and meat, and his own rags, all together, said:

'There! Now take me to the woman!'

As the Chemist, with a new-born dislike to touch him, sternly motioned him to follow, and was going out of the door, he trembled and stopped.

'The gift that I have given, you shall give again, go where you will.'

The Phantom's words were blowing in the wind, and the wind blew chill upon him.

'I'll not go there tonight,' he murmured faintly. 'I'll go nowhere tonight. Boy! straight down this long arched passage, and past the great dark door into the yard, you will see the fire shining on a window there.'

'The woman's fire?' inquired the boy.

He nodded, and the naked feet had sprung away. He came back with his lamp, locked his door hastily, and sat down in his chair, covering his face like one who was frightened at himself.

For now he was indeed alone. Alone, alone.

A small man sat in a small parlour, partitioned off from a small shop by a small screen, pasted all over with small scraps of newspapers. In company with the small man was almost any amount of small children you may please to name – at least, it seemed so; they made, in that very limited sphere of action, such an imposing effect, in point of numbers.

Of these small fry, two had, by some strong machinery, been got into bed in a corner, where they might have reposed snugly enough in the sleep of innocence, but for a constitutional propensity to keep awake, and also to scuffle in and out of bed. The immediate occasion of these predatory dashes at the waking world was the construction of an oyster-shell wall in a corner, by two other youths of tender age; on which fortification the two in bed made harassing descents (like those accursed Picts and Scots who beleaguer the early historical studies of most young Britons), and then withdrew to their own territory.

In addition to the stir attendant on these inroads, and the retorts of the invaded, who pursued hotly, and made lunges at the bedclothes, under which the marauders took refuge, another little boy, in another little bed, contributed his mite of confusion to the family stock, by casting his boots upon the waters; in other words, by launching these and several small objects, inoffensive in themselves, though of a hard substance considered as missiles, at the disturbers of his repose, who were not slow to return these compliments.

Besides which, another little boy – the biggest there, but still little – was tottering to and fro, bent on one side, and considerably affected in his knees by the weight of a large baby, which he was supposed, by a fiction that obtains sometimes in sanguine families, to be hushing to sleep. But oh! the inexhaustible regions of contemplation and watchfulness into which this baby's eyes were then only beginning to compose themselves to stare over his unconscious shoulder!

It was a very Moloch of a baby, on whose insatiate altar the whole existence of this particular young brother was offered up a daily sacrifice. Its personality may be said to have consisted in its never being quiet, in any one place, for five consecutive minutes, and never going to sleep when required. 'Tetterby's baby' was as well known in the neighbourhood as the postman or the potboy. It roved from door-step to door-step, in the arms of little Johnny Tetterby, and lagged heavily at the rear of troops of juveniles who followed the Tumblers or the Monkey, and came up, all on one side, a little too late for everything that was attractive, from Monday morning until Saturday night. Wherever childhood congregated to play, there was little Moloch making Johnny fag and toil. Wherever Johnny desired to stay, little Moloch became fractious, and would not remain. Whenever Johnny wanted to go out, Moloch was asleep, and must be watched. Whenever Johnny wanted to stay at home, Moloch was awake, and must be taken out. Yet Johnny was verily persuaded that it was a faultless baby, without its peer in the realm of England; and was quite content to catch meek glimpses of things in general from behind its skirts, or over its limp flapping bonnet, and to go staggering about with it like a very little porter with a very large parcel, which was not directed to anybody, and could never be delivered anywhere.

The small man who sat in the small parlour, making fruitless attempts to read his newspaper peaceably in the midst of this disturbance, was the father of the family, and the chief of the firm described in the inscription over the little shop-front, by the name and title of A. TETTERBY AND CO., NEWSMEN. Indeed, strictly speaking, he was the only personage answering to that designation; as Co. was a merely poetical abstraction, altogether baseless and impersonal.

Tetterby's was the corner shop in Jerusalem Buildings. There was a good show of literature in the window, chiefly consisting of picture-newspapers out of date, and serial pirates and footpads. Walking-sticks, likewise, and marbles, were included in the stock-in-trade. It had once extended into the light confectionary line; but it would seem that those elegancies of life were not in demand about Jerusalem Buildings, for nothing connected with that branch of commerce remained in the window, except a sort of small glass lantern containing a languishing mass of bull's-eyes, which had melted in the summer and congealed in the winter, until all hope of ever getting them out, or of eating them without eating the lantern too, was gone for ever. Tetterby's had tried its hand at several things. It had once made a feeble little dart at the toy business; for, in another lantern, there was a heap of minute wax dolls, all sticking together upside down, in the direst confusion, with their feet on one another's heads and a precipitate of broken arms and legs at the bottom. It had made a move in the millinery direction, which a few dry, wiry bonnet-shapes remained in a corner of the window to attest. It had fancied that a living might lie hidden in the tobacco trade, and had stuck up a representation of a native of each of the three integral portions of the British empire in the act of consuming that fragrant weed; with a poetic legend attached, importing that united in one cause they sat and joked, one chewed tobacco, one took snuff, one smoked: but nothing seemed to have come of it – except flies. Time had been when it had put a forlorn trust in imitative jewellery, for in one pane of glass there was a card of cheap seals, and another of pencil-cases, and a mysterious black amulet of inscrutable intention labelled ninepence. But, to that hour, Jerusalem Buildings had bought none of them. In short, Tetterby's had tried so hard to get a livelihood out of Jerusalem Buildings in one way or other, and appeared to have done so indifferently in all, that the best position in the firm was too evidently Co.'s; Co., as a bodiless creation, being untroubled with the vulgar inconveniences of hunger and thirst, being chargeable neither to the poor's rates nor the assessed taxes, and having no family to provide for.

Tetterby himself, however, in his little palour, as already mentioned, having the presence of a young family impressed upon his mind in a manner too clamorous to be disregarded, or to comport with the quiet perusal of a newspaper, laid down his paper, wheeled, in his distraction, a few times round the parlour like an undecided carrier pigeon, made an ineffectual rush at one or two flying little figures in bedgowns that skimmed past him, and then, bearing suddenly down upon the only unoffending member of the family, boxed the ears of little Moloch's nurse.

'You bad boy!' said Mr. Tetterby; 'haven't you any feeling for your poor father after the fatigues and anxieties of a hard winter's day. Since five o'clock in the morning, but must you wither his rest, and corrode his latest intelligence, with *your* vicious tricks? Isn't it enough, sir, that your brother 'Dolphus is toiling and moiling in the fog and cold, and you rolling in the lap of luxury with a – with a baby, and everything you can wish for,' said Mr. Tetterby, heaping this up as a great climax of blessings, 'but must you make a wilderness of home, and maniacs of your parents? Must you, Johnny? Hey?' At each interrogation, Mr. Tetterby made a feint of boxing his ears again, but thought better of it, and held his hand.

'Oh, father!' whimpered Johnny, 'when I was'nt doing anything, I'm sure, but taking such care of Sally, and getting her to sleep. Oh, father!'

'I wish my little woman would come home!' said Mr. Tetterby, relenting and repenting; 'I only wish my little woman would come home! I ain't fit to deal with 'em. They make my head go round, and get the better of me. Oh, Johnny! Isn't it enough that your dear mother has provided you with that sweet sister!' indicating Moloch; 'isn't it enough that you were seven boys before, without a ray of gal, and that your dear mother went through what she *did* go through, on purpose that you might all of you have a little sister, but must you so behave yourself as to make my head swim?'

Softening more and more as his own tender feelings, and those of his injured son, were worked on, Mr. Tetterby concluded by embracing him, and immediately breaking away to catch one of the real delinquents. A reasonably good start occurring, he succeeded, after a short but smart run, and some rather severe cross-country work under and over the bed-steads, and in and out among the intricacies of the chairs, in capturing this infant, whom he condignly punished, and bore to bed. This example had a powerful, and apparently mesmer-ic, influence on him of the boots, who instantly fell into a deep sleep, though he had been, but a moment before, broad awake, and in the highest possible feather. Nor was it lost upon the two architects, who retired to bed, in an adjoining

closet, with great privacy and speed. The comrade of the
Intercepted One also shrinking into his nest with similar
discretion, Mr. Tetterby, when he paused for breath, found
himself unexpectedly in a scene of peace.

'My little woman herself,' said Mr. Tetterby, wiping his
flushed face, 'could hardly have done it better! I only wish my
little woman had had it to do, I do indeed!'

Mr. Tetterby sought upon his screen for a passage appropri-
ate to be impressed upon his children's minds on the occasion,
and read the following: '"It is an undoubted fact that all
remarkable men have had remarkable mothers, and have
respected them in after life as their best friends." Think of
your own remarkable mother, my boys,' said Mr. Tetterby,
'and know her value while she is still among you!'

He sat down again in his chair by the fire, and composed
himself, cross-legged, over his newspaper.

'Let anybody, I don't care who it is, get out of bed again,'
said Tetterby as a general proclamation, delivered in a very
soft-hearted manner, 'and astonishment will be the portion of
that respected contemporary!' – which expression Mr. Tetterby selected from his screen. 'Johnny, my child, take care of
your only sister, Sally; for she's the brightest gem that ever
sparkled on your early brow.'

Johnny sat down on a little stool, and devotedly crushed
himself beneath the weight of Moloch.

'Ah, what a gift that baby is to you, Johnny!' said his father;
'and how thankful you ought to be! "It is not generally
known," Johnny,' – was now referring to the screen again –
'"but it is a fact ascertained, by accurate calculations, that the
following immense percentage of babies never attain to two
years old; that is to say —"'

'Oh, don't, father, please!' cried Johnny. 'I can't bear it
when I think of Sally.'

Mr. Tetterby desisting, Johnny, with a profounder sense of
his trust, wiped his eyes, and hushed his sister.

'Your brother 'Dolphus,' said his father, poking the fire, 'is
late tonight, Johnny, and will come home like a lump of ice.
What's got your precious mother?'

'Here's mother, and 'Dolphus too, father,' exclaimed Johnny, 'I think!'

'You're right!' returned his father, listening. 'Yes, that's the footstep of my little woman.'

The process of induction, by which Mr. Tetterby had come to the conclusion that his wife was a little woman, was his own secret. She would have made two editions of himself very easily. Considered as an individual, she was rather remarkable for being robust and portly; but, considered with reference to her husband, her dimensions became magnificent. Nor did they assume a less imposing proportion when studied with reference to the size of her seven sons, who were but diminutive. In the case of Sally, however, Mrs. Tetterby had asserted herself at last; as nobody knew better than the victim Johnny, who weighed and measured that exacting idol every hour in the day.

Mrs. Tetterby, who had been marketing, and carried a basket, threw back her bonnet and shawl, and sitting down, fatigued, commanded Johnny to bring his sweet charge to her straightway for a kiss. Johnny having complied, and gone back to his stool, and again crushed himself, Master Adolphus Tetterby, who had by this time unwound his torso out of a prismatic comforter, apparently interminable, requested the same favour. Johnny having again complied, and again gone back to his stool, and again crushed himself, Mr. Tetterby, struck by a sudden thought, preferred the same claim on his own paternal part. The satisfaction of this third desire, completely exhausted the sacrifice, who had hardly breath enough left to get back to his stool, crush himself again, and pant at his relations.

'Whatever you do, Johnny,' said Mrs. Tetterby, shaking her head, 'take care of her, or never look your mother in the face again.'

'Nor your brother,' said Adolphus.

'Nor your father, Johnny,' added Mr. Tetterby.

Johnny, much affected by this conditional renunciation of him, looked down at Moloch's eyes to see that they were all right, so far, and skilfully patted her back (which was uppermost), and rocked her with his foot.

'Are you wet, 'Dolphus, my boy?' said his father. 'Come and take my chair, and dry yourself.'

'No, father, thankee,' said Adolphus, smoothing himself

down with his hands. 'I an't very wet, I don't think. Does my face shine much, father?'

'Well, it *does* look waxy, my boy,' returned Mr. Tetterby.

'It's the weather, father,' said Adolphus, polishing his cheeks on the worn sleeve of his jacket. 'What with rain, and sleet, and wind, and snow, and fog, my face gets quite brought out into a rash sometimes. And shines, it does – oh, don't it, though!'

Master Adolphus was also in the newspaper line of life, being employed, by a more thriving firm than his father and Co., to vend newspapers at a railway station, where his chubby little person, like a shabbily-disguised Cupid, and his shrill little voice (he was not much more than ten years old), were as well known as the hoarse panting of the locomotives running in and out. His juvenility might have been at some loss for a harmless outlet, in this early application to traffic, but for a fortunate discovery he made of a means of entertaining himself, and of dividing the long day into stages of interest, without neglecting business. This ingenious invention, remarkable, like many great discoveries, for its simplicity, consisted in varying the first vowel in the word 'paper,' and substituting in its stead, at different periods of the day, all the other vowels in grammatical succession. Thus, before daylight in the winter-time, he went to and fro, in his little oil-skin cap and cape, and his big comforter, piercing the heavy air with his cry of 'Morn-ing Pa-per!' which, about an hour before noon, changed to 'Morn-ing Pepper!' which, at about two, changed to 'Morn-ing Pipper!' which, in a couple of hours, changed to 'Morn-ing Pop-per!' and so declined with the sun into 'Eve-ning Pup-per!' to the great relief and comfort of this young gentleman's spirits.

Mrs. Tetterby, his lady mother, who had been sitting with her bonnet and shawl thrown back, as aforesaid, thoughtfully turning her wedding-ring round and round upon her finger, now rose, and, divesting herself of her out-of-door attire, began to lay the cloth for supper.

'Ah, dear me, dear me, dear me!' said Mrs. Tetterby. 'That's the way the world goes!'

'Which is the way the world goes, my dear?' asked Mr. Tetterby, looking around.

'Oh, nothing!' said Mrs. Tetterby.

Mr. Tetterby elevated his eyebrows, folded his newspaper afresh, and carried his eyes up it, and down it, and across it, but was wandering in his attention, and not reading it.

Mrs. Tetterby, at the same time, laid the cloth, but rather as if she were punishing the table than preparing the family supper; hitting it unnecessarily hard with the knives and forks, slapping it with the plates, dinting it with the salt-cellar, and coming heavily down upon it with the loaf.

'Ah, dear me, dear me, dear me!' said Mrs. Tetterby. 'That's the way the world goes!'

'My duck,' returned her husband, looking round again, 'you said that before. Which is the way the world goes?'

'Oh, nothing!' said Mrs. Tetterby.

'Sophia!' remonstrated her husband, 'you said *that* before, too.'

'Well, I'll say it again if you like,' returned Mrs. Tetterby. 'Oh, nothing – there! And again if you like. Oh, nothing – there! And again if you like. Oh, nothing – now then!'

Mr. Tetterby brought his eye to bear upon the partner of his bosom, and said, in mild astonishment: 'My little woman what has put you out?'

'I'm sure *I* don't know,' she retorted. 'Don't ask me. Who said I was put out at all? *I* never did.'

Mr. Tetterby gave up the perusal of his newspaper as a bad job, and, taking a slow walk across the room, with his hands behind him, and his shoulders raised – his gait according perfectly with the resignation of his manner – addressed himself to his two eldest offspring.

'Your supper will be ready in a minute, 'Dolphus,' said Mr. Tetterby. 'Your mother has been out in the wet, to the cook's shop, to buy it. It was very good of your mother so to do. *You* shall get some supper too, very soon, Johnny. Your mother's pleased with you, my man, for being so attentive to your precious sister.'

Mrs. Tetterby, without any remark, but with a decided subsidence of her animosity towards the table, finished her preparations, and took from her ample basket a substantial slab of hot pease-pudding wrapped in paper, and a basin covered with a saucer, which, on being uncovered, sent forth an odour so agreeable, that the three pair of eyes in the two beds opened wide, and fixed themselves upon the banquet. Mr. Tetterby, without regarding this tacit invitation to be seated, stood repeating slowly, 'Yes, yes, your supper will be ready in a minute, 'Dolphus – your mother went out in the wet, to the cook's shop, to buy it. It was very good of your mother so to do' – until Mrs. Tetterby, who had been exhibiting sundry tokens of contrition behind him, caught him round the neck, and wept.

'Oh, 'Dolphus!' said Mrs. Tetterby, 'how could I go and behave so?'

This reconciliation affected Adolphus the younger and Johnny to that degree, that they both, as with one accord, raised a dismal cry, which had the effect of immediately shutting up the round eyes in the beds, and utterly routing the two remaining little Tetterbys, just then stealing in from the adjoining closet to see what was going on in the eating way.

'I am sure, 'Dolphus,' sobbed Mrs. Tetterby, 'coming home, I had no more idea than a child unborn —'

Mr. Tetterby seemed to dislike this figure of speech, and observed, 'Say than the baby, my dear.'

'— Had no more idea than the baby,' said Mrs. Tetterby. 'Johnny, don't look at me, but look at her, or she'll fall out of your lap and be killed, and then you'll die in agonies of a broken heart, and serve you right. No more idea, I hadn't than that darling, of being cross when I came home; but somehow 'Dolphus —' Mrs. Tetterby paused, and again turned her wedding-ring round and round upon her finger.

'I see!' said Mr. Tetterby. 'I understand! My little woman was put out. Hard times, and hard weather, and hard work, make it trying now and then. I see, bless your soul! No wonder! 'Dolf, my man,' continued Mr. Tetterby, exploring the basin with a fork, 'here's your mother been and bought, at the cook's shop, besides pease-pudding, a whole knuckle of a lovely roast leg of pork, with lots of crackling left upon it, and with seasoning, gravy, and mustard quite unlimited. Hand in your plate, my boy, and begin while it's simmering.'

Master Adolphus, needing no second summons, received his portion with eyes rendered moist by appetite, and, with-drawing to his particular stool, fell upon his supper tooth and nail. Johnny was not forgotten, but received his rations on bread, lest he should, in a flush of gravy, trickle any on the baby. He was required, for similar reasons, to keep his pudding, when not on active service, in his pocket.

There might have been more pork on the knuckle-bone – which knuckle-bone the carver at the cook's shop had assuredly not forgotten in carving for previous customers – but there was no stint of seasoning, and that is an accessory dreamily suggesting pork, and pleasantly cheating the sense of taste. The pease-pudding, too, the gravy and mustard, like the Eastern rose in respect of the nightingale, if they were not absolutely pork, had lived near it; so, upon the whole, there was the flavour of a middle-sized pig. It was irresistible to the Tetterbys in bed, who, though professing to slumber peacefully, crawled out when unseen by their parents, and silently appealed to their brothers for any gastronomic token of fraternal affection. They, not hard of heart, presenting scraps in return, it resulted that a party of light skirmishers in nightgowns were careering about the parlour all through supper, which harassed Mr. Tetterby exceedingly, and once or twice imposed upon him the necessity of a charge, before which these guerrilla troops retired in all directions, and in great confusion.

Mrs. Tetterby did not enjoy her supper. There seemed to be something on Mrs. Tetterby's mind. At one time she laughed without reason, and at another time she cried without reason, and at last she laughed and cried together in a manner so very unreasonable that her husband was confounded.

'My little woman,' said Mr. Tetterby, 'if the world goes that way, it appears to go the wrong way, and to choke you.'

'Give me a drop of water,' said Mrs. Tetterby, struggling with herself, 'and don't speak to me for the present, or take any notice of it. Don't do it!'

Mr. Tetterby, having administered the water, turned suddenly on the unlucky Johnny (who was full of sympathy), and demanded why he was wallowing there in gluttony and idleness, instead of coming forward with the baby, that the sight of her might revive his mother. Johnny immediately approached, borne down by its weight; but Mrs. Tetterby holding out her hand to signify that she was not in a condition to bear that trying appeal to her feelings, he was interdicted from advancing another inch, on pain of perpetual hatred from all his dearest connections; and accordingly retired to his stool again, and crushed himself as before.

After a pause Mrs. Tetterby said she was better now, and began to laugh.

'My little woman,' said her husband dubiously, 'are you quite sure you're better? Or are you, Sophia, about to break out in a fresh direction?'

'No, 'Dolphus, no,' replied his wife. 'I'm quite myself.' With that, settling her hair, and pressing the palms of her hands upon her eyes, she laughed again.

'What a wicked fool I was to think so for a moment!' said Mrs. Tetterby. 'Come nearer, 'Dolphus, and let me ease my mind, and tell you what I mean. Let me tell you all about it.'

Mr. Tetterby bringing his chair closer, Mrs. Tetterby laughed again, gave him a hug, and wiped her eyes.

'You know, 'Dolphus, my dear,' said Mrs. Tetterby, 'that when I was single, I might have given myself away in several directions. At one time, four after me at once; two of them were sons of Mars.'

'We're all sons of Ma's, my dear,' said Mr. Tetterby, 'jointly with Pa's.'

'I don't mean that,' replied his wife; 'I mean soldiers – sergeants.'

'Oh!' said Mr. Tetterby.

'Well, 'Dolphus, I'm sure I never think of such things now, to regret them; and I'm sure I've got as good a husband, and would do as much to prove that I was fond of him, as —'

'As any little woman in the world,' said Mr. Tetterby. 'Very good. *Very* good.'

If Mr. Tetterby had been ten feet high, he could not have expressed a gentler consideration for Mrs. Tetterby's fairy-like stature; and, if Mrs. Tetterby had been two feet high she could not have felt it more appropriately her due.

'But you see, 'Dolphus,' said Mrs. Tetterby, 'this being Christmas-time, when all people who can, make holiday, and when all people who have got money like to spend some, I did, somehow, get a little out of sorts when I was in the streets just now. There were so many things to be sold – such delicious things to eat, such fine things to look at, such delightful things to have – and there was so much calculating and calculating necessary, before I durst lay out a sixpence for the commonest thing; and the basket was so large, and wanted so much in it; and my stock of money was so small, and would go such a little way — You hate me, don't you, 'Dolphus?'

'Not quite,' said Mr. Tetterby, 'as yet.'

'Well! I'll tell you the whole truth' pursued his wife penitently, 'and then perhaps you will. I felt all this so much, when I was trudging about in the cold, and when I saw a lot of other calculating faces and large baskets trudging about too, that I began to think whether I mightn't have done better, and been happier, if I hadn't —' The wedding-ring went round again, and Mrs. Tetterby shook her downcast head as she turned it.

'I see,' said her husband quietly; 'if you hadn't married at all, or if you had married somebody else?'

'Yes,' sobbed Mrs. Tetterby. 'That's really what I thought. Do you hate me now, 'Dolphus?'

'Why, no,' said Mr. Tetterby, 'I don't find that I do as yet.'

Mrs Tetterby gave him a thankful kiss, and went on.

'I begin to hope you won't, now, 'Dolphus, though I am afraid I haven't told you the worst. I can't think what came over me. I don't know whether I was ill, or mad, or what I was, but I couldn't call up anything that seemed to bind us to each other, or to reconcile me to my fortune. All the pleasures and enjoyments we had ever had – *they* seemed so poor and insignificant, I hated them. I could have trodden on them. And I could think of nothing else except our being poor, and the number of mouths there were at home.'

'Well, well, my dear,' said Mr. Tetterby, shaking her hand encouragingly, 'that's truth, after all. We *are* poor, and there *are* a number of mouths at home here.'

'Ah! but, Dolf, Dolf!' cried his wife, laying her hands upon his neck, 'my good, kind, patient fellow, when I had been at home a very little while – how different! Oh, Dolf dear, how different it was! I felt as if there was a rush of recollection on me, all at once, that softened my hard heart, and filled it up till it was bursting. All our struggles for a livelihood, all our cares

and wants since we have been married, all the times of
sickness, all the hours of watching, we have ever had, by one
another, or by the children, seemed to speak to me, and say
that they had made us one, and that I never might have been,
or could have been, or would have been, any other than the
wife and mother I am. Then the cheap enjoyments that I could
have trodden on so cruelly, got to be so precious to me – oh,
so priceless and dear! – that I couldn't bear to think how much
I had wronged them; and I said, and say again a hundred
times, how could I ever behave so, 'Dolphus? how could I
ever have the heart to do it?'

The good woman, quite carried away by her honest tenderness and remorse, was weeping with all her heart, when she
started up with a scream, and ran behind her husband. Her cry
was so terrified, that the children started from their sleep and
from their beds, and clung about her. Nor did her gaze belie
her voice as she pointed to a pale man in a black cloak who had
come into the room.

'Look at that man! Look there! What does he want?'

'My dear,' returned her husband, 'I'll ask him if you'll let
me go. What's the matter? How you shake!'

'I saw him in the street when I was out just now. He looked
at me, and stood near me. I am afraid of him.'

'Afraid of him! Why?'

'I don't know why – I – stop! husband!' for he was going
towards the stranger.

She had one hand pressed upon her forehead, and one upon
her breast; and there was a peculiar fluttering all over her, and
a hurried unsteady motion of her eyes, as if she had lost
something.

'Are you ill, my dear?'

'What is it that is going from me again?' she muttered in a
low voice. 'What *is* this that is going away?'

Then she abruptly answered: 'Ill? No, I am quite well,' and
stood looking vacantly at the floor.

Her husband, who had not been altogether free from the
infection of her fear at first, and whom the present strangeness
of her manner did not tend to reassure, addressed himself to
the pale visitor in the black cloak, who stood still, and whose
eyes were bent upon the ground.

'What may be your pleasure, sir,' he asked, 'with us?'

'I fear that my coming in unperceived,' returned the visitor, 'has alarmed you; but you were talking, and did not hear me.'

'My little woman says – perhaps you heard her say it,' returned Mr. Tetterby, 'that it's not the first time you have alarmed her tonight.'

'I am sorry for it. I remember to have observed her, for a few moments only, in the street. I had no intention of frightening her.'

As he raised his eyes in speaking, she raised hers. It was extraordinary to see what dread she had of him, and with what dread he observed it – and yet how narrowly and closely.

'My name,' he said, 'is Redlaw. I come from the old College hard by. A young gentleman, who is a student there, lodges in your house, does he not?'

'Mr Denham?' said Tetterby.

'Yes.'

It was a natural action, and so slight as to be hardly noticeable; but the little man, before speaking again, passed his hand across his forehead, and looked quickly round the room, as though he were sensible of some change in its atmosphere. The Chemist, instantly transferring to him the look of dread he had directed towards the wife, stepped back, and his face turned paler.

'The gentleman's room,' said Tetterby, 'is upstairs, sir. There's a more convenient private entrance; but, as you have come in here, it will save your going out into the cold, if you'll take this little staircase,' showing one communicating directly with the parlour, 'and go up to him that way, if you wish to see him.'

'Yes, I wish to see him,' said the Chemist. 'Can you spare a light?'

The watchfulness of his haggard look, and the inexplicable distrust that darkened it, seemed to trouble Mr. Tetterby. He paused; and, looking fixedly at him in return, stood for a minute or so, like a man stupefied or fascinated.

At length he said, 'I'll light you, sir, if you'll follow me.'

'No,' replied the Chemist, 'I don't wish to be attended, or announced to him. He does not expect me. I would rather go alone. Please to give me the light, if you can spare it, and I'll find the way.'

In the quickness of his expression of this desire, and in taking the candle from the newsman, he touched him on the breast. Withdrawing his hand hastily, almost as though he had wounded him by accident (for he did not know in what part of himself his new power resided, or how it was communicated, or how the manner of its reception varied in different persons), he turned and ascended the stair.

But, when he reached the top, he stopped and looked down. The wife was standing in the same place, twisting her ring round and round upon her finger. The husband, with his head bent forward on his breast, was musing heavily and sullenly. The children, still clustering about the mother, gazed timidly after the visitor, and nestled together when they saw him looking down.

'Come!' said the father roughly. 'There's enough of this. Get to bed here!'

'The place is inconvenient and small enough,' the mother added, 'without you. Get to bed!'

The whole brood, scared and sad, crept away: little Johnny and the baby lagging last. The mother glancing contemptuously round the sordid room, and tossing from her the fragments of her meal, stopped on the threshold of her task of clearing the table, and sat down, pondering idly and dejectedly. The father betook himself to the chimney-corner, and, impatiently raking the small fire together, bent over it as if he would monopolise it all. They did not interchange a word.

The Chemist, paler than before, stole upward like a thief; looking back upon the change below, and dreading equally to go on or return.

'What have I done?' he said confusedly. 'What am I going to do?'

'To be the benefactor of mankind,' he thought he heard a voice reply.

He looked round, but there was nothing there; and a passage now shutting out the little parlour from his view, he went on, directing his eyes before him at the way he went.

'It is only since last night,' he muttered gloomily, 'that I have remained shut up, and yet all things are strange to me. I am strange to myself. I am here as in a dream. What interest have I in this place, or in any place that I can bring to my remembrance? My mind is going blind!'

There was a door before him, and he knocked at it. Being invited, by a voice within, to enter, he complied.

'Is that my kind nurse?' said the voice. 'But I need not ask her. There was no one else to come here.'

It spoke cheerfully, though in a languid tone, and attracted his attention to a young man lying on a couch, drawn before the chimney-piece, with the back towards the door. A meagre, scanty stove, pinched and hollowed like a sick man's cheeks, and bricked into the centre of a hearth that it could scarcely warm, contained the fire, to which his face was turned. Being so near the windy housetop, it wasted quickly, and with a busy sound, and the burning ashes dropped down fast.

'They chink when they shoot out here,' said the student, smiling; 'so, according to the gossips, they are not coffins, but purses. I shall be well and rich yet, some day, if it please God, and shall live, perhaps, to love a daughter Milly, in remembrance of the kindest nature and the gentlest heart in the world.'

He put up his hand as if expecting her to take it, but, being weakened, he lay still, with his face resting on his other hand, and did not turn round.

The Chemist glanced about the room; at the student's books and papers, piled upon a table in a corner, where they, and his extinguished reading-lamp, now prohibited and put away, told of the attentive hours that had gone before this illness, and perhaps caused it; at such signs of his old health and freedom as the out-of-door attire that hung idle on the wall; at those remembrances of other and less solitary scenes, the little miniatures upon the chimney-piece, and the drawing of home; at that token of his emulation, perhaps, in some sort, of his personal attachment, too, the framed engraving of himself, the looker-on. The time had been, only yesterday, when not one of these objects, in its remotest association of interest with the living figure before him, would have been lost on Redlaw. Now, they were but objects; or, if any gleam of such connection shot upon him, it perplexed, and not enlightened him, as he stood looking round with a dull wonder.

The student, recalling the thin hand which had remained so

long untouched, raised himself on the couch, and turned his head.

'Mr Redlaw!' he exclaimed, and started up.

Redlaw put out his arm.

'Don't come near to me. I will sit here. Remain you where you are!'

He sat down on a chair near the door, and, having glanced at the young man standing leaning with his hand upon the couch, spoke with his eyes averted towards the ground.

'I heard, by an accident, by what accident is no matter, that one of my class was ill and solitary. I received no other description of him than that he lived in this street. Beginning my inquiries at the first house in it, I have found him.

'I have been ill, sir,' returned the student, not merely with a modest hesitation, but with a kind of awe of him, 'but am greatly better. An attack of fever – of the brain, I believe – has weakened me, but I am much better. I cannot say I have been solitary in my illness, or I should forget the ministering that has been near me.'

'You are speaking of the keeper's wife?' said Redlaw.

'Yes.' The student bent his head, as if he rendered her some silent homage.

The Chemist, in whom there was a cold, monotonous apathy, which rendered him more like a marble image on the tomb of the man who had started from his dinner yesterday at the first mention of this student's case, than the breathing man himself, glanced again at the student leaning with his hand upon the couch, and looked upon the ground, and in the air, as if for light for his blinded mind.

'I remembered your name,' he said, 'when it was mentioned to me downstairs just now; and I recollect your face. We have held but very little personal communication together?'

'Very little.'

'You have retired and withdrawn from me, more than any of the rest, I think?'

The student signified assent.

'And why?' said the Chemist; not with the least expression of interest, but with a moody, wayward kind of curiosity. 'Why? How comes it that you have sought to keep especially from me the knowledge of your remaining here, at this season, when all the rest have dispersed, and of your being ill? I want to know why this is?'

The young man, who had heard him with increasing agitation, raised his downcast eyes to his face, and, clasping his hands together, cried with sudden earnestness, and with trembling lips:

'Mr. Redlaw! You have discovered me. You know my secret!'

'Secret?' said the Chemist harshly. '*I* know?'

'Yes! Your manner, so different from the interest and sympathy which endear you to so many hearts, your altered voice, the constraint there is in everything you say, and in your looks,' replied the student, 'warn me that you know me. That you would conceal it, even now, is but a proof to me (God knows I need none!) of your natural kindness, and of the bar there is between us.'

A vacant and contemptuous laugh was all his answer.

'But Mr. Redlaw,' said the student, 'as a just man, and a good man, think how innocent I am, except in name and descent, of participation in any wrong inflicted on you, or in any sorrow you have borne.'

'Sorrow!' said Redlaw, laughing. 'Wrong! What are those to me?'

'For Heaven's sake,' entreated the shrinking student, 'do not let the mere interchange of a few words with me change you like this sir! Let me pass again from your knowledge and notice. Let me occupy my old reserved and distant place among those whom you instruct. Know me only by the name I have assumed, and not by that of Langford —'

'Langford!' exclaimed the other.

He clasped his head with both his hands, and for a moment turned upon the young man his own intelligent and thought-ful face. But the light passed from it like the sunbeam of an instant, and it clouded as before.

'The name my mother bears, sir,' faltered the young man, 'the name she took, when she might, perhaps, have taken one more honoured. Mr. Redlaw,' hesitating, 'I believe I know that history. Where my infomation halts, my guesses at what is wanting may supply something not remote from the truth. I am the child of a marriage that has not proved itself a

well-assorted or a happy one. From infancy I have heard you
spoken of with honour and respect – with something that was
almost reverence. I have heard of such devotion, of such
fortitude and tenderness, of such rising up against the obstacles which press men down, that my fancy, since I learnt my
little lesson from my mother, has shed a lustre on your name.
At last, a poor student myself, from whom could I learn but
you?'

Redlaw, unmoved, unchanged, and looking at him with a
staring frown, answered by no word or sign.

'I cannot say,' pursued the other, 'I should try in vain to say,
how much it has impressed me, and affected me, to find the
gracious traces of the past, in that certain power of winning
gratitude and confidence which is associated among us students (among the humblest of us most) with Mr. Redlaw's
generous name. Our ages and positions are so different, sir,
and I am so accustomed to regard you from a distance, that I
wonder at my own presumption when I touch, however
lightly, on that theme. But to one who – I may say, who felt
no common interest in my mother once – it may be something
to hear, now that is all past, with what indescribable feelings
of affection I have, in my obscurity, regarded him; with what
pain and reluctance I have kept aloof from his encouragement,
when a word of it would have made me rich; yet how I have
felt it fit that I should hold my course, content to know him,
and to be unknown. Mr. Redlaw,' said the student faintly,
'what I would have said, I have said ill, for my strength is
strange to me as yet; but, for anything unworthy in this fraud
of mine, forgive me, and for all the rest forget me!'

The staring frown remained on Redlaw's face, and yielded
to no other expression until the student, with these words,
advanced towards him, as if to touch his hand, when he drew
back and cried to him:

'Don't come nearer to me!'

The young man stopped, shocked by the eagerness of his
recoil, and by the sternness of his repulsion; and he passed his
hand thoughtfully across his forehead.

'The past is past,' said the Chemist. 'It dies like the brutes.
Who talks to me of its traces in my life? He raves or lies! What
have I to do with your distempered dreams? If you want

money, here it is. I came to offer it; and that is all I came for.
There can be nothing else that brings me here,' he muttered,
holding his head again with both his hands. 'There *can* be
nothing else, and yet —'

He had tossed his purse upon the table. As he fell into this
dim cogitation with himself, the student took it up, and held it
out to him.

'Take it back, sir,' he said proudly, though not angrily. 'I
wish you could take from me, with it, the remembrance of
your words and offer.'

'You do?' he retorted, with a wild light in his eyes. 'You
do?'

'I do!'

The Chemist went close to him for the first time, and took
the purse, and turned him by the arm, and looked him in the
face.

'There is sorrow and trouble in sickness, is there not?' he
demanded with a laugh.

The wondering student answered, 'Yes.'

'In its unrest, in its anxiety, in its suspense, in all its train of
physical and mental miseries?' said the Chemist with a wild,
unearthly exultation. 'All best forgotten, are they not?'

The student did not answer, but again passed his hand
confusedly across his forehead. Redlaw still held him by the
sleeve, when Milly's voice was heard outside.

'I can see very well now,' she said, 'thank you, Dolf. Don't
cry, dear. Father and mother will be comfortable again
tomorrow, and home will be comfortable too. A gentleman
with him, is there?'

Redlaw released his hold as he listened.

'I have feared, from the first moment,' he murmured to
himself, 'to meet her. There is a steady quality of goodness in
her that I dread to influence. I may be the murderer of what is
tenderest and best within her bosom.'

She was knocking the door.

'Shall I dismiss it as an idle foreboding, or still avoid her?' he
muttered, looking uneasily around.

She was knocking at the door again.

'Of all the visitors who could come here,' he said in a
hoarse, alarmed voice, turning to his companion, 'this is the

one I should desire most to avoid. Hide me!'

The student opened a frail door in the wall, communicating, where the garret roof began to slope towards the floor, with a small inner room. Redlaw passed in hastily, and shut it after him.

The student then resumed his place upon the couch, and called to her to enter.

'Dear Mr. Edmund,' said Milly, looking round, 'they told me there was a gentleman here.'

'There is no one here but I.'

'There has been someone?'

'Yes, yes, there has been someone.'

She put her little basket on the table, and went up to the back of the couch, as if to take the extended hand – but it was not there. A little surprised, in her quiet way, she leaned over to look at his face, and gently touching him on the brow.

'Are you quite as well tonight? Your head is not so cool as in the afternoon.'

'Tut!' said the student petulantly, 'very little ails me.'

A little more surprise, but no reproach, was expressed in her face, as she withdrew to the other side of the table, and took a small packet of needlework from her basket. But she laid it down again, on second thoughts, and going noiselessly about the room, set everything exactly in its place, and in the neatest order; even to the cushions on the couch, which she touched with so light a hand, that he hardly seemed to know it, as he lay looking at the fire. When all this was done, and she had swept the hearth, she sat down, in her modest little bonnet, to her work, and was quietly busy on it directly.

'It's the new muslin curtain for the window, Mr. Edmund,' said Milly, stitching away as she talked. 'It will look very clean and nice, though it costs very little, and will save your eyes, too, from the light. My William says the room should not be too light just now, when you are recovering so well, or the glare might make you giddy.'

He said nothing; but there was something so fretful and impatient in his change of position, that her quick fingers stopped, and she looked at him anxiously.

'The pillows are not comfortable,' she said, laying down her work and rising. 'I will soon put them right.'

'They were very well,' he answered. 'Leave them alone, pray. You make so much of everything.'

He raised his head to say this, and looked at her so thanklessly, that, after he had thrown himself down again, she stood timidly pausing. However, she resumed her seat, and her needle, without having directed even a murmuring look towards him, and was soon as busy as before.

'I have been thinking, Mr. Edmund, that *you* have been often thinking of late, when I have been sitting by, how true the saying is, that adversity is a good teacher. Health will be more precious to you, after this illness, than it has ever been. And years hence, when this time of year comes round, and you remember the days when you lay here sick, alone, that the knowledge of your illness might not afflict those who are dearest to you, your home will be doubly dear and doubly blessed. Now, isn't that a good, true thing?''

She was too intent upon her work, and too earnest in what she said, and too composed and quiet altogether, to be on the watch for any look he might direct towards her in reply; so the shaft of his ungrateful glance fell harmless, and did not wound her.

'Ah!' said Milly, with her pretty head inclining thoughtfully on one side, as she looked down, following her busy fingers with her eyes. 'Even on me – and I am very different from you, Mr. Edmund, for I have no learning, and don't know how to think properly – this view of such things has made a great impression since you have been lying ill. When I have seen you so touched by the kindness and attention of the poor people down-stairs, I have felt that you thought even that experience some repayment for the loss of health, and I have read in your face, as plain as if it was a book, that but for some trouble and sorrow we should never know half the good there is about us.'

His getting up from the couch interrupted her, or she was going on to say more.

'We needn't magnify the merit, Mrs. William,' he rejoined slightingly. 'The people downstairs will be paid in good time, I dare say, for any little extra service they may have rendered me; and perhaps they anticipate no less. I am much obliged to you, too.'

Her fingers stopped, and she looked at him.

'I can't be made to feel the more obliged by your exaggerating the case,' he said. 'I am sensible that you have been interested in me, and I say I am much obliged to you. What more would you have?'

Her work fell on her lap, as she still looked at him walking to and fro with an intolerant air, and stopping now and then.

'I say again, I am much obliged to you. Why weaken my sense of what is your due in obligation, by preferring enormous claims upon me? Trouble, sorrow, affliction, adversity! One might suppose I had been dying a score of deaths here.'

'Do you believe, Mr. Edmund,' she asked, rising and going nearer to him, 'that I spoke of the poor people of the house with any reference to myself? To me?' laying her hand upon her bosom with a simple and innocent smile of astonishment.

'Oh! I think nothing about it, my good creature,' he returned. 'I have had an indisposition, which your solicitude – observe! I say solicitude – makes a great deal more of than it merits; and it's over, and we can't perpetuate it.'

He coldly took a book, and sat down at the table.

She watched him for a little while, until her smile was quite gone, and then, returning to where her basket was, said gently:

'Mr. Edmund, would you rather be alone?'

'There is no reason why I should detain you here,' he replied.

'Except —' said Milly, hesitating, and showing her work.

'Oh! the curtain,' he answered with a supercilious laugh. 'That's not worth staying for.'

She made up the little packet again, and put it in her basket. Then, standing before him with such an air of patient entreaty that he could not choose but look at her, she said: 'If you should want me, I will come back willingly. When you did want me I was quite happy to come; there was no merit in it. I think you must be afraid that, now you are getting well, I may be troublesome to you; but I should not have been, indeed, I should have come no longer than your weakness and confinement lasted. You owe me nothing; but it is right that you should deal as justly by me as if I was a lady – even the very lady that you love; and, if you suspect me of meanly making

much of the little I have tried to do to comfort your
sick-room, you do yourself more wrong than ever you can do
me. That is why I am sorry. That is why I am very sorry.'

If she had been as passionate as she was quiet, as indignant as
she was calm, as angry in her look as she was gentle, as loud of
tone as she was low and clear, she might have left no sense of
her departure in the room, compared with that which fell
upon the lonely student when she went away.

He was gazing drearily upon the place where she had been,
when Redlaw came out of his concealment, and came to the
door.

'When sickness lays its hand on you again,' he said looking
fiercely back at him – 'may it be soon! – die here! Rot here!'

'What have you done?' returned the other catching at his
cloak. 'What change have you wrought in me? What curse
have you brought upon me? Give me back myself!'

'Give me back *myself*!' exclaimed Redlaw like a madman.
'I am infected. I am infectious! I am charged with poison for
my own mind, and the minds of all mankind. Where I
felt interest, compassion, sympathy, I am turning into
stone. Selfishness and ingratitude spring up in my blighting
footsteps. I am only so much less base than the wretches
whom I make so, that in the moment of their transforma-
tion I can hate them.'

As he spoke – the young man still holding to his cloak – he
cast him off, and struck him; then wildly hurried out into the
night air where the wind was blowing, the snow falling, the
cloud-drift sweeping on, the moon dimly shining; and where,
blowing in the wind, falling with the snow, drifting with the
clouds, shining in the moonlight, and heavily looming in the
darkness, were the Phantom's words, 'The gift that I have
given, you shall give again, go where you will!'

Whither he went he neither knew nor cared, so that he
avoided company. The change he felt within him made the
busy streets a desert, and himself a desert, and the multitude
around him, in their manifold endurances and ways of life, a
mighty waste of sand, which the winds tossed into unintelligible heaps, and made a ruinous confusion of. Those traces in his
breast which the Phantom had told him would 'die out soon'
were not, as yet, so far upon their way to death, but that he

understood enough of what he was, and what he made of
others, to desire to be alone.

This put it in his mind – he suddenly bethought himself, as
he was going along, of the boy who had rushed into his room.
And then he recollected that, of those with whom he had
communicated since the Phantom's disappearance, that boy
alone had shown no sign of being changed.

Monstrous and odious as the wild thing was to him, he
determined to seek it out, and prove if this were really so; and
also to seek it with another intention, which came into his
thoughts at the same time.

So, resolving with some difficulty where he was, he
directed his steps back to the old College, and to that part of it
where the general porch was, and where, alone, the pavement
was worn by the tread of students' feet.

The keeper's house stood just within the iron gates, forming
a part of the chief quadrangle. There was a little cloister
outside, and from that sheltered place he knew he could look
in at the window of their ordinary room, and see who was
within. The iron gates were shut, but his hand was familir
with the fastening, and, drawing it back by thrusting in his
wrist between the bars, he passed through softly, shut it again,
and crept up to the window, crumbling the thin crust of snow
with his feet.

The fire, to which he had directed the boy last night,
shining brightly through the glass, made an illuminated place
upon the ground. Instinctively avoiding this, and going round
it, he looked in at the window. At first he thought that there
was no one there, and that the blaze was reddening only the
old beams in the ceiling and the dark walls; but, peering in
more narrowly, he saw the object of his search coiled asleep
before it on the floor. He passed quickly to the door, opened
it, and went in.

The creature lay in such a fiery heat, that, as the Chemist
stooped to rouse him, it scorched his head. So soon as he was
touched, the boy, not half awake, clutched his rags together
with the instinct of flight upon him, half rolled and half ran
into a distant corner of the room, where, heaped upon the
ground, he stuck his foot out to defend himself.

'Get up!' said the Chemist. 'You have not forgotten me?'

'You let me alone!' returned the boy. 'This is the woman's house – not yours.'

The Chemist's steady eye controlled him somewhat, or inspired him with enough submission to be raised upon his feet, and looked at.

'Who washed them, and put those bandages where they were bruised and cracked?' asked the Chemist, pointing to their altered state.

'The woman did.'

'And is it she who has made you cleaner in the face, too?'

'Yes, the woman.'

Redlaw asked these questions to attract his eyes towards himself, and, with the same intent, now held him by the chin, and threw his wild hair back, though he loathed to touch him. The boy watched his eyes keenly, as if he thought it needful to his own defence, not knowing what he might do next; and Redlaw could see well that no change came over him.

'Where are they?' he inquired.

'The woman's out.'

'I know she is. Where is the old man with the white hair, and his son?'

'The woman's husband, d'ye mean?' inquired the boy.

'Ay. Where are those two?'

'Out. Something's the matter somewhere. They were fetched out in a hurry, and told me to stop here.'

'Come with me,' said the Chemist, 'and I'll give you money.'

'Come where? and how much will you give?'

'I'll give you more shillings than you ever saw, and bring you back soon. Do you know your way to where you came from?'

'You let me go,' returned the boy, suddenly twisting out of his grasp. 'I'm not a-going to take you there. Let me be, or I'll heave some fire at you!'

He was down before it, and ready, and with his savage little hand, to pluck the burning coals out.

What the Chemist had felt, in observing the effect of his charmed influence stealing over those with whom he came in contact, was not nearly equal to the cold vague terror with which he saw this baby-monster put in at defiance. It chilled his blood to look on the immovable, impenetrable thing, in the likeness of a child, with its sharp malignant face turned up to his, and its almost infant hand ready at the bars.

'Listen, boy!' he said. 'You shall take me where you please, so that you take me where the peole are very miserable or very wicked. I want to do them good, and not to harm them. You shall have money, as I have told you, and I will bring you back. Get up! Come quickly!' He made a hasty step towards the door, afraid of her returning.

'Will you let me walk by myself, and never hold me, nor yet touch me?' said the boy, slowly withdrawing the hand with which he threatened, and beginning to get up.

'And let me go before, behind, or anyways I like?'

'I will!'

'Give me some money first, then, and I'll go.'

The Chemist laid a few shillings, one by one, in his extended hand. To count them was beyond the boy's knowledge, but he said, 'one,' every time, and avariciously looked at each as it was given, and at the donor. He had nowhere to put them, out of his hand, but in his mouth; and he put them there.

Redlaw then wrote with his pencil, on a leaf of his pocket-book, that the boy was with him; and, laying it on the table, signed to him to follow. Keeping his rags together, as usual, the boy complied, and went out with his bare head and his naked feet into the winter night.

Preferring not to depart by the iron gate by which he had entered, where they were in danger of meeting her whom he so anxiously avoided, the Chemist led the way, through some of those passages among which the boy had lost himself, and by that portion of the building where he lived, to a small door of which he had the key. When they got into the street, he stopped to ask his guide – who instantly retreated from him – if he knew where they were.

The savage thing looked here and there, and at length, nodding his head, pointed in the direction he designed to take. Redlaw going on at once, he followed, somewhat less suspiciously; shifting his money from his mouth into his hand, and back again into his mouth, and stealthily rubbing it bright upon his shreds of dress, as he went along.

Three times, in their progress, they were side by side. Three times they stopped, being side by side. Three times the Chemist glanced down at his face, and shuddered as it forced upon him one reflection.

The first occasion was when they were crossing an old churchyard, and Redlaw stopped among the graves, utterly at a loss how to connect them with any tender, softening, or consolatory thought.

The second was when the breaking forth of the moon induced him to look up at the heavens, where he saw her in her glory, surrounded by a host of stars he still knew by the names and histories which human science has appended to them; but where he saw nothing else he had been wont to see, felt nothing he had been wont to feel, in looking up there on a bright night.

The third was when he stopped to listen to a plaintive strain of music, but could only hear a tune, made manifest to him by the dry mechanism of the instruments and his own ears, with no address to any mystery within him, without a whisper in it of the past, or of the future, powerless upon him as the sound of last year's running water, or the rushing of last year's wind.

At each of these three times he saw, with horror, that in spite of the vast intellectual distance between them, and their being unlike each other in all physical respects, the expression on the boy's face was the expression on his own.

They journeyed on for some time – now through such crowded places, that he often looked over his shoulder, thinking he had lost his guide, but generally finding him within his shadow on his other side; now by ways so quiet, that he could have counted his short, quick, naked footsteps coming on behind – until they arrived at a ruinous collection of houses, and the boy touched him and stopped.

'In there!' he said, pointing out one house where there were scattered lights in the windows, and a dim lantern in the doorway, with 'Lodgings for Travellers' painted on it.

Redlaw looked about him; from the houses, to the waste piece of ground on which the houses stood, or rather, did not altogether tumble down, unfenced, undrained, unlighted, and bordered by a sluggish ditch; from that, to the sloping line of arches, part of some neighbouring viaduct or bridge with which it was surrounded, and which lessened gradually towards them, until the last but one was a mere kennel for a dog, the last a plundered little heap of brick; from that, to the child, close to him, cowering and trembling with the cold, and limping on one little foot, while he coiled the other round his leg to warm it, yet staring at all these things with that frightful likeness of expression so apparent in his face, that Redlaw started from him.

'In there!' said the boy, pointing out the house again. 'I'll wait.'

'Will they let me in?' asked Redlaw.

'Say you're a doctor,' he answered with a nod. 'There's plenty ill here.'

Looking back on his way to the house-door, Redlaw saw him trail himself upon the dust, and crawl within the shelter of the smallest arch, as if he were a rat. He had no pity for the thing, but he was afraid of it; and when it looked out of its den at him, he hurried to the house as a retreat.

'Sorrow, wrong, and trouble,' said the Chemist, with a painful effort at some more distinct remembrance, 'at least haunt this place darkly. He can do no harm who brings forgetfulness of such things here!'

With these words he pushed the yielding door, and went in.

There was a woman sitting on the stairs, either asleep or forlorn, whose head was bent down on her hands and knees. As it was not easy to pass without treading on her, and as she was perfectly regardless of his near approach, he stopped, and touched her on the shoulder. Looking up, she showed him quite a young face, but one whose bloom and promise were all swept away, as if the haggard winter should unnaturally kill the spring.

With little or no show of concern on his account, she moved nearer to the wall to leave him a wider passage.

'What are you?' said Redlaw, pausing, with his hand upon the broken stair-rail.

'What do you think I am?' she answered, showing him her face again.

He looked upon the ruined temple of God, so lately made, so soon disfigured; and something, which was not compassion – for the springs in which a true compassion for such miseries has its rise were dried up in his breast – but which was nearer to it, for the moment, than any feeling that had lately struggled into the darkening, but not yet wholly darkened, night of his mind – mingled a touch of softness with his next words.

'I am come here to give relief, if I can,' he said. 'Are you thinking of any wrong?'

She frowned at him, and then laughed; and then her laugh prolonged itself into a shivering sigh, as she dropped her head again, and hid her fingers in her hair.

'Are you thinking of a wrong?' he asked once more.

'I am thinking of my life,' she said with a momentary look at him.

He had a perception that she was one of many, and that he saw the type of thousands when he saw her drooping at his feet.

'What are your parents?' he demanded.

'I had a good home once. My father was a gardener, far away into the country.'

'Is he dead?'

'He's dead to me. All such things are dead to me. You a gentleman, and not know that!' She raised her eyes again, and laughed at him.

'Girl!' said Redlaw sternly, 'before this death of all such things was brought about, was there no wrong done to you? In spite of all that you can do, does no remembrance of wrong cleave to you? Are there not times upon times when it is misery to you?'

So little of what was womanly was left in her appearance, that now, when she burst into tears, he stood amazed. But he was more amazed, and much disquieted, to note, in her awakened recollection of this wrong, the first trace of her old humanity and frozen tenderness appeared to show itself.

He drew a little off, and, in doing so, observed that her arms were black, her fact cut, and her bosom bruised.

'What brutal hand has hurt you so?' he asked.

'My own. I did it myself!' she answered quickly.

'It is impossible.'

'I'll swear I did! He didn't touch me. I did it to myself in a passion, and threw myself down here. He wasn't near me. He never laid a hand upon me!'

In the white determination of her face, confronting him with this untruth, he saw enough of the last perversion and distortion of good surviving in that miserable breast, to be stricken with remorse that he had ever come near here.

'Sorrow, wrong, and trouble!' he muttered, turning his fearful gaze away. 'All that connects her with the state from which she has fallen has those roots! In the name of God, let me go by!'

Afraid to look at her again, afraid to touch her, afraid to think of having sundered the last thread by which she held upon the mercy of Heaven, he gathered his cloak about him, and glided swiftly up the stairs.

Opposite to him, on the landing, was a door, which stood partly open, and which, as he ascended, a man with a candle in his hand came forward from within to shut. But this man, on seeing him, drew back, with much emotion in his manner, and, as if by a sudden impulse, mentioned his name aloud.

In the surprise of such a recognition there, he stopped, endeavouring to recollect the wan and startled face. He had no time to consider it, for, to his yet greater amazement, old Philip came out of the room, and took him by the hand.

'Mr Redlaw,' said the old man, 'this is like you, this is like you, sir! You have heard of it, and have come after us to render any help you can. Ah, too late, too late!'

Redlaw, with a bewildered look, submitted to be led into the room. A man lay there on a truckle-bed, and William Swidger stood at the bedside.

'Too late!' murmured the old man, looking wistfully into the Chemist's face; and the tears stole down his cheeks.

'That's what I say, father,' interposed his son in a low voice. 'That's where it is exactly. To keep as quiet as ever we can while he's dozing is the only thing to do. You're right, father!'

Redlaw paused at the bedside, and looked down on the figure that was stretched upon the mattress. It was that of a man who should have been in the vigour of his life, but on whom it was not likely that the sun would ever shine again. The vices of his forty or fifty years' career had so branded him, that, in comparison with their effects upon his face, the heavy hand of time upon the old man's face who watched him had been merciful and beautifying.

'Who is this?' asked the Chemist, looking round.

'My son George, Mr. Redlaw,' said the old man, wringing his hands. 'My eldest son, George, who was more his mother's pride than all the rest!'

Redlaw's eyes wandered from the old man's grey head, as he laid it down upon the bed, to the person who had recognised him, and who had kept aloof in the remotest corner of the room. He seemed to be about his own age; and, although he knew no such hopeless decayed and broken man as he appeared to be, there was something in the turn of his figure, as he stood with his back towards him, and now went out at the door, that made him pass his hand uneasily across his brow.

'William,' he said in a gloomy whisper, 'who is that man?'

'Why, you see, sir,' returned Mr. William, 'that's what I say myself. Why should a man ever go and gamble, and the like of that, and let himself down inch by inch till he can't let himself down any lower?'

'Has *he* done so?' asked Redlaw, glancing after him with the same uneasy action as before.

'Just exactly that, sir,' returned William Swidger, 'as I'm told. He knows a little about medicine, sir, it seems; and having been wayfaring towards London with my unhappy brother that you see here,' – Mr. William passed his coat-sleeve across his eyes – 'and being lodging upstairs for the night – what I say, you see, is, that strange companions come together here sometimes – he looked in to attend upon him, and came for us at his request. What a mournful spectacle, sir! But that's where it is. It's enough to kill my father!'

Redlaw looked up at these words, and, recalling where he was and with whom, and the spell he carried with him – which his surprise had obscured – retired a little, hurriedly, debating with himself whether to shun the house that moment, or remain.

Yielding to a certain sullen doggedness, which it seemed to be part of his condition to struggle with, he argued for remaining.

'Was it only yesterday,' he said, 'when I observed the

memory of this old man to be a tissue of sorrow and trouble, and shall I be afraid, tonight, to shake it? Are such remembrances as I can drive away so precious to this dying man, that I need fear for *him*? No, I'll stay here.'

But he stayed in fear and trembling none the less for these words; and, shrouded in his black cloak with his face turned from them, stood away from the bedside, listening to what they said, as if he felt himself a demon in the place.

'Father!' murmured the sick man, rallying a little from his stupor.

'My boy! My son George!' said old Philip.

'You spoke, just now, of my being mother's favourite long ago. It's a dreadful thing to think, now, of long ago!'

'No, no, no!' returned the old man. 'Think of it. Don't say it's dreadful. It's not dreadful to me, my son.'

'It cuts you to the heart, father.' For the old man's tears were falling on him.

'Yes, yes,' said Philip, 'so it does; but it does me good. It's a heavy sorrow to think of that time, but it does me good, George. Oh, think of it too, think of it too, and your heart will be softened more and more! Where's my son William? William, my boy, your mother loved him dearly to the last, and with her latest breath said, "Tell him I forgave him, blessed him, and prayed for him." Those were her words to me. I have never forgotten them, and I'm eighty-seven!'

'Father!' said the man upon the bed, 'I am dying, I know. I am so far gone, that I can hardly speak, even of what my mind most runs on. Is there any hope for me beyond this bed?'

'There is hope,' returned the old man, 'for all who are softened and penitent. There is hope for all such. Oh!' he exclaimed, clasping his hands and looking up, 'I was thankful, only yesterday, that I could remember this unhappy son when he was an innocent child. But what a comfort is it, now, to think that even God himself has that remembrance of him!'

Redlaw spread his hands upon his face, and shrunk like a murderer.

'Ah!' feebly moaned the man upon the bed. 'The waste since then, the waste of life since then!'

'But he was a child once,' said the old man. 'He played with children. Before he lay down on his bed at night, and fell into his guiltless rest, he said his prayers at his poor mother's knee. I have seen him do it many a time; and seen her lay his head upon her breast and kiss him. Sorrowful as it was to her, and to me, to think of this, when he went so wrong, and when our hopes and plans for him were all broken, this gave him still a hold upon us, that nothing else could have given. Oh, Father, so much better than the fathers upon earth! Oh, Father, so much more afflicted by the errors of thy children! take this wanderer back! Not as he is, but as he was then, let him cry to thee, as he has so often seemed to cry to us!'

As the old man lifted up his trembling hands, the son, for whom he made the supplication, laid his sinking head against him for support and comfort, as if he were indeed the child of whom he spoke.

When did man ever tremble as Redlaw trembled in the silence that ensued? He knew it must come upon them, knew that it was coming fast.

'My time is very short, my breath is shorter,' said the sick man, supporting himself on one arm, and with the other groping in the air, 'and I remember there is something on my mind concerning the man who was here just now. Father and William – wait! – is there really anything in black out there?'

'Yes, yes, it is real,' said his aged father.

'Is it a man?'

'What I say myself George,' interposed his brother, bending kindly over him. 'It's Mr. Redlaw.'

'I thought I had dreamed of him. Ask him to come here.'

The Chemist, whiter than the dying man, appeared before him. Obedient to the motion of his hand, he sat upon the bed.

'It·has been so ripped up tonight, sir,' said the sick man, laying his hand upon his heart, with a look in which the mute, imploring agony of his condition was concentrated, 'by the sight of my poor old father, and the thought of all the trouble I have been the cause of, and all the wrong and sorrow lying at my door that —'

Was it the extremity to which he had come, or was it the dawning of another change, that made him stop?

'— that what I *can* do right, with my mind running on so much, so fast, I'll try to do. There was another man here. Did you see him?'

Redlaw could not reply by any word; for when he saw that
fatal sign he knew so well now, of the wandering hand upon
the forehead, his voice died at his lips. But he made some
indication of assent.

'He is penniless, hungry, and destitute. He is completely
beaten down, and has no resource at all. Look after him! Lose
no time! I know he has it in his mind to kill himself.'

It was working. It was on his face. His face was changing,
hardening, deepening in all its shades, and losing all its
sorrow.

'Don't you remember? Don't you know him?' he pursued.

He shut his face out for a moment with the hand that again
wandered over his forehead and then it lowered on Redlaw,
reckless, ruffianly, and callous.

'Why, d—n you!' he said, scowling round, 'what have you
been doing to me here? I have lived bold, and I mean to die
bold. To the Devil with you!'

And so he lay down upon his bed, and put his arms up over
his head and ears, as resolute from that time to keep out all
access, and to die in his indifference.

If Redlaw had been struck by lightning, it could not have
struck him from the bedside with a more tremendous shock.
But the old man, who had left the bed while his son was
speaking to him, now returning, avoided it quickly likewise,
and with abhorrence.

'Where's my boy William?' said the old man hurriedly.
'William, come away from here. We'll go home.'

'Home, father!' returned William. 'Are you going to leave
your own son?'

'Where's my own son?' replied the old man.

'Where? Why, there!'

'That's no son of mine,' said Philip, trembling with resentment. 'No such wretch as that has any claim on me. My
children are pleasant to look at, and they wait upon me, and
get my meat and drink ready, and are useful to me. I've a right
to it! I'm eighty-seven!'

'You're old enough to be no older,' muttered William,
looking at him grudgingly, with his hands in his pockets. 'I
don't know what good you are myself. We could have a deal
more pleasure without you.'

'*My* son, Mr. Redlaw!' said the old man. '*My* son, too! The boy talking to me of *my* son! Why, what has he ever done to give me any pleasure, I should like to know?'

'I don't know what you have ever done to give *me* any pleasure,' said William sulkily.

'Let me think,' said the old man. 'For how many Christmas-times running have I sat in my warm place, and never had to come out in the cold night air; and have made good cheer, without being disturbed by any such uncomfortable, wretched sight as him there? Is it twenty, William?'

'Nigh forty, it seems,' he muttered. 'Why, when I look at my father, sir, and come to think of it,' addressing Redlaw with an impatience and an irritation that were quite new, 'I'm whipped if I can see anything in him but a calendar of ever so many years of eating, and drinking, and making himself comfortable over and over again.'

'I – I'm eighty-seven,' said the old man, rambling on, childishly and weakly, 'and I don't know as I ever was much put out by anything. I'm not-a-going to begin now, because of what he calls my son. He's not my son. I've had a power of pleasant times. I recollect once – no, I don't – no, it's broken off. It was something about a game of cricket and a friend of mine, but it's somehow broken off. I wonder who he was – I suppose I liked him? And I wonder what became of him – I suppose he died? But I don't know. And I don't care, neither; I don't care a bit.'

In his drowsy chuckling, and the shaking of his head, he put his hands into his waistcoat pockets. In one of them he found a bit of holly (left there, probably, last night), which he now took out, and looked at.

'Berries, eh?' said the old man. 'Ah! It's a pity they're not good to eat. I recollect when I was a little chap about as high as that, and out a walking with – let me see – who was I out a walking with? – no, I don't remember how that was. I don't remember as I ever walked with any one particular, or cared for any one, or any one for me. Berries, eh? There's good cheer when there's berries. Well, I ought to have my share of it, and to be waited on, and kept warm and comfortable; for I'm eighty-seven, and a poor old man. I'm eighty-seven. Eighty-seven!'

The drivelling, pitiable manner in which, as he repeated this, he nibbled at the leaves, and spat the morsels out; the cold, uninterested eye with which his youngest son (so changed) regarded him; the determined apathy with which his eldest son lay hardened in his sin; impressed themselves no more on Redlaw's observation; for he broke his way from the spot to which his feet seemed to have been fixed, and ran out of the house.

His guide came crawling forth from his place of refuge, and was ready for him before he reached the arches.

'Back to the woman's?' he inquired.

'Back quickly!' answered Redlaw. 'Stop nowhere on the way!'

For a short distance the boy went on before; but their return was more like a flight than a walk, and it was as much as his bare feet could do to keep pace with the Chemist's rapid strides. Shrinking from all who passed, shrouded in his cloak, and keeping it drawn closely about him, as though there were mortal contagion in any fluttering touch of his garments, he made no pause until they reached the door by which they had come out. He unlocked it with his key, went in, accompanied by the boy, and hastened through the dark passages to his own chamber.

The boy watched him as he made the door fast, and withdrew behind the table when he looked round.

'Come!' he said. 'Don't you touch me! You've not brought me here to take my money away.'

Redlaw threw some more upon the ground. He flung his body on it immediately, as if to hide it from him, less the sight of it should tempt him to reclaim it; and not until he saw him seated by his lamp, with his face hidden in his hands, began furtively to pick it up. When he had done so, he crept near the fire, and, sitting down in a great chair before it, took from his breast some broken scraps of food, and fell to munching, and to staring at the blaze, and now and then to glancing at his shillings, which he kept clenched up in a bunch in one hand.

'And this,' said Redlaw, gazing on him with increasing repugnance and fear, 'is the only one companion I have left on earth!'

How long it was before he was aroused from his contemplation of this creature whom he dreaded so – whether half an hour, or half the night – he knew not. But the stillness of the room was broken by the boy (whom he had seen listening) starting up, and running towards the door.

'Here's the woman coming!' he exclaimed.

The Chemist stopped him on his way, at the moment when she knocked.

'Let me go to her, will you?' said the boy.

'Not now,' returned the Chemist. 'Stay here. Nobody must pass in or out of the room now. Who's that?'

'It's I, sir,' cried Milly. 'Pray, sir, let me in.'

'No! not for the world!' he said.

'Mr. Redlaw, Mr. Redlaw, pray, sir, let me in!'

'What is the matter?' he said, holding the boy.

'The miserable man you saw is worse, and nothing I can say will wake him from his terrible infatuation. William's father has turned childish in a moment. William himself is changed. The shock has been too sudden for him; I cannot understand him: he is not like himself. Oh, Mr. Redlaw, pray advise me, help me!'

'No! No! No!' he answered.

'Mr. Redlaw! Dear sir! George has been muttering in his doze about the man you saw there, who, he fears, will kill himself.'

'Better he should do it than come near me!'

'He says, in his wandering, that you know him; that he was your friend once, long ago; that he is the ruined father of a student here – my mind misgives me, of the young gentleman who has been ill. What is to be done? How is he to be followed? How is he to be saved? Mr. Redlaw, pray, oh, pray advise me! Help me!'

All this time he held the boy, who was half mad to pass him, and let her in.

'Phantoms! Punishers of impious thoughts!' cried Redlaw, gazing round in anguish. 'Look upon me! From the darkness of my mind, let the glimmering of contrition that I know is there, shine up and show my misery! In the material world, as I have long taught, nothing can be spared; no step or atom in the wondrous structure could be lost, without a blank being made in the great universe. I know, now, that it is the same with good and evil, happiness and sorrow, in the memories of men. Pity me! Relieve me!'

There was no response but her 'Help me, help me, let me in!' and the boy's struggling to get to her.

'Shadow of myself! Spirit of my darker hours!' cried Redlaw in distraction. 'Come back, and haunt me day and night, but take this gift away! Or, if it must still rest with me, deprive me of the dreadful power of giving it to others. Undo what I had done. Leave me benighted, but restore the day to those whom I have cursed. As I have spared this woman from the first, and as I never will go forth again, but will die here, with no hand to tend me, save this creature's who is proof against me – hear me!'

The only reply still was, the boy struggling to get to her, while he held him back; and the cry increasing in its energy, 'Help! let me in! He was your friend once: how shall he be followed, how shall he be saved? They are all changed, there is no one else to help me: pray, pray let me in!'

Night was still heavy in the sky. On open plains, from hill-tops, and from the decks of solitary ships at sea, a distant low-lying line, that promised by-and-by to change to light, was visible in the dim horizon; but its promise was remote and doubtful, and the moon was striving with the night clouds busily.

The shadows upon Redlaw's mind succeeded thick and fast to one another, and obscured its light as the night clouds hovered between the moon and earth, and kept the latter veiled in darkness. Fitful and uncertain as the shadows which the night clouds cast were their concealments from him, and imperfect revelations to him; and, like the night clouds still, if the clear light broke forth for a moment, it was only that they might sweep over it, and make the darkness deeper than before.

Without, there was a profound and solemn hush upon the ancient pile of building, and its buttresses and angles made dark shapes of mystery upon the ground, which now seemed to retire into the smooth white snow, and now seemed to come out of it, as the moon's path was more or less beset. Within, the Chemist's room was indistinct and murky, by the light of the expiring lamp; a ghostly silence had succeeded to the knocking and the voice outside; nothing was audible but, now and then, a low sound among the whitened ashes of the fire, as of its yielding up its last breath. Before it, on the ground, the boy lay fast asleep. In his chair the Chemist sat, as he had sat there since the calling at his door had ceased – like a man turned to stone.

At such a time the Christmas music he had heard before began to play. He listened to it, at first, as he had listened in the churchyard; but presently – it playing still, and being borne towards him on the night air, in a low, sweet melancholy strain – he rose, and stood stretching his hands about him, as if there were some friend approaching within his reach, on whom his desolate touch might rest, yet do no harm. As he did this, his face became less fixed and wondering; a gentle trembling came upon him; and at last his eyes filled with tears, and he put his hands before them, and bowed down his head.

His memory of sorrow, wrong, and trouble had not come back to him; he knew that it was not restored; he had no passing belief or hope that it was. But some dumb stir within him made him capable, again, of being moved by what was hidden, afar off, in the music. If it were only that it told him sorrowfully the value of what he had lost, he thanked Heaven for it with a fervent gratitude.

As the last chord died upon his ear, he raised his head to listen to its lingering vibration. Beyond the boy, so that his sleeping figure lay at its feet, the Phantom stood, immovable and silent, with its eyes upon him.

Ghastly it was, as it had ever been, but not so cruel and relentless in its aspect – or he thought or hoped so, as he looked upon it, trembling. It was not alone, but in its shadowy hand it held another hand.

And whose was that? Was the form that stood beside it indeed Milly's, òr but her shade and picture? The quiet head was bent a little, as her manner was and her eyes were looking down, as if in pity, on the sleeping child. A radiant light fell on her face, but did not touch the Phantom; for, though close beside her, it was dark and colourless as ever.

'Spectre!' said the Chemist, newly troubled as he looked, 'I have not been stubborn or presumptuous in respect of her. Oh, do not bring her here! Spare me that!'

'This is but a shadow,' said the Phantom; 'when the morning shines, seek out the reality whose image I present before you.'

'Is it my inexorable doom to do so?' cried the Chemist.

'It is,' replied the Phantom.

'To destroy her peace, her goodness; to make her what I am myself, and what I have made of others?'

'I have said, "Seek her out,"' returned the Phantom. 'I have said no more.'

'Oh, tell me!' exclaimed Redlaw, catching at the hope which he fancied might lie hidden in the words. 'Can I undo what I have done?'

'No,' returned the Phantom.

'I do not ask for restoration to myself,' said Redlaw. 'What I abandoned, I abandoned of my own will, and have justly lost. But for those to whom I have transferred the fatal gift; who never sought it; who unknowingly received a curse of which they had no warning, and which they had no power to shun; can I do nothing?'

'Nothing,' said the Phantom.

'If I cannot, can anyone?'

The Phantom, standing like a statue, kept its gaze upon him for awhile; then turned its head suddenly, and looked upon the shadow at its side.

'Ah! Can she?' cried Redlaw, still looking upon the shade.

The Phantom released the hand it had retained till now, and softly raised its own with a gesture of dismissal. Upon that, her shadow, still preserving the same attitude, began to move or melt away.

'Stay!' cried Redlaw with an earnestness to which he could not give enough expression. 'For a moment! As an act of mercy! I know that some change fell upon me when those sounds were in the air just now. Tell me, have I lost the power of harming her? May I go near her without dread? Oh, let her give me any sign of hope!'

The Phantom looked upon the shade as he did – not at him – and gave no answer.

'At least, say this – has she, henceforth, the consciousness of any power to set right what I have done?'

'She has not,' the Phantom answered.

'Has she the power bestowed on her without the consciousness?'

The Phantom answered: 'Seek her out.' And her shadow slowly vanished.

They were face to face again, and looking on each other as intently and awfully as at the time of the bestowal of the gift, across the boy who still lay on the ground between them, at the Phantom's feet.

'Terrible instructor,' said the Chemist, sinking on his knee before it in an attitude of supplication, 'by whom I was renounced, but by whom I am revisited (in which, and in whose milder aspect, I would fain believe I have a gleam of hope), I will obey without inquiry, praying that the cry I have sent up in the anguish of my soul has been, or will be, heard on behalf of those whom I have injured beyond human reparation. But there is one thing –'

'You speak to me of what is lying here, the Phantom interposed, and pointed with its finger to the boy.

'I do,' returned the Chemist. 'You know what I would ask. Why has this child alone been proof against my influence, and why, why have I detected in its thoughts a terrible companionship with mine?'

'This,' said the Phantom, pointing to the boy, 'is the last, completest illustration of a human creature utterly bereft of such remembrances as you have yielded up. No softening memory of sorrow, wrong, or trouble enters here, because this wretched mortal from his birth has been abandoned to a worse condition than the beasts, and has, within his knowledge, no one contrast, no humanising touch to make a grain of such a memory spring up in his hardened breast. All within this desolate creature is barren wilderness. All within the man bereft of what you have resigned is the same barren wilderness. Woe to such a man! Woe, tenfold, to the nation that shall count its monsters such as this, lying here by hundreds and by thousands!'

Redlaw shrunk, appalled, from what he heard.

'There is not,' said the Phantom, 'one of these – not one – but sows a harvest that mankind *must* reap. From every seed of evil in this boy a field of ruin is grown that shall be gathered in, and garnered up, and sown again in many places in the world, until regions are overspread with wickedness enough to raise the waters of another Deluge. Open and unpunished murder in a city's streets would be less guilty in its daily toleration than one such spectacle as this.'

It seemed to look down upon the boy in his sleep. Redlaw, too, looked down upon him with a new emotion.

'There is not a father,' said the Phantom, 'by whose side, in his daily or his nightly walk, these creatures pass; there is not a mother among all the ranks of loving mothers in this land; there is no one risen from the state of childhood, but shall be responsible in his or her degree for this enormity. There is not a country throughout the earth on which it would not bring a curse. There is no religion upon earth that it would not deny; there is no people upon earth it would not put to shame.'

The Chemist clasped his hands, and looked, with trembling fear and pity, from the sleeping boy to the Phantom, standing above him with its finger pointing down.

'Behold, I say,' pursued the Spectre, 'the perfect type of what it was your choice to be. Your influence is powerless here, because from this child's bosom you can banish nothing. His thoughts have been in "terrible companionship" with yours, because you have gone down to his unnatural level. He is the growth of man's indifference; you are the growth of man's presumption. The beneficent design of Heaven is, in each case, overthrown, and from the two poles of the immaterial world you come together.'

The Chemist stooped upon the ground beside the boy, and, with the same kind of compassion for him that he now felt for himself, covered him as he slept, and no longer shrunk from him with abhorrence or indifference.

Soon, now, the distant line on the horizon brightened, the darkness faded, the sun rose red and glorious, and the chimney-stacks and gables of the ancient building gleamed in the clear air, which turned the smoke and vapour of the city into a cloud of gold. The very sun-dial in his shady corner, where the wind was used to spin with such unwindy constancy, shook off the finer particles of snow that had accumulated on his dull old face in the night, and looked out at the little white wreaths eddying round and round him. Doubtless some blind groping of the morning made its way down into the forgotten crypt, so cold and earthy, where the Norman arches were half buried in the ground, and stirred the dull sap in the lazy vegetation hanging to the walls, and quickened the slow principle of life within the little world of wonderful and delicate creation which existed there, with some faint knowledge that the sun was up.

The Tetterbys were up, and doing. Mr. Tetterby took down the shutters of the shop, and, strip by strip, revealed the treasures of the window to the eyes, so proof against their seductions, of Jerusalem Buildings. Adolphus had been out so long already, that he was half-way on to Morning Pepper. Five small Tetterbys, whose ten round eyes were much

inflamed by soap and friction, were in the tortures of a cool
wash in the back-kitchen; Mrs. Tetterby presiding. Johnny,
who was pushed and hustled through his toilet with great
rapidity when Moloch chanced to be in an exacting frame of
mind (which was always the case), staggered up and down
with his charge before the shop-door, under greater difficulties than usual; the weight of Moloch being much increased by
a complication of defences against the cold, composed of
knitted worsted-work, and forming a complete suit of chain-
armour, with a head-piece and blue gaiters.

It was a peculiarity of this baby to be always cutting teeth.
Whether they never came, or whether they came and went
away again, is not in evidence; but it had certainly cut enough,
on the showing of Mrs. Tetterby, to make a handsome dental
provision for the sign of the Bull and Mouth. All sorts of
objects were impressed for the rubbing of its gums, notwithstanding that it always carried, dangling at its waist (which
was immediately under its chin), a bone ring, large enough to
have represented the rosary of a young nun. Knife handles,
umbrella tops, the heads of walking-sticks selected from the
stock, the fingers of the family in general, but especially of
Johnny, nutmeg-graters, crusts, the handles of doors, and the
cook knobs on the tops of pokers, were among the commonest instruments indiscriminately applied for this baby's
relief. The amount of electricity that must have been rubbed
out of it in a week is not to be calculated. Still Mrs. Tetterby
always said 'it was coming through, and then the child would
be herself;' and still it never did come through, and the child
continued to be somebody else.

The tempers of the little Tetterbys had sadly changed with a
few hours. Mr. and Mrs. Tetterby themselves were not more
altered than their offspring. Usually they were an unselfish,
good-natured, yielding little race, sharing short commons
when it happened (which was pretty often) contentedly, and
even generously, and taking a great deal of enjoyment out of a
very little meat. But they were fighting now, not only for the
soap-and-water, but even for the breakfast which was yet in
perspective. The hand of every little Tetterby was against the
other little Tetterbys; and even Johnny's hand – the patient,
much-enduring, and devoted Johnny – rose against the baby!

Yes. Mrs. Tetterby, going to the door by a mere accident, saw him viciously pick out a weak place in the suit of armour, where a slap would tell, and slap that blessed child.

Mrs. Tetterby had him into the parlour, by the collar, in that same flash of time, and repaid him the assault with usury thereto.

'You brute, you murdering little boy!' said Mrs. Tetterby. 'Had you the heart to do it?'

'Why don't her teeth come through, then,' retorted Johnny in a loud rebellious voice, 'instead of bothering me? How would you like it yourself?'

'Like it, sir!' said Mrs. Tetterby, relieving him of his dishonoured load.

'Yes, like it,' said Johnny. 'How would you? Not at all. If you was me, you'd go for a soldier. I will, too. There an't no babies in the army.'

Mr. Tetterby, who had arrived upon the scene of action, rubbed his chin thoughtfully, instead of correcting the rebel, and seemed rather struck by this view of a military life.

'I wish I was in the army myself, if the child's in the right,' said Mrs. Tetterby, looking at her husband, 'for I have no peace in my life here. I'm a slave – a Virginia slave,' some indistinct association with their weak descent on the tobacco trade, perhaps, suggested this aggravated expression to Mrs. Tetterby. 'I never have a holiday, or any pleasure at all, from year's end to year's end! Why, Lord bless and save the child,' said Mrs. Tetterby, shaking the baby with an irritability hardly suited to so pious an aspiration, 'what's the matter with her now?'

Not being able to discover, and not rendering the subject much clearer by shaking it, Mrs. Tetterby put the baby away in a cradle, and, folding her arms, sat rocking it angrily with her foot.

'How you stand there, 'Dolphus!' said Mrs. Tetterby to her husband. 'Why don't you do something?'

'Because I don't care about anything,' Mr. Tetterby replied.

'I'm sure I don't,' said Mrs. Tetterby.

'I'll take my oath I don't,' said Mr. Tetterby.

A diversion arose here among Johnny and his five younger brothers, who, in preparing the family breakfast-table, had fallen to skirmishing for the temporary possession of the loaf, and were buffering one another with great heartiness; the smallest boy of all, with precocious discretion, hovering outside the knot of combatants, and harassing their legs. Into the midst of this fray Mr. and Mr. Tetterby both precipitated themselves with great ardour, as if such ground were the only ground on which they could now agree; and having, with no visible remains of their late soft-heartedness, laid about them without any lenity, and done much execution, resumed their former relative positions.

'You had better read your paper than do nothing at all,' said Mrs. Tetterby.

'What's there to read in a paper?' returned Mr. Tetterby with excessive discontent.

'What?' said Mrs. Tetterby. 'Police.'

'It's nothing to me,' said Tetterby. 'What do I care what people do, or are done to?'

'Suicides,' suggested Mrs. Tetterby.

'No business of mine,' replied her husband.

'Births, deaths, and marriages, are those nothing to you?' said Mrs. Tetterby.

'If the births were all over for good and all today; and the deaths were all to begin to come off tomorrow; I don't see why it should interest me, till I thought it was a-coming to my turn,' grumbled Tetterby. 'As to marriages, I've done it myself. I know quite enough about *them*.'

To judge from the dissatisfied expression of her face and manner, Mrs. Tetterby appeared to entertain the same opinions as her husband; but she opposed him, nevertheless, for the gratification of quarrelling with him.

'Oh! you're a consistent man,' said Mrs. Tetterby, 'an't you? You, with the screen of your own making there, made of nothing else but bits of newspapers, which you sit and read to the children by the half-hour together!'

'Say used to, if you please,' returned her husband. 'You won't find me doing so any more. I'm wiser now.'

'Bah! Wiser, indeed!' said Mrs. Tetterby. 'Are you better?'

The question sounded some discordant note in Mr. Tetterby's breast. He ruminated dejectedly, and passed his hand across and across his forehead.

'Better!' murmured Mr. Tetterby. 'I don't know as any of us are better, or happier either. Better is it?'

He turned to the screen, and traced about it with his finger, until he found a certain paragraph of which he was in quest.

'This used to be one of the family favourites, I recollect,' said Tetterby in a forlorn and stupid way, 'and used to draw tears from the children, and make 'em good, if there was any little bickering or discontent among 'em, next to the story of the robin redbreasts in the wood. "Melancholy case of destitution. Yesterday a small man, with a baby in his arms, and surrounded by half-a-dozen ragged little ones, of various ages between ten and two, the whole of whom were evidently in a famishing condition, appeared before the worthy magistrate, and made the following recital." Ha! I don't understand it, I'm sure,' said Tetterby; 'I don't see what it has got to do with us.'

'How old and shabby he looks!' said Mrs. Tetterby, watching him. 'I never saw such a change in a man. Ah! dear me, dear me, dear me, it was a sacrifice!'

'What was a sacrifice?' her husband sourly inquired.

Mrs. Tetterby shook her head; and, without replying in words, raised a complete sea-storm about the baby by her violent agitation of the cradle.

'If you mean your marriage was a sacrifice, my good woman –' said her husband.

'I *do* mean it,' said his wife.

'Why, then, I mean to say,' pursued Mr. Tetterby as sulkily and surlily as she, 'that there are two sides to that affair; and that *I* was the sacrifice; and that I wish the sacrifice hadn't been accepted.'

'I wish it hadn't, Tetterby, with all my heart and soul, I do assure you,' said his wife. 'You can't wish it more than I do, Tetterby.'

'I don't know what I saw in her,' muttered the newsman, 'I'm sure; certainly, if I saw anything, it's not there now. I was thinking so last night, after supper, by the fire. She's fat, she's ageing, she won't bear comparison with most other women.'

'He's common-looking, he has no air with him, he's small, he's beginning to stoop, and he's getting bald,' muttered Mrs. Tetterby.

'I must have been half out of my mind when I did it,' muttered Mr. Tetterby.

'My senses must have forsook me. That's the only way in which I can explain it to myself,' said Mrs. Tetterby with elaboration.

In this mood they sat down to breakfast. The little Tetter-bys were not habituated to regard that meal in the light of a sedentary occupation, but discussed it as a dance or trot; rather resembling a savage ceremony, in the occasional shrill whoops and brandishings of bread-and-butter with which it was accompanied, as well as in the intricate filings off into the street and back again, and the hoppings up and down the doorsteps, which were incidental to the performance. In the present instance, the contentions between these Tetterby children for the milk-and-water jug, common to all, which stood upon the table, presented so lamentable an instance of angry passions risen very high indeed, that it was an outrage on the memory of Doctor Watts. It was not until Mr. Tetterby had driven the whole herd out of the front-door that a moment's peace was secured; and even that was broken by the discovery that Johnny had surreptitiously come back, and was at that instant choking in the jug like a ventriloquist, in his indecent and rapacious haste.

'These children will be the death of me at last!' said Mrs. Tetterby after banishing the culprit. 'And the sooner the better I think.'

'Poor people,' said Mr. Tetterby, 'ought not to have children at all. They give *us* no pleasure.'

He was at that moment taking up the cup which Mrs. Tetterby had rudely pushed towards him, and Mrs. Tetterby was lifting her own cup to her lips, when they both stopped, as if they were transfixed.

'Here! Mother! Father!' cried Johnny, running into the room. 'Here's Mrs. William coming down the street!'

And if ever, since the world began, a young boy took a baby from a cradle with the care of an old nurse, and hushed and soothed it tenderly, and tottered away with it cheerfully, Johnny was that boy, and Moloch was that baby, as they went out together.

Mr. Tetterby put down his cup; Mrs. Tetterby put down

her cup. Mr. Tetterby rubbed his forehead; Mrs. Tetterby
rubbed hers. Mr. Tetterby's face began to smooth and bright-
en; Mrs. Tetterby's began to smooth and brighten.

'Why, Lord forgive me,' said Mr. Tetterby to himself,
'what evil tempers have I been giving way to? What has been
the matter here?'

'How could I ever treat him ill again, after all I said and felt
last night?' sobbed Mrs. Tetterby, with her apron to her eyes.

'Am I a brute,' said Mr. Tetterby, 'or is there any good in
me at all? Sophia! My little woman!'

''Dolphus dear!' returned his wife.

'I – I've been in a state of mind,' said Mr. Tetterby, 'that I
can't bear to think of, Sophy.'

'Oh! It's nothing to what I've been in, Dolf,' cried his wife
in a great burst of grief.

'My Sophia,' said Mr. Tetterby, 'don't take on! I never shall
forgive myself. I must have nearly broke your heart, I know.'

'No, Dolf, no. It was me! Me!' cried Mrs. Tetterby.

'My little woman,' said her husband, 'don't. You make me
reproach myself dreadful when you show such a noble spirit.
Sophia, my dear, you don't know what I thought. I showed it
bad enough, no doubt; but what I thought, my little
woman —'

'Oh dear Dolf, don't! Don't!' cried his wife.

'Sophia,' said Mr. Tetterby, 'I must reveal it. I couldn't rest
in my conscience unless I mentioned it. My little woman —'

'Mrs. William's very nearly here!' screamed Johnny at the
door.

'My little woman, I wondered how,' gasped Mr. Tetterby,
supporting himself by his chair, 'I wondered how I had ever
admired you – I forgot the precious children you have brought
about me, and thought you didn't look as slim as I could wish.
I – I never gave a recollection,' said Mr. Tetterby with severe
self-accusation, 'to the cares you've had as my wife, and along
of me and mine, when you might have had hardly any with
another man, who got on better and was luckier than me
(anybody might have found such a man easily, I am sure); and
I quarrelled with you for having aged a little in the rough years
you've lightened for me. Can you believe it, my little woman?
I hardly can myself.'

Mrs. Tetterby, in a whirlwind of laughing and crying, caught his face within her hands, and held it there.

'Oh, Dolf!' she cried. 'I am so happy that you thought so; I am so grateful that you thought so! For I thought that you were common-looking, Dolf; and so you are, my dear, and may you be the commonest of all sights in my eyes, till you close them with your own good hands! I thought that you were small; and so you are, and I'll make much of you because you are, and more of you because I love my husband. I thought that you began to stoop; and so you do, and you shall lean on me, and I'll do all I can to keep you up. I thought there was no air about you; but there is, and it's the air of home, and that's the purest and the best there is, and *God* bless home once more, and all belonging to it, Dolf!'

'Hurrah! Here's Mrs. William!' cried Johnny.

So she was, and all the children with her; and, as she came in, they kissed her, and kissed one another, and kissed the baby, and kissed their father and mother, and then ran back and flocked and danced about her, trooping on with her in triumph.

Mr. and Mrs. Tetterby were not a bit behind-hand in the warmth of their reception. They were as much attracted to her as the children were; they ran towards her, kissed her hands, pressed round her, could not receive her ardently or enthusiastically enough. She came among them like the spirit of all goodness, affection, gentle consideration, love, and domesticity.

'What! are *you* all so glad to see me, too, this bright Christmas morning?' said Milly, clapping her hands in a pleasant wonder. 'Oh dear, how delightful this is!'

More shouting from the children, more kissing, more trooping round her, more happiness, more love, more joy, more honour, on all sides, than she could bear.

'Oh dear!' said Milly, 'what delicious tears you make me shed! How can I ever have deserved this? What have I done to be so loved?'

'Who can help it?' cried Mr. Tetterby.

'Who can help it?' cried Mrs. Tetterby.

'Who can help it?' echoed the children in a joyful chorus. And they danced and trooped about her again, and clung to her, and laid their rosy faces against her dress, and kissed and fondled it, and could not fondle it, or her, enough.

'I never was so moved,' said Milly, drying her eyes, 'as I have been this morning. I must tell you as soon as I can speak – Mr. Redlaw came to me at sunrise, and with a tenderness in his manner, more as if I had been his darling daughter than myself, implored me to go with him to where William's brother George is lying ill. We went together, and all the way along he was so kind, and so subdued, and seemed to put such trust and hope in me, that I could not help crying with pleasure. When we got to the house, we met a woman at the door (somebody had bruised and hurt her, I am afraid), who caught me by the hand, and blessed me as I passed.'

'She was right,' said Mr. Tetterby. Mrs. Tetterby said she was right. All the children cried out she was right.

'Ah! but there's more than that,' said Milly. 'When we got upstairs into the room, the sick man, who had lain for hours in a state from which no effort could rouse him, rose up in his bed, and, bursting into tears, stretched out his arms to me, and said that he had led a mis-spent life, but that he was truly repentant now in his sorrow for the past, which was all as plain to him as a great prospect from which a dense black cloud had cleared away, and that he entreated me to ask his poor old father for his pardon and his blessing, and to say a prayer beside his bed. And, when I did so, Mr. Redlaw joined in it so fervently, and then so thanked and thanked me, and thanked Heaven, that my heart quite overflowed, and I could have done nothing but sob and cry, if the sick man had not begged me to sit down by him – which made me quiet, of course. As I sat there, he held my hand in his until he sunk in a doze; and even then, when I withdrew my hand to leave him to come here (which Mr. Redlaw was very earnest indeed in wishing me to do), his hand felt for mine, so that some one else was obliged to take my place, and make believe to give him my hand back. Oh dear oh dear!' said Milly, sobbing. 'How thankful and how happy I should feel, and do feel, for all this!'

While she was speaking Redlaw had come in, and, after pausing for a moment to observe the group of which she was the centre, had silently ascended the stairs. Upon those stairs he now appeared again; remaining there while the young student passed him, and came running down.

'Kind nurse, gentlest, best of creatures,' he said, falling on his knee to her, and catching at her hand, 'forgive my cruel ingratitude!'

'Oh dear, oh dear!' cried Milly innocently, 'here's another of them! Oh dear, here's somebody else who likes me! What shall I ever do?'

The guileless, simple way in which she said it, and in which she put her hands before her eyes and wept for very happiness, was as touching as it was delightful.

'I was not myself,' he said. 'I don't know what it was – it was some consequence of my disorder, perhaps – I was mad. But I am so no longer. Almost as I speak I am restored. I heard the children crying out your name, and the shade passed from me at the very sound of it. Oh, don't weep! Dear Milly, if you could read my heart, and only know with what affection and what grateful homage it is glowing, you would not let me see you weep. It is such deep reproach.'

'No, no,' said Milly, 'it's not that. It's not, indeed. It's joy. It's wonder that you should think it necessary to ask me to forgive so little, and yet it's pleasure that you do.'

'And will you come again? and will you finish the little curtain?'

'No,' said Milly, drying her eyes, and shaking her head. 'You won't care for *my* needlework now.'

'Is it forgiving me to say that?'

She beckoned him aside, and whispered in his ear.

'There is news from your home, Mr. Edmund.'

'News? How?'

'Either your not writing when you were very ill, or the change in your handwriting when you began to be better, created some suspicion of the truth. However, that is — But you're sure you'll not be the worse for any news, if it's not bad news?'

'Sure.'

'Then there's some one come!' said Milly.

'My mother?' asked the student, glancing round involuntarily towards Redlaw, who had come down from the stairs.

'Hush! No,' said Milly.

'It can be no one else.'

'Indeed!' said Milly. 'Are you sure?'

'It is not —' Before he could say more, she put her hand upon his mouth.

'Yes, it is!' said Milly. 'The young lady (she is very like the miniature, Mr. Edmund, but she is prettier) was too unhappy to rest without satisfying her doubts, and came up last night, with a little servant-maid. As you always dated your letters from the College, she came there; and, before I saw Mr. Redlaw this morning, I saw her. *She* likes me too!' said Milly. 'Oh dear, that's another!'

'This morning! Where is she now?'

'Why, she is now,' said Milly advancing her lips to his ear, 'in my little parlour in the Lodge, and waiting to see you.'

He pressed her hand, and was darting off, but she detained him.

'Mr. Redlaw is much altered, and has told me this morning that his memory is impaired. Be very considerate to him, Mr. Edmund; he needs that from us all.'

The young man assured her, by a look, that her caution was not ill bestowed; and, as he passed the Chemist on his way out, bent respectfully and with an obvious interest before him.

Redlaw returned the salutation courteously, and even humbly, and looked after him as he passed on. He dropped his head upon his hand too, as if trying to re-awaken something he had lost. But it was gone.

The abiding change that had come upon him since the influence of the music, and the Phantom's reappearance, was, that now he truly felt how much he had lost, and could compassionate his own condition, and contrast it, clearly, with the natural state of those who were around him. In this, an interest in those who were around him was revived, and a meek, submissive sense of his calamity was bred, resembling that which sometimes obtains in age, when its mental powers are weakened without insensibility or sullenness being added to the list of its infirmities.

He was conscious that, as he redeemed, through Milly, more and more of the evil he had done, and as he was more and more with her, this change ripened itself within him. Therefore, and because of the attachment she inspired him

with (but without other hope), he felt that he was quite
dependent on her, and that she was his staff in his affliction.

So, when she asked him whether they should go home now
to where the old man and her husband were, and he readily
replied, 'Yes' – being anxious in that regard – he put his arm
through hers, and walked beside her; not as if he were the
wise and learned man to whom the wonders of nature were
an open book, and hers were the uninstructed mind, but as
if their two positions were reversed, and he knew nothing,
and she all.

He saw the children throng about her, and caress her, as he
and she went away together thus out of the house; he heard the
ringing of their laughter, and their merry voices; he saw their
bright faces clustering round him like flowers, he witnessed
the renewed contentment and affection of their parents; he
breathed the simple air of their poor home, restored to its
tranquillity; he thought of the unwholesome blight he had
shed upon it, and might, but for her, have been diffusing then;
and perhaps it is no wonder that he walked submissively
beside her, and drew her gentle bosom nearer to his own.

When they arrived at the Lodge, the old man was sitting in
his chair in the chimney-corner, with his eyes fixed on the
ground, and his son was leaning against the opposite side of
the fire-place, looking at him. As she came in at the door, both
started and turned round towards her, and a radiant change
came upon their faces.

'Oh dear, dear, dear, they are pleased to see me, like the
rest!' cried Milly, clapping her hands in an ecstasy, and
stopping short. 'Here are two more!'

Pleased to see her! Pleasure was no word for it. She ran into
her husband's arms, thrown wide open to receive her, and he
would have been glad to have her there, with her head lying
on his shoulder, through the short winter's day. But the old
man couldn't spare her. He had arms for her too, and he
locked her in them.

'Why, where has my quiet Mouse been all this time?' said
the old man. 'She has been a long while away. I find that it's
impossible for me to get on without Mouse. I – where's my
son William? – I fancy I have been dreaming, William.'

'That's what I say myself, father,' returned his son. '*I* have been in an ugly sort of dream, I think. How are you, father? Are you pretty well?'

'Strong and brave, my boy,' returned the old man.

It was quite a sight to see Mr. William shaking hands with his father, and patting him on the back, and rubbing him gently down with his hand, as if he could not possibly do enough to show an interest in him.

'What a wonderful man you are, father! How are you father? Are you really pretty hearty, though?' said William, shaking hands with him again, and patting him again, and rubbing him gently down again.

'I never was fresher or stouter in my life, my boy.'

'What a wonderful man you are, father! But that's exactly where it is,' said Mr. William with enthusiasm. 'When I think of all that my father's gone through, and all the chances and changes, and sorrows and troubles, that have happened to him in the course of his long life, and under which his head has grown grey, and years upon years have gathered on it, I feel as if we couldn't do enough to honour the old gentleman, and make his old age easy. How are you, father? Are you really pretty well, though?'

Mr. William might never have left off repeating his inquiry and shaking hands with him again, and patting him again, and rubbing him down again, if the old man had not espied the Chemist, whom until now he had not seen.

'I ask your pardon, Mr. Redlaw,' said Philip, 'but didn't know you were here, sir, or should have made less free. It reminds me, Mr. Redlaw, seeing you here on a Christmas morning, of the time when you was a student yourself, and worked so hard that you was backwards and forwards in our library even at Christmas-time. Ha, ha! I'm old enough to remember that; and I remember it right well, I do, though I am eighty-seven. It was after you left here that my poor wife died. You remember my poor wife, Mr. Redlaw?'

The Chemist answered, 'Yes.'

'Yes,' said the old man. 'She was a dear creetur. — I recollect you come here one Christmas morning with a young lady – I ask your pardon Mr. Redlaw, but I think it was a sister you was very much attached to?'

The Chemist looked at him, and shook his head. 'I had a

sister,' he said vacantly. He knew no more.

'One Christmas morning,' pursued the old man, 'that you come here with her – and it began to snow, and my wife invited the young lady to walk in, and sit by the fire that is always a burning on Christmas Day in what used to be, before our ten poor gentlemen commuted, our great Dinner Hall. I was there; and I recollect, as I was stirring up the blaze for the young lady to warm her pretty feet by, she read the scroll out loud, that is underneath that picter. "Lord, keep my memory green!" She and my poor wife fell a talking about it; and it's a strange thing to think of, now, that they both said (both being so unlike to die) that it was a good prayer, and that it was one they would put up very earnestly, if they were called away young, with reference to those who were dearest to them. "My brother," says the young lady – "My husband," says my poor wife – "Lord, keep his memory of me green, and do not let me be forgotten!"'

Tears more painful and more bitter than he had ever shed in all his life coursed down Redlaw's face. Philip, fully occupied in recalling his story, had not observed him until now, nor Milly's anxiety that he should not proceed.

'Philip!' said Redlaw, laying his hand upon his arm, 'I am a stricken man, on whom the hand of Providence has fallen heavily, although deservedly. You speak to me, my friend, of what I cannot follow; my memory is gone.'

'Merciful power!' cried the old man.

'I have lost my memory of sorrow, wrong, and trouble,' said the Chemist; 'and with that I have lost all man would remember!'

To see old Philip's pity for him, to see him wheel his own great chair for him to rest in, and look down upon him with a solemn sense of his bereavement, was to know, in some degree, how precious to old age such recollections are.

The boy came running in, and ran to Milly.

'Here's the man,' he said, 'in the other room. I don't want *him*.'

'What man does he mean?' asked Mr. William.

'Hush!' said Milly.

Obedient to a sign from her, he and his old father softly

withdrew. As they went out unnoticed, Redlaw beckoned to the boy to come to him.

'I like the woman best,' he answered holding to her skirts.

'You are right,' said Redlaw with a faint smile. 'But you needn't fear to come to me. I am gentler than I was. Of all the world, to you, poor child!'

The boy still held back at first; but yielding little by little to her urging, he consented to approach, and even to sit down at his feet. As Redlaw laid his hand upon the shoulder of the child, looking on him with compassion and a fellow-feeling, he put out his other hand to Milly. She stooped down on that side of him, so that she could look into his face; and, after silence, said: 'Mr. Redlaw, may I speak to you?'

'Yes,' he answered, fixing his eyes upon her. 'Your voice and music are the same to me.'

'May I ask you something?'

'What you will.'

'Do you remember what I said when I knocked at your door last night? About one who was your friend once, and who stood on the verge of destruction?'

'Yes. I remember,' he said with some hesitation.

'Do you understand it?'

He smoothed the boy's hair – looking at her fixedly the while, and shook his head.

'This person,' said Milly in her clear, soft voice, which her mild eyes, looking at him, made clearer and softer, 'I found soon afterwards. I went back to the house, and, with Heaven's help, traced him. I was not too soon. A very little, and I should have been too late.'

He took his hand from the boy, and, laying it on the back of that hand of hers, whose timid and yet earnest touch addressed him no less appealingly than her voice and eyes, looked more intently on her.

'He *is* the father of Mr. Edmund, the young gentleman we saw just now. His real name is Langford. – You recollect the name?'

'I recollect the name.'

'And the man?'

'No, not the man. Did he ever wrong me?'

'Yes!'

'Ah! Then it's hopeless – hopeless.'

He shook his head, and softly beat upon the hand he held, as though mutely asking her commiseration.

'I did not go to Mr. Edmund last night,' said Milly. 'You will listen to me just the same as if you did remember all?'

'To every syllable you say.'

'Both because I did not know, then, that this really was his father, and because I was fearful of the effect of such intelligence upon him, after his illness, if it should be. Since I have known who this person is, I have not gone either; but that is for another reason. He has long been separated from his wife and son – has been a stranger to his home almost from his son's infancy, I learn from him – and has abandoned and deserted what he should have held most dear. In all that time he has been falling from the state of a gentleman, more and more, until —' She rose up hastily, and, going out for a moment, returned, accompanied by the wreck that Redlaw had beheld last night.

'Do you know me?' asked the Chemist.

'I should be glad,' returned the other, 'and that is an unwonted word for me to use, if I could answer no.'

The Chemist looked at the man standing, in self-abasement and degradation before him, and would have looked longer, in an ineffectual struggle for enlightenment, but that Milly resumed her late position by his side, and attracted his attentive gaze to her own face.

'See how low he is sunk, how lost he is!' she whispered, stretching our her arm towards him, without looking from the Chemist's face. 'If you could remember all that is connected with him, do you not think it would move your pity to reflect that one you ever loved (do not let us mind how long ago, or in what belief that he has forfeited), should come to this?'

'I hope it would,' he answered. 'I believe it would.'

His eyes wandered to the figure standing near the door, but came back speedily to her, on whom he gazed intently, as if he strove to learn some lesson from every tone of her voice, and every beam of her eyes.

'I have no learning, and you have much,' said Milly; 'I am not used to think, and you are always thinking. May I tell you

why it seems to me a good thing for us to remember wrong
that has been done us?'

'Yes.'

'That we may forgive it.'

'Pardon me, great Heaven!' said Redlaw, lifting up his eyes,
'for having thrown away thine own high attribute!'

'And if,' said Milly, 'if your memory should one day be
restored, as we will hope and pray it may be, would it not be a
blessing to you to recall at once a wrong and its forgiveness?'

He looked at the figure by the door, and fastened his
attentive eyes on her again. A ray of clearer light appeared to
him to shine into his mind from her bright face.

'He cannot go to his abandoned home. He does not seek to
go there. He knows that he could only carry shame and
trouble to those he has so cruelly neglected; and that the best
reparation he can make them now is to avoid them. A very
little money, carefully bestowed, would remove him to some
distant place, where he might live and do no wrong, and make
such atonement as is left within his power for the wrong he
has done. To the unfortunate lady who is his wife, and to his
son, this would be the best and kindest boon that their best
friend could give them – one, too, that they need never know
of; and to him, shattered in reputation, mind, and body, it
might be salvation.'

He took her head between his hands, and kissed it, and said:
'It shall be done. I trust to you to do it for me, now and
secretly; and to tell him that I would forgive him, if I were so
happy as to know for what.'

As she rose, and turned her beaming face towards the fallen
man, implying that her mediation had been successful, he
advanced a step, and, without raising his eyes, addressed
himself to Redlaw.

'You are so generous,' he said, 'you ever were – that you
will try to banish your rising sense of retribution in the
spectacle that is before you. I do not try to banish it from
myself, Redlaw. If you can, believe me.'

The Chemist entreated Milly, by a gesture, to come nearer
to him; and, as he listened, looked in her face, as if to find in it
the clue to what he heard.

'I am too decayed a wretch to make professions; I recollect

my own career too well to array any such before you. But
from the day on which I made my first step downward, in
dealing falsely by you, I have gone down with a certain,
steady, doomed progression. That I say.'

Redlaw, keeping her close at his side, turned his face
towards the speaker, and there was sorrow in it. Something
like mournful recognition too.

'I might have been another man, my life might have been
another life, if I had avoided that first fatal step. I don't know
that it would have been. I claim nothing for the possibility.
Your sister is at rest, and better than she could have been with
me, if I had continued even what you thought me: even what I
once supposed myself to be.'

Redlaw made a hasty motion with his hand, as if he would
have put that subject on one side.

'I speak,' the other went on, 'like a man taken from the
grave. I should have made my own grave last night, had it not
been for this blessed hand.'

'Oh dear, he likes me too!' sobbed Milly under her breath.
'That's another!'

'I could not have put myself in your way last night, even for
bread. But, today, my recollection of what has been between
us is so strongly stirred, and is presented to me, I don't know
how, so vividly, that I have dared to come at her suggestion,
and to take your bounty, and to thank you for it, and beg you,
Redlaw, in your dying hour, to be as merciful to me in your
thoughts as you are in your deeds.'

He turned towards the door, and stopped a moment on his
way forth.

'I hope my son may interest you, for his mother's sake. I
hope he may deserve to do so. Unless my life should be
preserved a long time, and I should know that I have not
misused your aid, I shall never look upon him more.'

Going out, he raised his eyes to Redlaw for the first time.
Redlaw, whose steadfast gaze was fixed upon him, dreamily
held out his hand. He returned and touched it – little more –
with both his own – and, bending down his head, went slowly
out.

In the few moments that elapsed while Milly silently took
him to the gate, the Chemist dropped into his chair, and

covered his face with his hands. Seeing him thus when she came back, accompanied by her husband and his father (who were both greatly concerned for him), she avoided disturbing him, or permitting him to be disturbed; and kneeled down near the chair to put some warm clothing on the boy.

'That's exactly where it is. That's what I always say, father!' exclaimed her admiring husband. 'There's a motherly feeling in Mrs. William's breast that must and will have went!'

'Ay, ay,' said the old man; 'you're right. My son William's right!'

'It happens all for the best, Milly dear, no doubt,' said Mr. William tenderly, 'that we have no children of our own; and yet I sometimes wish you had one to love and cherish. Our little dead child that you built such hopes upon, and that never breathed the breath of life – it has made you quiet-like, Milly.'

'I am very happy in the recollection of it, William dear,' she answered. 'I think of it every day.'

'I was afraid you thought of it a good deal.'

'Don't say afraid; it is a comfort to me; it speaks to me in so many ways. The innocent thing that never lived on earth is like an angel to me, William.'

'You are like an angel to father and me,' said Mr. William softly. 'I know that.'

'When I think of all those hopes I built upon it, and the many times I sat and pictured to myself the little smiling face upon my bosom, that never lay there, and the sweet eyes turned up to mine that never opened to the light,' said Milly, 'I can feel a greater tenderness, I think, for all the disappointed hopes in which there is no harm. When I see a beautiful child in its fond mother's arms, I love it all the better, thinking that my child might have been like that, and might have made my heart as proud and happy.'

Redlaw raised his head, and looked towards her.

'All through life, it seems by me,' she continued, 'to tell me something. For poor neglected children my little child pleads as if it were alive, and had a voice I knew, with which to speak to me. When I hear of youth in suffering or shame, I think that my child might have come to that, perhaps, and that God took it from me in his mercy. Even in age and grey hair, such as father's, it is present: saying that it too might have lived to be old, long and long after you and I were gone, and to have needed the respect and love of younger people.'

Her quiet voice was quieter than ever as she took her husband's arm, and laid her head against it.

'Children love me so, that sometimes I half fancy – it's a silly fancy, William – they have some way I don't know of, of feeling for my little child, and me, and understanding why their love is precious to me. If I have been quiet since, I have been more happy, William, in a hundred ways. Not least happy, dear, in this – that even when my little child was born and dead but a few days, and I was weak and sorrowful, and could not help grieving a little, the thought arose that, if I tried to lead a good life, I should meet in Heaven a bright creature who would call me Mother!'

Redlaw fell upon his knees with a loud cry.

'O Thou,' he said, 'who, through the teaching of pure love, hast graciously restored me to the memory which was the memory of Christ upon the cross, and of all the good who perished in His cause, receive my thanks, and bless her!'

Then he folded her to his heart; and Milly, sobbing more than ever, cried, as she laughed. 'He is come back to himself! He likes me very much indeed, too! Oh dear, dear, dear me, here's another!'

Then, the student entered, leading by the hand a lovely girl, who was afraid to come. And Redlaw, so changed towards him, seeing in him, and in his youthful choice, the softened shadow of that chastening passage in his own life, to which, as to a shady tree, the dove so long imprisoned in his solitary ark might fly for rest and company, fell upon his neck, entreating them to be his children.

Then, as Christmas is a time in which, of all times in the year, the memory of every remediable sorrow, wrong, and trouble in the world around us, should be active with us, not less than our own experiences, for all good, he laid his hand upon the boy, and, silently calling Him to witness who laid His hand on children in old time, rebuking, in the majesty of His prophetic knowledge, those who kept them from him, vowed to protect him, teach him, and reclaim him.

Then, he gave his right hand cheerily to Philip, and said that they would that day hold a Christmas dinner in what used to

be, before the ten poor gentlemen commuted, their great
Dinner Hall; and that they would bid to it as many of that
Swidger family, who, his son had told him, were so numerous
that they might join hands and make a ring round England, as
could be brought together on so short a notice.

And it was that day done. There were so many Swidgers
there, grown up and children, that an attempt to state them in
round numbers might engender doubts, in the distrustful, of
the veracity of this history. Therefore the attempts shall not be
made. But there they were, by dozens and scores – and there
was good news and good hope there, ready for them, of
George, who had been visited again by his father and brother,
and by Milly, and again left in a quiet sleep. There, present at
the dinner too, were the Tetterbys, including young Adolphus, who arrived in his prismatic comforter, in good time for
the beef. Johnny and the baby were too late, of course, and
came in all on one side, the one exhausted, the other in a
supposed state of double-tooth; but that was customary, and
not alarming.

It was sad to see the child who had no name or lineage
watching the other children as they played, not knowing how
to talk with them, or sport with them, and more strange to the
ways of childhood than a rough dog. It was sad, though in a
different way, to see what an instinctive knowledge the
youngest child there had of his being different from the rest,
and how they made timid approaches to him with soft words
and touches, and with little presents, that he might not be
unhappy. But he kept by Milly, and began to love her – that
was another, as she said! – and, as they all liked her dearly,
they were glad of that, and when they saw him peeping at
them from behind her chair, they were pleased that he was so
close to it.

All this the Chemist, sitting with the student and his bride
that was to be, and Philip, and the rest, saw.

Some people have said since that he only thought what has
been herein set down; others, that he read it in the fire, one
winter night about the twilight-time; others, that the Ghost
was but the representation of his gloomy thoughts, and Milly
the embodiment of his better wisdom. *I* say nothing.

— Except this. That as they were assembled in the old Hall,

by no other light than that of a great fire (having dined early), the shadows once more stole out of their hiding-places, and danced about the room, showing the children marvellous shapes and faces on the walls, and gradually changing what was real and familiar there to what was wild and magical. But that there was one thing in the Hall to which the eyes of Redlaw, and of Milly and her husband, and of the old man, and of the student, and his bride that was to be, were often turned, which the shadows did not obscure or change. Deepened in its gravity by the fire-light, and gazing from the darkness of the panelled wall like life, the sedate face in the portrait, with the beard and ruff, looked down at them from under its verdant wreath of holly, as they looked up at it, and, clear and plain below, as if a voice had uttered them, were the words:

'Lord, keep my Memory Green!'

THE HAUNTED HOUSE

THE MORTALS IN THE HOUSE

Under none of the accredited ghostly circumstances, and environed by none of the conventional ghostly surroundings, did I first make acquaintance with the house which is the subject of this Christmas piece. I saw it in the daylight, with the sun upon it. There was no wind, no rain, no lightning, no thunder, no awful or unwonted circumstance, of any kind, to heighten its effect. More than that: I had come to it direct from a railway station: it was not more than a mile distant from the railway station; and, as I stood outside the house, looking back upon the way I had come, I could see the goods train running smoothly along the embankment in the valley. I will not say that everything was utterly commonplace, because I doubt if anything can be that, except to utterly commonplace people – and there my vanity steps in; but, I will take it on myself to say that anybody might see the house as I saw it, any fine autumn morning.

The manner of my lighting on it was this.

I was travelling towards London out of the North, intending to stop by the way, to look at the house. My health required a temporary residence in the country; and a friend of mine who knew that, and who had happened to drive past the house, had written to me to suggest it as a likely place. I had got into the train at midnight, and had fallen asleep, and had woke up and had sat looking out of window at the brillant Northern Lights in the sky, and had fallen asleep again, and had woke up again to find the night gone, with the usual discontented conviction on me that I hadn't been to sleep at all; – upon which question, in the first imbecility of that condition, I am ashamed to believe that I would have done wager by battle with the man who sat opposite me. That opposite man had had, through the night – as that opposite man always has – several legs too many, and all of them too long. In addition to this unreasonable conduct (which was only to be expected of

him), he had had a pencil and a pocket-book, and had been
perpetually listening and taking notes. It had appeared to me
that these aggravating notes related to the jolts and bumps of
the carriage, and I should have resigned myself to his taking
them, under a general supposition that he was in the civil-
engineering way of life, if he had not sat staring straight over
my head whenever he listened. He was a goggly-eyed gentleman of a perplexed aspect, and his demeanour became unbear-
able.

It was a cold, dead morning (the sun not being up yet), and
when I had out-watched the paling light of the fires of the iron
country, and the curtain of heavy smoke that hung at once
between me and the stars and between me and the day, I
turned to my fellow-traveller and said:

'I *beg* your pardon, Sir, but do you observe anything
particular in me?' For, really, he appeared to be taking down,
either my travelling-cap or my hair, with a minuteness that
was a liberty.

The goggle-eyed gentleman withdrew his eyes from behind
me, as if the back of the carriage were a hundred miles off, and
said, with a lofty look of compassion for my insignificance:

'In you, Sir? – B.'

'B, Sir?' said I, growing warm.

'I have nothing to do with you, Sir,' returned the gentleman; 'pray let me listen – O.'

He enunciated this vowel after a pause, and noted it down.

At first I was alarmed, for an Express lunatic and no
communication with the guard, is a serious position. The
thought came to my relief that the gentleman might be what is
popularly called a Rapper: one of a sect for (some of) whom I
have the highest respect, but whom I don't believe in. I was
going to ask him the question, when he took the bread out of
my mouth.

'You will excuse me,' said the gentleman contemptuously,
'if I am too much in advance of common humanity to trouble
myself at all about it. I have passed the night – as indeed I pass
the whole of my time now – in spiritual intercourse.'

'O!' said I, something snappishly.

'The conferences of the night began,' continued the gentleman, turning several leaves of his note-book, 'with this

message: "Evil communications corrupt good manners."'

'Sound,' said I; 'but, absolutely new?'

'New from spirits,' returned the gentleman.

I could only repeat my rather snappish 'O!' and ask if I might be favoured with the last communication.

"A bird in the hand," said the gentleman, reading his last entry with great solemnity, "is worth two in the Bosh."

'Truly I am of the same opinion,' said I; 'but shouldn't it be Bush?'

'It came to me, Bosh,' returned the gentleman.

The gentleman then informed me that the spirit of Socrates had delivered this special revelation in the course of the night, 'My friend, I hope you are pretty well. There are two in this railway carriage. How do you do? There are seventeen thousand four hundred and seventy-nine spirits here, but you cannot see them. Pythagoras is here. He is not at liberty to mention it, but hopes you like travelling.' Galileo likewise had dropped in, with this scientific intelligence. 'I am glad to see you, *amico*. *Come sta?* Water will freeze when it is cold enough. *Addio!*' In the course of the night, also, the following phenomena had occurred. Bishop Butler had insisted on spelling his name, 'Bubler,' for which offence against orthography and good manners he had been dismissed as out of temper. John Milton (suspected of wilful mystification) had repudiated the authorship of Paradise Lost, and had introduced, as joint authors of that poem, two Unknown gentlemen, respectively named Grungers and Scadgingtone. And Prince Arthur, nephew of King John of England, had described himself as tolerably comfortable in the seventh circle, where he was learning to paint on velvet, under the direction of Mrs. Trimmer and Mary Queen of Scots.

If this should meet the eye of the gentleman who favoured me with these disclosures, I trust he will excuse my confessing that the sight of the rising sun, and the contemplation of the magnificent Order of the vast Universe, made me impatient of them. In a word, I was so impatient of them, that I was mightily glad to get out at the next station, and to exchange these clouds and vapours for the free air of Heaven.

By that time it was a beautiful morning. As I walked away among such leaves as had already fallen from the golden,

brown, and russet trees; and as I looked around me on the
wonders of Creation, and thought of the steady, unchanging,
and harmonious laws by which they are sustained; the gentleman's spiritual intercourse seemed to me as poor a piece of
journey-work as ever this world saw. In which heathen state
of mind, I came within view of the house, and stopped to
examine it attentively.

It was a solitary house, standing in a sadly neglected garden:
a pretty even square of some two acres. It was a house of about
the time of George the Second; as stiff, as cold, as formal, and
in as bad taste, as could possibly be desired by the most loyal
admirer of the whole quartet of Georges. It was uninhabited,
but had, within a year or two, been cheaply repaired to render
it habitable; I say cheaply, because the work had been done in a
surface manner, and was already decaying as to the paint and
plaster, though the colours were fresh. A lop-sided board
drooped over the garden wall, announcing that it was 'to let
on very reasonable terms, well furnished.' It was much too
closely and heavily shadowed by trees, and, in particular,
there were six tall poplars before the front windows, which
were excessively melancholy, and the site of which had been
extremely ill chosen.

It was easy to see that it was an avoided house – a house that
was shunned by the village, to which my eye was guided by a
church spire some half a mile off – a house that nobody would
take. And the natural inference was, that it had the reputation
of being a haunted house.

No period within the four-and twenty hours of day and
night is so solemn to me, as the early morning. In the summer
time, I often rise very early, and repair to my room to do a
day's work before breakfast, and I am always on those
occasions deeply impressed by the stillness and solitude
around me. Besides that there is something awful in the being
surrounded by familiar faces asleep – in the knowledge that
those who are dearest to us and to whom we are dearest, are
profoundly unconscious of us, in an impassive state, anticipa-
tive of that mysterious condition to which we are all tending –
the stopped life, the broken threads of yesterday, the deserted
seat, the closed book, the unfinished but abandoned occupation, all are images of Death. The tranquillity of the hour is the

tranquillity of Death. The colour and the chill have the same association. Even a certain air that familiar household objects take upon them when they first emerge from the shadows of the night into the morning, of being newer, and as they used to be long ago, has its counterpart in the subsidence of the worn face of maturity or age, in death, into the old youthful look. Moreover, I once saw the apparition of my father, at this hour. He was alive and well, and nothing ever came of it, but I saw him in the daylight, sitting with his back towards me, on a seat that stood beside my bed. His head was resting on his hand, and whether he was slumbering or grieving, I could not discern. Amazed to see him there, I sat up, moved my position, leaned out of bed, and watched him. As he did not move then, I became alarmed and laid my hand upon his shoulder, as I thought – and there was no such thing.

For all these reasons, and for others less easily and briefly statable, I find the early morning to be my most ghostly time. Any house would be more or less haunted, to me, in the early morning; and a haunted house could scarcely address me to greater advantage than then.

I walked on into the village, with the desertion of this house upon my mind, and I found the landlord of the little inn, sanding his doorstep. I bespoke breakfast, and broached the subject of the house.

'Is it haunted?' I asked.

The landlord looked at me, shook his head, and answered, 'I say nothing.'

'Then it is haunted?'

'Well!' cried the landlord, in a outburst of frankness that had the appearances of desperation – 'I wouldn't sleep in it.'

'Why not?'

'If I wanted to have all the bells in a house ring, with nobody to ring 'em; and all the doors in a house bang, with nobody to bang 'em; and all sorts of feet treading about, with no feet there; why, then,' said the landlord. 'I'd sleep in that house.'

'Is anything seen there?'

The landlord looked at me again, and then, with his former appearance of desperation, called down his stable-yard for 'Ikey!'

The call produced a high-shouldered young fellow, with a round red face, a short crop of sandy hair, a very broad humerous mouth, a turned-up nose, and a great sleeved waistcoat of purple bars, with mother-of-pearl buttons, that seemed to be growing upon him, and to be in a fair way – if it were not pruned – of covering his head and overrunning his boots.

'This gentleman wants to know,' said the landlord, 'if anything's seen at the Poplars.'

"Ooded woman with a howl,' said Ikey, in a state of great freshness.

'Do you mean a cry?'

'I mean a bird, Sir.'

'A hooded woman with an owl. Dear me! Did you ever see her?'

'I seen the howl.'

'Never the woman?'

'Not so plain as the howl, but they always keeps together.'

'Has anybody ever seen the woman as plainly as the owl?'

'Lord bless you, Sir! Lots.'

'Who?'

'Lord bless you, Sir! Lots.'

'The general-dealer opposite, for instance, who is opening his shop?'

'Perkins? Bless you, Perkins wouldn't go a-nigh the place. No!' observed the young man, with considerable feeling; 'he an't over wise, an't Perkins, but he an't such a fool as *that*.'

(Here, the landlord murmured his confidence in Perkins's knowing better.)

'Who is – or who was – the hooded woman with the owl? Do you know?'

'Well!' said Ikey, holding up his cap with one hand while he scratched his head with the other, 'they say, in general, that she was murdered, and the howl he 'ooted the while.'

This very concise summary of the facts was all I could learn, except that a young man, as hearty and likely a young man as ever I see, had been took with fits and held down in 'em, after seeing the hooded woman. Also, that a personage, dimly described as 'a hold chap, a sort of one-eyed tramp, answering to the name of Joby, unless you challenged him as Greenwood, and then he said, 'Why not? and even if so, mind your own business,'' had encountered the hooded woman, a matter of five or six times. But, I was not materially assisted by these witnesses: inasmuch as the first was in California, and the last was, as Ikey said (and he was confirmed by the landlord), Anywheres.

Now, although I regard with a hushed and solemn fear, the mysteries, between which and this state of existence is interposed the barrier of the great trial and change that fall on all the things that live; and although I have not the audacity to pretend that I know anything of them; I can no more reconcile the more banging of doors, ringing of bells, creaking of boards, and such-like insignificances, with the majestic beauty and pervading analogy of all the Divine rules that I am permitted to understand, than I had been able, a little while before, to yoke the spiritual intercourse of my fellow-traveller to the chariot of the rising sun. Moreover, I had lived in two haunted houses – both abroad. In one of these, an old Italian palace, which bore the reputation of being twice abandoned on that account, I lived eight months, most tranquilly and pleasantly: notwithstanding that the house had a score of mysterious bedrooms, which were never used, and possessed, in one large room in which I sat reading, times out of number at all hours, and next to which I slept, a haunted chamber of the first pretensions. I gently hinted these considerations to the landlord. And as to this particular house having a bad name, I reasoned with him, Why, how many things had bad names undeservedly, and how easy it was to give bad names, and did he not think that if he and I were persistently to whisper in the village that any weird-looking old drunken tinker of the neighbourhood had sold himself to the Devil, he would come in time to be suspected, of that commercial venture! All this wise talk was perfectly ineffective with the landlord, I am bound to confess, and was as dead a failure as ever I made in my life.

To cut this part of the story short, I was piqued about the haunted house, and was already half resolved to take it. So, after breakfast, I got the keys from Perkins's brother-in-law (a whip and harness maker, who keeps the Post Office, and is under submission to a most rigorous wife of the Doubly

Seceding Little Emmanuel persuasion), and went up to the house, attended by my landlord and by Ikey.

Within, I found it, as I had expected, transcendently dismal. The slowly changing shadows waved on it from the heavy trees, were doleful in the last degree; the house was ill-placed, ill-built, ill-planned, and ill-fitted. It was damp, it was not free from dry rot, there was a flavour of rats in it, and it was the gloomy victim of that indescribable decay which settles on all the work of man's hands whenever it is not turned to man's account. The kitchens and offices were too large, and too remote from each other. Above stairs and below, waste tracts of passage intervened between patches of fertility represented by rooms; and there was a mouldy old well with a green growth upon it, hiding like a murderous trap, near the bottom of the back stairs, under the double row of bells. One of these bells was labelled, on a black ground in faded white letters, MASTER B. This, they told me, was the bell that rang the most.

'Who was Master B.?' I asked. 'Is it known what he did while the owl hooted?'

'Rang the bell,' said Ikey.

I was rather struck by the prompt dexterity with which this young man pitched his fur cap at the bell, and rang it himself. It was a loud, unpleasant bell, and made a very disagreeable sound. The other bells were inscribed according to the names of the rooms to which their wires were conducted: as 'Picture Room,' 'Double Room,' 'Clock Room,' and the like. Following Master B.'s bell to its source, I found that young gentleman to have had but indifferent third-class accommodation in a triangular cabin under the cock-loft, with a corner fireplace which Master B. must have been exceedingly small if he were ever able to warm himself at, and a corner chimneypiece like a pyramidal staircase to the ceiling for Tom Thumb. The papering of one side of the room had dropped down bodily, with fragments of plaster adhering to it, and almost blocked up the door. It appeared that Master B., in his spiritual condition, always made a point of pulling the paper down. Neither the landlord nor Ikey could suggest why he made such a fool of himself.

Except that the house had an immensely large rambling loft

at top, I made no other discoveries. It was moderately well furnished, but sparely. Some of the furniture – say, a third – was as old as the house; the rest was of various periods within the last half-century. I was referred to a corn-chandler in the market-place of the country town to treat for the house. I went that day, and I took it for six months.

It was just the middle of October when I moved in with my maiden sister (I venture to call her eight-and-thirty, she is so very handsome, sensible, and engaging). We took with us, a deaf stable-man, my bloodhound Turk, two women servants, and a young person called an Odd Girl. I have reason to record of the attendant last enumerated, who was one of the Saint Lawrence's Union Female Orphans, that she was a fatal mistake and a disastrous engagement.

The year was dying early, the leaves were falling fast, it was a raw cold day when we took possession, and the gloom of the house was most depressing. The cook (an amiable woman, but of a weak turn of intellect) burst into tears on beholding the kitchen, and requested that her silver watch might be delivered over to her sister (2 Tuppintock's Gardens, Liggs's Walk, Clapham Rise), in the event of anything happening to her from the damp. Streaker, the housemaid, feigned cheerfulness, but was the greater martyr. The Odd Girl, who had never been in the country, alone was pleased and made arrangements for sowing an acorn in the garden outside the scullery window, and rearing an oak.

We went, before dark, through all the natural – as opposed to supernatural – miseries incidental to our state. Dispiriting reports ascended (like the smoke) from the basement in no rolling-pin, there was no salamander (which failed to surprise me, for I don't know what it is), there was nothing in the house, what there was, was broken, the last people must have lived like pigs, what could the meaning of the landlord be? Through these distresses, the Odd Girl was cheerful and exemplary. But within four hours after dark we had got into a supernatural groove, and the Odd Girl had seen 'Eyes,' and was in hysterics.

My sister and I had agreed to keep the haunting strictly to ourselves, and my impression was, and still is, that I had not left Ikey, when he helped to unload the cart, alone with the woman, or any one of them, for one minute. Nevertheless, as I say, the Odd Girl had 'seen Eyes' (no other explanation could ever be drawn from her), before nine, and by ten o'clock had had as much vinegar applied to her as would pickle a handsome salmon.

I leave a discerning public to judge of my feelings, when, under these untoward circumstances, at about half-past ten o'clock Master B.'s bell began to ring in a most infuriated manner, and Turk howled until the house resounded with his lamentations!

I hope I may never again be in a state of mind so unchristian as the mental frame in which I lived for some weeks, respecting the memory of Master B. Whether his bell was rung by rats, or mice, or bats, or wind, or what other accidental vibration or sometimes by one cause, sometimes another, and sometimes by collusion, I don't know; but, certain it is, that it did ring two nights out of three, until I conceived the happy idea of twisting Master B.'s neck – in other words, breaking his bell short off – and silencing that young gentleman, as to my experience and belief, for ever.

But, by that time, the Odd Girl had developed such improving powers of catalepsy, that she had become a shining example of that very inconvenient disorder. She would stiffen, like a Guy Fawkes endowed with unreason, on the most irrelevant occasions. I would address the servants in a lucid manner, pointing out to them that I had painted Master B.'s room and balked the paper, and taken Master B.'s bell away and balked the ringing, and if they could suppose that that confounded boy had lived and died, to clothe himself with no better behaviour than would most unquestionably have brought him and the sharpest particles of a birch-broom into close acquaintance in the present imperfect state of existence, could they also suppose a mere poor human being, such as I was, capable by those contemptible means of counteracting and limiting the powers of the disembodied spirits of the dead, or of any spirits? – I say I would become emphatic and cogent, not to say rather complacent, in such an address, when it would all go for nothing by reason of the Odd Girl's suddenly stiffening from the toes upward, and glaring amoung us like a parochial petrifaction.

Streaker, the housemaid, too, had an attribute of a most discomfiting nature. I am unable to say whether she was of an unusually lymphatic temperament, or what else was the matter with her, but this young woman became a mere Distillory for the production of the largest and most transparent tears I ever met with. Combined with these characteristics, was a peculiar tenacity of hold in those specimens, so that they didn't fall, but hung upon her face and nose. In this condition, and mildly and deplorably shaking her head, her silence would throw me more heavily than the Admirable Crichton could have done in a verbal disputation for a purse of money. Cook, likewise, always covered me with confusion as with a garment, by neatly winding up the session with the protest that the Ouse was wearing her out, and by meekly repeating her last wishes regarding her silver watch.

As to our nightly life, the contagion of suspicion and fear was among us, and there is no such contagion under the sky. Hooded woman? According to the accounts, we were in a perfect Convent of hooded women. Noises? With that contagion downstairs, I myself have sat in the dismal parlour, listening, until I have heard so many and such strange noises, that they would have chilled my blood if I had not warmed it by dashing out to make discoveries. Try this in bed, in the dead of the night; try this at your own comfortable fireside, in the life of the night. You can fill any house with noises, if you will, until you have a noise for every nerve in your nervous system.

I repeat; the contagion of suspicion and fear was among us, and there is no such contagion under the sky. The women (their noses in a chronic state of excoriation from smelling-salts) were always primed and loaded for a swoon, and ready to go off with hair-triggers. The two elder detached the Odd Girl on all expeditions that were considered doubly hazardous, and she always established the reputation of such adventures by coming back cataleptic. If Cook or Streaker went overhead after dark, we knew we should presently hear a bump on the ceiling; and this took place so constantly, that it was as if a fighting man were engaged to go about the house, administering a touch of his art which I believe is called The Auctioneer, to every domestic he met with.

It was in vain to do anything. It was in vain to be frightened, for the moment in one's own person, by a real owl, and then to show the owl. It was in vain to discover, by striking an accidental discord on the piano, that Turk always howled at particular notes and combinations. It was in vain to be a Rhadamanthus with the bells, and if an unfortunate bell rang without leave, to have it down inexorably and silence it. It was in vain to fire up chimneys, let torches down the well, charge furiously into suspected rooms and recesses. We changed servants, and it was no better. The new set ran away, and a third set came, and it was no better. At last, our comfortable housekeeping got to be so disorganised and wretched, that I one night dejectedly said to my sister: 'Patty, I begin to despair of our getting people to go on with us here, and I think we must give this up.'

My sister, who is a woman of immense spirit, replied, 'No, John, don't give it up. Don't be beaten, John. There is another way.'

'And what is that?' said I.

'John,' returned my sister, 'if we are not to be driven out of this house, and that for no reason whatever, that is apparent to you or me, we must help ourselves and take the house wholly and solely into our own hands.'

'But, the servants,' said I.

'Have no servants,' said my sister, boldly.

Like most people in my grade of life, I had never thought of the possibility of going on without those faithful obstructions. The notion was so new to me when suggested, that I looked very doubtful.

'We know they come here to be frightened and infect one another, and we know they are frightened and do infect one another,' said my sister.

'With the exception of Bottles,' I observed, in a meditative tone.

(The deaf stable-man. I kept him in my service, and still keep him, as a phenomenon of moroseness not to be matched in England.)

'To be sure, John,' assented by sister; 'except Bottles. And what does that go to prove? Bottles talks to nobody, and hears nobody unless he is absolutely roared at, and what alarm has Bottles ever given, or taken? None.'

This was perfectly true; the individual in question having retired, every night at ten o'clock, to his bed over the coach-house, with no other company than a pitchfork and a pail of water. That the pail of water would have been over me, and the pichfork through me, if I had put myself without announcement in Bottles's way after that minute, I had deposited in my own mind as a fact worth remembering. Neither had Bottles ever taken the least notice of any of our many uproars. An imperturbable and speechless man, he had sat at his supper, with Streaker present in a swoon, and the Odd Girl marble, and had only put another potato in his cheek, or profited by the general misery to help himself to beefsteak pie.

'And so,' continued my sister, 'I exempt Bottles. And considering, John, that the house is too large, and perhaps too lonely, to be kept well in hand by Bottles, you, and me, I propose that we cast about among our friends for a certain selected number of the most reliable and willing – form a Society here for three months – wait upon ourselves and one another – live cheerfully and socially – and see what happens.'

I was so charmed with my sister, that I embraced her on the spot, and went into her plan with the greatest ardour.

We were then in the third week of November; but, we took our measures so vigorously, and were so well seconded by the friends in whom we confided, that there was still a week of the month unexpired, when our party all came down together merrily, and mustered in the haunted house.

I will mention, in this place, two small changes that I made while my sister and I were yet alone. It occurring to me as not improbable that Turk howled in the house of night, partly because he wanted to get out of it, I stationed him in his kennel outside, but unchained; and I seriously warned the village that any man who came in his way must not expect to leave him without a rip in his own throat. I then casually asked Ikey if he were a judge of a gun? On his saying, 'Yes, Sir, I knows a good gun when I sees her.' I begged the favour of his stepping up to the house and looking at mine.

'She's a true one, Sir,' said Ikey, after inspecting a double-barrelled rifle that I bought in New York a few years ago. 'No mistake about *her*, Sir.'

'Ikey,' said I, 'don't mention it; I have seen something in this house.'

'No, Sir?' he whispered, greedily opening his eyes. ''Ooded lady, Sir?'

'Don't be frightened,' said I. 'It was a figure rather like you.'

'Lord, Sir?'

'Ikey!' said I, shaking hands with him warmly: I may say affectionately; 'if there is any truth in these ghost-stories, the greatest service I can do you, is, to fire at that figure. And I promise you, by Heaven and earth, I will do it with this gun if I see it again!'

The young man thanked me, and took his leave with some little precipitation, after declining a glass of liquor. I imparted my secret to him, because I had never quite forgotten his throwing his cap at the bell; because I had, on another occasion, noticed something very like a fur cap, lying not far from the bell, one night when it had burst out ringing; and because I had remarked that we were at our ghostliest whenever he came up in the evening to comfort the servants. Let me do Ikey no injustice. He was afraid of the house, and believed in its being haunted; and yet he would play false on the haunting side, so surely as he got an opportunity. The Odd Girl's case was exactly similar. She went about the house in a state of real terror, and yet lied monstrously and wilfully, and invented many of the alarms she spread, and made many of the sounds we heard. I had had my eye on the two, and I know it. It is not necessary for me, here to account for this preposterous state of mind; I content myself with remarking that it is familiarly known to every intelligent man who has had fair medical, legal, or other watchful experience; that it is as well established and as common a state of mind as any with which observers are acquainted; and that it is one of the first elements, above all others, rationally to be suspected in, and strictly looked for, and separated from, any question of this kind.

To return to our party. The first thing we did when we were all assembled, was, to draw lots for bedrooms. That done, and every bedroom, and indeed, the whole house, having been minutely examined by the whole body, we allotted the various household duties, as if we had been on a gipsy party, or a yachting party, or a hunting party, or were shipwrecked. I then recounted the floating rumours concerning the hooded lady, the owl, and Master B.: with others, still more filmy, which had floated about during our occupation, relative to some ridiculous old ghost of the female gender who went up and down, carrying the ghost of a round table; and also to an impalpable Jackass, whom nobody was ever able to catch. Some of these ideas I really believe our people below had communicated to one another in some diseased way, without conveying them in words. We then gravely called one another to witness, that we were not there to be deceived, or to deceive – which we considered pretty much the same thing – and that, with a serious sense of responsibility, we would be strictly true to one another, and would strictly follow out the truth. The understanding was established, that any one who heard unusual noises in the night, and who wished to trace them, should knock at my door; lastly, that on Twelfth Night, the last night of holy Christmas, all our individual experiences since that then present hour of our coming together in the haunted house, should be brought to light for the good of all; and that we would hold our peace on the subject till then, unless on some remarkable provocation to break silence.

We were, in number and in character, as follows:

First – to get my sister and myself out of the way – there were we two. In the drawing of lots, my sister drew her own room, and I drew Master B.'s. Next, there was our first cousin John Herschel, so called after the great astronomer: than whom I suppose a better man at a telescope does not breathe. With him, was his wife: a charming creature to whom he had been married in the previous spring. I thought him (under the circumstances) rather imprudent to bring her, because there is no knowing what even a false alarm may do at such a time; but I suppose he knew his own business best, and I must say that if she had been *my* wife, I never could have left her endearing and bright face behind. They drew the Clock Room. Alfred Starling, an uncommonly agreeable young fellow of eight-and-twenty for whom I have the greatest liking, was in the Double Room; mine, usually, and designated by that name from having a dressing-room within it, with two large and cumbersome windows, which no wedges I was ever able to make, would keep from shaking, in any weather, wind or no wind. Alfred is a young fellow who pretends to be 'fast' (another word for loose, as I understand the term), but who is much too good and sensible for that nonsense, and who would have distinguished himself before now, if his father had not unfortunately left him a small independence of two hundred a year, on the strength of which his only occupation in life has been to spend six. I am in hopes, however, that this Banker may break, or that he may enter into some speculation guaranteed to pay twenty per cent.; for, I am convinced that if he could only be ruined, his fortune is made. Belinda Bates, bosom friend of my sister, and a most intellectual, amiable, and delightful girl, got the Picture Room. She has a fine genius for poetry, combined with real business earnestness, and 'goes in' – to use an expression of Alfred's – for Woman's mission, Woman's rights, Woman's wrongs, and everything that is woman's with a capital W, or is not and ought to be, or is and ought not to be. 'Most praiseworthy, my dear, and Heaven prosper yet!' I whispered to her on the first night of my taking leave of her at the Picture-Room door, 'but don't overdo it. And in respect of the great necessity there is, my darling, for more employ-ments being within the reach of Woman than our civilisation has as yet assigned to her, don't fly at the unfortunate men, even those men who are at first sight in your way, as if they were the natural oppressors of your sex; for, trust me, Belinda, they do sometimes spend their wages among wives and daughters, sisters, mothers, aunts, and grandmothers; and the play is, really, not all Wolf and Red Riding-Hood, but has other parts in it. However, I digress.

Belinda, as I have mentioned, occupied the Picture Room. We had but three chambers: the Corner Room, the Cupboad Room, and the Garden Room. My old friend, Jack Governor, 'slung his hammock,' as he called it, in the Corner Room. I have always regarded Jack as the finest-looking sailor that ever sailed. He is gray now, but as handsome as he was a quarter of a century ago – nay, handsomer. A portly, cheery, well-built figure of a broad-shouldered man, with a frank smile, as brilliant dark eye, and a rich dark eyebrow. I remember those under darker hair, and they look all the better for their silver setting. He has been wherever his Union namesake flies, has Jack, and I have met old shipmates of his, away in the Mediterranean and on the other side of the Atlantic, who have beamed and brightened at the casual mention of this name, and have cried, 'You know Jack Governor? Then you know a prince of men!' That he is! And so unmistakably a naval officer, that if you were to meet him coming out of an Esquimaux snow-hut in seal's skins, you would be vaguely persuaded he was in full naval uniform.

Jack once had that bright clear eye of his on my sister; but, it fell out that he married another lady and took her to South America, where she died. This was a dozen years ago or more. He brought down with him to our haunted house a little cask of salt beef; for, he is always convinced that all salt beef not of his own pickling, is mere carrion, and invariably, when he goes to London, packs a piece in his portmanteau. He had also volunteered to bring with him one 'Nat Beaver,' an old comrade of his, captain of a merchantman. Mr. Beaver, with a thick-set wooden face and figure, and apparently as hard as a block all over, proved to be an intelligent man, with a world of watery experiences in him, and great practical knowledge. At times, there was a curious nervousness about him, apparently the lingering result of some old illness; but, it seldom lasted many minutes. He got the Cupboard Room, and lay there next to Mr. Undery, my friend and solicitor: who came down, in an amateur capacity, 'to go through with it,' as he said, and who plays whist better than the whole Law List, from the red cover at the beginning to the red cover at the end.

I never was happier in my life, and I believe it was the universal feeling among us. Jack Governor, always a man of wonderful resources, was Chief Cook, and made some of the best dishes I ever ate, including unapproachable curries. My sister was pastrycook and confectioner. Starling and I were Cook's Mate, turn and turn about, and on special occasions the chief cook 'pressed' Mr. Beaver. We had a great deal of out-door sport and exercise, but nothing was neglected within, and there was no ill-humour or misunderstanding among us, and our evenings were so delightful that we had at least one good reason for being reluctant to go to bed.

We had a few night alarms in the beginning. On the first night, I was knocked up by Jack with a most wonderful ship's lantern in his hand, like the gills of some monster of the deep, who informed me that he 'was going aloft to the main truck,' to have the weathercock down. It was a stormy night, and I remonstrated; but Jack called my attention to its making a sound like a cry of despair, and said somebody would be 'hailing a ghost' presently, if it wasn't done. So, up to the top of the house, where I could hardly stand for the wind, we went, accompanied by Mr. Beaver; and there Jack, lantern and all, with Mr. Beaver after him, swarmed up to the top of a cupola, some two dozen feet above the chimneys, and stood upon nothing particular, coolly knocking the weathercock off, until they both got into such good spirits with the wind and the height, that I thought they would never come down. Another night, they turned out again, and had a chimney-cowl off. Another night, they cut a sobbing and gulping water-pipe away. Another night, they found out something else. On several occasions, they both, in the coolest manner, simultaneously dropped out of their respective bedroom windows, hand over hand by their counterpanes, to 'overhaul' something mysterious in the garden.

The engagement among us was faithfully kept, and nobody revealed anything. All we knew was, if any one's room were haunted, no one looked the worse for it.

When I established myself in the triangular garret which had gained so distinguished a reputation, my thoughts naturally turned to Master B. My speculations about him were uneasy and manifold. Whether his Christian name was Benjamin, Bissextile (from his having been born in Leap Year), Barth-olomew, or Bill. Whether the initial letter belonged to his family name, and that was Baxter, Black, Brown, Barker, Buggins, Baker, or Bird. Whether he was a foundling, and had been baptized B. Whether he was a lion-hearted boy, and B. was short for Briton, or for Bull. Whether he could possibly have been kith and kin to an illustrious lady who brightened my own childhood, and had come of the blood of the brilliant Mother Bunch?

With these profitless meditations I tormented myself much. I also carried the mysterious letter into the appearance and pursuits of the deceased; wondering whether he dressed in Blue, wore Boots (he couldn't have been Bald), was a boy of Brains, liked Books, was good at Bowling, had any skill as a Boxer, even in his Buoyant Boyhood Bathed from a Bathing-machine at Bognor, Bangor, Bournemouth, Brighton, or Broadstairs, like a Bounding Billiard Ball?

So, from the first, I was haunted by the letter B.

It was not long before I remarked that I never by any hazard had a dream of Master B., or of anything belonging to him. But, the instant I awoke from sleep, at whatever hour of the night, my thoughts took him up, and roamed away, trying to attach his initial letter to something that would fit it and keep it quiet.

For six nights, I had been worried thus in Master B.'s room, when I began to perceive that things were going wrong.

The first appearance that presented itself was early in the morning when it was but just daylight and no more. It was standing shaving at my glass, when I suddenly discovered, to my consternation and amazement, that I was shaving – not myself – I am fifty – but a boy. Apparently Master B.!

I trembled and looked over my shoulder; nothing there. I looked again in the glass, and distinctly saw the features and expression of a boy, who was shaving, not to get rid of a beard, but to get one. Extremely troubled in my mind, I took a few turns in the room, and went back to the looking-glass, resolved to steady my hand and complete the operation in which I had been disturbed. Opening my eyes, which I had shut while recovering my firmness, I now met in the glass, looking straight at me, the eyes of a young man of four or five and twenty. Terrified by this new ghost, I closed my eyes, and made a strong effort to recover myself. Opening them again, I saw, shaving his cheek in the glass, my father, who has long been dead. Nay, I even saw my grandfather too, whom I never did see in my life.

Although naturally much affected by these remarkable visitations, I determined to keep my secret, until the time agreed upon for the present general disclosure. Agitated by a multitude of curious thoughts, I retired to my room, that night, prepared to encounter some new experience of a spectral character. Nor was my preparation needless, for, waking from an uneasy sleep at exactly two o'clock in the morning, what were my feelings to find that I was sharing my bed with the skeleton of Master B.!

I sprang up, and the skeleton sprang up also. I then heard a plaintive voice saying, 'Where am I! What is become of me?' and, looking hard in that direction, perceived the ghost of Master B.

The young spectre was dressed in an obsolete fashion: or rather, was not so much dressed as put into a case of inferior pepper-and-salt cloth, made horrible by means of shining buttons. I observed that these buttons went, in a double row, over each shoulder of the young ghost, and appeared to descend his back. He wore a frill round his neck. His right hand (which I distinctly noticed to be inky) was laid upon his stomach; connecting this action with some feeble pimples on his countenance, and his general air of nausea, I concluded this ghost to be the ghost of a boy who had habitually taken a great deal too much medicine.

'Where am I?' said the little spectre, in a pathetic voice. 'And why was I born in the Calomel days, and why did I have all that Calomel given me?'

I replied, with sincere earnestness, that upon my soul I couldn't tell him.

'Where is my little sister,' said the ghost, 'and where my angelic little wife, and where is the boy I went to school with?'

I entreated the phantom to be comforted, and above all things to take heart respecting the loss of the boy he went to school with. I represented to him that probably that boy never did, within human experience, come out well, when disco-vered. I urged that I myself had, in later life, turned up several boys whom I went to school with, and none of them had at all answered. I expressed my humble belief that the boy never did answer. I represented that he was a mythic character, a delusion, and a snare. I recounted how, the last time I found him, I found him at a dinner party behind a wall of white cravat, with an inconclusive opinion on every possible subject, and a power of silent boredom absolutely Titanic. I related how, on the strength of our having been together at 'Old Doylance's,' he had asked himself to breakfast with me (a social offence of the largest magnitude); how, fanning my weak embers of belief in Doylance's boys, I had let him in; and how, he had proved to be a fearful wanderer about the earth, pursuing the race of Adam with inexplicable notions concern-ing the currency, and with a proposition that the Bank of England should, on pain of being abolished, instantly strike off and circulate, God knows how many thousand millions of ten-and-sixpenny notes.

The ghost heard me in silence, and with a fixed stare. 'Barber!' it apostrophised me when I had finished.

'Barber?' I repeated – for I am not of that profession.

'Condemned,' said the ghost, 'to shave a constant change of customers – now, me – now, a young man – now, thyself as thou art – now, thy father – now, thy grandfather; conde-mned, too, to lie down with a skeleton every night, and to rise with it every morning –'

(I shuddered on hearing this dismal announcement).

'Barber! Pursue me!'

I had felt, even before the words were uttered, that I was

under a spell to pursue the phantom. I immediately did so, and was in Master B.'s room no longer.

Most people knew what long and fatiguing night journeys had been forced upon the witches who used to confess, and who, no doubt, told the exact truth – particularly as they were always assisted with leading questions, and the Torture was always ready. I asseverate that, during my occupation of Master B.'s room, I was taken by the ghost that haunted it, on expeditions fully as long and wild as any of those. Assuredly, I was presented to no shabby old man with a goat's horns and tail (something between Pan and an old clothesman), holding conventional receptions, as stupid as those of real life and less decent; but, I came upon other things which appeared to me to have more meaning.

Confident that I speak the truth and shall be believed, I declare without hesitation that I followed the ghost, in the first instance on a broom-stick, and afterwards on a rocking-horse. The very smell of the animal's paint – especially when I brought it out, by making him warm – I am ready to swear to. I followed the ghost, afterwards, in a hackney coach; an institution with the peculiar smell of which, the present generation is unacquainted, but to which I am again ready to swear as a combination of stable, dog with the mange, and very old bellows. (In this, I appeal to previous generations to confirm or refute me.) I pursued the phantom, on a headless donkey: at least, upon a donkey who was so interested in the state of his stomach that his head was always down there, investigating it; on ponies, expressly born to kick up behind; on roundabouts and swings, from fairs; in the first cab – another forgotten institution where the fare regularly got into bed, and was tucked up with the driver.

Not to trouble you with a detailed account of all my travels in pursuit of the ghost of Master B., which were longer and more wonderful than those of Sinbad the Sailor, I will confine myself to one experience from which you may judge of many.

I was marvellously changed. I was myself, yet not myself. I was conscious of something within me, which has been the same all through my life, and which I have always recognised under all its phases and varieties as never altering, and yet I was not the I who had gone to bed in Master B.'s room. I had the smoothest of faces and the shortest of legs, and I had taken another creature like myself, also with the smoothest of faces and the shortest of legs, behind a door, and was confiding to him a proposition of the most astounding nature.

This proposition was, that we should have a Seraglio.

The other creature assented warmly. He had no notion of respectability, neither had I. It was the custom of the East, it was the way of the good Caliph Haroun Alraschid (let me have the corrupted name again for once, it is so scented with sweet memories!), the usage was highly laudable, and most worthy of imitation. 'O, yes! Let us,' said the other creature with a jump, 'have a Seraglio.'

It was not because we entertained the faintest doubts of the meritorious character of the Oriental establishment we proposed to import, that we perceived it must be kept a secret from Miss Griffin. It was because we knew Miss Griffin to be bereft of human sympathies, and incapable of appreciating the greatness of the great Haroun. Mystery impenetrably shrouded from Miss Griffin then, let us entrust it to Miss Bule.

We were ten in Miss Griffin's establishment by Hampstead Ponds; eight ladies and two gentlemen. Miss Bule, whom I judged to have attained the ripe age of eight or nine, took the lead in society. I opened the subject to her in the course of the day, and proposed that she should become the Favourite.

Miss Bule, after struggling with the diffidence so natural to, and charming in, her adorable sex, expressed herself as flattered by the idea, but wished to know how it was proposed to provide for Miss Pipson? Miss Bule – who was understood to have vowed towards that young lady, a friendship, halves, and no secrets, until death, on the Church Service and Lessons complete in two volumes with case and lock – Miss Bule said she could not, as the friend of Pipson, disguise from herself, or me, that Pipson was not one of the common.

Now, Miss Pipson, having curly light hair and blue eyes (which was my idea of anything mortal and feminine that was called Fair), I promptly replied that I regarded Miss Pipson in the light of a Fair Circassian.

'And what then?' Miss Bule pensively asked.

I replied that she must be inveigled by a Merchant, brought to me veiled, and purchased as a slave.

[The other creature had already fallen into the second male place in the State, and was set apart for Grand Vizier. He afterwards resisted this disposal of events, but had his hair pulled until he yielded.]

'Shall I not be jealous?' Miss Bule inquired, casting down her eyes.

'Zobeide, no,' I replied; 'you will ever be the favourite Sultana; the first place in my heart, and on my throne, will be ever yours.'

Miss Bule, upon that assurance, consented to propound the idea to her seven beautiful companions. It occurring to me, in the course of the same day, that we knew we could trust a grinning and good-natured soul called Tabby, who was the serving drudge of the house, and had no more figure than one of the beds, and upon whose face there was always more or less black-lead, I slipped into Miss Bule's hand after supper, a little note to that effect: dwelling on the black-lead as being in a manner deposited by the finger of Providence, pointing Tabby out for Mesrour, the celebrated chief of the Blacks of the Hareem.

There were difficulties in the formation of the desired institution, as there are in all combinations. The other creature showed himself of a low character, and, when defeated in aspiring to the throne, pretended to have conscientious scruples about prostrating himself before the Caliph; wouldn't call him Commander of the Faithful; spoke of him slightingly and inconsistently as a mere 'chap;' said he, the other creature, 'wouldn't play' – Play! and was otherwise coarse and offensive. This meanness of disposition was, however, put down by the general indignation of an united Seraglio, and I became blessed in the smiles of eight of the fairest of the daughters of men.

The smiles could only be bestowed when Miss Griffin was looking another way, and only then in very wary manner, for there was a legend among the followers of the Prophet that she saw with a little round ornament in the middle of the pattern on the back of her shawl. But every day after dinner, for an hour, we were all together, and then the Favourite and the rest of the Royal Hareem competed who should most beguile the leisure of the Serene Haroun reposing from the cares of State –

which were generally, as in most affairs of State, of an arithmetical character, the Commander of the Faithful being a fearful boggler at a sum.

On these occasions, the devoted Mesrour, chief of the Blacks of the Hareem, was always in attendance (Miss Griffin usually ringing for that officer, at the same time, with great vehemence), but never acquitted himself in a manner worthy of his historical reputation. In the first place, his bringing a broom into the Divan of the Caliph, even when Haroun wore on his shoulders the red robe of anger (Miss Pipson's pelisse), though it might be got over for the moment, was never to be quite satisfactorily accounted for. In the second place, his breaking out into grinning exclamations of 'Lork you pretties!' was neither Eastern nor respectful. In the third place, when specially instructed to say 'Bismillah!' he always said 'Hallelujah!' This officer, unlike his class, was too good-humoured altogether, kept his mouth open far too wide, expressed approbation to an incongruous extent, and even once – it was on the occasion of the purchase of the Fair Circassian for five hundred thousand purses of gold, and cheap, too – embraced the Slave, the Favourite, and the Caliph, all round. (Parenthetically let me say God bless Mesrour, and may there have been sons and daughters on that tender bosom, softening many a hard day since!)

Miss Griffin was a model of propriety, and I am at a loss to imagine what the feelings of the virtuous woman would have been, if she had known, when she paraded us down the Hampstead-road two and two, that she was walking with a stately step at the head of Polygamy and Mahomedanism. I believe that a mysterious and terrible joy with which the contemplation of Miss Griffin, in this unconscious state, inspired us, and a grim sense prevalent among us that there was a dreadful power in our knowledge of what Miss Griffin (who knew all things that could be learnt out of book) didn't know, were the mainspring of the preservation of our secret. It was wonderfully kept, but was once upon the verge of self-betrayal. The danger and escape occurred upon a Sunday. We were all ten ranged in a conspicuous part of the gallery at church, with Miss Griffin at our head – as we were every Sunday – advertising the establishment in an unsecular sort of way – when the description of Solomon in his domestic glory happened to be read. The moment that monarch was thus referred to, conscience whispered me, 'Thou, too, Haroun!' The officiating minister had a cast in his eye, and it assisted conscience by giving him the appearance of reading personally at me. A crimson blush, attended by a fearful perspiration, suffused my features. The Grand Vizier become more dead than alive, and the whole Seraglio reddened as if the sunset of Bagdad shone direct upon their lovely faces. At this portentous time the awful Griffin rose, and balefully surveyed the children of Islam. My own impression was, that Church and State had entered into a conspiracy with Miss Griffin to expose us, and that we should all be put into white sheets, and exhibited in the centre aisle. But, so Westerly – if I may be allowed the expression as opposite to Eastern associations – was Miss Griffin's sense of rectitude, that she merely suspected Apples, and we were saved.

I have called the Seraglio, united. Upon the question, solely, whether the Commander of the Faithful durst exercise a right of kissing in that sanctuary of the palace, were its peerless inmates divided. Zobeide asserted a counter-right in the Favourite to scratch, the fair Circassian put her face, for refuge, into a green baize bag, originally designed for books. On the other hand, a young antelope of transcendent beauty from the fruitful plains of Camdentown (whence she had been brought, by traders, in the half-yearly caravan that crossed the intermediate desert after the holidays), held more liberal opinions, but stipulated for limiting the benefit of them to that dog, and son of a dog, the Grand Vizier – who had no rights, and was not in question. At length, the difficulty was compromised by the installation of a very youthful slave as Deputy. She, raised upon a stool, officially received upon her cheeks the salutes intended by the gracious Haroun for other Sultanas, and was privately rewarded from the coffers of the Ladies of the Hareem.

And now it was, at the full height of enjoyment of my bliss, that I became heavily troubled. I began to think of my mother, and what she would say to my taking home at Midsummer eight of the most beautiful of the daughers of men, but all unexpected. I though of the number of beds we made up at our house, of my father's income, and of the baker, and my despondency redoubled. The Seraglio and malicious Vizier, divining the cause of their Lord's unhappiness, did their utmost to augment it. They professed unbounded fidelity, and declared that they would live and die with him. Reduced to the utmost wretchedness by these protestations of attachment, I lay awake, for hours at a time, ruminating on my frightful lot. In my despair, I think I might have taken an early opportunity of falling on my knees before Miss Griffin, avowing my resemblance to Solomon, and praying to be dealt with according to the outraged laws of my country, if an unthought-of means of escape had not opened before me.

One day, we were out walking, two and two – on which occasion the Vizier had his usual instructions to take note of the boy at the turnpike, and if he profanely gazed (which he always did) at the beauties of the Hareem, to have him bow-strung in the course of the night – and it happened that our hearts were veiled in gloom. An unaccountable action on the part of the antelope had plunged the State into disgrace. That charmer, on the representation that the previous day was her birthday, and that vast treasures had been sent in a hamper for its celebration (both baseless assertions), had secretly but most pressingly invited thirty-five neighbouring princes and princesses to a ball and supper: with a special stipulation that they were 'not to be fetched till twelve.' This wandering of the antelope's fancy, led to the surprising arrival at Miss Griffin's door, in divers equipages and under various escorts, of a great company in full dress, who were deposited on the top step in a flush of high expectancy, and who were dismissed in tears. At the beginning of the double knocks attendant on these cere-monies, the antelope had retired to a back attic, and bolted herself in; and at every new arrival Miss Griffin had gone so much more and more distracted, that at last she had been seeen to tear her front. Ultimate capitulation on the part of the offender, had been followed by solitude in the linen-closet, bread and water and a lecture to all, of vindictive length, in which Miss Griffin had used expressions: Firstly, 'I believe you all of you knew of it;' Secondly, 'Every one of you is as wicked as another;' Thirdly, 'A pack of little wretches.'

Under these circumstances, we were walking drearily

along; and I especially, with my Moosulmaun responsibilities
heavy on me, was in a very low state of mind; when a strange
man accosted Miss Griffin, and, after walking on at her side
for a little while and talking with her, looked at me. Supposing him to be a minion of the law, and that my hour was
come, I instantly ran away, with the general purpose of
making for Egypt.

. The whole Seraglio cried out, when they saw me making
off as fast as my legs would carry me (I had an impression that
the first turning on the left, and round by the public-house,
would be the shortest way to the Pyramids), Miss Griffin
screamed after me, the faithless Vizier ran after me, and the
boy at the turnpike dodged me into a corner, like a sheep, and
cut me off. Nobody scolded me when I was taken and brought
back; Miss Griffin only said, with a stunning gentleness, This
was very curious! Why had I run away when the gentleman
looked at me?

If I had had any breath to answer with, I dare say I should
have made no to answer; having no breath, I certainly made
none. Miss Griffin and the strange man took me between
them, and walked me back to the palace in a sort of state; but
not at all (as I couldn't help feeling, with astonishment), in
culprit state.

When we got there, we went into a room by ourselves, and
Miss Griffin called in to her assistance, Mesrour, chief of the
dusky guards of the Hareem. Mesrour, on being whispered
to, began to shed tears.

'Bless you, my precious!' said that officer, turning to me;
'your pa's took bitter bad!'

I asked, with a fluttered heart, 'Is he very ill?'

'Lord temper the wind to you, my lamb!' said the good
Mesrour, kneeling down, that I might have a comforting
shoulder for my head to rest on, 'your pa's dead!'

Haroun Alraschid took to flight at the words; the Seraglio
vanished; from that moment, I never again saw one of the
eight of the fairest of the daughters of men.

I was taken home, and there was Debt at home as well as
Death, and we had a sale there. My own little bed was so
superciliously looked upon by a Power unknown to me,
hazily called 'The Trade,' that a brass coal-scuttle, a roasting-

jack, and a birdcage, were obliged to be put into it to make a Lot of it, and then it went for a song. So I heard mentioned and I wondered what song, and thought what a dismal song it must have been to sing!

Then, I was sent to a great, cold, bare, school of big boys; where everything to eat and wear was thick and clumpy, without being enough; where everybody, large and small, was cruel; where the boys knew all about the sale, before I got there, and asked me what I had fetched, and who had bought me, and hooted at me. 'Going, going, gone!' I never whispered in that wretched place that I had been Haroun or had had a Seraglio: for, I knew that if I mentioned my reverses, I should be so worried, that I should have to drown myself in the muddy pond near the playground, which looked like the beer.

Ah me, ah me! no other ghost has haunted the boy's room, my friends, since I have occupied it, than the ghost of my own childhood, the ghost of my own innocence, the ghost of my own airy belief. Many a time have I pursued the phantom: never with this man's stride of mine to come up with it, never with these man's hands of mine to touch it, never more to this man's heart of mine to hold it in its purity. And here you see me working out, as cheerfully and thankfully as I may, my doom of shaking in the glass a constant change of customers, and of lying down and rising up with the skeleton allotted to me for my mortal companion.

THE DICKENS FELLOWSHIP

The Dickens Fellowship exists to promote an interest in Charles Dickens, and a knowledge and appreciation of his writing.

Information about the Fellowship, which arranges meetings, 'at homes', conferences and lectures, may be obtained from:

Mr Edward G. Preston
Honorary General Secretary
The Dickens Fellowship
The Dickens House,
48 Doughty Street
LONDON WC1N 2LF